I0635692

Hands
of the
Architects

Book Two

Pretty Faces and Peculiar Places

A novel by

Brian Harmon

Hands of the Architects

Book Two

Pretty Faces and Peculiar Places

Copyright © 2018 Brian Harmon

Published by Brian Harmon

Cover Images and Design by Candorem

All rights reserved.

This book is a work of fiction. All names, characters, places and events are products of the author's imagination. Any resemblance to actual persons, places and events is entirely coincidental.

ISBN: 1-945559-09-8

ISBN-13: 978-1-945559-09-9

Also by Brian Harmon

For Nathan

Chapter 1

"See? This is what I'm talking about."

Piper looked up from her book, confused. She hadn't been paying attention.

"*This,*" said Meg, wagging a manicured finger back and forth, indicating the two of them, as if that in any way explained anything.

"Huh?"

"You and me. Hanging out. You know. Girl time. Don't you miss that?"

Piper's pretty face scrunched into an expression of complete bewilderment. How was this girl time? She was trying to enjoy her new book and Meg wouldn't shut up. She wasn't even talking *to* her. She was just ranting in her general direction. She'd been rambling on for most of the last hour, complaining about everyone she knew. The last thing she remembered was her droning on about how stupid and stuck-up Melanie was.

She didn't even *know* Melanie.

"Come on, Pipes." Meg had been lying stretched out on the couch, taking up the whole thing. Now she sat up, brushed her shiny, black curls from her face and fixed her with those piercing blue eyes. "We're like a team. We're *besties*. Don't pretend like you don't miss me."

Piper raised an eyebrow. She wasn't pretending anything. She *didn't* miss her. How could she, when she couldn't seem to make her *leave*? She'd been here every day this week. This morning she showed up at seven o'clock! And they certainly weren't "besties." They never had been. They might've been friends occasionally, but mostly they'd only ever been roommates. Meg was far too self-centered and fake to be anyone's BFF. Those weren't even her natural hair and eye colors. Regardless of how much she swore otherwise, her real hair was limp and sandy-colored and her real eyes were a muddy shade of brown. The *real* Meg was sort of mousy-looking.

But she didn't say any of this. She didn't say *anything*. She lowered her gaze back to her book again without commenting at all.

Meg rolled her eyes. "Auuuuugh."

Piper had no idea what you called that sound she made, but it was textbook Meg. It was deep and throaty, not quite a moan but not quite a growl, either. And utterly obnoxious. She did it whenever she was irritated, which was pretty well all the time.

She thrust her feet out in front of her and dropped her heels onto the coffee table, nearly knocking over a cup of colored pencils in the process. "I can't believe you won't just let me move back in."

"I already have a roommate."

"*I'm* your roommate."

"You *were* my roommate," corrected Piper without taking her eyes off her book. "Then you moved out. I found a new roommate. Now there's no room."

"Auuuuugh."

That sound had never not been annoying in all the time she'd known her. And today it was giving her a headache. A sharp pain was beginning to take root just behind her left temple.

"That's bullshit, Pipes. You know it. I was here first."

"And then you left." It was all she said. It was all she should've needed to say. It was as simple as that. Meg had announced her intention to move in with her boyfriend, Martin, without warning and then immediately began packing out all her stuff. Just like that, Piper had been stuck with no roommate and all the bills. As far as she was concerned, Meg surrendered any claim to this apartment the first time she didn't pay her share of the rent. The fact that she and Martin had barely lasted six months living under the same roof didn't change that.

It simply wasn't Piper's problem.

But Meg didn't see it that way. "We've been friends for years. That doesn't count for anything?"

Of course it did. It was why she hadn't kicked her out. But again, she kept this to herself and instead replied, "It's not personal."

"Isn't it?" She wasn't even looking at her. She was playing with the pendant on her necklace. She always did stuff like that. She couldn't ever seem to give anyone her full attention. She always had to be occupying herself with something.

Piper was convinced she had ADHD.

"You know it's not," she replied.

"Then what is it?"

"It's just what it is," replied Piper.

11

"What does that even mean?" She let the pendant drop back onto her chest and sat up again. This time, she succeeded in kicking the cup off the coffee table. Colored pencils spilled onto the floor. "Why the hell does she have to leave all her junk everywhere?" she snapped. "She's a total slob." She kicked a sketch pad that was lying beside the pencil cup, knocking it onto the floor, too.

Piper tried to concentrate on her book, but it was getting harder. That headache was getting worse. And the ceiling fan was making an irritating buzzing sound. That wasn't helping things at all.

Meg didn't seem to notice the sound. She turned and stretched out on the couch again and went back to fiddling with her necklace. "I don't know how you live like this."

Piper still refused to comment. Seph wasn't the tidiest person she'd ever known, but she was by no means a slob. It wasn't like she left dirty cereal bowls and empty soda cans lying around. It was just her art supplies. They didn't bother her. And it was no different, really, than the way Meg always used to leave her dirty socks lying around when she lived here.

"I mean what *is* all this stuff, anyway?" she asked, gesturing at a painting on the wall. "Have you ever even *looked* at it? It's *hideous.*"

There was lots of artwork displayed throughout the apartment, in all manner of styles and mediums. Much of it was fantasy art. Comic book-like stuff. Seph had a thing for comic books and superhero movies. She loved science fiction and fantasy. But the image in question was a large and haunting depiction of the Grim Reaper wielding his legendary scythe in a dramatic pose as he cut down a horde of shrieking, shadowy figures.

"Seriously, Pipes. There is something *wrong* with her."

Piper held her book a little higher to hide her smirk. Like everyone else who'd ever visited and gazed upon that painting, Meg had no idea of the true meaning behind the reaper. Seph painted it shortly after they became roommates, following the weird events that took place in November. It was something of a private joke. A portrait of a secret.

If you looked closely enough—and nobody ever had so far—you might notice that Death had the subtle figure of a woman...

"It's not healthy to expose yourself to people like that," said Meg.

Piper heard the bedroom door open and glanced up from her book as Seph walked into the room and picked up her purse. She was dressed nice for her breakfast date. Black skirt and black button-down shirt. Black sandals. Seph wore a lot of black. Even her glasses frames were black. All of it matching her raven black hair.

"I'll be back later," she announced.

"Say hi to your mom for me," said Piper.

"Sure."

"Hey, my friend Evie broke up with her fiancé last week," blurted Meg. She thrust her arm up over the back of the couch and pointed at Seph, making her bracelets clatter together. "She's going to be looking for a new roommate."

"Awesome," said Seph. "That should be perfect for you."

"Not for *me*," she spat, sounding exasperated. "I couldn't stand living with Evie. She's a total drama whore. Everyone says so."

"Huh," was all Seph said, but she glanced over at Piper, clearly annoyed.

Piper shrugged and dived back into her book. Invisible to everyone in the world but Seph, the luminescent ears on top of her head drooped.

"You'd probably like her, though," continued Meg. "She's all artsy. She's way into those adult coloring books."

"Right," said Seph. "Because that's totally the same thing."

"Right?" agreed Meg, who didn't have the best ear for sarcasm.

"I'm not moving out," she said as she walked through the door. "Later Peps."

"Bye-bye," chirped Piper.

Meg rolled her eyes again.

Piper pretended not to notice and went back to reading her book.

"She's rude. I hate rude people."

Piper raised an unamused eyebrow at her and then returned her attention to her book again.

Was that damned buzzing getting louder? It was really irritating. Her headache was getting worse.

"You're *selfish*. You know that, right?"

This made her lower the book. "What?"

"You didn't used to be selfish. She's a bad influence on you. I can tell."

It was Piper's turn to roll her eyes. She wished Meg would just shut up for a while. But of course, she wouldn't. She never did. Not when she was in one of these kinds of moods.

"I'm your best friend, Pipes. Trust me. You don't need people like that in your life."

Nobody ever called Piper by her name. Everyone always called her by nicknames. She wasn't sure why. It wasn't like "Piper" was some cumbersome mouthful of a name. Even if it was, not all the cutesy nicknames people came up with saved them any breath. Lately Seph had taken to calling her "Pepper" for some reason, which was basically the same name. She had no idea what the point even was.

"I have to pee," blurted Meg. She stood up and walked off toward the bathroom. "Seriously," she called back as she disappeared down the hallway, "people like her are toxic. They're not your friends. They just want to use you."

Unseen from her chair, Piper stuck out her tongue and made a face at her. She knew good and well who *really* cared about her.

Seph wasn't always the *nicest* person. She was sarcastic and usually not particularly concerned with sparing people's feelings. Especially obnoxious, deceitful people like Meg. But she was a good friend. Her *real* best friend. Seph would never do anything to hurt her.

Meg was the toxic one. *She* was selfish, not Piper. All she cared about was getting her old room back. And she was getting downright vile about it.

She tried to forget about Meg and focus on her book, but she was having trouble concentrating, even without her ex-roommate's constant, self-centered droning.

It was that stupid noise.

She looked up at the ceiling fan, wondering what was wrong with it, but she realized that it wasn't coming from there.

Confused, she closed her book and looked around. Was it coming from the air conditioning vents? The refrigerator? What else made that kind of buzzing noise?

Maybe there was a light bulb getting ready to go out. Sometimes they made irritating buzzing noises right before they blew.

She stood up and walked around the apartment, listening for it. It wasn't coming from the living room…or the kitchen…or the hallway…or from *anywhere*, as far as she could tell. She stopped and turned around, puzzled. She couldn't even determine which *direction* it was coming from. Regardless of where she went, it didn't get any louder or softer. It remained perfectly and perplexingly constant.

It didn't make sense. It had to be coming from *somewhere*. Didn't it? What kind of sound didn't have a source?

But as she passed the mirror on the living room wall, she paused and stared at her reflection.

Unless it was a different kind of sound…

She couldn't see anything unremarkable. She looked precisely the way she always looked when she gazed at herself in a mirror, precisely the way almost everyone else in the world saw her. She had long, light blonde hair, fair features and soft, blue eyes. All her life, people had been telling her that she was exceptionally pretty, so she probably was, but she didn't care to think that she was exceptionally *anything*. She certainly didn't *feel* exceptional. She'd always felt like she was perfectly *average*, which was all she needed to feel good about herself.

And yet, as she found out when she first met Seph, she was anything *but* average.

Seph saw the difference. She had a gift. She could see things no one else on earth could see. And when she looked at Piper, what she saw was ghostly, animal ears protruding from the top of her head.

No one else could see them, not even Piper. And not even Seph could *feel* them. If she tried, her fingers would pass through them as if they weren't even there. But they were real. She knew because sometimes they allowed her to *hear* things other people couldn't.

That was what was happening now, she realized. The reason she couldn't pinpoint the source of the buzzing was because she was listening with the wrong ears. It wasn't going to get any louder or softer, no matter where she went, because it didn't have volume. It wasn't a sound. Not in the way that most people heard sounds. She was going to have to listen with her spirit ears.

But she hadn't used them since that day at Shawbeck Ranch. She wasn't sure she remembered how. And besides that, she didn't *want* to use them. Her heart was already pounding. Her mouth had gone dry. A growing anxiety gripped her, closing in around her lungs, rapidly swelling into a smothering dread. The last time she heard something with her spirit ears, she ended up nearly dying. *Repeatedly.* And *horribly.* She still had nightmares about the things she witnessed on that terrifying journey.

She turned away from the mirror and glanced around at the quiet apartment. Absently, she reached up and pinched her lower lip, twisting it as she pondered her situation. It was what Seph called her "thinking face."

She wished Seph were here. She'd know what to do. Maybe. At the very least the two of them could figure it out together. But

Seph wouldn't be back for at least a couple hours.

She was on her own.

Well…there was Meg. But Meg was useless. She couldn't handle most of the *normal* things the world threw at her. She certainly didn't possess the emotional capacity to deal with things like mall wraiths, flock goats and fringe cats.

She walked to the window and peered out into the bright, morning sunlight. There was nothing that wasn't supposed to be there. No shadowy forms or vicious creatures were prowling the property. At least, not in plain sight.

But they wouldn't be in plain sight. They'd be hidden somewhere, watching, waiting… Or, for all she knew, they might be invisible. Nothing was impossible. That was one thing she'd learned back in November.

November also taught her that you couldn't ever run away. Not really. You could run from all the monsters out there, you could even run from yourself, but you couldn't run from your future. That, you were always running toward, even when standing still.

She closed her eyes and forced herself to take a deep, calming breath. It was okay. It was just a noise. (Well, sort of…) It didn't mean the horrors were beginning again.

She crossed the room, opened the door and peered out into the empty hallway, listening.

It felt different here. She wasn't sure *how* it was different because it still *sounded* the same, probably because her brain still didn't know how to process this strange, new input.

She glanced at the table next to the door. Her purse was sitting on it.

She shouldn't follow it. That would be a bad idea. The things she heard with her spirit ears had always led her to trouble. And this time Seph wasn't here to protect her.

But the "buzzing" pulled at her, compelling her to follow...

With a groan, she turned and plucked the keys from her purse. Then she stepped into her flip-flops and walked out into the hallway.

She *really* hoped this wasn't like November. It took three days to complete that strange journey to Shawbeck Ranch. And she didn't want to have to call into work this soon after changing jobs. She'd only been working at Victoria's Secret for about a month now. It'd look bad if she had to call in and make up some sob story.

She paused to listen again. After a moment, she shook her head. No. She was doing it wrong. She was listening for a sound. This wasn't a sound. It was...well...she didn't really know *what* it was... But it wasn't a sound.

She tried again. She closed her eyes and focused on that irritating "buzzing" sensation.

Was it stronger here? Was she closer to the source? It was hard to tell, but she thought it was. It seemed more... More *something*. Not louder, certainly, but maybe sharper? More intense?

The headache was getting worse.

She set off down the steps, trying to focus on the buzzing, on listening with her spirit ears and not her human ears. It wasn't easy. She was used to having only five senses. She wished she could remember what she did last time.

How long had it been? It was July now, so... She did the math in her head. Eight months? Had it really been that long? It didn't seem possible.

At the bottom of the steps, she stopped and looked around again. There was definitely a change in the "buzzing" now. She still wasn't sure how to describe it, but she was increasingly sure that she was getting closer to the source.

And it was changing, too. Or maybe it was only that she was beginning to understand what she was hearing. It wasn't so much a buzzing as it was a sort of garbled static. Like the noise between radio stations.

Were there voices in the static? Or was that only her imagination?

She walked toward the front door, but after just a few steps, she stopped again. No... Not that way. She turned and looked the other way, toward the back door. There? It wasn't really a conscious realization, but rather a sort of gut feeling. She wasn't sure if she was learning to use these queer ears or if it was some deep-down, primal instinct. Either way, she was sure the source was coming from that direction.

But even as she began walking toward it, an uneasy feeling crept through her.

Something wasn't right.

That anxiety she'd been feeling had fully bloomed into dread by now, and that dread was rapidly swelling into stark terror. She kept telling herself that it couldn't be happening again. They accomplished their task in Nebraska. They *won*. And yet she was also certain that her spirit ears didn't lie.

Something unnatural awaited her somewhere on the other side

of that door.

She paused before reaching for the handle.

That static-like sensation in her brain was strangely frantic. The headache had grown into a constant pounding, making it harder to think straight.

She shouldn't be doing this. Not without Seph. They were a team. Neither of them would've survived that business with the shepherd on her own. It was the way it was supposed to be, the way fate intended. Seph had the prophet sight. She could see what no one else could. And Piper had the spirit ears. She could hear what Seph couldn't.

But did this queer static really have anything to do with those events in November? The shepherd was gone. *Destroyed*. He wasn't coming back. Not ever.

And yet she *really* didn't want to open that door...

In fact, she took a step backward. Although she couldn't possibly explain how or why, she was certain that something horrible was standing just on the other side.

Inside that static, she could definitely hear a voice.

Well...not *hear*, exactly... (This was so confusing!) But it was there, just the same. She couldn't understand what it was saying, but there was something incredibly creepy about it.

She took another step back.

Her heart was racing now.

She reached into the pocket of her shorts and pulled out her cell phone. She should call Seph. And she should run away, of course. Back to the safety of her apartment. Or at least whatever *illusion* of safety it offered her. If this really was anything like the last time she heard things with her spirit ears, then nowhere would truly be safe.

But she didn't run. She was frozen in place, her eyes fixed on the lower portion of the door.

Was that the sound of something scratching?

Inside her head, she was screaming at herself. *Run away! Run away before it opens the door!* But she couldn't run. She couldn't even move. She was too afraid.

Then the door flew open.

Chapter 2

"I'm sorry."

"It's okay," Seph assured her. "Don't worry about it."

"But you drove all the way here."

"I live fifteen minutes away. It's *nothing*. Seriously, don't worry about it."

Seph hesitated to sit down. She'd never particularly liked being inside her mother's apartment. Besides being quite small, the place was sparsely decorated, rather dark and stank of cigarette smoke. As an artist, she liked to be surrounded by color and imagery. She liked light. She liked things that engaged her creativity. To her, these empty walls and dark curtains were as depressing and oppressive as a prison cell, completely devoid of warmth and life. It didn't feel like a home. It felt *generic*, little more than a place to sleep off a hangover…which might not have been too far off base, considering that the woman who lived here had spent most of the past two decades adrift in an ugly sea of substance addictions.

But this wasn't turning out to be one of those visits where she could just stand and wait by the door, so she seated herself in the ugly, salmon-colored armchair, willing herself not to make a face at the tobacco stench it exhaled as the cushion compacted beneath her butt.

"I wanted to call and tell you not to come, but I can't find where I left my phone. I swear I've looked everywhere."

Like a lot of people Seph knew, Buffy Kipp didn't have a landline. Her cell phone was her only means of communication with the outside world. And it was all she needed, really. She didn't have any other family. Her entire social life consisted of the occasional meal out with her daughter and her various support groups.

"It's okay," Seph assured her again. "I would've come to check up on you anyway."

Buffy gave her a tired smile. "You're sweet. But I don't want to get *you* sick."

"I'll be fine," she insisted. "You need to worry about yourself."

Seph had never seen her mother look this way. She was lying on the couch, clutching a light blanket in spite of the July heat outside. She looked pale and gaunt, with dark circles under her eyes. She was a very thin woman anyway, and today she looked almost emaciated.

She kept saying it was the flu, and she was probably right, but even for the flu, she looked bad.

"When did you start getting sick?"

She thought about it for a moment. "Wednesday, I think it was. I started to feel gross after dinner. But it wasn't anything I couldn't handle. I wasn't even feeling all that bad when I woke up this morning. Just sort of tired and achy. It only *really* hit me about an hour ago."

Seph nodded. She hadn't contracted the flu in years. She was probably way overdue and just asking for it by hanging around here. But she remembered it coming on hard and fast, without any warning. If she started feeling sick three days ago, why was she just now suddenly getting the brunt of it? Maybe it was different for different people. More likely, it was something else altogether, hopefully something that cleared up a little more quickly than the flu.

Any way you looked at it, she clearly wasn't in any condition to go out for breakfast.

Buffy closed her eyes and lay her head back against the cushion. "I'm so disappointed. All I could think was, 'It's my me-and-Seph day!'"

"We'll have more days," promised Seph.

Everyone had always called her Seph. No one ever called her Persephone. At least, not until she met Piper. Piper was the only person she'd ever known who preferred for some reason to call her by all four syllables of her real name.

Her gaze washed across her mother's pallid face. She'd never seen her look so frail. But then again, she never saw much of her at all until just a few years ago. For most of her childhood, she didn't have a mom.

The ugly truth was that she'd *always* been weak. Whenever things got tough, Buffy could always be counted on to run away, usually straight for the bottom of a liquor bottle. She'd never been able to handle the daily struggle of adult life. She surrounded herself with loud music and strangers, the better to drown out the nagging voice of responsibility. When that didn't work, she sought refuge in the numbing embrace of drugs and distracted herself in the company of questionable men.

This was how she spent many of those missed years while Seph was growing up. She was weak and childish, afraid of the world and all it expected of her, utterly incapable of shouldering any kind of responsibility. She didn't know how to control life, so she ran away from it. And she embraced the things she *could* control. Like how she looked. She dyed her hair. She pierced her nose. She chose the tattoos that decorated her skin. And even all that was nothing more than another attempt to run away and hide. If she didn't look like the same little girl who never grew up, who never stopped being afraid, then maybe life wouldn't find her.

Buffy wasn't even her real name. It wasn't even a nickname. It wasn't short for anything. It wasn't a pet name that anybody gave her. Her real name was Marianne. She just decided one day that she wanted to be a Buffy and insisted that everyone start calling her that.

The woman was a total mess.

But she was her mother. And she *was* trying.

Seph's father had already been gone five years now. Buffy was all the family she had. That was a blessing, as far as she was concerned. It didn't matter how damaged she was.

Buffy withdrew her arm from under the blanket and brushed her unkempt hair from her forehead.

"Where did you get those bruises?" asked Seph.

"What bruises?"

"On your arm."

She held up her arm, twisting it this way and that, trying to see

26

all of it. "I don't know. Where?"

"Right there." Seph stood up and leaned over her, but stopped as she realized that she no longer saw any bruises. She hovered there for a moment, confused. "Huh…" was all she could think to say. "Weird. Must've been a trick of the light." She sat back down in the chair, puzzled. She supposed it was only the gloom of this unhappy little apartment, but for a moment there, she was sure she'd seen dark bruises running up and down her forearm.

"I *feel* like I'm covered in bruises," said Buffy, rubbing at her arms.

"My imagination," said Seph, more to herself than to her mother.

"You really don't have to babysit me. Travis promised he'd come by again tonight."

Seph pushed the curious hallucination from her thoughts and smiled. "Oh yeah. *Travis.* I was going to ask how things were going." Travis was Buffy's new boyfriend. They'd been seeing each other since right around their last mother-daughter breakfast date, a couple weeks ago, From the way she'd talked about him over the phone, she seemed to be fairly smitten with him.

Seph hadn't met him yet, and Buffy hadn't said much about him other than that he was a realtor and, in her words, "a gentleman."

Buffy looked embarrassed. "He's so sweet. He keeps finding reasons to stop by. He brought me lunch yesterday. And the night before that he came over with a new light bulb for the refrigerator, just because I told him I kept forgetting to buy one at the store."

"Sounds like he's really into you."

She shrugged. It was a cute, girlish gesture. Seph thought she even blushed a little. "I think it's going good. He…" She pulled the blanket up to her chin, even more embarrassed. In a very small voice, she said, "He might have…stayed over last night."

Seph gave her a scandalized look. "*No!*"

She lifted the blanket all the way over her face. "I know!"

Seph laughed. "Good for you."

"Are you really okay with it?" she asked, emerging from the blanket again.

"Why wouldn't I be?"

"I don't know. I'm your mom. I thought it might be weird."

"It's fine!"

Buffy shrugged again. "Besides…I'm not exactly known for making good choices when it comes to men. The only good one I ever found was your dad and we both know how I messed *that* up."

"It's *fine.*" And it was. First of all, they weren't your typical mother and daughter. There were no traditional family dynamics in place. They never even lived together, not while she was old enough to remember it. And it was never going to feel like she was cheating on her dad because she didn't remember her ever *being* with her dad. Their relationship was *friendly*, not maternal. "You're allowed to be happy."

A bright smile spread across Buffy's face, but Seph's smile immediately melted away. Before her eyes, dark bruises blossomed beneath the skin around her mother's mouth and on the sides of her neck.

She closed her eyes tight and then opened them again, trying to clear her vision. The bruises were fainter, but they were still there, and now her eyes looked dark and sunken, almost corpse-like.

Buffy didn't notice the look of shock and horror on her face. She was staring across the room, distracted. "You're so sweet. I don't deserve it."

The bruises faded completely away again. The dark circles around her eyes softened a little. But as she watched, a trickle of blackish blood from her nose began to slide down her lip.

"It figures, doesn't it. I finally meet a nice guy and I go and get myself sick." She looked up at her, finally noticing her expression. "Are you okay?"

Seph gestured at her own nose. "You've got…uh…"

Buffy wiped at her nose, smearing the blood across her lip and onto her fingers, but when she looked at her hand, she didn't seem to see anything there. "What?" she asked, wiping at it again.

Even as she watched, it evaporated from her mother's face and hand, disappearing into thin air, as if it were never there.

"Did I get it?"

Seph nodded. "Yeah…" she replied. "It's… Yeah. You got it."

"Sorry. I'm gross."

"No you're not." And she wasn't. Even the dark circles around her eyes had vanished. She looked perfectly lifelike again. A little under the weather, but certainly not *corpselike*.

"I totally am. You probably shouldn't hang around here. I really don't want to get you sick."

Seph barely heard her. This wasn't the first time she'd seen something that others couldn't.

An old man in Minnesota once told her it was called "prophet sight" and suggested that it might be one of the rarest abilities in human history. It'd allowed her to find hidden places and to read ancient writings invisible to the rest of the world and even to see ghosts.

Well...*a* ghost, anyway. Although it was possible she'd seen more and simply didn't know it, she supposed.

This was like that, she realized. These bruises. The black and sunken eyes. The blood. She wasn't seeing these things with her human eyes. That was merely how her brain was perceiving it.

But what did it mean?

She stared at her mother, an even greater horror rising deep inside her. Was it possible that her prophet sight could perceive a person's imminent death? Was this what it looked like when she gazed upon a person who was dying?

No. She couldn't accept that.

Buffy hadn't exactly been there for her. When she was little and really needed a mother, she was nowhere to be found. But she was better now. She was really trying.

And she was the only family she had left.

No, this had to be something else.

It had to be...

And yet, as she watched, the bruises blossomed across her skin again, creeping down her neck, across her chest and out of sight beneath her shirt. Her skin paled and thinned, becoming paper-like. Black blood dripped down her chin. Her eyes grew dim. Even her hair seemed to gray before her eyes.

"You should go," insisted Buffy. "I'll be fine. I just need to get some sleep."

She *did* want to go. The sooner she could get out of that gloomy, cramped apartment the better. But she also didn't want to leave her there.

"And I don't want to be the reason you miss breakfast," she added.

Seph forced a smile. "Well I *am* hungry," she said. It was a lie. Her appetite was long gone. But she needed to get out for a little bit. She needed to go somewhere and think.

And she needed to talk to Piper. She probably wouldn't know what was going on either, but at least she'd understand. Maybe together they could figure out what to do next.

"I'll check in on you again later," she promised.

"Don't bother yourself. Travis promised to come take care of me this evening."

"Tomorrow, then."

Buffy smiled. "Don't worry about me. Really. I'll be fine." And yet, when she smiled up at her, the flesh of her face had shriveled, clinging to the contours of her skull. A visage of stark death stared back at her.

She was looking at a corpse.

Somehow, she managed not to cry out at the horrid sight. She even forced a smile. "You call me if you need anything."

"I will," she promised.

Just as quickly as it came, the vision was gone and Seph was only looking at her mother again, ill but alive. She pretended to have forgotten that Buffy told her she lost her cell phone. She could come back later and help her look for it. Right now, she needed to get out of this stuffy apartment for a little while.

She stepped out into the July heat and then stood there for a moment, giving her pounding heart time to ease and pondering what she'd seen. Was she hallucinating? She wanted desperately to believe that she was, that it was only a queer trick of her mind, but she knew better than that. She'd been down that road before.

"You saw something, didn't you?"

Seph jumped, startled, and turned to find her path blocked by a strikingly handsome man in a crisp, white tee shirt and faded jeans. He was tall and muscular, with perfect, almost chiseled features. Even his sandy blond hair was perfect. For a moment, she was so taken back that she could only stand there and stare at him.

"I'm sorry. I didn't mean to scare you."

She couldn't remember the last time she ran into a man this attractive. Not in real life, outside of a movie screen. He was surprisingly distracting. "That's... Um... It's okay. I'm just..." She shook her head, confused. "What...what did you just say?"

"I said, 'You saw something.' And you did, didn't you?" He gestured at the door. "In there."

Seph squinted at him. "What do you...?"

"She's someone special to you, isn't she?"

She glanced back at the door. "She's my mom," she replied. "Why? What are you talking about?"

"It's not your imagination," he told her. "What you saw was a manifestation of the poison in her soul."

"A manifestation..." She scrunched up her face, confused. "Poison? What are you talking about?"

The stranger met her eyes with a piercing gaze. They were the deepest shade of blue she'd ever seen and they carried a strange sort of weight as he spoke. "She's dying."

Chapter 3

Piper screamed.

What happened next was like something out of a nightmare. Not a violent or bloody nightmare. Not even a really scary, something-is-chasing-you-and-you-can't-get-away kind of nightmare. It was more like one of those really embarrassing, *you-forgot-your-pants-again* nightmares.

She stood there like an idiot, her hand clamped over her mouth, her eyes wide, her face burning, turning ever-hotter, ever-brighter shades of red.

Standing in the doorway, staring back at her with an equally startled expression, was not a monster come to suck the marrow from her shattered bones and devour her still-beating heart, but her neighbor, Gavin Ledlow.

Gavin lived a few doors down from her. He was a really nice guy. And he was very attractive. She had a little crush on him. (Just a little one; she was pretty sure he had a girlfriend.) But she'd been known to go out of her way to check the mail when she saw him at the boxes, just to say hi, even when she'd already brought in the mail for the day.

And now he thought she was a raving lunatic.

Awesome.

"I'm sorry," he said. "Didn't mean to…uh…startle you."

"*I'm* sorry," she countered, still blushing. "My fault. Totally. I didn't mean to…you know…scream at you…" (*Oh god…*)

"It's all right," he assured her, although he didn't look very convincing. He looked like someone who just walked into his own apartment building and was immediately screamed at by the resident psycho girl. He gave her a sort of awkward smile and then hurried past her.

Piper watched him walk away. When he was out of earshot, she groaned and smacked her forehead with the heel of her hand. That was *really* embarrassing. And it wasn't the first time she'd done something like that. It was pretty much exactly how she first met Seph.

Seph…

She turned and looked at the door again, but that feeling that something was lurking on the other side was gone. In fact, it was *all* gone. The strange, static-like noise. The pain behind her left temple. All of it had just vanished.

It was like waking from a dream. That strange certainty had vanished like smoke, leaving nothing behind, making her wonder if anything had ever really been there in the first place.

She pushed open the door and squinted into the bright sunlight. It was already so hot today. The heat rolled over her skin, nearly taking her breath away.

There was nothing out there.

She walked out of the building, letting the door swing closed behind her, listening, but all she heard was the perfectly ordinary sounds of the city. Traffic. A lawnmower. A distant train whistle. A barking dog. The world appeared to have reverted to normal again.

She looked down at her phone. Should she still call Seph? She didn't want to bother her needlessly. She was with her mom. It might not seem like a big deal to some people, but Piper understood how much these mother-daughter dates meant to her.

She slipped it back into her pocket. The buzzing/static sensation had stopped, so it was reasonable to assume that whatever was causing it had gone away.

Right?

She rubbed thoughtfully at the place behind her left temple where the headache first started. Maybe she really *had* just imagined the whole thing.

But before she could return to the air-conditioned hallway, she heard something new. A *real* sound this time, with her human ears, but one that didn't belong. She cocked her head and listened closer.

It was faint, but it was distinct. A small whimper. A quiet sob.

She turned and surveyed her surroundings. Her apartment building was one part of a larger complex of six buildings, constructed in pairs. Each of them stood back-to-back with the next one in line, mirror images of each other. Between each pair was a narrow, grassy lawn and a small, fenced-in structure where the dumpsters were located. The crying seemed to be coming from there.

It sounded like a child.

She scanned the area once more, but everything else remained quiet. The static hadn't started again. Whatever danger had been lurking out here a moment ago now seemed to be gone.

But if she didn't imagine it…and she didn't really believe that she did…could it have hurt someone?

Fresh fear blossoming in her heart, she crossed the lot, following the sound.

"Hello?"

No one answered, but that pitiful whimpering continued.

She peered through the gate. "Are you okay?"

The child sat with her back against the side of the dumpster, her knees drawn up to her chest, her head buried in her arms. Thick, brown hair spilled down her back. She appeared to be no more than five or six years old.

Immediately, Piper felt a sense of wrongness about the scene. It was her clothes. The heavy, long-sleeved dress. The dirty, white tights. She wasn't dressed for summer at all, much less the intense heat and humidity of this particular summer day.

For that matter, she didn't exactly look dressed for *any* season. The clothes looked strangely out of time, like something she might've seen in old photographs.

She felt a powerful urge to turn and flee, but she fought it. Out of place or not, this was a child, and she might yet need help. She forced herself to take a step closer. "Hi there," she said. "What's your name?"

The little girl didn't answer. Instead, that awful static sensation began again, stronger than ever. A piercing pain shot through her head. Alarmed, she began to back away.

The little girl lifted her face and looked at her. She had no eyes. There was only an empty blackness there, an inky, hellish void.

Piper tried to scream, but all that escaped her was a shrill sort of squeak.

She'd seen people with black eyes before, people possessed by a strange, shadowy entity that was once their ally. But she immediately knew that this was different. There was something evil about this child's eyes. Something beyond that threatening static sensation in her brain. Deep down, she understood that she was in grave danger.

She turned and fled, but halfway back to the building she realized that her way was blocked. Two more oddly-dressed children, one boy and one girl, stood in front of the door, staring back at her, an impossible blackness shining back where their eyes should be.

Her voice was a little louder when she screamed this time, but not much. She turned again and ran, intending to circle around the building. Surely the front doors wouldn't be blocked by freaky kids. They'd be in plain sight of the parking lot. Someone would see.

But before she could reach the end of the building, another creepy little boy walked around the corner.

She stopped and turned back, but now there were half a dozen terrifying children closing in on her from that direction.

They were all like the first one, dressed head-to-toe in heavy, thick fabric, like something from old, black-and-white photographs. Each of them had thick, bushy hair, as if it were a family trait.

This was apparently not a day for wearing flip-flops.

Still clutching her phone, she turned and sprinted across the lot, circling wide around the freaky little boy at the corner of the building.

Two more little girls were lurking over here.

Her screams were getting louder. At this rate, someone might actually hear her soon.

Luckily, none of the little creeps seemed to be very fast on their feet. She dodged both little girls and ran to the parking lot.

She fumbled her keys from her pants pocket and mashed the button to unlock the doors. Once inside, she should be able to lock herself in and call Seph. Or at least drive somewhere safe enough to call her.

No terrifying children were lurking in the parking lot, at least. She glanced behind her to see three of them ambling toward her from the side of the building.

Was anybody else seeing this? Surely there had to be someone around.

But it was such a hot day. Most people were at home behind closed curtains, enjoying the air conditioning. She didn't even see anyone on the streets right now.

She opened the driver's door of the SUV and jumped up into the seat, only to find herself staring into the black, empty eyes of a little boy.

This time, her scream was loud and piercing.

But still no one heard it.

Chapter 4

Seph stared at the handsome stranger, horrified. Did he really just tell her that her mother was *dying*? What was she even supposed to say to such a thing? "How…?" She gave her head a firm shake, as if she could just wake herself up and make this weirdness go away. "*Who are you?*"

"I'm a friend. My name is Ian Heffler. Miss Shawbeck sent me."

"Shawbeck?" asked Seph. For a moment, she was confused. Her thoughts were spinning. First those bizarre, deathly hallucinations of her mother and now this guy appearing out of nowhere… It felt as if she'd lost control of the world and couldn't quite regain her grasp on what was real. Then she remembered where she knew that name from. "You mean Amethyst?"

He shrugged. "To be honest, I can't really keep up with all her aliases. I just know her as Miss Shawbeck."

That certainly sounded like her. Amethyst Wilhoit was Seph's quirky college roommate, back before she started her job at Vertical Design and moved in with Piper. But as she later found out, Amethyst was only a mask. She never existed. She was really Lyla Shawbeck, the enigmatic owner of a mysterious, Nebraskan ranch that was home to a large menagerie of otherworldly beasts and the hiding place for an ancient gateway to one of the most powerful objects in existence.

(It was a very long story…)

But she wasn't even Lyla Shawbeck. That was just one of her many names. One of many *masks*. Seph had no idea who the woman really was. And she didn't care. She hadn't heard from Amethyst/Lyla/*whatever* since the day she learned the truth about her secret other life. Apparently, she didn't consider living together for four years reason enough to bother with a phone call once in a while. Not even, as it turned out, to let her know that this guy was coming.

Not that it really mattered, since those four years had all been one big lie. She wasn't sure what she would've said if she *had* called, to be honest.

So maybe she couldn't blame her for just sending this guy to do the talking for her.

But who was he? He wasn't at the ranch that day. You'd think she'd send someone she'd recognize.

She took off her glasses and wiped at a bead of sweat that was trickling into the corner of her eye. The heat today was intense. It made her head feel fuzzy. It was hard to make sense of all this. "I don't understand… What do you mean she's *dying*?"

"I mean precisely what I said," replied Ian. "She's dying. And she doesn't have much time left."

"But…" She shook her head again. "*No*. It's… It's just the flu."

41

"You know it's not. You saw it yourself. I saw it on your face when you walked out of there. You saw it with your *gift*."

It felt as if her heart were sinking deeper and deeper into a cold, dark pit. He was right, of course. That was no trick of the light. It wasn't her imagination. It was her prophet sight again, showing her things that no one else could see. This time, it had showed her that something was dreadfully wrong with Buffy.

She returned her glasses to her face. "How?" she demanded.

"Your mother's fallen victim to an incubus."

Seph stared at him, her mouth half-open. Did he really just say "incubus"? That was beyond absurd. It had to be a joke. But there was no humor in Ian's expression when he said it, and there was none there now as he gazed back at her.

"Don't pretend it's impossible," he said. "Two years ago, you found and wielded the Grim Reaper's scythe."

He had her there. That was a pretty rock-solid point.

This guy knew a lot about her. Not many people besides Amethyst should know anything about the scythe.

"But an *incubus*?" She shook her head. "Like...those demons that rape women in their sleep?"

"Not in their sleep," corrected Ian. "And not rape. Not exactly, anyway. More like seduction. The incubus is a patient deceiver. Women give themselves to it willingly."

"Why would anyone do that?"

"Because they never see it for what it is. It doesn't just creep into their bedrooms at night. It takes a human form. It creates a convincing identity. It inserts itself into their lives. It becomes what they want and need."

Seph let this sink in for a moment. "Wait… Do you mean…?" She turned and looked back at the apartment door, horrified. "Do you mean *Travis*?"

Ian shrugged. "It can call itself anything it wants. It's a demon. A nameless, shapeshifting thing from a dead and ancient universe."

Her mother's "gentleman" boyfriend, with whom she'd gotten much closer this past week. He'd even stayed over last night, she'd said.

And this morning, probably right after he left, her "flu" took a sudden turn for the worse.

That son of a bitch…

"It's not too late to save her," said Ian.

Seph turned to face him again.

"This isn't an accident. I don't think for a second that it's a coincidence that it picked your mother of all people."

"You mean it's trying to get at *me*?"

"It knows what you did last year."

"The scythe?"

Ian nodded.

"But I don't have it anymore! It disappeared after I claimed it!"

"Yes, but it's not the scythe it wants. It's *you*. You *found* the scythe. That means that you can find the other two tools."

Realization bloomed. "It wants the other Hands of the Architects…"

Two more were still out there, hidden somewhere. Immensely powerful instruments, thought to have been forged by God, Himself, for the sole purpose of creating the universes.

The first Hand had turned out to be the Grim Reaper's scythe. Of course, there was no such thing as the Grim Reaper. (At least, she didn't think so…) It was just one of many stories that had evolved from the original truth. The second and third Hands would no doubt be based on similar myths and legends. They could be King Arthur's Excalibur and Paul Bunyan's axe, for all she knew. And even then, they wouldn't be what she expected. After all, the scythe was no scythe at all. It was made of living water and only even took the vague shape of a scythe when she used it to dispatch the shepherd. Even then, it probably only took that shape because that was what Seph imagined it would look like.

"My guess," said Ian, "is that it intends to force you into searching for the second Hand to save your mother."

"It'll leave my mom alone if I find the next Hand?"

"Not likely. It'll just kill you both once it has what it wants."

"Oh…"

"But if *you* claim it," he went on, "you can use it to defeat the incubus and then save her yourself."

Seph glanced back at the apartment again. "Defeating Travis will save her?"

"Well, no…" said Ian. "It's extremely likely that she'll die anyway at this point, even if you did manage to destroy the incubus."

She turned back and stared at him, confused. This guy was a lousy salesman. "So how do I save her, then?"

"The second tool of the Architects is said to have the power to transform anything."

"Transform?" Seph considered this. As she understood it, the three tools each had a specific purpose in building a universe. The first one created, the second one shaped and the third one trimmed away the unwanted. She'd already found the third one. The scythe. What Ian was describing was the second Hand of the Architects.

"It can turn a mountain range into an ocean or a desert into a rain forest," he explained. "It can turn cold stone into living, breathing creatures. It can turn poisonous gas into clean air."

It made sense. The scythe wasn't just for chopping off rough corners. It had the power to erase anything it was used on from existence. This next tool would be just as terrifyingly powerful. It didn't just shape the universe, like a mere whittling knife. It probably changed it at the atomic level. This was a tool that could transform any landscape, any person, any *reality* into anything the wielder chose. The idea of *anyone* acquiring that kind of power, much less a *demon*, was horrifying.

Ian raised an eyebrow at her and added, "And it can turn a very sick woman healthy again."

Seph stared at him.

"Take your time," he told her. "It's a lot, I know."

If this guy was telling the truth, her mother was in terrible danger. And she was literally the only one who could save her.

With the second of the three Hands of the Architects…

That was the plan? Just take off again on another ridiculous adventure to find another of God's epic-ass gardening tools? Even assuming that she'd know how to use such a thing when she found it, she still had to locate it. If it was anything like the scythe, it was going to be buried somewhere no one had been able to reach since the dawn of the universe, maybe billions of years ago. It would be guarded by horrific traps and hidden in places the rest of the world was incapable of seeing or hearing.

And then she'd have to deal with the incubus itself.

Travis.

She clenched her fists. It infuriated her to think that the nice guy who'd been making Buffy so happy lately was really a murderous monster from hell.

She couldn't say no. It was her mother they were talking about. She turned and looked at the apartment door. "How long does she have?"

"Maybe a week."

She sighed. "That little?"

"That much," he countered. "As I heard, it only took you a couple of days to track down the first one."

That was true, she supposed. She turned and met his piercing eyes again. "So where do I find the second Hand?"

Ian managed to look embarrassed. "Well, that's the thing. We don't know."

"*What?*" Last time she did this, the entire journey ended up feeling like a colossal waste of time. In the end, Amethyst knew where it was hidden all along. Didn't they have someone somewhere guarding the second one, too?

"After the Hands of the Architects were passed down to the protectors," he explained, "they were each taken to separate vaults hidden where only the seekers could one day find them. One of those three vaults, as you know, was located in what is now Northern Nebraska, under the protection of Miss Shawbeck. But she wouldn't have any knowledge about the whereabouts of the other two vaults, or the identities of the other vault guards."

Her thoughts racing, Seph looked out at the passing cars, at an old woman walking her dog, at a mail carrier making his way up the street. That made sense. But it was a big world out there. How the hell was she supposed to find something that could literally be anywhere? "So what are we supposed to do?"

"Not 'we.' I can offer some guidance and a little bit of protection, but little more. The only ones capable of finding the Hands are the seekers."

The seekers. Her and Piper.

"But where do I even begin?" she asked. "In case you haven't noticed, it's a really big world out there. It could literally be anywhere right now."

"True," said Ian. "And even if I could tell you where it was hidden, it wouldn't do you any good. There's a process that must be followed."

She frowned. "That's right…" She recalled the events of those weird, November days. "There were three markers. Amethyst…or whatever the hell her name is…said there were three things we needed in order to enter the vault."

"The gateway, the gate and the key."

She tried to remember the conversation they had with Amethyst. It wasn't easy. She hadn't thought much about it since then. It still pissed her off to think about her ex-roommate and all the lies she'd told.

"It'll be like last time. There will be a tomb, which will act as the gateway. The vault guardian will likely act as the gate, itself, opening the door for you. And you, yourselves, will be the key."

Now she remembered. "But we couldn't just go straight there.

47

We had to go to Messing Knob and Muntony to find the Keeper's markers. That was how we were able to become the key."

"So you don't have to find the vault," he reasoned. "You only have to find the first marker. That doesn't sound quite as tough, does it?"

"Again," she said, dabbing at her sweaty forehead, hoping she didn't look as gross as she was feeling, "it's a big world out there."

"Yes, but that's why Miss Shawbeck sent *me*. I may know a place. Its location is along the approximate route we think the second Hand was taken. And it's a place that was once known to be associated with the Keeper."

"Let me guess... It's somewhere halfway across the country."

"No. It's only about an hour from here."

Chapter 5

Seph shifted her truck into gear and sped off toward home.

Was this really happening again?

The events of November felt like a distant dream, a strange, twisted fantasy, and yet her life had changed so drastically because of those things that she couldn't even pretend that none of it ever happened. She only had to stop and look around. The proof was everywhere. Her home. Her job. Her best friend. All of the things she surrounded herself with on a daily basis was hers *because* of November. Even the very truck she was driving still bore the scars of an encounter with something impossible.

Even if she wanted to, she couldn't deny that these things were real.

And she was about to get neck deep in them again.

According to Ian, the first marker for the second Hand of the Architects was hidden somewhere in Sukmukwe Mounds State Park, about halfway to Madison from here. *Maybe*. "Might be," were the actual words he'd used. When she pressed him on the matter, he confessed that he wasn't entirely sure. "Only the seekers could ever really be certain," he'd explained.

Seekers. She and Piper. That's what people who knew about the true weirdness of the world kept calling them. According to these people, only *they*, with their special gifts, had the ability to find and obtain the Hands of the Architects. This was the Keeper's design, the mechanism that kept them from falling into the wrong hands until it was time to start building the next universe.

Why the unfathomable forces looking down upon this world would choose two unremarkable Wisconsin girls as the only two people in the entire *history* of an entire *universe* capable of finding the three most powerful objects ever created was so far beyond her imagining that it hurt her head to even attempt to contemplate it. It made absolutely no sense. There had to be literally *millions* of people out there far more suited for things like this than her and Piper. People with any kind of basic combat training, for example? Marines? Navy SEALs? Government agents? MMA fighters? Even a couple of nightclub bouncers would be better suited than Persephone Kipp and Piper Holleworth. They weren't fighters. They didn't know how to defend themselves. Seph's father had at least taught her some basic self-defense, enough to thwart a common mugger or a would-be rapist. But that wouldn't protect her against a *demon*.

An incubus… A year ago, she would've laughed at something so absurd. But the truth was that an incubus wouldn't even be the strangest thing she'd ever seen.

She turned onto Lodwyn Road and headed south as she contemplated her encounter with Ian. How much did she trust this man? She was still angry at Amethyst for lying to her all those years, but she didn't believe for a second that she would do anything to actually harm her. If Amethyst—or Lyla or whatever the hell she was calling herself today—sent Ian to help them find the next Hand, then Ian was someone they could trust.

But Amethyst also trusted the librarian in Muntony.

Until she knew for sure who this Ian Heffler really was, she intended to keep a close eye on him...which wouldn't be too much of a chore, she supposed. He wasn't exactly hard to look at.

She called Piper's cell phone as she turned off Lodwyn onto Pinewest Avenue, but after ringing a few times, it went to voicemail.

She wouldn't have thought twice about this on any other day. Piper wasn't as attached to her cell phone as a lot of people she knew. She frequently left it on the charger and forgot about it for hours at a time. She also had a habit of leaving it on the end table or the arm of the couch and then wandering off to make herself a snack or use the bathroom. But this time, she couldn't help feeling anxious. Her imagination was quick to suggest about a dozen horrible things that might've happened to her in the short time she'd been away.

Seph turned onto Kourtney Drive. This was her street. She could see her apartment building from here. And yet the urge to push the accelerator all the way to the floor only grew.

It's fine, she told herself as she killed the engine and jumped out into the stifling heat. *Everything's okay.* But as she hurried into the building, she couldn't help but look out over the lawns, half-expecting to see the unnatural form of a wraith melting into the grass.

There shouldn't be any more wraiths. Amethyst had assured them that they wouldn't be a problem anymore. Seph had wielded the scythe, the only object they feared, and now they'd associate it with her, regardless of the fact that she'd only possessed it for a moment before it vanished. They'd never come near either of them again. But she found that she still couldn't help looking over her shoulder whenever she thought about the foul things.

They were still out there, after all. Somewhere.

What if they stopped being afraid of the scythe?

And even if Amethyst was right about them, what *other* horrors were lurking out there?

She ran up the stairs and threw open her apartment door.

The book Piper was reading was resting on the arm of the chair, but Piper, herself, was nowhere to be seen.

"Where did you go?" snapped Meg. All that was visible of her was one bare foot sticking up over the back of the couch, resting on the cushion. She'd made herself comfortable and was watching one of those stupid daytime talk shows on the television.

Seph ignored her and walked to the hallway. "Peps?" she called.

"Ugh…" groaned Meg. "It's *you*."

Ditto, thought Seph. The bathroom light was on, but the door was open. She could see from the living room that she wasn't in there, so she made her way to Piper's bedroom and checked the door. It was unlocked. "Pepper?"

"She's not here, *obviously*," grunted Meg.

Sure enough, the bedroom was deserted. She turned and walked back to the living room. "Where'd she go?"

"I don't know. I went and took a pee and when I came back, she was just gone. *Rude*."

Seph rolled her eyes. Classy as always.

And why did everything that came out of Meg's mouth have to sound so bitchy? Did the girl even *know* how to use a polite tone?

She called Piper's cell phone again. As she listened to it ring, her eyes drifted to the table next to the door.

Piper's purse was still here.

As the call went to voicemail again, she crossed the room and opened it. Her wallet was still inside, as were her emergency snacks and her sunglasses. Only her keys seemed to be missing.

And her cell phone.

And *her*.

She wouldn't have gone far without her purse. Her driver's license was in there. Had she decided she needed to take a walk? It was awful hot out for a stroll, but it wasn't impossible. Seph sometimes felt like she'd risk taking a walk in a *hailstorm* if it meant a break from Meg.

"You're almost out of those iced cappuccino bottles, by the way," said Meg. "Get the mocha ones next time. Those're better."

Seph left the apartment again before she said something one of them would regret.

She walked back down the stairs, glanced around to make sure Piper wasn't hanging around down here somewhere—sometimes she liked to loiter around the mailboxes for some reason—and then walked back outside and looked around.

There was still no sign of her.

Her Grand Cherokee was still here. She couldn't have gone far in this heat on foot. Piper wasn't exactly known for her love of rigorous fitness. She hated getting sweaty.

She made her way slowly back toward her truck and tried once more to call Piper's cell phone. Halfway there, she froze as a familiar ring tone cut through the humid air.

Chapter 6

Seph's heart dropped.

Piper's cell phone was lying on the ground next to her SUV.

She walked over and picked it up. It didn't appear to be damaged. Her own name and number were displayed across the screen for a moment before the voicemail took over.

She turned and scanned the lawns, the trees, the bushes, but there didn't appear to be a single leaf out of place. There was no sign of a struggle. No blood, thankfully, but nothing else, either, that could shed light on what had happened out here.

A closer inspection of the vehicle revealed that the door was ajar. She opened it and peered inside. Empty. Like the cold, awful feeling that had begun to swim through her belly.

Piper…

Relax, she thought. It was as if the voice in her head belonged to someone else, because she wasn't fully aware that she was panicking until the word crossed her mind. Her heart was racing. She was close to hyperventilating. She turned and leaned against the hot door, her eyes flitting across the lawn. "Oh god…" she sighed. "Oh god…" *It's okay*, she thought at herself. *She's okay. She's got to be okay.*

There was a perfectly reasonable explanation for all of this. There had to be. "Relax," she said aloud. "Relax and breathe. Just breathe. Just…" *Oh god…*

This wasn't right. Everything was already spinning out of control. She *needed* Piper. And not just for her strange, ghostly ears. Piper was her best friend. They gave each other strength.

She wasn't sure she could do this without her.

Keep it together!

She forced herself to take slow, steady breaths. It was okay. Everything was going to be just fine.

Then her gaze drifted toward the roof of the building.

There was a man standing on the ledge up there, staring down at her.

It wasn't fear that gripped her so much as an intense feeling of distracted befuddlement as she squinted back at him. Why was there a man on the roof of her apartment building? How did he get up there? Who was he? She couldn't make out any of his features from here. The bright sun washed out everything but his outline. He was nothing more than a silhouette against the blazing sky. Was he a maintenance man? Was he thinking about jumping?

Several seconds passed in frozen silence as the two of them stared at each other.

Then, with terrifying speed, the man on the roof dropped over the ledge and began to crawl head-first down the brick wall like some kind of freaky, human-shaped lizard.

The weirdness of the sight was so overwhelming that the man had nearly reached the ground before it occurred to her that she needed to be running away. And even when she realized the imminent threat, she found herself frozen there, unsure what she should do. Run, sure, but where? He was *between* her and the building. And her truck was parked too far away. Would she be able to make it in time?

He was so fast...

Indecision locked her legs. She couldn't make herself go.

He jumped the last few feet to the ground, twisting himself upright in a strange sort of rolling bounce. Then he was moving straight toward her, closing the distance at an alarming speed.

Two things became apparent as she stood staring at the approaching stranger. First, he didn't run like a man, upright with arms pumping. Instead, his back was bent, his arms flopping at his sides as if they were too heavy for him to lift. And he had a strange, almost hopping sort of gait that reminded her more of an ape than a man. Second, and far more alarming, this guy was much *bigger* than she first realized. And he seemed to be getting bigger with each step he took.

She was little more than a ragdoll to a man that size.

And for some reason she was *still* just standing here like an idiot as the lunatic rushed straight toward her.

Finally, she managed to break her paralysis and run. She couldn't make it to her own truck, she was certain, so she jumped into Piper's SUV and locked the doors.

Crouching there in the driver's seat, she stared out at the fast-approaching madman, her heart hammering in her chest. Time seemed to slow down as her artist's brain processed every small, horrific detail. His hair was ghastly white. He was dressed in nothing but a pair of tattered jeans and almost every inch of his naked flesh appeared to be covered in a vast array of ugly scars. There was something dreadfully wrong about his body, but she couldn't at first understand what it was. It was subtle. Something about the *shape* of him, the way his muscles moved... It was like when she made a mistake in one of her drawings and couldn't quite tell where she went wrong. His *anatomy* wasn't quite right.

Second by frantic second, it was becoming clear that this was no man at all. It was a *monster*.

She wasn't safe in Piper's Jeep. It wouldn't protect her from that thing. She'd be lucky if it even slowed it down. It might rip the door right off. Or it might simply pick the entire vehicle up off the ground and smash it against the building until her broken body spilled out of the shattered windows. She needed to be ready to go out the other side. But it was like moving underwater. She couldn't seem to get control of herself. Even if she managed to slip out and make a run for the apartment or her truck, there was no way she'd be fast enough to escape.

As the thing closed the last few yards between them, the vehicle was suddenly rocked hard on its shocks, startling a shrill scream from her. In the same instant, Ian dropped to the ground in front of her, colliding with the approaching monster and sending it rolling across the pavement.

She stared out at him. Where did he come from? Did he just vault over the top of the SUV? She turned and looked back at the empty parking lot behind her, then up at the Jeep's moonroof.

The monster sprang back to its feet and launched itself at Ian.

It was definitely not a man. Its body didn't move the way a human body did. Its muscles didn't *flex*, but instead *stretched*. Each time the thing lashed out at Ian, it distorted itself, like a rubber doll.

But as she watched, she discovered that Ian, too, was a monster. He crouched low to the ground and shrugged his shoulders. A strange darkness spread across his muscular arms, seeming to sprout from his skin like hair. And the shape of his body changed, becoming rigid. Dark, reddish horns sprang up from his shoulders, bursting from his tee shirt. His hands bristled into long, spiny claws.

With blinding speed, he leapt forward and slashed open the other monster's throat.

Again, her artist's brain took over the moment and she watched in gruesome slow-motion as its blood sprayed high into the air, gleaming in the blistering sunlight.

The white-haired man-monster should've been dead. Or at the very least dying, its life blood gushing onto the steaming pavement. But the thing was still on its feet. It was clutching at its shredded throat as gore ran between its fingers. The battle was over. It had lost the fight, but somehow not its life. Its strange, yellowish eyes fixed on her as it backed away, as if sending her a message. "Next time…" perhaps. Then it turned and fled, vanishing around the corner of the building.

Ian remained where he was for a moment, crouched down, those wicked spikes bristling along his shoulders and back. Then, slowly, he stood up straight. The horns shrank away, his body softened and that creepy darkness vanished, leaving him human again.

Finally, he turned and looked at her.

She didn't move. She stared out at him, still cowering behind the Grand Cherokee's safety glass. She expected him to yell at her, to demand to know what she was thinking by coming back here when she was supposed to be on her way to Sukmukwe to find the first marker.

It wasn't entirely irrational. Last time she did this, someone was sent to watch over her, too. A body-snatching thing that called itself Warner Harr. It wasn't a very nice babysitter. In fact, it was downright mean. The queer creature berated them almost constantly for taking too long as they made their weird journey west toward the first vault.

Ian, however, didn't look angry. He looked only concerned.

"Are you all right?" he asked.

For a moment, she found herself unable to respond. The fear had melted away and she found herself trapped in his gaze, too distracted to move, lost in those deep, blue eyes…

Maybe it was the heat. It was hot as hell in here.

She shook it off and opened the door. "I'm fine." She jumped out of the sweltering vehicle, embarrassed. "What *was* that thing? Was that the incubus?" He *did* tell her it was a shapeshifter, so it could be a giant, white-haired, wall-crawling lunatic if it wanted to be.

Ian glanced off in the direction the creature had run. "No. An incubus is a very powerful demon. We wouldn't have stood a chance. That was just a revenant."

She wiped at the sweat on her face. "Okay. Then what's a revenant? And what's it doing *here*?"

"Revenants are essentially reanimated souls. Typically souls that have been claimed by a demon and tortured and mutilated into something monstrous. In this case, it's a fully corrupted soul that's been forced into a cursed corpse, making it virtually impossible to kill."

A cursed corpse? She recalled the horrid scars that covered its body, almost as if it had been carved up and then sewn back together, Frankenstein style. "Oh good," she grumbled. "I was worried it was going to be something *scary.*"

"Indeed."

"Why would the incubus send something like that to attack me? I thought he *wanted* me to find the Hand."

"Well, it could be a diversion to keep you moving. If you're constantly scared and on the run, you'll be easier to control."

That did make sense, she guessed. It was basically the same strategy the shepherd used last November when it sent those wraiths after them.

"Or maybe someone else sent it here. The incubus isn't the only one with an interest in interfering with the cycle. Someone might be trying to stop you. You'd do well not to assume that everyone wants to keep you alive."

She didn't like the sound of that one bit.

He offered her a reassuring smile. "I'll do my best to watch your back, but you should be careful, okay?"

"What are you?" she asked, staring at him. "How did you change just now?"

He managed to look embarrassed. "Well…the truth is, I'm like *him.* I'm a demon."

"*You're* an incubus?"

"No. I'm a different kind of demon." He cocked his head to one side. "My kind is related, though. So we have a similar sort of...*pheromone* effect on people. Lots of people find me very attractive."

"Oh," she said, still staring into those deep, blue eyes. Then she shook it off and forced herself to look away. "I see. I mean, I guess. I didn't really notice."

She looked at the spilled blood on the pavement. She wondered who was going to clean that up. What were people going to think when they saw it? It looked like someone had been murdered out here.

But as she watched, she realized that something was happening to the blood. Small curls of smoke were rising off of it, like the mist rolling off the surface of a lake in the early morning.

The color was changing, too, darkening from crimson to black.

"You don't have to worry about the mess," promised Ian. "Revenants aren't a part of this world. They don't belong here, so their remains don't linger."

Sure enough, the bloody stains on the asphalt and Piper's vehicle were turning to ash. It was still visible, but it already didn't look like blood.

"But I'm certain it'll be back again. You need to focus on getting to Sukmukwe."

She nodded. Sukmukwe. Right. She turned and looked at Piper's SUV, at the crimson spatters that had become dry, black flakes. She looked down at the phone she was still clutching in her hand. "Peps..." She looked off in the direction the revenant ran, suddenly afraid. "You don't think it hurt her, do you?"

"Not likely," said Ian. "As I said, the incubus wants you to find the Hand. And it knows you can't do that without her."

Seph stared at the phone. "Then where is she?"

"She'll turn up, I'm sure. Miss Shawbeck speaks very highly of both of you and your talent for getting out of trouble."

"Does she?" She wasn't particularly flattered. She didn't really care what Amethyst said about her. Just hearing someone call her by one of her other names was only a reminder that she was a manipulative liar who only *pretended* to be her friend. The Amethyst she trusted and cared about never even existed.

Ian didn't seem to notice the venom in her voice. "I'll stay here for a little while longer to make sure she's not in trouble. In the meantime, get to Sukmukwe."

Seph didn't want to leave without Piper, but she couldn't deny that things were rapidly spiraling out of her control.

He was right. Piper would turn up. She was resourceful. She was clever.

She was just going to have to trust Ian on this one.

Chapter 7

There was something about a frenzied knocking at one's front door that unfailingly instilled a deep and gut-wrenching sense of dread, no matter whether it was the middle of the night or, in Wanda Janger's case that hot, Mid-July morning, just past nine.

Her heart thumping in her breast, she abandoned the last few bites of her bagel and rushed to the door, terrified of what might be waiting for her there.

What she found was her childhood best friend, gasping for breath, sweating profusely and looking as if the devil, himself had chased her here.

"*Babs*?" she sputtered, staring at her.

"I'm sorry!" gasped Piper.

Wanda looked out at the street, confused to find no sign of Piper's familiar Jeep, or any other apparent mode of transportation. "Did you *run* here? In this heat?"

"I didn't…know where…else…"

"Holy hell, Babs!" She took Piper by the arm and practically yanked her into the air conditioning. "What happened to you?"

Like everyone else Piper knew, Wanda never called her Piper.

But unlike anyone else in the world, Wanda didn't call her by any variation of her real name. She called her "Babs." And she wouldn't say why no matter how much anyone pressed her to explain it. As far as anyone could figure, she just simply decided one day that she wanted Piper to be Babs and that was it.

When it came to personality, Wanda had plenty to spare. She'd always been boisterous, loud and unreserved. Even her style was attention-grabbing. She was fond of pinup fashion and today she was wearing rolled-up, denim capris, a white, sleeveless top with half the buttons undone, revealing the canvas of tattoos that covered her left shoulder and arm. She had flashy Chuck Taylors on her feet and a bright red bandana in her tied-back hair. Even her makeup fit the look. Dark, smoky cat eyes and bright red lipstick.

She was as beautiful and confident as ever. And Piper was wheezing and soaking in her own stinking sweat…

Gross.

"Did you break down somewhere?"

Piper shook her head as she dropped onto the couch.

"You didn't come here all the way from your apartment, did you?"

She nodded and coughed.

"You live, like, three miles from here!"

"I'm sorry," she gasped.

"Stop saying you're sorry! Just…stay there. I'll get you some water."

She nodded again as Wanda hurried to the kitchen. "Thank you," she gasped. It felt like her heart was about to give out. She couldn't remember the last time she'd had such a vigorous workout.

Her hair was plastered to her face. The pits of her tee shirt were soaked.

Did she even remember to put on deodorant this morning? She thought she did, but she wasn't planning on leaving the apartment, so she might've overlooked it. Even if she did, she'd used it up.

So gross.

She didn't know where else to go. One of those freaky kids with the black eyes was waiting for her in the front seat of her Grand Cherokee. The little monster nearly had her. She left more than a few strands of hair in his chubby little psycho fists. She managed to run away, but she dropped her phone when she fell out of the Jeep, and before she knew what had happened, she was alone on the streets of Cakwetak, sweating, out of breath and probably looking like a total freak.

Without her phone, she couldn't call for help. She had friends who lived closer to her than Wanda did, but they were in the opposite direction she'd run, meaning she'd have to go back past her devil-children-infested apartment complex, so she came here instead.

She didn't see any more of those freaky kids along the way, but neither did she linger to let them catch up. She ran all the way here, praying her poor heart would hold out and that Wanda would actually be home when she got here. She knew she wouldn't be working. She was a bartender and only worked nights. But she also had a life.

Wanda hurried back into the room with a bottle of water. Piper drained it all at once and then gasped for air and belched.

"I'm sorry!" she gasped. "Excuse me!"

Wanda waved it away. "You want to tell me what's going on? Are you in some kind of trouble? Do I need to kick somebody's ass? Because I'll totally mess up anyone who messes with my Babs."

Piper wiped at the sweat on her forehead and grimaced. She felt so…*greasy*! Seriously, did she look as gross as she felt? This was definitely not one of her prettier days. But there was no time to be concerned with that sort of thing. "I need to use your phone. Please."

"Sure." She pulled her cell phone from her pocket and handed it to her. "Nine-one-one?"

Piper shook her head as she fumbled with the phone's contact list. "Persephone."

"Seph?" Wanda wrinkled her nose at her, confused. "Is *she* okay?"

"I hope so." She found Seph's number and made the call, then she pressed it to her ear and closed her eyes. "Please pick up…" she whispered.

Wanda bit her lip and sat down on the edge of the chair facing her. What happened? Was she attacked? Was there an accident? What was going on?

"Hello?" said Seph.

"Oh my gosh! Thank goodness!"

"Peps? Where are you? Are you okay?"

"I'm okay. But something seriously messed-up is going on."

"Yeah, I know."

Piper scrunched up her face. "You do?"

"It's kind of a long story. I was just at home looking for you. I found your phone."

"You did? Did you see any of those freaky kids?"

"Freaky kids? What freaky kids?"

Piper brushed a stiff strand of hair from her cheek and frowned. She didn't see any of those weird children? Where did they go? Her eyes twitched toward the windows, half-expecting to see them staring in at her with those eerie black eyes.

"Never mind," said Seph. "Did Ian find you?"

Piper's face scrunched up again. "Who's Ian?"

"Guess not… Where are you right now?"

"I'm at Wanda's place. Where're *you*?"

"I'm on the interstate, heading toward Madison."

"What? *Why*? I thought you were having breakfast with your mom."

"My mom's in trouble."

"What's wrong?"

"It's…complicated. But Pi…it has to do with the *Hands*."

Piper closed her eyes for a moment. She couldn't honestly say she was surprised. This whole mess *did* start with her spirit ears, after all. "What do we do?" she asked.

"Can you get to Sukmukwe Mounds State Park?"

"Sukmukwe? Near Pasoken?"

"That's the one."

Piper looked up at Wanda. "I need to go to Pasoken. Right now."

Wanda stared back at her for a moment, bemused. "Okay… Let me grab my purse."

Chapter 8

Piper assured her repeatedly that she didn't need to go to any trouble, but Wanda insisted on driving her to Sukmukwe. And in all honesty, Piper wasn't sure what other option she had. She couldn't just *walk* all the way to Pasoken. And going home to get her Jeep just seemed like a really bad idea. The only possible alternative was to borrow Wanda's car and she didn't really feel right doing that, either. She'd feel awful if it came back looking like Seph's poor Ford, with its banged-up fender and tailgate.

Wanda was quirky, but in a good way. Almost everyone liked her. Even Seph really liked her. She was a good friend. And she was clever. Of all Piper's friends, Wanda was the only one who seemed to notice a change since last November.

And she *had* changed. How could she not after all she went through? And it wasn't easy keeping such an enormous secret. The Architects. The Grim Reaper's scythe. Mankind's never-ending migration from one universe to the next. It was all so wondrous. It was all so *big*. She'd stumbled upon some of the most profound secrets of the universe! Keeping it to themselves seemed... *wrong*.

Except for the fact that no one in their right mind would believe a word of it. They couldn't very well go around telling everybody these things. That was how people ended up in straightjackets.

November had changed her life. She was different now than she used to be. In lots of small ways. And in at least a few *big* ways, too, she thought.

No one else seemed to notice anything. If she seemed a little different it was probably because she had Seph around now. They lived together. They spent a lot of time together. She was pretty sure that every person you met in your life changed you in some small way or another. That was the true beauty of making friends. And Seph had quickly become her very *best* friend.

But Wanda wasn't like the other people in Piper's life. She was a lot smarter, for one thing. She was a lot more observant. She noticed all those little things that other people ignored. She even seemed to know that Seph was more than just some random woman who answered an online ad for a roommate. And what Wanda was hoping for now was the chance to finally figure out what was really going on with the two of them.

And Piper had no idea how to keep it from her anymore.

She slid into the passenger's seat of Wanda's shiny little Volkswagen Beetle. Super cute car, bright yellow with a big, pink, custom bow painted on the trunk. But adorable or not, Piper didn't think she could feel comfortable driving something this small around. It seemed like all those big trucks would just run right over her.

Wanda started the engine and cranked up the air conditioning. "So are you going to tell me what's really going on, or what?"

Piper already felt small crammed inside this tiny little car, but she shrank even more as she slouched down in the seat. "It's complicated…"

"Obviously. What's going on with Seph? Why do you need to be in Pasoken so badly? And who were you running from?"

She was an extraordinarily good liar. When she needed to, she could be very convincing. And she was extremely good at making things up on the fly. It was something of a defense mechanism, really. Sometimes it was easier to tell a convincing white lie than to risk an awkward confrontation, which she really, *really* hated. But she didn't think she could lie her way out of this one. "Bunch of kids," she replied, looking out the window.

"Kids?" Wanda frowned. She *did* say something about "those freaky kids" when she was talking to Seph. "*What* kids? Like a gang or something?"

"It's *really* complicated," said Piper. "And it's a really long story. I really need you to trust me, okay?"

Wanda stared at her.

"Please?"

She sighed. "Fine. But it's going to get really hard to keep trusting you if you won't stop keeping secrets from me."

"I know. I'm sorry."

Wanda shook her head and steered the bug toward the street. She pulled up to the curb and looked out the window for oncoming traffic. "Uh…what the hell is *that*?"

Piper leaned forward and looked past her. About twenty yards away, crouched on the sidewalk under the shade of a large oak tree, was a strange, black figure. It looked sort of like a man crouching down on all fours, but it had no discernable features. In spite of the bright sunlight, it was shrouded in an impossible darkness. "That's probably not good," she sighed.

"Is that one of those freaky kids you were talking about?"

"No. That's...something different."

Back in November, the creature that called itself Warner Harr had looked sort of like that when it was finally forced to reveal its true form. But she was immediately certain that this wasn't Warner. Although also impossibly black and featureless, Warner had constantly shifted in and out of view, as if he only barely existed in this world. And what could be seen was definitively *not* human. This thing had a more distinctly human shape, like a living, three-dimensional shadow.

"What's it doing here?" asked Wanda, a clear note of fear in her usually unshakable voice.

"I don't know." But if Seph were here, she'd likely say that it probably wasn't here to deliver a singing telegram. "We need to go the other direction. *Now.*"

Wanda twirled the wheel and turned right. As soon as the Beetle started rolling, the thing sprang to its feet and ran after them. She screamed and stomped the accelerator all the way to the floor.

That same, unnerving static that filled Piper's head in the presence of those creepy children was suddenly back. She pressed her fingers against her temple and rubbed at the pain that had blossomed there as she watched the thing through the back window. Was it somehow related to those kids? Was it one of them? A more advanced form, more suitable for chasing down faster prey?

It reminded her of Peter Pan's wandering shadow. Except this thing was exponentially more terrifying.

And it was *fast*. It was quickly catching up to them, even as the bug's speedometer crept past forty.

"Try to lose it!"

"*Really?*" snapped Wanda. "I thought I'd stop and ask if it needed a ride!" She turned at the next street and sped away, and the shadowy runner disappeared from view.

Piper watched the intersection, waiting for the thing to run into view after them, but it didn't follow the road. It darted out from beside them instead, having cut the corner through someone's yard. This unexpected appearance, as well as the fact that it was much closer to them now, startled a scream from her.

"*What does it want?*" shrieked Wanda.

Piper didn't want to say what she thought it wanted. There was no reason for it to want Wanda. And she couldn't picture the thing driving around in a bright yellow bug with a big pink bow on its butt. Just like those freaky, black-eyed children, it could only be after *her*.

Why was this stuff happening again?

Wanda made a hard right onto another street.

Again, the runner disappeared from view, only to reappear even closer from an open driveway.

Wanda made another hard, right turn, then a left, running both stop signs.

The runner cut across the street and vanished from view again. A pickup truck going the other way slammed on its brakes. A mail carrier stopped what she was doing to turn and watch the thing, her shocked expression clear even from this distance.

Piper found it somewhat reassuring that they weren't the only ones who were seeing the thing. But reassurances wouldn't amount for much if it actually caught them.

Wanda made another hard left just as the runner darted out onto the street, passing close enough this time to touch the bug's bow.

Piper watched as it reached out its hand. Its fingers were longer than they should be. And there were too many of them. They made her think of the reaching branches of those creepy old trees in children's books that always scratched at your window on dark and stormy nights.

"What *is* that thing?" squealed Wanda.

Piper didn't have an answer for her. But whatever it was, it was showing the same sort of relentless intention as those freaky children.

It was just like the mall wraiths back in November…

A red light loomed ahead of them. That was the Trawling Road intersection, one of the main city streets. Wanda slowed down as she approached, studying the traffic. It wasn't too heavy this time of day. There was an opening. She floored it.

Piper thrust her hands against the dashboard. Thankfully, she always buckled up, or she was sure she'd have ended up in Wanda's lap.

When the inertia eased, she looked out the window. She didn't see the runner anywhere. Had they lost it?

"We need to get onto the interstate," said Wanda. "Where I can really put the peddle to the metal." They'd been lucky so far. The traffic was light. But that luck wouldn't hold out much longer.

Ahead of them was another red light. That was the intersection of Trawling and Lodwyn. Traffic was always much heavier there. They weren't going to be able to avoid stopping.

Piper nodded. "Preferably heading for Pasoken."

"What do we do?" asked Wanda.

Piper didn't know. She turned and looked behind them, searching for any sign of the speedy, black creature. "Maybe we lost it?" But as they passed a thick grove of trees on the right, she looked out and caught sight of something sprinting through the shade.

Wanda pressed her foot down on the brake as they approached the intersection. The light turned green, but it was still going to take a few seconds for the traffic in front of them to begin moving again. "What happens if that thing catches us?"

"I don't really want to find out."

"This is crazy! What is going on with you? Are you in some kind of trouble? What did you do?"

"Overdue library books?" replied Piper.

"I'm serious!"

"*Way* overdue library books?" she squeaked.

"You and I are going to have a seriously long talk if we get out of this mess!"

She shrank down in her seat again. "I know…"

As they slowed to a stop, Piper scanned the passing parking lots, trying to catch another glimpse of the runner.

There was a little old lady strolling slowly down the sidewalk. She looked up at the bug and met Piper's gaze. She gave her a kind smile.

"Come on!" groaned Wanda. She checked all her mirrors. She looked over both shoulders.

Piper looked back at the road behind them.

No runner.

Where did it go?

Finally, the car in front of them began to crawl forward.

"Come on, come on, come on!" groaned Wanda, still checking her rearview.

"I don't see it anymore," said Piper, turning around in her seat again.

"Where'd it go?"

"Maybe it's all the traffic. I mean, it'd make sense, right? For something like that to exist and no one to know about it, it couldn't go running out onto busy roads. Especially with everyone carrying around cell phone cameras."

Wanda glanced over at her. "I don't know. Maybe. I guess?"

Or maybe that was just wishful thinking. Piper wasn't sure. And she wasn't ready to let her guard down. She kept looking out her window, watching the spaces between the buildings as they passed.

But they reached the westbound onramp without incident and sped off down the interstate.

"I think we might be okay now," said Wanda.

"Don't let your guard down, though. Those kinds of things like to let you think you lost them and then jump out in front of you."

It didn't make sense. Why would the runner chase them this far just to give up? Was it just toying with them? Something just didn't seem right.

Wanda glanced over at her. "I'll stay on guard. *You* tell me why we're suddenly in a horror movie."

Piper glanced over at her, sheepish. "You're not going to believe it."

She raised an eyebrow. "How 'bout you just try me?"

Chapter 9

Sukmukwe Mounds State Park was easy enough to find. There was no shortage of signs pointing the way. The real problem, Seph realized as she pulled into the main parking lot, was where to go now that she was here.

There were two roads leading farther into the park. The signs informed her that one would take her to the West Mound picnic area and the Sukmukwe Campground, while the other would take her to the East Mound picnic area and river access.

Directly in front of her, between the two roads, was a huge, sprawling field surrounded by lush forest and dotted with the ant-like forms of a couple dozen park visitors wandering along the many winding paths.

She'd heard about the Sukmukwe Mounds pretty much all her life, but she'd never actually been here. Hiking had never really appealed to her, and there was little else to do in a place like this.

From what she knew—which admittedly wasn't much—this was the site of some ancient, Native American city. The mounds, according to experts, were originally the bases of religious temples and other important buildings.

She sat behind the wheel, looking out at the open field. There were several mounds out there, she saw, but two of them stood out from the rest. One on either side, opposite each other. The East Mound and the West Mound, mentioned on the signs.

Even squinting at them, she couldn't see anything that resembled a city. They just looked like hills. Sure, they were squared off and perfectly flat on top, but otherwise they weren't all that impressive. How did they even spot those back when this area was covered in trees and brush?

She glanced around at the quiet parking lot. What was she supposed to do now? Should she wait here for Piper? It was highly likely that finding whatever was hidden here would require both of their special senses. And if the revenant that showed up at their apartment was any indication, they didn't have any time to spare. Inaction didn't seem like an option, but where was she supposed to go? The West Mound? Or the East Mound? Or to some other far corner of the park? It was a lot of ground to cover.

If Piper were here, maybe she could use her spirit ears. The first marker on the path to the scythe emitted a signal that only she could hear. It led them to the exact spot where it was buried and then, with the location narrowed down, Seph had been able to see through the Keeper's illusion to the entrance. Without Piper, she was sure she never would have been able to find it.

She could feel the seconds ticking away. At this very moment, something terrible was probably moving toward her as she sat here wondering where to begin.

She killed the engine and stepped out into the sweltering heat.

The most productive thing she could think to do was just walk out there and have a look around. With enough luck, maybe she'd catch sight of something before Piper showed up, saving them some precious time.

But as she set off along the walking trail, she realized that her mind hadn't fully comprehended the true size of the park, in spite of how tiny all those people looked as they wandered from mound to mound.

It could take all day and all night to search all of Sukmukwe. And that was probably a grossly optimistic estimate.

She began to feel the weight of the ordeal she was facing. Not just the task of finding some long-hidden secret in this vast sea of grass and dirt, but the realization that she was all that stood between her mother and a cruel, withering death.

Travis.

That bastard.

When she thought about how happy Buffy seemed whenever she talked about him… What kind of monster would do something like that? How could anyone, even a *demon*, find pleasure in such cruelty?

The worst part was that even if she succeeded, there'd be no happy ending for poor Buffy. She'd live, sure, assuming everything went as planned…but her "gentleman" boyfriend would be lost. Seph would only have two choices: she could tell her the weird truth, that Travis was really a demon from hell who'd been slowly killing her all this time because that's how incubi got their sick kicks…or she could *not* sound like a raving lunatic. If she kept her mouth shut, the world would go on, but Buffy would never know why the first guy who'd made her feel like a human being in almost a quarter of a century had disappeared off the face of the earth without a word. Knowing her, she'd probably sink into another of her crippling depressions and spiral back into that ugly, self-destructive cycle she'd been trying so hard to climb out of.

But the truth... Would she even believe it? Would it make anything better if she did?

She didn't know what to do.

She swatted at something that was buzzing around her ear. A mosquito? God, she hated those things.

Something small leaped out of the grass and landed on her arm. She squealed and brushed it away. It was probably a grasshopper. Nothing that would bother any normal person. Except she wasn't exactly normal when it came to bugs. It didn't matter what kind it was.

She stepped wide of a bumble bee that was hovering over the path, then squealed again as another grasshopper sailed in front of her face.

She stopped and forced herself to clear her mind.

It was okay. She was fine. She could do this.

She took a deep breath and looked around.

The place didn't seem any smaller out here. If anything, it looked bigger the farther she walked.

It made sense, she supposed. It was a city, after all. A sprawling metropolis. Once upon a long-forgotten time.

Something buzzed in her ear again. She flapped her hand at it and started walking faster this time. She just needed to hurry. That was all. The sooner she found what was hidden here, the sooner she could get back into her truck and leave this bug-infested place.

How did her prophet sight work again? On one hand, she used it every single day. Every time she looked at Piper she could see those iridescent ears poking out of the top of her head. She saw them automatically, and without effort, as if they were as real as her nose or her fingers. The same had been true at each of the three markers they visited in November. The writing on the black cube, the map disk and the tomb had appeared to her without any effort at all on her part. But there were other things that her special sense had showed her that *didn't* come to her effortlessly. The hidden tunnel opening in Messing Knob, the secret passage in the Muntony Public Library basement, even the sickening truth about Pappy Stan's horrific diner had remained frustratingly elusive until it was almost too late.

That was how this was going to be. She was sure of it. She could be walking right past a great big doorway right now and her stupid prophet sight might be passing right over it.

There was some sort of trick to it, she thought, but she'd never been able to figure out what it was. She found herself squinting at her surroundings, but that didn't feel right. Looking *harder* wasn't the answer.

Was she supposed to relax?

It had something to do with the right mindset, she thought.

Did it work better when she let her mind wander? When she let herself get distracted?

She swatted at another mosquito and then jumped as something stirred the grass a short distance from where she was walking.

She stopped and turned around, scanning her surroundings.

This wasn't going to work. Even if she found the right mindset, there was a good chance she wasn't anywhere near it. She needed to narrow down this thing's location first.

What she needed was a better view.

She looked ahead again. The path she was on was veering toward the East Mound.

She hesitated for a moment, wondering if she should go back to her truck and drive over there. It was considerably closer to go back than forward. But what if the thing she was looking for turned out to be between here and the East Mound?

Wouldn't she do better, logically, to keep moving and cover as much ground as possible?

She continued forward, picking up her pace.

Where was Ian? Was he still searching Cakwetak for Piper? Did he know she was safe and on her way here? Surely he did. He seemed to know enough to be able to locate her outside Buffy's apartment. And he knew just when and where to come to her aid when that revenant showed up.

She wished he was here. Maybe he could give her some sort of clue about what it was she was looking for. But that wasn't the way it worked, was it? That wasn't how Warner handled things last time. Ian had even told her as much. He was only allowed to watch over them and occasionally offer advice, which seemed like a load of bull to her, but what did she know?

By the time she reached the base of the East Mound, she was already winded and sweating. She wasn't dressed for this kind of activity. She was dressed for a nice breakfast at her favorite, air-conditioned café near the university. She was wearing her cute sandals, not her comfortable running shoes. And this skirt wasn't doing her any favors, either.

She supposed Piper was right. She really *should* own more clothes that weren't black. She could feel the hot sun soaking into the cloth, slowly baking her.

As she climbed the steep steps toward the top of the East Mound, she undid two of the buttons on her shirt and tried to let out some of the heat.

This sucked. She couldn't believe people came here and did this crap for fun.

Finally, she reached the top and stopped to rest. There were several people already up here. A young couple was standing on the far side, holding hands and enjoying the view. A family with two hyperactive boys was just setting off down the other set of steps. An old woman was wandering around, a serene sort of smile on her face, as if this place held precious memories. And a middle-aged man in a straw hat was taking pictures with a very expensive-looking camera.

None of them looked like they were breaking a sweat in this heat, and Seph found herself compelled to stand up straight and try to not look like the wimp in the group.

Forcing herself to breathe as normally as possible, and doing her best to ignore all the spiders and ticks her mind insisted were crawling around on her bare legs, she made her way to the side of the mound overlooking the majority of the park.

It was pretty out here. The sun shined down across the fields. The breeze sent ripples across the grass. There were birds flying above. Somewhere, children were playing. But she still couldn't see what the big deal was. Sure, someone had clearly *made* the mounds.

Now that she was looking at them like this, they didn't look natural at all. They were completely out of place in this otherwise flat area. But other than that, what made them so special? Sure, maybe they were important sites a long time ago. Maybe to generations of people these mounds represented God and heaven. Maybe these were where the priests prayed and made offerings.

Or maybe, with no internet or action movies or video games, they just got bored and made a bunch of really big piles of dirt.

Focus, she thought. She concentrated on the view in front of her. She squinted.

No. Not like that.

She forced herself to relax. Instead of looking harder, she let her gaze drift out over the grassy fields. She let herself feel the breeze. She let herself feel the sunshine as it beat down on her. She noticed the color of the sky. The soft clouds above.

She cleared her mind.

She let it come to her.

Finally, she saw…nothing.

It was still just a big field full of big, pointless hills.

Frustrated, she turned and walked all the way around the top of the mound, letting her gaze drift out over the grounds.

By the time she'd returned to where she started, she was already sick of this place.

Maybe she was at the wrong mound.

But that one was so far away… And she was so hot…

Her hair was plastered to her forehead. She probably looked like something that crawled out of a drain pipe.

This was stupid.

"It's fascinating, isn't it?"

She turned to find that the old woman had stepped up beside her, her smiling eyes looking out over the park. "Huh?"

"A thousand years ago, this was a thriving city. Generation after generation of people spent their entire lives here. To them, this was the whole world. Everything else was just a frightening mystery."

Seph stared at her, unsure what to say to that.

"And today, the only things left of all those people are these mounds. Nothing more than a footprint left behind in the mud. We don't know who they were. Their names. What they looked like. But they lived and fought and loved and struggled just like any of us." She smiled and turned her wistful gaze on Seph. "Sometimes I wish I could see it. Just once. Back in time. Back when the footprint was still fresh."

Seph still wasn't sure what to say.

"Sorry. Sometimes I just lose myself in thought."

"It's okay. I don't mind."

She smiled again. Then she tilted her head a little, as if really seeing her for the first time. "Aren't you hot in all that black?"

Seph blinked, surprised.

The old woman turned and walked away. "You should find some shade soon. Pretty little thing like you'll wilt in this heat."

She watched her amble off toward the steps. She moved slow and steady, but managed those steps without so much as a totter.

Her cell phone alerted her to a new text message. It was Piper, asking where she was.

She texted back that she was in Sukmukwe, on the East

Mound.

Piper texted right back that she and Wanda weren't far away. Another five or ten minutes.

She pocketed the phone and looked out at the park again.

Hills. Mounds. Piles of stuff. It looked to her like those ancient people had just lifted up the lawn and swept all their junk under it before leaving.

That was it. Mystery solved.

She chuckled a little to herself at the thought.

But the humor faded as she stared out over the park again. What was it the old lady said? A footprint?

She supposed it *was* like that, now that she thought about it. Wipe away all the man-made stuff and this was what was left. This was where it all used to sit.

She tried to picture this place as it might've been a thousand years ago. People wandering around, working, playing, socializing. Farmers and hunters and gatherers. Mothers and fathers and children. She recalled pictures she'd seen in museums of the people in this area, dressed in deer hides and living in grass huts. Was that an accurate representation, she wondered, or mere assumption?

She gazed out at the farther mound and imagined a building there. Mud and logs, grass roof, smoke curling up. It wasn't so hard. She *was* an artist, after all. Imagining things and then bringing them to life was what she did.

Footprint.

She stared out at it all, taking it all in. The footprint of a city. The footprint of an entire civilization.

She felt her heart leap in her chest. The hair on her arms and neck stood up. A fierce tingle ran all the way up her spine, cutting through the heat like a cold blade.

The footprint of a city...

She could see it.

It was so subtle, almost completely lost beneath the waving grass, beneath a thousand years of accumulated soil. Beneath the very weight of *time*.

Many *centuries* had slowly scrubbed away at it, trying to erase it from existence. But she could see it now. The faint lines that once made up the foundations of buildings and walls. The flat, packed earth of roads. The scars left by posts driven into the earth, now long-since rotted. Dimples in the ground where fire pits once burned for countless hours. Subtle depressions. Nearly-invisible shapes.

It was like looking at one of those Magic Eye illusions. Look at it only on the surface and it was nothing more than a two-dimensional scene, but focus your eyes just so, and move your head a little...and suddenly you were peering into a three-dimensional space.

But this wasn't as simple as the difference between two dimensions and three. This was like looking through time, itself.

The paths that people were walking on today were all wrong. The real streets ran in straight lines, leading to and from the mounds...but also to many other structures, only a very few of which stood on mounds.

The city had a purposeful, geometric layout to it, centered between the two mounds, with three circular courtyards at its center.

In November, she and Piper were told that this wasn't the first universe and wouldn't be the last. They were told that mankind had migrated here when the last universe began to wither and die, and that they'd done so many times before that, too. Compared to the idea that her ancestors had been around throughout the lifespan of many universes, the thought of thousand-year-old Native American cities just didn't have the same kind of magic about it.

But standing here now, watching the past unravel before her, she couldn't help but feel an almost overwhelming sense of awe.

She could see so much... So many places where human feet had trampled down the earth. So many living souls had wandered this land.

So many homes had been built here. The land was dotted with the shadows of so many of them. The more she looked, the more she saw. They seemed to overlap each other, as if built one on top of another.

No...

What she was seeing was *time*.

Not all those homes existed at once. Old ones were torn down, or burned down, or collapsed, replaced by newer ones, not always in the same place, not always of the same size or shape, so that over the centuries, a vast amount of buildings had existed in this area.

She could see the entire history of the Sukmukwe city. And *beyond*.

There was a city here before they built theirs.

And another city before that.

People had been here a very, *very* long time.

And she could see it all.

The longer she looked, the farther back she could see. Below the streets of ancient Sukmukwe to the underlying shadows.

All the way back.

Until...

Her gaze slid to the far side of the park, along a faint shadow of an invisible path, to the edge of the woods that separated the fields from the river.

Over there...

Chapter 10

Even as Wanda turned off the highway, Piper knew they were where they were supposed to be. A strangely ominous "humming" sensation had suddenly blossomed in her brain.

It was different from the "static" in her apartment that led her to those scary kids, though she couldn't quite explain *how* it was different. This one was less irritating, somehow, but more *insistent*...if that made any sense. And, of course, it didn't. None of this stuff ever made any sense.

It was also different, she thought, from the Messing Knob Broadcast Signal, which made her feel sick, and the humming chicken at Harv Tottlestep's farm in Minnesota, which was just...*weird*.

This sound sort of *thrummed*. It reminded her of those booming bass speakers some people had in their cars. She could feel it inside her head, a faint and unpleasant sort of pounding sensation.

"Isn't that Seph's truck?" asked Wanda. It was the first thing she'd said in a while. She was still processing all the things she'd just been told.

Piper looked up. "It is." She'd recognize that dented tailgate anywhere. "A monster did that," she said, gesturing at it. "Big, wooly, buffalo kind of thing. Huge tusks."

"Oh..." She stared at the damaged vehicle, surprised. "I...uh...always sort of assumed she was just a really bad driver."

"No. She's a good driver. It was the monster's fault."

"Huh." Wanda parked next to the big Ford pickup. Her head was spinning. Multiple universes? World-crafting giants? Godlike weapons of mass...*creation*? Ghostly animal ears and hordes of monsters? The *Grim Reaper's scythe*? It was absurd. *Never-before-seen levels* of absurdity. And yet, less than an hour ago, she was chased several city blocks by an inhumanly fast, black figure.

"She said she was at the East Mound," said Piper, squinting out at the two large mounds and wondering which of those distant, human shapes was her roommate. "I'll call her and see if she's still there."

Wanda nodded and passed her her cell phone. She didn't say anything. She was still trying to understand what was happening. The most logical explanation was that this was all some stupid prank. Babs and her new friends were obviously trying to pull one over on her with this insane story and a bunch of guys in black morph suits.

Except it didn't *feel* like a prank. For one thing, it was going on way too long. Why would they bring her all the way to Pasoken just to humiliate her?

Also, although Babs had always been a suspiciously good liar and a pretty fantastic actress, pranks weren't exactly her thing. She was too nice of a girl to pull something as mean as this.

Most of all, however, it was the runner.

The stubbornly logical part of her mind told her that it was just a guy in a morph suit or some other costume. *Several* guys, stationed at different points along the road, each jumping out in turn, giving the illusion of a single, supernatural thing fast enough to keep up with a speeding car.

But that didn't really make any sense. For one thing, it was *dangerous*. How many traffic laws did she break trying to escape? And how would they've known which way she'd go? And then there was the feeling she got when she first saw the thing... That was no guy in a morph suit. She'd seen people in morph suits and they didn't make the hair on the back of her neck stand up.

Whatever the runner was, it'd seriously given her the willies.

"Where are you?" answered Seph.

"We're parked next to your truck," replied Piper. "Are you still at the East Mound?"

"No. I'm crossing the field now. Meet me on the other side instead."

"Did you see anything?"

"Uh... It's sort of hard to explain. But I think what we're looking for may be in the woods near the West Mound campsite. *Hurry*."

"Okay." She disconnected the call and handed the phone back to Wanda. "The west one."

Wanda pocketed the phone and shifted the bug into reverse without a word.

Piper stared out across the field. Was that her? The one by herself and dressed in black? She thought it was, but she couldn't be sure from this distance.

"Thanks for not telling me I'm crazy."

Wanda glanced over at her, surprised. "What?"

"I know how it all sounds. It's why we agreed never to tell anyone about it. Persephone and me."

"Yeah… I guess I probably wouldn't tell anyone either."

"You wouldn't have believed me."

"No. I wouldn't have."

"You don't even really believe me now."

Wanda started to tell her that she was wrong. Of course she believed her. But it was a lie she didn't think she could pull off. Instead, she said, "It does kind of go against everything we've grown up believing."

Piper chuckled. "Believe me, I know. For me, a big part of growing up was finally convincing myself that there aren't any monsters out there. Not under your bed, not in your closet, not squeezed into that little space behind your dresser…" She stared out the window, her thoughts roaming. She was the worst about that when she was a girl. She used to make her dad check every inch of her room before turning out the light. And then last November came around… Suddenly, she discovered that monsters *were* real. And it didn't matter how thoroughly Daddy checked your room because they could hide in the walls and ceilings. They could hide in the pipes in the bathroom. Under the appliances in the kitchen. Inside the air ducts. *Anywhere.* They could hide in your shadow if they wanted to. Worse still, they didn't need to hide at all. They could just wait until all the lights were off and seep right through the window screen. Or they could just appear at the foot of your bed while you slept. "Monsters are real." She turned her gaze back to Wanda. "I didn't want you to have to know that. It's better not to. I'm so sorry."

For some reason, these words gave her a fiercer chill than the runner.

Perhaps it was the brutal honesty in her eyes.

Wanda turned her attention to the road in front of her. "Forget it," she said. "It's not like I believe you anyway."

Piper smiled. "Right. So it doesn't really matter, does it."

"Not in the least."

"Good." She turned her attention back to the park, her smile melting away. "We're getting closer."

Wanda looked out over the open fields. "How can you tell?"

"I can hear it."

"I don't hear anything."

"I hear it with my spirit ears."

She looked at her friend. "Oh yeah. Those." They'd known each other since they were little. They went to school together. And Piper had never once had a pair of animal ears poking out of the top of her head. But that wasn't really surprising because only Seph could see them. Apparently. "So…what does it sound like?"

"Like whispered screams and angry laughing."

Wanda stared at her a moment longer, then turned her attention back to the road. "Oh," was all she could think to say.

Chapter 11

It wasn't easy following the old path. It kept blending into the terrain and vanishing, forcing her to stop and search for it.

She shouldn't have even been able to see it. This wasn't a path that was built by the people of Sukmukwe. It wasn't even built by the people who came *before* the Sukmukwe. Or the people who came before *them*.

It wasn't even *built*. It was just a trail worn through the grass.

Maybe not even that.

It may have been nothing more than a single set of footprints.

She had no idea how it was she could see something like ancient footprints. She could almost understand seeing the layout of the ancient city from the top of the East Mound. Something like that left actual scars in the earth. They had technology now that could see things like that. It didn't seem like such a stretch that her prophet sight could do the same. But to see *this* far back? And to see something so faint across so many ages?

It was a lot to take in. She wasn't entirely sure how to feel about being able to do these things. It was a little overwhelming.

But she didn't have time to dwell on the matter. The incubus had made certain of that.

She didn't run. Ian warned her that the revenant would come back and she wanted to make sure she conserved enough energy to put plenty of distance between her and it when it did. But she didn't dare take her time either. She knew that every second that passed was another second something terrible drew closer.

And yet she couldn't help stopping every few steps to escape one of the millions of disgusting bugs that infested this stupid field...

God, she hated bugs!

Finally, she reached the edge of the woods and stopped.

This was a strangely creepy place. It was dense and wild here, meant to serve as a barrier between the natural, pristine features of the mounds and the modern picnic area beyond it. But it was more than that, too. There was something about this place. It wasn't just shaded. It was unnaturally dark. There was a coldness about these woods, even in spite of the sweltering heat.

Her mysterious prophet sight failed her here. The ghostly shapes she'd followed to this place broke apart in the tangled underbrush and vanished completely.

She'd lost the trail.

"Persephone!"

She turned to see Piper and Wanda running toward her. *Perfect timing*, she thought.

"Oh my gosh! I was so worried about you!"

"I'm fine," Seph assured her. "I was worried about *you*."

"I'm okay."

"What kind of trouble have you gotten my Babs into?" demanded Wanda.

Seph stared back at her, surprised. "Uh…"

"Um, yeah…" said Piper. "I kind of told her everything."

"Everything?"

"Well, most of it, I guess. What I had time for, really. I just kind of…summarized."

Seph nodded. There was nothing they could do about it. "We have to hurry. That revenant could be here any minute."

"Revenant?"

"Long story. I'll fill you in later."

"Is that what the black thing was that chased my car?" asked Wanda.

Seph looked back and forth between the two of them. "Black thing?"

"Long story," said Piper. "Is this the place?"

"I think so." She turned and walked to the edge of the woods and peered through the foliage, but she still couldn't see anything beyond where the trees started. "I found a hidden path leading to this spot."

"Something's in there," confirmed Piper. "I can hear it."

Seph sighed. "I'm *so* not dressed for this."

Piper made her way along the edge of the woods, focusing on the unpleasant pounding in her brain. It was a lot stronger now than it was at the front of the park. Was this getting easier? Was she starting to learn how this worked? It was hard to tell.

"So…what're we doing?" asked Wanda.

"Looking for the first marker," replied Seph.

"Right. And the marker points the way to a…a *hand*, is it?"

"The Hands of the Architects. It's a metaphor. We're not looking for their actual, dismembered hands, only their tools."

"Oh. Well, that's good to know. Tools sound a lot better than hands."

Seph followed Piper as she made her way along the edge of the woods, her eyes fixed on those ghostly ears. They were an iridescent gray, ghostly, like shimmering fog. She used to think they glowed, because she could see them even in the dark, but she didn't think that was exactly right. They always looked exactly the same, regardless of the light, because she didn't see them with her real eyes. Her brain only seemed to process them the same way. These things never appeared brighter or darker because they didn't reflect visible light. Brightness was, after all, nothing more than a measurement of light.

It was the same way the things Piper heard with those ears didn't have volume.

She'd first described them to Piper as looking like cat ears, but that wasn't exactly right. They didn't precisely look like any particular animal's ears. But they were probably more similar to a cat's ears than anything else.

She'd drawn and painted a number of pictures of them so Piper could see what she looked like from her perspective, but she didn't think she'd ever quite gotten it right. For some reason, it was really hard to reproduce.

"So…" said Wanda. "She can *hear* it? This marker thing?"

"It gives off a signal that she can follow with her spirit ears."

Piper stopped and turned her head, studying that queer thrumming.

"Too far," deduced Seph.

Piper nodded and turned. She pointed into the forest. "That way? No…" She turned a little, pointing a few degrees to the right."

"No," said Seph. "This way."

Again, she nodded. This time she pointed a few degrees to the left. "There," she said with confidence.

"Right."

"You can hear it, too?" asked Wanda.

"No. Only *she* can hear these things. But when she's listening, her ears rotate toward the sounds they hear. Like a cat. So I can *see* where the sound's coming from that she's hearing."

"Oh…"

Her prophet sight only began working a few weeks before she first met Piper. In that time she saw two other people who had the same kind of ghostly ears on their heads. She thought at first that she was hallucinating, a symptom of the combination of too much stress and too little sleep at a time when she was pushing herself in hopes of landing a promising job. But both of those people had later turned up dead, hunted down by the wraiths that had apparently been following her all that time. It was the reason she felt compelled to approach Piper when she first caught sight of her. She couldn't bear the thought of seeing another brutal murder on the news and wondering if she could've prevented it. In the months since then, however, she'd only caught sight of one other person with these bizarre spirit ears. A skinny, middle-aged woman in bohemian style clothes with what appeared to be luminescent rabbit ears sticking straight up through the top of her floppy hat. She only saw the woman for a moment, and only from behind the wheel of her truck as she sat waiting at a stop light. She'd worried that the woman would meet the same gruesome fate as those first two men, but she never turned up on the news. Now that she'd found Piper, it didn't seem that the other spirit-eared people out there in the world were in any danger. And that was an immense relief.

She turned and looked out into the woods where Piper's spirit ears were now fixed. She *really* didn't want to go in there. It was probably *crawling* with bugs. Way more than there were in the field. And they'd probably be nastier, too. "Is there a better way in over there?"

Piper scanned the tree line in front of her. "No." She walked straight toward the source of the "sound" and began pushing her way through the dense brush.

It was harder than it looked, especially in flip-flops. She didn't get far before one of them got caught on a stick and she lost it. And when she bent over to pick it up again, a low branch snagged her hair and instantly became tangled.

It occurred to her fairly quickly that this would be a terrible time for that runner or those black-eyed kids to pop up again. For a moment, she couldn't even stand up straight, much less run away.

"Here," said Seph. She reached in, careful to check for any spider webs, and snapped off the twig. "Maybe you should put your hair up."

"I didn't bring any hair thingies."

Right. Like last time, they didn't exactly have a chance to prepare for any of this. At least *she* had her purse. Poor Piper left the house with nothing but her keys and phone, which reminded her: "By the way, don't let me forget to give you back your phone."

"Oh yeah. Thanks for finding it."

After checking for any bugs, she pushed her way into the brush behind her. "Thanks for not being *dead*. Seriously, it kind of scared the hell out of me when I found it on the ground."

"Sorry. It was those kids' fault."

"Kids?"

"Yeah. A bunch of them. Ow! Stupid branches. They were dressed weird and had these creepy, all-black eyes. *Ow…*"

"Black-eyed children? Like, the ones they talk about on the internet?"

"You know about them?"

"Just what I've seen online. Scary kids with black eyes that try to get you to invite them into your house or car. I thought they were just creepypasta."

"Creepy what?"

"Like an urban legend, but on the internet."

"Oh."

"Like Slender Man."

"Please tell me *he's* not out here somewhere, too," said Piper.

"Slender Man's not real. He was made up to scare people on the internet."

"But black-eyed children are real?"

Seph stopped and swatted at another mosquito. "Uh…"

"You know what? Maybe let's not talk about more creepy stuff right now."

"Deal."

Wanda turned and looked out across the open field as her friends pushed their way deeper into the forest. Were they supposed to be doing this? Could they get in trouble? Obviously, this part of the park wasn't maintained for visitors.

At least there wasn't any sign of the runner.

"Ow…" groaned Piper as she pushed her way through a tangle of wild grapevines. "Owie… Ow! *Ouch*!"

Seph followed behind her, trying to bend back as many of the branches as she could and keeping an eye out for cobwebs. "*So* not the right shoes for this."

Finally, the woods began to thin out a little. Piper stumbled out into an opening that wasn't quite a clearing, but was thin enough to at least walk through. She looked down at her stinging legs and found that she was bleeding in several places. "Watch out for thorns," she called back.

"Too late…" grunted Seph. She stumbled out of the brush behind her, rubbing at a painful scrape on her right cheek.

Piper plucked a twig off her shoulder and then cocked her head again, listening. The thrumming was stronger now. They were closer.

Seph gave a hard shudder and brushed herself off. It was impossible not to imagine that there were bugs crawling all over her now. She was probably covered in ticks. And something was still buzzing around her head. She could hear it.

Wanda let out a sharp cry behind her. "Little help, please?"

Seph turned to find her tangled in vines. A stray branch had snagged her shirt and was pulling it back, exposing her bra. Another had her by the hair. "You probably should've just waited for us back there."

"No way! What if that runner thing came back?"

"What's a 'runner thing'?"

"Kind of hard to describe," explained Piper. "Sort of human-shaped, but all black."

"It chased my car," said Wanda as Seph unhooked her shirt from the branch.

A shadowy runner, black-eyed children *and* a revenant?

"Thank you," said Wanda. She stepped out into the clearing and looked around as she fixed her hair again. "That really sucked."

"Life of a seeker, I guess," grumbled Seph.

"Oh look." Wanda pointed into the woods ahead of them. There was an opening there, with picnic tables and trash cans just visible through the leaves. "All we had to do was walk around and come in that way."

"Aw!" said Piper.

"Of course," grunted Seph. She turned and looked at Piper. "Where is it?"

"Um…" She turned her head this way and that, focusing on that weird hum. "I think it's…"

"This way," said Seph.

"Yeah."

Wanda looked in the direction Seph was pointing. "There's nothing here."

"That's just what it wants you to think," replied Seph.

Piper began walking in that direction, following the "sound" of the humming. If the unpleasantness of it was any indication, they were definitely getting close. She caught herself clenching her teeth against it. It was definitely one of the most unpleasant sounds she'd ever heard.

Seph followed behind her, keeping her eyes on those iridescent ears.

After a moment, they began to twitch left and right, as if confused.

"You passed it," said Seph. "It's around here somewhere."

Piper stopped and turned around, scanning the surrounding woods. "I don't see anything. Your turn?"

"Probably." She turned in a circle, taking in her surroundings.

"What's going on?" asked Wanda.

"I can follow the sound to the general area of the marker," explained Piper, "but only *she* can see the entrance. It's hidden. Like my ears."

"Oh. Okay."

Seph ignored them and tried to clear her mind. It seemed to work best when she didn't try too hard.

But it was hard to clear your head when there were things hunting you.

And Wanda wasn't helping much, either.

It wasn't that Seph didn't want her here. She liked Wanda just fine. She was a good person. She was a great friend to Piper. She was fun to have around. And compared to Meg, the woman was a saint and a genius. It was just that she was worried about her. She wasn't sure if she was capable of handling things like demons, revenants and black-eyed children. It was a lot to take in, after all.

She should know.

"What do you see?" asked Piper.

Seph frowned. There were footprints here, too. But they were so faint. They were buried deep in the earth, way back in time. And beneath nature. It was difficult to be sure. The road didn't run straight here. It sort of dispersed. It became muddled somewhere between here and the edge of the wood.

She closed her eyes and tried to relax.

Forget Ian. Forget Travis. Forget the revenant. Focus only on this place. Something was hidden here. She just had to find it.

When she opened her eyes, nothing had changed.

"Anything?" pressed Piper.

Seph looked back at her, frustrated. She looked out into the woods behind her. She looked down at her own feet, as if she might have been standing on it this whole time. She even looked up into the trees.

Nothing.

"What happens if she can't see it?" whispered Wanda.

"She'll see it," Piper assured her. "Just watch."

Seph wished she had that much faith in herself. She scanned the woods again.

Maybe a different perspective would help.

She turned and took a step to her left, and with a sharp scream, she fell into a hole.

Chapter 12

"Are you okay?" asked Piper.

Seph was fine. The hole wasn't very deep. And it was filled with dirt and leaves, providing a fairly soft landing. But as she pushed herself up off the ground, she caught sight of a fat spider scurrying out from under her. She cried out and scrambled to her feet, brushing at her clothes and hair.

"Was this here the whole time?" asked Wanda.

"Weird, isn't it?" said Piper.

"Is it, like, an optical illusion or something?"

"Something."

The hole was about the size of Seph's pickup, longer than it was wide, only a few inches deep on this end, but sloping down to about four feet on the other side. It might've been a natural sinkhole of some sort, except for the carefully laid stones that lined its walls.

"Is this what we were looking for?" asked Piper.

"Unless you think there's another suspicious hole around here somewhere I should fall into instead," replied Seph. "But personally I think this one's enough for one day."

There was a large, flat stone laid across the other side, half-buried in the earth so that the hole they were standing on sloped off into darkness beneath it.

Seph and Piper made their way down the slope to the edge of the stone and peered under it. Seph shined her cell phone light into the darkness.

"What do you see?" asked Wanda.

"Spiders," said Seph, eying the curtains of cobwebs that filled the cavity beneath the stone.

Piper stood up and searched the nearby trees.

"Spiders?" said Wanda.

"She hates spiders," explained Piper as she climbed out of the hole and broke off a suitable branch. "They *really* creep her out."

"Well, lots of people are scared of spiders," reasoned Wanda.

"Not like Persephone. And it's not just spiders. All bugs. Even butterflies."

"Seriously?"

"I can't help it!" snapped Seph.

Piper dropped back into the hole and used the branch to sweep the opening clean. "She's totally phobic. It's kind of adorable, really."

"I'm *not* adorable," she grumbled as she peered into the shadowy hole beneath the rock again.

"It was kind of an adorable scream you made when you fell in there," recalled Wanda. "Very girlish."

"I'm not girlish."

"Whatever. What do you see?"

The stone that rested over the other side of the hole was set into the earth considerably farther back than it appeared from up top. The opening reached back another ten feet. And at the very back…

"Another hole," reported Piper.

This one was round, about three feet across, set directly into the ground.

Piper ducked under the rock and crept toward it, using the branch to sweep away the remaining cobwebs.

Seph followed behind her, taking extra care to make sure there was nothing squirmy where she placed her hand and knees. She really hated this sort of thing.

The hole dropped about six feet straight down, into a small tunnel with a shallow, underground stream running along the floor.

"Wait," said Seph. "Do we actually have to go down there?"

"It's just water," said Piper.

Seph groaned.

Wanda stepped down into the hole and approached the opening, peering under at them. "You guys can't be serious."

"We don't really have a choice," said Piper.

"I know," relented Seph.

"I totally don't know which sounds worse," said Wanda, "following you guys down there or waiting up here for that black thing to show up again."

"She should probably stay with us," said Piper.

"Not a good idea," said Seph.

"We can't just leave her out here."

"Of course we can. Don't you remember what happened last time? Those zombie things?"

"Zombies?" said Wanda. "Like…*real* zombies?"

"You think there'll be something like that down there?" asked Piper.

"Probably. What if taking her down there sets off another trap?"

"But Amethyst told us that only a malicious intruder could set off the traps. Wanda's not malicious. She should be safe."

"Maybe. But what if that revenant shows up while we're down there? Or more of your black-eyed children? Do you think she could handle a giant zombie worm?"

Both of them turned and looked back at Wanda.

She stared back at them from the far side of the hole, her eyes wide. "You know what? You guys go ahead. Maybe just take some pictures for me or something, okay?"

Seph glanced at Piper. "Wouldn't hurt to have a lookout."

"But will she be safe out here?"

"Probably as safe as she'd be with us."

"You guys are starting to freak me out," said Wanda. "You know that, right?"

"Let's just get this over with," said Seph, peering down into the hole. "You first."

"Why me?"

"*Spiders!*" she whined.

Piper shot her a dirty look. She didn't mind getting rid of spiders and other creepy crawlies for her friends, but she was getting a little tired of having to always go into the scary, monster-filled holes first. But there was no point in arguing over it, so she said nothing.

There wasn't any good way down into the stream. The Keeper, or whoever had built this place, had neglected to include any kind of ladder or steps. All she could do was sit on the edge with her feet dangling and then hop down into the water.

It wasn't very deep, only about an inch, but it was surprisingly cold. She let out a squeal as it splashed up her bare legs.

Not for the first time, she wished she'd taken the time to put on her sneakers instead of these flip-flops.

Seph handed her cell phone down to her. "What do you see?"

She switched on the flashlight and shined it one way and then the other. "It narrows off really fast downstream," she reported. "So I guess we don't have to waste time wondering which way to go."

"Are there spiders?"

"Just give me my branch," she grumbled.

Seph handed it down to her and then hopped in after her.

"Be careful!" called Wanda. "Hurry back! Please…"

The tunnel wasn't quite tall enough to walk upright in. They had to crouch down a little. And Seph was *very* aware of all the horrid little things that were crawling around on the walls and ceiling.

"How long has this been here?" wondered Piper.

"I don't know. Almost as long as the world, I assume. Maybe hundreds of millions of years."

"You'd think if water had been running through here for that long, it would've eroded the floor away. Isn't that how water and rock work?"

"The world was built by three giants," Seph reminded her. "And one of them was carrying the Grim Reaper's scythe. I don't think physical science applies as much as we used to think it did."

111

"Fair point."

The tunnel shouldn't have been very long. According to Piper's ears, the signal it gave off in the form of that queer "thrumming" was only coming from a point about twenty yards from here. But the tunnel didn't run straight. It curved to the right, then back to the left again. Then it just kept turning left…

Piper's ears kept twitching toward the inner wall.

They were circling around the source of the signal, spiraling inward toward the marker.

Seph looked back the way they came, concerned by the distance they were putting between themselves and the exit.

Something was probably going to happen down here.

Something always happened in places like these.

Finally, Piper's light fell on an opening. "That's it," she announced. "That's where the sound is coming from."

Chapter 13

At the center of the spiraling, underground stream was a small, domed chamber, only slightly taller than the tunnel, allowing them to stand up straight again, but with only a few inches to spare. The walls were solid stone, with several curved, black beams set into them, converging at the very top, like the bars on a birdcage. The water they'd been wading through appeared to be seeping right out of the stone and trickling down the walls.

"This place is going to make me have to pee," said Piper.

"We're probably the first people to set foot in here in who knows how long and *that's* the first thing that crosses your mind?"

Piper shrugged. She reached out and brushed her fingertips across one of the black beams. It was cold and smooth, like polished obsidian, utterly featureless. It was identical to the cube at the center of the *other* first chamber, back in November. Touching that cube had shut down the signal, clearing her head of the disorienting noise. The same didn't happen here. That curious thrumming sensation went on and on.

It wasn't nearly as bad as the sickening sensation of the Messing Knob Broadcast Signal, fortunately, but she still didn't think she wanted to linger at the center of it for very long. It made her feel uneasy.

She turned and looked at Seph. "Is there writing?"

Seph was already studying the black surface. "Yeah."

"Is it the same as last time?"

"I think so."

"What's it say?"

"Give me a minute."

Piper nodded and said no more. Only Seph's prophet sight could detect the invisible writing on the markers. To everyone else, the surface was utterly blank. Curiously, though, the symbols were not only visible to Seph, they were carved into the very surface of the stone. She could feel them beneath her fingers when she touched them.

She still couldn't wrap her head around how *that* worked…

She glanced around the small chamber, nervous. The first time they found a place like this, a dozen freaky, mutant zombies burst from the walls and attacked them. The experience was so terrifying, neither of them had been able to move at first. She could clearly remember standing there, screaming her head off, unable to make herself run away as they shambled toward her. If not for Seph, who knows what might've become of her.

The walls in that chamber were cobbled together from small stones. These walls were apparently porous enough to let a spring seep through, but it didn't look like rotting corpses would be able to break through it.

She reached out and tapped on it, just to be sure.

It seemed solid enough.

But the walls weren't the only concern she had. She aimed her light down at her feet.

The second marker on the way to the scythe was a much larger room hidden under a seemingly ordinary library in South Dakota. Those walls had been solid, too. It was the *floor* that opened up to reveal the undead monster lurking there: a gigantic, festering, slime-covered worm.

They hadn't fared a whole lot better against *that* thing than they did the mutant zombies in Messing Knob.

The floor of this chamber seemed to be made of the same, porous stone as the walls, as if the entire room had been carved from it.

Was this chamber similarly boobytrapped? And if so, what manner of horror was slumbering here?

And from where would it emerge?

She suddenly realized that her heart was racing. She was terrified.

Seph ran her fingers across the black stone. She could feel the lines etched into the surface. These symbols looked real. They *felt* real. And yet, they were only real to her. She snapped a picture with her cell phone just to prove it to herself. Just like last time, the photo revealed exactly what Piper and presumably everyone else in the world would've seen: featureless, black stone.

It defied reason.

But in a world filled with monsters and demons and Keepers and world-crafting giants, she supposed reason was overrated.

For a frustrating couple of minutes, she could make no sense of the symbols. But she remained patient. It took a little while in November, too. She just had to keep looking.

Sure enough, after a while she caught sight of something.

It was the same language as last time. Or at least the same *sort* of language. It wasn't the symbols themselves, but rather their arrangement. If she looked at these markings up here…then down at these…then there on the next beam…

She circled the room, her fingers dancing from beam to beam, sliding up and down, back and forth.

"Evil."

Piper glanced over at her, startled. "What?"

"I see evil."

"Like, the *word* evil?"

Seph frowned. "Not exactly. More like…the *concept* of evil."

"How do you read a concept?"

"It doesn't read in words. It's more like…" she struggled with her own words for a moment, unsure how to describe it, "…like it reads in *ideas*."

Piper scrunched up her face as she tried to wrap her head around that.

"I don't think there're any words to describe it, exactly. It's like…" She reached over and ran her fingers down one of the beams. "Over here there's this…I don't know… I get this really strong feeling like everything's slowly getting dark. In an *ominous* sort of way. That's the idea I get." She turned around and touched the top of the dome, near where the beams met. "And up here…it's like…like when people just turn away and ignore the bad things that happen." She turned around and pointed at another beam. "This is fear. Like…deep-in-your-gut kind of fear." She turned again and knelt down, touching another beam near the bottom. "And this feels like…" She paused for a moment, distracted. "It's like…like hope dying. Like…you can't feel joy anymore…" Her eyes drifted to the next beam. "Emptiness. Despair. Tears. It's like…" She stood up straight again, but her eyes lingered on that spot, on that *idea*. "It's like how it felt when my dad died…"

Piper reached out and touched her shoulder.

"It's okay," said Seph. "It just feels bad. *Worse* than bad. Like, I can't really put it into words. It's like all those things, but on this really *epic* scale. It feels like the world coming to an end. It feels… It feels like *evil*."

"It's almost like it's talking about the state of the world."

Seph glanced back at her, surprised.

"Like, the way there's always something horrible in the news. And the way the whole country seems to be divided on, like, every issue."

"Yeah… Sort of. I guess." She turned and looked at the beam again. "I mean, that's kind of a depressing way to think about it…"

"Does it say anything else?"

She turned back to the beams, scanning the hundreds of symbols. A painfully slow minute passed. Then, finally, she said, "Se-crets."

"Secrets?"

"I think so. Maybe? It's…complicated." She turned and scanned the beams. "Hidden things. Like…hidden *truth*, maybe?"

"You mean, like, *lies*?"

She gave her head an indecisive sort of wobble. "Sort of. Maybe."

"What else?"

She turned around again. Then she looked up at the ceiling where the beams met. "Army."

"Army?"

"Soldier, maybe?"

"Soldier?"

"No. That's not right. It's less specific than that. It's more like…*protector*."

"Oh."

"It doesn't quite translate. Maybe it's talking about Ian? He protected me from that revenant."

Piper considered this for a moment. "Maybe it's talking about the Keeper."

"Yeah. It could be him, too."

"Does anything tell you where we should go next?"

Seph frowned. "I don't see anything." She turned and scanned the beams, searching for anything else that might help point the way forward.

"There has to be something," reasoned Piper.

Did there? Seph wasn't so sure. Last time they did this, they didn't leave the first marker with any clear answers. It was the mysterious hitchhiker who pointed the way forward. It was only in hindsight that the random words carved into that mysterious cube made any sense.

Something caught her eye. This time, it wasn't an idea. It seemed to be an actual word. But she had no idea what it meant. "'Tane,'" she read.

"Huh?"

"Tane," she said again.

"What's a tane?"

"I have no idea."

"Are you sure you're reading it right?"

"Of course I am. I think. Maybe…"

Piper stared at her.

"How should *I* know?"

"There has to be more." She leaned close to one of the beams, squinting at it, but she still couldn't see any writing on that polished surface. "Doesn't there?"

Seph shook her head and scanned the room again. Evil. Secrets. Protector. Tane. What the hell did any of that even mean? Tane wasn't even a real word.

It was as she was pondering the meaning of this unfamiliar word that something else caught her eye. It began at the very top of the dome, at the very center of where the beams merged, and spiraled downward, jumping from one beam to the next, much like the stream that led them here.

She turned in a circle, following the strange symbols.

Like the first message that spelled out "evil" in a series of unhappy feelings, the chamber told her a story.

"A city in the earth," she said.

Piper looked up, surprised.

"Permanent midnight." She turned all the way around, her gaze sinking lower and lower. "Dirt and stone. Guardians of water." She bent lower, following the queer message. "Angels?" And at the very bottom: "Something about…dark…*strangers*? That's not right. I'm not sure I can translate that. It doesn't make sense. I just see…these dark shapes…and get this really weird, creepy feeling."

"Persephone…"

"Yeah?"

"*Persephone…*"

"*What?*" She looked up, annoyed, to find Piper staring at something behind her. Startled, she turned and looked.

A streak of crimson had blossomed between two of the beams and was running down the wall.

A stream of blood seemed to have cut the crystal-clear water in two and was now flowing from the chamber, snaking its way through the stream.

The smell of it filled the air. It was crisp and coppery.

Something was oozing out of the wall. A lump, like a great, bloody boil, swelled from the stone, then broke into several long, dripping fingers.

A hand stretched out into the chamber, attached to a long, bony arm.

Then another hand.

Then a great, yawning face appeared.

The thing let out a terrible howl and Seph's paralysis finally broke. She took Piper's hand and dragged her back down the spiraling tunnel, splashing through bloody water.

"*What was that thing?*" screamed Piper.

"*How should I know? Just run!*"

But it was hard to run very fast in flip-flops, through water, while crouching down to keep from hitting your head on a low ceiling.

The smell of blood still permeated the dank air, following them as they fled.

Seph dared a look back over her shoulder and immediately regretted it.

There, just visible in the light of her cell phone, was a ghastly, bloody thing dragging itself after them on long, dripping arms. Its face was still stretched into a silent scream.

With a startled cry, she picked up her pace, nearly dragging Piper along.

Ahead of them, muted sunlight shined down from the surface. Somehow it seemed surreal. Surely they'd gone deeper into the earth than that. Surely nothing as strange as that domed chamber or as terrible as the bloody thing pursuing them through this tunnel could exist so close to the sun and the sky.

Somehow, they reached the exit unscathed.

"What's happening?" asked Wanda. "What did you find?"

Piper and Seph climbed up out of the tunnel and then crawled out from under the stone on their hands and knees before turning and looking back.

They could hear it coming. It was splashing through the water, getting louder and louder.

"Guys...?" croaked Wanda, her eyes glued to the shadowy cave from which her friends had just crawled.

Piper and Seph both began scooting backward, away from the tunnel entrance, their wide eyes fixed on the ominous darkness.

It was very close now.

Just a few more seconds and it would launch itself through that opening and grab them with its huge, bloody hands. Then it would drag them both screaming back down into that hellish darkness, never to be seen again.

Closer.

Closer.

It was directly under the opening.

Wanda began backing away, but tripped over the rim of the hole and sat down hard on the forest floor.

Then there was only silence.

Seph's heart was thundering. She knew what happened next. This was the part of the movie where the monster suddenly went quiet, as if had vanished. It would give them just a few seconds to think it was gone. Then it would leap from the shadows with a heart-stopping scream and rip them to pieces.

Any second now...

But nothing more happened.

The seconds kept ticking by.

Exhausted, Seph flopped onto her back and stared up into the branches. "I know he's supposed to be on our side, but I'm pretty sure the Keeper's a psychopath."

Piper nodded. Her gaze remained fixed on the hole, still not convinced that the bloody creeper wasn't going to leap out and drag them back into that darkness to devour their souls.

Wanda stood up and brushed off the seat of her pants. "Are you guys okay?"

"Assuming I'm not having a heart attack right now," replied Seph. "Yes."

"What the hell *was* that down there?"

"I don't know," said Piper. "But I'm pretty sure I'll be seeing it in my nightmares for the next few weeks."

Seph closed her eyes and tried to calm down. It was over.

They'd survived another of the Keeper's stupid traps. Now they could hurry on to the next stop before something else showed up.

Except, she still had no idea where to go next.

The words in the domed chamber never told her that. Not in any words that she yet understood.

She opened her eyes and turned her head, looking out into the forest.

There, crawling through the brush on all fours like a predator on the prowl, was the revenant, its wild, not-quite human eyes glaring back at her.

Chapter 14

Seph screamed and jumped to her feet.

Piper and Wanda saw it a second later and then they, too, screamed.

The monster crawled forward only another couple steps, then it stopped, its deathly eyes fixed on Seph. Crouched there in the grass, she was reminded of how it had looked when it crawled down the side of the building, like a great, fleshy lizard.

"What *is* that thing?" stammered Wanda. She was backing away from it, stumbling through the brush.

"Revenant," said Seph. She stood frozen, her eyes locked on the monster's. She didn't dare turn away, convinced that the moment she did it would launch itself at her. She'd seen it move. It was too fast. She had no chance of outrunning it. Especially in all this underbrush.

Slowly, the monster rose to its feet. She'd forgotten how big it was. Up close, it towered over them.

It was still injured. Its throat was tattered and bloody. Its chest and belly were covered in gore. And it didn't appear to have forgotten about that last encounter. It looked positively murderous as it took hold of a large branch that blocked its path and snapped it from the tree as if it were merely a twig.

They were no match for this thing. It was as strong as a machine. It was insanely fast. And it could scale sheer walls. It was like something right out of her nightmares. And she'd had some epically scary nightmares.

"That thing does *not* look happy, you guys," said Wanda.

It certainly didn't. And Seph couldn't really blame it. That neck injury looked like it hurt. The closer it got, the worse it looked. There was blood oozing from the corners of its mouth. And there was an ugly, wet, wheezing noise coming from the gash in its throat that she didn't want to think too much about.

Its yellow, ghoulish eyes were fixed on her.

Piper took another step back and, like Wanda, tripped over the rim of the hole. She fell onto her butt with a yelp.

Seph couldn't move at all. She was convinced that the moment she turned to run, it would pounce on her and tear *her* throat out.

Its movements were so odd. Every step was strangely stretched out of proportion. *Exaggerated.* It made her think for some reason of stop-motion animation, as if the thing were nothing more than a very large and very scary puppet.

And now that she was thinking about it...wasn't that pretty much what Ian told her it was? According to him, a revenant was a tortured and corrupted soul placed inside a reanimated corpse. Was that what she was looking at? A dead body being awkwardly driven by the insane spirit crammed inside it?

The monster opened its mouth and made a strangled sort of

snarling noise.

At least, that's what Seph and Wanda heard. Piper, with her spirit ears laid flat atop her head, heard something else. There was a voice buried inside that snarl. A single, terrible word blew through her brain like a sour wind.

...kill...

"Guys!" whined Wanda. "Why aren't we running away? We should really be running away now!"

The revenant suddenly gave its head a violent shake and lurched forward, snarling.

All three of them screamed.

Wanda turned and fled through the woods, terrified.

Piper tried to get to her feet, but only stumbled again and fell in the underbrush.

Seph's feet still seemed to be anchored to the ground. All she could do was stand there and scream.

Then Ian was there. He stepped out of a sudden breeze, his body bristling with those strange, reddish spikes.

The two monsters collided.

The revenant slammed both of its fists against the side of Ian's head, knocking him aside.

Ian slashed at it with his strange, spiny claws, tearing fresh wounds into the soft flesh of the monster's face.

It stumbled backward, snarling. Then it lifted its face and let out a furious howl.

Piper clasped her hands over her ears as that word filled her head again. *KILL!*

Ian took advantage and drove his horned shoulders into the

monster's exposed belly, goring it.

The revenant staggered backward again, its yellow eyes filled with hatred. Then it turned and bolted away, melting back into the trees like a wild animal.

Ian watched after the creature for a moment, making sure it was really gone, then he turned to face them, his clean, white shirt freshly torn by his otherworldly spikes and stained with the revenant's stale blood. "You girls okay?"

"I think so," replied Seph.

Piper stared up at him, her eyes wide. "Wow..." Then she blushed and said, "I mean... Uh... *Hi.*"

"This is Ian," said Seph. "He's the one who saved me last time that thing showed up. He's a demon."

"Oh..." said Piper. "That's...um..."

"It's okay," she assured her. "He's a *nice* demon, apparently."

"There're nice demons?"

"A demon isn't necessarily evil," Ian explained. "And something evil isn't necessarily a demon. There *are* exceptions to almost everything."

"Oh." Suddenly, Piper felt bad. Did she just stereotype him? That was *way* uncool.

"Is that thing going to follow us everywhere we go?" asked Seph.

"Most likely," replied Ian. "Like I told you before, it's nearly indestructible. All I can do is hurt it and send it away for a while."

"How did it even get here?"

"Things like that have ways of traveling. It would take too long to explain. Just know you'll need to be very careful. Don't spend too long in one place if you can help it."

"Right, because it's just that simple, isn't it?"

Ian smiled. "True. It's not like the Keeper was kind enough to put up signs for you, is it?"

"That *would* have been helpful," agreed Piper.

He turned his smile on her. "If it were that easy, I suppose anyone could do it."

She stared back at him, distracted. "I'm Piper, by the way."

"Yes. Miss Shawbeck told me about you."

"Amethyst?"

He shrugged. "Sure."

"Whatever her name is," grumbled Seph. She turned and looked around. "Uh… Where's Wanda?"

Piper turned and looked behind her.

She was gone.

"I think your friend ran away about the time I arrived," said Ian. "She looked pretty scared."

"Will she be okay?" asked Seph. "That thing won't hurt her, will it?"

"Not likely. A revenant is technically a sort of supernatural mercenary. It's not interested in anything but its target. Unless someone were to intentionally put themselves between it and you, like I did just now, it'll ignore anyone else." He turned and looked out into the woods. "Are you going to need her to help you find the Hand?"

"No," replied Seph. "We should probably let her go. I don't want her getting hurt."

"What about those things that were chasing me?" asked Piper.

"*They* won't hurt her, will they?"

"Nothing should harm her if you just leave her behind."

"Then it's settled," decided Seph.

"Yeah," agreed Piper as she reached for her phone. "But I should let her know we're all right. So she doesn't worry." As she began typing a text message she said, "You know we're going to have to tell her everything, right?"

"I know."

"Did you find what you were looking for down there?" asked Ian.

"I don't know," confessed Seph. "We were interrupted by that...*thing.*"

"The revenant must've set off the Keeper's trap," he reasoned. "But they shouldn't be able to hurt you."

"I don't know," said Seph. "It sure seemed like it wanted to hurt us."

"I'm sure it would've been fine," he insisted. "What you need to focus on is what the marker told you. You *did* find the marker, didn't you?"

"Yeah," replied Seph. "But we didn't find out where to go next."

"I see. What *did* you find?"

"A whole lot of something really *evil*," she recalled.

"That was kind of creepy," said Piper, remembering all those eerie feelings she'd described.

"That's not surprising," said Ian. "There's an evil force at work trying to obtain the Hand. And as this universe ages and decays, it'll naturally breed more evil. It's a part of the cycle, unfortunately."

"Well *that's* a disturbing thought," said Piper.

"Yeah…" said Seph.

"What else did you see?"

"Something about a secret, I think. Or some kind of hidden thing, anyway. That's probably the Hand, right?"

"Or the vault where the Hand is hidden," he agreed, sounding impatient. "What else?"

"Something about a city in the earth," recalled Piper.

Seph nodded. "A city in the earth. Permanent midnight. Angels and dark shadows. It was all kinda weird."

"And that word we didn't know," said Piper. "Tane."

Ian looked over at her, surprised. "Tane? You actually saw his name?"

"Name?" said Seph.

He suddenly looked concerned. "Janon Tane… We had our suspicions, but we couldn't be sure. If he's involved… Well, that would be bad."

"Who's Janon Tane?" asked Seph.

"It would take too long to explain. Tane is *bad*. That's all you need to know."

"Worse than the incubus?" asked Seph.

Piper glanced at her. "Incubus?"

"*Much* worse. If Tane's involved, then it's much bigger than *any* demon." He turned and scanned the woods around them, as if suddenly paranoid.

Seph found that she didn't care much for the sight of Ian uneasy. This was a demon, after all. Although he admitted to being no match for Travis, he'd pretty well owned that revenant twice now. If this Tane guy frightened him this much, then did they even stand a chance against him?

"We need to keep moving," he said, turning his attention back to them. "Did you see anything else while you were down there?"

Seph considered it. An overwhelming sense of something evil. Some sort of protector. Secrets of some sort.

"You said something about a city in the earth?" prodded Ian.

"That's right," said Piper. "Dirt and stone."

"Permanent midnight," recalled Seph. "Someplace underground? A subterranean city?"

Ian considered this. "That doesn't narrow it down much."

"An underground city doesn't narrow it down much?" said Seph, surprised.

"It's a big world. Almost every modern city sits on some kind of buried system, whether it's sewers or steam tunnels or subways or something."

"But we aren't looking for anything modern," reasoned Piper.

"No. But often times a modern city was built on the ruins of an older one, much like this place was. And there are plenty of places, even here in the Midwest, that are as old as this world."

"Seriously?"

"Migration routes used by the first people to cross over from the last universe were often constructed underground. Most of those doorways were sealed afterward, but there're still remains buried all over the world, some of them still functional, even still inhabited by the descendants of the caretakers placed there by the Architects' engineers."

"And nobody's found any of these places after all this time?" asked Seph.

"The Architects had engineers?" asked Piper.

Ian ignored them and continued to ponder the underground city. "I find it highly doubtful that the Architects would've constructed the vaults in one of those places. What we're looking for is likely someplace far more discrete." He stared at Seph. "Can you remember any other details from that chamber?"

Seph considered it. "I don't think so... A city in the earth... Permanent midnight... Dirt and stone..." She cocked her head. "Oh, and something about guardians?"

"Oh yeah," said Piper. "Something like, guardians and water?"

"Guardians of Water..." sighed Ian, his blue eyes widening.

"Yeah, that."

"What is it?" asked Seph.

He considered all of this for a moment and then nodded. "It's a lot closer than I would've thought, but that has to be it."

"*What?*"

"The Guardians of Water are an entirely forgotten name for three lakes in Northern Illinois. They were considered sacred by more than one tribe of Native Americans in the distant past."

"That's where the next marker is?" asked Seph.

"The city that's built there today sits on top of a network of old tunnels."

"An underground city," said Piper. "Just like the marker said."

"Exactly," agreed Ian. "What you're looking for is almost certainly under the streets of Avelby, Illinois."

Chapter 15

By the time she crossed the wide-open lawns of Sukmukwe for the third time, Seph could barely breathe. She stopped beside the Ford, gasping for breath, sweat running down her face. Her shirt was plastered to her skin. She unlocked the door and heaved herself into the sweltering cab. "I've *got* to get more cardio!" she gasped as she started the engine and cranked up the air conditioning.

Piper melted into the passenger seat and nodded. She felt so gross. Why did this stuff have to happen on such a hot day? She had sweat stains on her tee shirt and her bra was beginning to chafe. She felt like she was starting to smell like the gym. "I really hope Wanda's okay," she panted. "She still hasn't texted me back…"

With no idea which way Wanda might've gone after she fled from the revenant, and with no time to waste looking for her, they made the decision to head straight for the front parking lot.

"She'll be fine. She knows how to take care of herself." Seph fanned herself with a Chinese takeout menu from the console between the seats. "Besides, Ian said nothing'll hurt her."

"Those things know where she lives," said Piper. "That runner was waiting for us outside her apartment."

"It wasn't after her. It was after *you*."

"But what if it hurts her to try to get to us?"

Seph glanced over at her. It was a good question. After all, wasn't that precisely what was happening to Buffy? "It won't," she insisted, hoping she sounded more confident than she felt. "Ian said so."

Of course, Ian also warned them to do their best to stay out of trouble. "I've got some business to attend to before I meet you in Avelby," he'd said. "I might not be there next time something shows up."

Right. Because they were *so* good at that.

"How much do we trust Ian, anyway?" asked Piper. "I mean, Amethyst never mentioned him, did she?"

"Amethyst never mentioned a *lot* of things," grumbled Seph.

Piper kept her mouth shut. She'd almost forgotten what a sore subject Seph's ex-roommate was.

"And he's saved me from that revenant twice now."

Piper nodded. That was true.

"Besides," she added. "He's kind of all we've got right now."

Also true.

"We'll go to Avelby and check out these guardian lakes," said Seph, trying to sound confident. "We'll find the second Hand, kick Travis' demonic ass and be back to our normal lives by this time tomorrow."

Piper scrunched her face at her. "Who's Travis?"

"Right. You weren't there." She dropped the takeout menu

back into the console and fastened her seatbelt. Then she backed out of the parking space, taking one last look at Sukmukwe and its mysterious mounds before she aimed the Ford toward the park exit and drove away.

"Oh yeah! You said something happened to your mom. Is she okay?"

"No. She's not. It's…" She shook her head. "She's really sick. She thinks it's just the flu, but it's not. I could see it. The way I could see the words in that chamber."

"Oh my gosh…"

"Ian says she's been poisoned by an incubus pretending to be her boyfriend, Travis. If we don't find the next Hand…"

Piper didn't bother questioning the part about the incubus. Because why not? In a world where reality was periodically rebuilt by giant, godlike Architects, horny demons didn't seem all that improbable. "But we can save her, right?"

"Ian says the next Hand has the power we need. It can make her healthy again. It's the only chance she has."

Piper considered this for a moment. "So it's just like last time. It's like those wraiths."

"Yeah. It's exactly like that."

The Grim Reaper's scythe was the only weapon in the world capable of stopping the wraiths. Without it, those monstrous spirits would've stalked them to the ends of the earth. Giving up had never been a choice. Not for a single second. And it was the same thing now.

Only the monsters had changed.

"Is that Ian guy really a demon?"

135

"That's what he said. I didn't really have any reason not to believe him. I mean, you saw the way he transformed back there."

Piper stared at her, confused. "Transformed?"

Seph squinted back at her, just as confused. "You...didn't see all those spikes pop out of him?"

Piper's bewildered expression told her all she needed to know.

"You *didn't* see him change..." she realized. "Only *I* could see it?"

"I guess. I mean, that's kind of your thing, isn't it? Seeing things no one else can?"

"Apparently..."

"I mean, I saw *something*. But I don't know what. When he first appeared he was sort of...I don't know...*blurry*, I guess."

"Blurry?"

"Like a movie shifting in and out of focus. It was kind of weird." She pinched her lower lip as she recalled what she witnessed in those woods. "I couldn't really see what happened. Everything went all wonky and then that monster was injured and backing away."

Seph drove on in silence for a moment as she considered this. It *did* make sense, given how her prophet sight seemed to work. If demons were real and walking around among us, completely unnoticed, then it made sense that people might not see them for what they really were. And if she could see spirit ears, phantom writing and ghosts, then why couldn't she see a demon's hidden form?

Piper glanced over at her. "He's really...um..."

"Scary?" said Seph, nodding.

"I was gonna say 'hot.'"

Seph glanced over at her, surprised.

"Well he *was*! Didn't you think so?"

She shook her head, flustered. "He's a *demon*. He has these crazy pheromone powers. It's just in your head."

Piper watched her as she spoke, the way the color filled her cheeks. "So you *do* think he's hot."

"*What*? Can we stay on task, please?"

"Sorry." She turned and looked out the window for a moment. "I was just thinking it must be nice. You know, him coming to your rescue twice now like that."

Seph's face flushed a shade brighter. "What're you talking about?"

But before either of them could say another word on the subject, Piper's phone rang. "Oh!" She put it on speaker and held it out in front of her. "Wanda?"

"Where'd you guys go?" She sounded worried and out of breath.

"We're on our way out of the park," replied Piper. "Are you okay?"

"I'm fine. I mean, I'm kind of freaking out right now... Did you say you guys are *leaving*?"

Piper bit her lip and glanced over at Seph. "We didn't know where you went."

"You sort of left us back there," Seph reminded her.

"Yeah..." said Wanda. "That wasn't...um...my coolest moment."

"You're forgiven," said Piper. "Things got pretty freaky back there. You're not used to that sort of thing."

"*We're* not exactly used to that sort of thing, either," said Seph.

"True... And I'm sorry we didn't try harder to find you. But you'll be safer not coming with us to Illinois."

"Why Illinois?" asked Wanda, sounding as if that were the most absurd place in the world for them to go right now.

"That's where the pretty demon man told us to go," replied Piper.

"The *what?*"

"That's right," said Seph. "You ran away before he showed up."

"I'm so confused..."

"You get used to that," said Seph.

"Eventually," agreed Piper.

Seph turned onto the main road and sped off toward the interstate. She checked her mirrors and saw no bloody, crawling monsters, white-haired revenants or black-eyed children chasing after them. After the day she'd had, she decided to take this as a sign that their luck was improving.

"What do you guys want *me* to do?" asked Wanda.

"Just go home," said Seph.

"We don't want you getting hurt," said Piper. "None of those things will bother you if we leave."

Wanda was silent for a moment.

"Don't worry about us," said Piper. "We'll be fine. We've kind of done this before."

"This is really crazy, Babs."

"I know," said Piper.

"I mean, *really* crazy."

"I know."

"Like, my Aunt Doreen has *nothing* on you guys."

Piper nodded. "Yeah…"

"Go big or go home," agreed Seph. She'd heard about Wanda's crazy Aunt Doreen. She had a ton of stories about the woman. If even half of them were true, then out-crazying Aunt Doreen was a nearly epic accomplishment. She couldn't decide whether to be concerned or proud…

"When you get back, you have to promise me you'll tell me everything."

"We promise."

"*Everything*," she stressed.

"We promise," said Seph. And she meant it. There didn't seem to be much point in keeping it from her. It wasn't like she was going to think they were crazy now, and that was the only real reason for keeping all this stuff to themselves.

The thought of having someone else out there who they could actually talk to about this stuff was actually kind of nice.

Wanda sighed. "Call me if you need anything, okay? Promise me."

"We promise," said Piper.

"Be careful."

"We will."

Piper disconnected the call and looked over at Seph. "I *really* hope she'll be okay."

"She'll be fine. I'm sure of it." But she *wasn't* sure. She wasn't sure of anything. And she wasn't nearly as good a liar as Piper. "We need to focus on what we're doing right now," she said, changing the subject. "Like, what happened to you after I left to see my mom? Tell me about those black-eyed children."

Piper leaned back in the seat and pinched her lower lip again as she recalled the events leading up to those monstrous kids. "It was really freaky. I kept hearing this—" She winced and grabbed at her belly. A second later, it gave a loud gurgle.

Seph looked over at her, alarmed. *"You haven't eaten?"*

She bit her lip, embarrassed. "I totally forgot… I was a little distracted!"

"What about your…" She shook her head. She was going to say, "What about your emergency snacks?" but then she remembered that Piper's purse was still at home. "Don't worry. We'll get you something." She turned the truck around and headed back toward Pasoken, instead. It was only a couple miles away and there was a McDonald's right on the edge of town.

Piper's spirit ears weren't her only oddity. She also had a very peculiar condition. As odd as it sounded, she became extremely ill if she went too long without eating meat. (Even after all this time, it still baffled Seph, but it was true.) She'd been eating around eleven and it was already well past that. Given how much energy she'd exerted this morning already, it was amazing she'd lasted this long.

"I'm sorry."

"Don't apologize for something you can't control."

"I should've had Wanda stop somewhere on the way here," she lamented. Then she remembered that she didn't have any money, either. Her wallet was in her purse with her jerky. Seph was going to have to buy lunch for her. And she really hated making her do that.

Seph pushed the truck's speedometer right up to sixty-five and held it there all the way to the city limits of Pasoken.

The McDonald's drive-through line was longer than she would've liked, but it moved quickly enough. She ordered Piper a double quarter-pounder meal and a ten-piece Mcnugget meal for herself. (She didn't care about paying; Piper was her best friend, after all, and she needed to eat.) Then she backed into a parking spot at the rear of the lot where she could both eat and keep an eye out for monsters.

She'd been living with Piper for the past eight months. During that time, she'd almost never missed a meal. When she kept to her schedule, she had perfectly ladylike manners. She was neat and polite and almost obnoxiously girlish when she ate. She even ate Doritos in small bites, which just seemed kind of ridiculous, if she were to be honest.

But on those rare occasions when she ate late, the difference was so drastic that one had to see it to truly believe it.

She watched as Piper tore open her sandwich box and attacked her burger.

This was meat-deprived Piper in all her…uh…glory? She wasn't being disgusting, really. Seph had known quite a few guys who ate like this all the time. It was the stark contrast between the polite and girlish Piper that the world saw and the ravenous, meat-deprived Piper that was shocking to behold.

Personally, after these past eight months, she found the whole thing rather amusing.

Piper took her third huge bite and then froze as she caught Seph watching her. She blushed and shrank back into the seat.

"Doan ach ee ee!" she cried with her mouth full, which translated to, "Don't watch me eat!"

Seph turned and looked out the window. "Sorry!"

Piper swallowed most of what was in her mouth and said, "You know I hate that."

"I can't help it. You're cute when you make a pig of yourself."

"*Ood!*" she said as she took another bite. ("*Rude!*")

Seph chuckled and took a bite of one of her Mcnuggets. She didn't really want them. She still felt gross from being out in that heat. But it would do her good to eat something. There was no way to know when she'd get another chance.

Piper gulped down some soda and burped. "Ugh… Why do I have to be like this?"

"Karma. It's what you get for being prettier than the rest of us girls. You have to be a were-carnivore."

"Ash jush shtupid," she grumbled around another bite. She wasn't prettier than anyone. Certainly not Seph.

Seph popped the rest of the Mcnugget into her mouth and adjusted the air conditioning vent again. Then she looked down at her arms. "I think I might've got a sunburn."

"Oo shu illy ooze shunsheen," said Piper.

"I didn't exactly have a chance to put on sunscreen, did I? I was going to breakfast. I didn't schedule getting attacked by monsters until *next* weekend."

Piper giggled. Then a glob of ketchup dropped into her lap. "*Aw…*"

Seph chuckled again and looked out across the parking lot. As her gaze passed over the building, she caught sight of a small kid staring back at them from one of the windows of the playroom.

Black-eyed children... she thought, recalling what Piper had told her.

That child probably didn't have black eyes. He seemed to belong to a family who was sitting at the table with him. But Seph decided it was time to go anyway. They'd wasted enough time here.

Chapter 16

"She needs to get it through her head that she's not moving back in," said Seph.

"I know," replied Piper. "I'm *trying*." She stared out the window at the passing farm fields. She hated being in this situation. It was true that it wasn't fair to Seph, but she *hated* having to confront Meg about anything. She hated to confront *anyone* about anything, much less irrational *Meg*. There was simply no telling how she might react, except that it almost certainly wouldn't be with maturity and grace…

"*Keep* trying. I mean, does she think I haven't noticed that more of her stuff is in our apartment every day? It's like she thinks if she moves in slowly enough we won't notice."

Piper pouted. "I *know*. I just hate being mean."

"You *have* to be mean to some people."

She wanted to argue with that. It wasn't a very good attitude to have. You should never *have* to be mean to *anyone*. But it was getting harder and harder to defend her ex-roommate. She was being unreasonable. And she'd already pretty well taken over their living room.

"It's not like she doesn't have anywhere to go. She can move back in with her parents. I know they have room."

"She doesn't want to."

"I'm sorry, but I don't *care* what she wants. It's not our fault that most of her friends hate her."

"I don't think they *hate* her…"

"Seriously?"

"Okay, *some* of them probably hate her."

Seph rolled her eyes.

"Some of them *definitely* hate her," conceded Piper.

"Yeah."

The fact that Meg had made such a mess out of everything didn't exactly surprise Piper. She had a nasty habit of turning small problems into epic crises and then behaving like a total psychopath about them. Last Fall, just before Piper and Seph first met, she lost her laptop. Within hours, the situation had escalated to an obscene mess involving a lot of wild accusations and some impetuous revenge sex with Libby Voloner's boyfriend.

As Seph had put it once, that was some first-class bridge-burning.

She shuddered to think what she'd do to "a backstabbing roommate who kicked her out onto the street"—and there was zero chance she wouldn't take it that way.

What really astounded Piper about the whole thing was just how long she was able to keep so much of it swept under the rug. It took another six months for her relationship with Martin to completely fall apart.

And the whole time it was happening, she'd acted like it was *everyone else* who was behaving irrationally!

"Is this it?" asked Seph.

Piper sat up in her seat and looked around. "Already?" They'd only been on the road for an hour and a half.

"Ian said it was closer than he expected," recalled Seph. But last time they did this, they'd traveled all the way to South Dakota by the time they reached the second marker.

Piper was relieved to have an excuse to put the subject of Meg's gradual home invasion on hold, but she didn't think she was quite ready for whatever might be waiting for them in this city. She looked out the window again. There were farm fields as far as they could see on either side of them. The horizon was nearly flat, broken only by a few sparse patches of forest and the occasional barn or silo. Looking at it gave her the strangest feeling of isolation… It didn't feel like she was heading into a bustling city. It felt like she was about to be marooned on a dangerous island in the middle of an unforgiving sea.

Maybe she'd been reading too many dystopian adventure novels.

A road sign told them they were entering Avelby.

"That's it, all right," confirmed Seph.

Piper recalled the bloody creeper that oozed out of the wall in Sukmukwe. She recalled the mutant, bug-infested mummies in Messing Knob. She recalled the enormous, rotting, slime-covered zombie worm in Muntony.

She shrank down a little farther in her seat. She *definitely* wasn't ready for this.

But at least she knew Wanda was safe. She sent her a text

message just a little while ago letting her know that she made it home without any scary encounters. It seemed that Ian was right about the monsters not being interested in her.

That was one less worry on her mind.

Just beyond the city limit sign, the farm fields yielded to a modest, but sprawling commercial district featuring a Farm and Fleet, a Walgreen's and a bustling grocery store called The Avelby Market.

"Where should we start?"

Seph didn't have an answer for her. She'd never been here before. She had no idea what was here. She drove straight ahead, through the first intersection, and made her way down Main Street. It was a really pretty little city. Nice, clean architecture. Lots of trees and flowers. It didn't look like the kind of place that might have a giant zombie worm slumbering under its library. (But neither did Muntony.) She looked out at the passing buildings around her. This city was much bigger than Sukmukwe. And she didn't think she'd be able to see any "footprints" like she did in those wide-open fields. "Ian said there were tunnels under the city, right? So I guess that's where we start."

"Yeah, but how do we find our way into these tunnels?"

Seph frowned. That hadn't occurred to her. "Manholes?"

Piper wrinkled her nose. "Ew. No. We want tunnels, not sewers."

"Sewers *are* tunnels," grumbled Seph.

"There's got to be actual entrances somewhere."

"Do you hear anything?"

Piper cocked her head and listened. The ghostly ears atop her head twitched this way and that, but remained indecisive. "I don't think so."

"I guess we should find somewhere to get out and have a look around."

She drove through the next intersection and found the perfect place. The buildings parted and revealed sprawling lawns, a large, beautiful fountain, colorful playground equipment and majestic old trees. A fancy, wooden sign told her she was looking at Raindskenner Park. No doubt one of the city's proudest landmarks. She pulled into the lot and parked beneath the shade of a huge oak tree.

It was even hotter in Avelby than it was in Sukmukwe. She felt the sweat beading on her forehead as soon as she stepped out into the sunshine.

"Well we found the library," said Piper. She was shielding her eyes from the sun with one hand and pointing to a large, brick structure just past the far side of the park with the other.

"Too easy," replied Seph. Surely *both* of the second markers wouldn't be located under libraries.

"Probably," agreed Piper. She turned around, scanning the buildings around her. At the far corner, she could see the post office. There was a flooring company. A dentist office. A bar. Nothing special. Then she caught sight of a big, colorful sign. "Oh my gosh! That's adorable!"

Seph turned and followed her gaze. C-"Arf"-EE & Treats was the name of the place. There was a big picture of an extremely happy-looking dog. "I don't get it."

"It's a dog-friendly coffee shop!"

"You don't have a dog."

Piper shot her a dirty look. "You're totally missing the point. Come on, that's *adorable!*"

"I don't think coffee is good for dogs."

"The coffee's not for the—*argh!*"

Seph chuckled.

"Maybe I *should* trade you out for Meg."

"You wouldn't dare. Then you'd *really* be stuck with her."

That was true, she supposed. She turned and looked at the businesses across the street. "Hey, a bookshop! Can we go there?"

"We're not here to shop," Seph reminded her. She looked over at the store. Magic Portal Books. Right next to it was a placed called Pluto Is A Planet. Science and Educational Toys. "THINK FOR YOURSELF!" proclaimed a bright banner in the window. She couldn't help but smile a little. It was clever.

On the other side of the bookshop, on the corner, was a Chinese takeout place called Wok 911. There was a little restaurant called The Big Potato, an ice cream shop called Glacier Shakes and a bunch of little clothing boutiques scattered among the florists and hair salons and bars and lawyers' offices.

"This whole city is adorable!" squealed Piper.

"Of course it is. It'll make it that much more terrifying when we find whatever's hidden under it."

"Pessimism, Persephone."

"Pessimism is healthy. It keeps you out of trouble."

Piper made a face at her and set out across the park.

Seph pulled out her cell phone and searched for "Avelby, Illinois" and "tunnels" in her search engine.

"*There's* a tunnel," said Piper, pointing.

Seph looked up. "That was fast."

The park extended to the other side of Main Street. A small, decorative tunnel had been built to let people pass beneath the traffic. "I don't think there'll be anything hidden in it, though."

"No. Probably not." Seph returned her attention to her phone.

Piper stopped and listened. Her human ears could hear all the typical sounds of a city. The passing traffic. Barking dogs. Singing birds. Cicadas. The constant hum of air conditioners. Voices drifting on the breeze. The distant rumblings of factories and engines and machines. But not a single sound seemed to touch her other ears.

She shaded her eyes again and squinted at the businesses that bordered the other side of the street.

"Huh…" said Seph. "There's a whole page on here dedicated to something called the 'Avelby Underground.' It's all about the tunnels."

"That's convenient." Piper pulled out her own phone and began her own online search.

"Yeah. It doesn't look like it's exactly a secret. 'Tunnels stretching for miles,' she read. 'More found every few years.' 'Origins shrouded in mystery.' *Weekend tours?* It looks like they turned the whole thing into a tourist trap!"

Piper glanced up at the tunnel connecting the two sides of the park. "I believe it." She found her way to the page and began skimming it over. "I guess I could've been reading all this stuff while you were driving," she realized.

"That probably would've been smart."

"*You* didn't think of it, either," she grumbled.

"No, I didn't."

Piper stuck her tongue out at her and then went back to reading.

According to the page, there were hundreds of tunnels lying beneath the city, some of them modern, but many of them possibly dating back more than two hundred years.

"So it really is kind of a city in the earth," said Piper.

"Permanent midnight," recalled Seph. "A place where the sun never rises. A place where it's nothing but...*dirt and stone.*"

Piper looked up at her. "Why do you have to make it sound so creepy?"

"*I* didn't describe it that way. That's how I read it in that...water hole...place."

She looked back down at her cell phone. "There's a place called Avelby Underground Walking Tours."

"I saw that."

"Maybe we should start there."

"I don't think what we're looking for is going to be on any tour."

Piper raised an eyebrow at her. "You didn't think it'd be in a children's reading room of a small-town library, either."

"Touché. I guess we can check it out."

"What about this 'Tunnel Park' place?"

"What? Where?"

Piper held out her phone for her to see. "It says an old building burned down back in the eighties and they found a bunch of tunnels intersecting under it."

Seph skimmed over the article. "So they turned it into a park. Makes sense."

Piper turned her phone around and scrolled down, skimming the article. "It says you can explore the Avelby Underground there. There're five different tunnels."

"Those kinds of things are always disappointing. I'll bet none of those tunnels go anywhere. Why else would they actually let people go in them?"

"But if it's like the library in Muntony, it won't matter. Nobody but us would know if what we're looking for is there anyway."

Seph glanced over at her. She was right of course. What they were looking for was supposed to be hidden so that no one on earth except the seekers could find them. Chances were good that the specific tunnel they were looking for would be something that only she could see. If so, then getting inside the correct tunnel wouldn't be a problem. Finding the tunnel entrance, on the other hand, might be much more of a needle in a haystack. "Okay…so we start with Tunnel Park," she decided. "Maybe we'll get lucky and find it on the first try."

Piper looked out at all the little shops. "Can we at least pick up some new shoes?"

Seph looked down at Piper's flip-flops and then at her own sandals.

It *would* be nice to have something they could run in. If it was anything like last time, they'd be doing a *lot* of running.

"Maybe we could check out some of the boutiques. Maybe take a peek in that bookstore?"

"We're not here to shop," Seph said again.

"There's a comic book shop."

"What? Where?"

Chapter 17

Beyond the tunnel and across from the far corner of the park was a little shoe store called Cozy Feet. Both of them found a pair of comfortable running shoes and some socks. Piper, naturally, looked perfectly cute and casual, as if she'd planned from the start on spending an active day in the sun. Seph, on the other hand, couldn't help but feel that her feet and ankles now sorely clashed with the rest of her body.

It was a silly thought.

It wasn't like anyone was going to notice what she was wearing. And even if they did, what did she care? People who paid that much attention to the way other people dressed were shallow. Good people didn't notice meaningless things like that.

Except that she *did* care. She couldn't help it. She always felt self-conscious about how she looked. Part of it was being friends with Piper. And before Piper there was Amethyst. And Kaitlyn and Phoenix. And before them, even way back in high school, there was Valerie Grenlow. She had a strange habit of ending up with best friends who were almost obnoxiously attractive.

She'd always felt as if she could never stand out in a crowd, even if she wanted to. And if she *did* stand out, it would be for all the wrong reasons. She was afraid that if she tried to be as fashionable as her friends, she'd just end up looking like she was desperate for attention. She'd just embarrass herself.

And besides, she liked wearing black. It was simple. It was low key. It was professional. And it was flattering, dammit.

It wasn't her fault the stupid weather was so hot. *She* didn't pick today to do this nonsense.

"We should get you some athleticwear," decided Piper.

"I'm *fine*," insisted Seph, even as she felt the sweat running down her neck. She'd inherited her father's stubbornness, after all.

"Ooh, look!" Piper pointed across the street. "Another bookstore!"

Seph wiped at the sweat on her forehead and squinted in the glaring sunlight. "This town has *two* bookstores? How do they stay in business?"

Piper wrinkled her nose. "Oh. It's an *occult* bookstore. That's different."

Seph paused and stared at the sign. Everyday Magic. Occult books and gifts. "Huh. I wonder if anyone in there would know anything about the tunnel we're looking for."

"You think they might?"

"A place like that might have something about the *weird* side of this town's history."

"You think so?"

"Probably not, but it might be worth a try. It's not like we have any idea what we're doing."

Piper shrugged and started across the street.

Seph followed along behind her, her eyes drifting to the sign over the door of Your One Superpower. Comics and Collectibles. Piper was right. This town *was* pretty cool. She wished they had a few hours to actually shop. But she could feel the time slipping away from them. The revenant was still out there somewhere. So were the runner and those black-eyed children. They couldn't afford to get distracted. But they also couldn't stand around expecting the Hand to come to them.

Her eyes were drawn to a storm drain as she hurried across the street. What would they find inside the tunnels down there, she wondered. What kinds of nightmares lurked in that darkness?

Almost as if in answer, a big, black bug crawled out between the bars and into the sunlight. Revolted, she picked up her pace and followed Piper inside.

Everyday Magic smelled like sage and incense. It was dark and gloomy. Mysterious. It was pretty much exactly what Seph expected it to be.

There were books on display all over the store, but they were only a small portion of the shop's merchandise. There were tarot card decks, crystals, scrying mirrors, candles, incense, runes, bundles of dried sage, little bottles of oils, baggies full of herbs and a whole lot of rustic-looking jewelry. It was less a bookstore than a new age magic shop.

This was the sort of place Amethyst used to love. The Amethyst she thought she knew, anyway...

Piper bent over a display of stone pendants, examining them. She never saw the woman standing in front of her until she said in a faint, wispy voice, "You..."

She let out a startled, "Eep!" and jumped back, nearly knocking over a display of crystal pyramids.

Seph twirled around, startled.

Had the woman been standing there this whole time? She didn't have much of a presence. She was small, barely five feet tall, whisper thin, with an unruly mop of kinky hair so light blonde it was nearly white. A random assortment of small flowers had been woven into those curls, giving her a strangely child-like appearance, though she appeared to be in her late thirties. She wore a wispy, light gray dress and flowery sandals. Her skin was so pale she was almost ashen. Her eyes were a washed-out shade of blue that was almost gray. Even her smile was faint, her mouth small, her lips fine. She reminded Seph of those women in old, classical paintings. But had she really just melted into the background until now?

She turned those faint eyes on Seph now. "And you..." she said. Her voice was as slight as she was, little more than a whisper.

She stared back at her, unsure what to say. Did she know this woman?

"You're not like everyone else," she said, turning those mysterious eyes on Piper again.

Piper nudged one of the crystal pyramids away from the edge of its display shelf and stepped away from it. "What do you mean?"

"You're not like *anyone* else," said the woman. "You're different. Your *souls* are different."

"Different *how*?" pressed Piper. The woman was so slight, so soft-spoken, that she felt the need to lean forward to hear her.

The woman gave her that mysterious smile again and softly replied, "They *shine*."

"Okay," said Seph. "If you say so." She had no idea how a soul could shine. Or do anything else, for that matter. You couldn't *see* someone's soul, after all.

Or could you?

Her gaze drifted to Piper, to those mysterious, luminescent ears. It'd crossed her mind in the past that perhaps those could be an extension of her soul, that they stuck out like that because they didn't fit inside her mortal body.

"It's no coincidence that you're here today," said the woman.

"It's not?" asked Piper. Those ghostly ears perked up, intrigued.

"Not at all," said the woman. "It's destiny."

Piper glanced at Seph, her eyebrows lifting as if to say, "Is she for real?"

Seph wasn't convinced.

"The universe is awakening. It's speaking to me."

"The universe can talk?" asked Piper.

The woman turned and walked between them. She reached out with one small hand as she passed a bookshelf and righted a book about self-healing that had fallen over. A collection of bracelets jangled softly on her delicate wrist as she did so. "Nine days…" she sighed.

Seph cocked her head, confused. "What?"

"Nine days have passed since it happened."

"Since what happened?"

"Since the natural flow of magic was thrown into chaos. Since I felt the great surge in the south." She turned those pale eyes on Seph again. Dramatically, she whispered, "Something has happened… Surely you felt it, too."

Seph shook her head. She had no recollection of anything happening nine days ago. Nine days ago she would've been at work. Her team would've been finishing up on the marketing artwork for the new Fever Island sequel for Inky Net Games. Maybe if she'd said eight months ago…

The woman turned and looked back at Piper. "Nine days," she said, her voice so soft now that Piper again found herself leaning closer to hear her. "*Nine.*"

"You sure you're not burning too much incense in here?" asked Seph. "Maybe you should get some fresh air."

The woman didn't seem to hear her. She turned and floated toward the cash register, straightening merchandise along the way. She picked up a jar of pink Himalayan salt and peered into it. "Nine is thrice three, you know. *Very* significant."

"*Every* number is significant if you screw with it enough," grumbled Seph.

Still the woman ignored her. She returned the salt to its display and said "Nine days ago, I felt an eruption of magic power like I've never felt before… It was a sign. An *omen.*"

"I'm seeing signs of something, all right," muttered Seph.

The woman turned back to Piper again. "And now *you.*"

"Me?" squeaked Piper.

"You've come. You're here. That's no coincidence."

Piper stared into those mysterious eyes as if mesmerized.

She smiled that faint smile again and said, "Faith."

Piper blinked, confused. "Faith?"

"*I'm* Faith," clarified the woman. "Faith Drenage."

"Oh!"

She turned her mysterious smile on Seph and added, "I'm the witch of the Three Lakes."

"*Oh.*" Seph turned to Piper. "She's a *witch.*"

"You're a witch?" said Piper.

"*I am,*" whispered Faith in another dramatic hush. "I hear the voices on the winds that blow through this town. They tell me the secrets of the past, present and future."

"Right," said Seph. "Nothing concerning about hearing voices. Perfectly normal."

A witch? Really? Sure, she'd seen some pretty incredible things, but a *witch*? After seeing an actual thunderbird with her own eyes, she couldn't possibly deny that anything could be real, even witches. But this woman?

Faith stepped behind a display of Ouija boards and turned those faint eyes on Piper. "You're searching for something...aren't you?"

She stared back at her, transfixed. "How do you know?"

"*Everyone's* searching for *something.* And I can help you find it."

Piper leaned closer. "You can?"

Faith nodded. "You just need the right...*tools.*"

Her eyes widened. Tools?

"I have everything you could possibly need," she said, spreading her bejeweled arms and gesturing at the room around her. "Happiness. Health. Prosperity. Love. Whatever's missing in your life. I guarantee I can help you fill the void."

Piper blinked, confused. "Huh?"

Seph rolled her eyes. Just as she thought, this woman was

completely full of it. She was only trying to sucker them into buying something. Did she do this to every customer who wandered into her shop?

She took a step forward. "We really just wanted to know if you had any information on the underground tunnels we've heard about."

Faith turned and stared at her for a moment, as if she'd completely forgotten that she was there. "The tunnels?"

Seph nodded. "Yeah. Under the city. Do you know about them?"

"Of course. I know all about them."

This caught her off guard. "You do?"

"Oh, yes. Why do you want to know?"

"Uh…" She turned and looked at Piper. Why *did* they want to know? She hadn't thought that far ahead yet. Somehow, the truth just didn't seem like the right answer. Besides, where would she even start?

"We're doing research for my graduate thesis," Piper said without a hint of hesitation. "I'm studying how certain places breed reputations for mystery and superstition by preying on our primal instinct to fear the unknown."

"Oh," said Faith.

Seph stared at her. How did she do that? She could barely tell anyone her phone number if she wasn't ready for the question.

"That sounds fascinating," said Faith. "But if I were you, I'd stay out of those tunnels. It's not safe for the living."

Seph and Piper exchanged a surprised look. "What do you mean?" asked Seph.

"Avelby sits on a major crossroad. Rivers of spiritual energy course through the black passageways in the deepest depths of those tunnels. Any living creature that steps foot there will be swept away forever into the endless sea of the dead."

"Oh," said Seph. "That *does* sound like something we'd want to avoid."

She nodded. "Yes. Definitely."

Again, Seph looked at Piper, unsure what else to say.

"What about the other tunnels?" asked Piper. "The ones, um, *not* occupied by rivers of souls?"

"None of the tunnels are completely safe. The spiritual energy encompassing the three lakes is extremely exaggerated. Restless things roam the dark places here. If you go looking for them, you run the risk of angering them."

"Awesome," grumbled Seph. That sounded like just the sort of thing they were looking for. "Is there anything else hidden down there we should know about?"

"Well, almost everyone in town has an opinion of what might be down there." She leaned closer and whispered, "But most of those people are kind of *crazy*."

"Right," said Seph. "We don't want to deal with any *crazy* people."

"I'd like to talk to some other people," said Piper. "For my thesis. You know, these *crazy* stories people tell. How they cultivate urban legends and superstition."

Faith nodded thoughtfully. Then she smiled that curious little smile again and silently turned and walked away.

Seph watched her vanish through a curtained doorway, then

turned and looked at Piper.

Piper looked back at her, confused.

Then, just as quickly as she'd left, Faith fluttered back through the curtain and glided across the room, gracefully weaving through the crowded display stands, right up to where Seph was standing. "Look for the signs." she said, her voice filled with that same, dramatic wonder.

Seph stared back at her.

"*These* signs," she clarified, holding up a piece of paper she'd apparently just retrieved from the back room.

She took the paper and looked at it. It was a pamphlet. There was a picture of an actual sign that read "Official Avelby Underground Checkpoint!" on the front.

"If you see one of these in a window, it means that place of business is a member of the Avelby Underground Tourism Group. Anyone at one of these places will be happy to talk to you."

"Oh…"

"That's convenient," said Piper, looking over Seph's shoulder at the pamphlet. It was an introduction to the Avelby Underground. Most of the information was the same as from the website.

"It *is* fascinating," sighed Faith. "Miles and miles of darkness right beneath our feet. Countless secrets buried beneath earth and time alike." She smiled. "The mystery of it is so romantic, don't you think?"

"It's something, all right," said Seph.

Faith lifted her face and looked deep into her eyes. For a moment, she only stared at her, as if transfixed. Slowly, that curious smile melted away. Then, in her hauntingly faint and dramatic

163

voice, she said, "I see darkness stalking you. Unnatural things are being drawn your way. The shadows come alive and bare their teeth. A blackness creeps toward you. Something *unearthly* nears… Something…*alien*…"

Seph stared into those pale eyes, unable to even respond.

Then Faith blinked and her wispy smile reappeared. "We have protection stones half-price this week."

"Oh." She glanced over at Piper. "Um… Cool. I'll have to come back and look at those before I leave town."

"Please do." She turned her gaze back to Piper. "We're also having a sale on love charms. Guaranteed to get you out of any rut."

Piper stared back at her, surprised. "Why're you telling *me*?"

"We should really get going," said Seph. She took Piper by the arm and steered her toward the door. "Thank you," she said, waving to the witchy shopkeeper.

"Thanks for visiting," sang Faith as they hurried out of the store. "Please come again."

"Why'd she look at *me* when she said that?"

"Let's go," urged Seph, nudging her along.

They stepped out into the blinding sunlight and squinted out at the park.

"I'm not in a rut…" grumbled Piper.

"Don't sweat it. Come on. Let's get out of here."

Following the sidewalk, they began to circle back around the park, toward the truck.

"I'm just too busy to mess with some clingy boyfriend."

"I know."

"It's not easy working part-time and earning your master's degree."

"Uh huh."

Piper crossed her arms over her chest and pouted. "...don't need any stupid love charms..." she muttered.

Seph opened the pamphlet and scanned the material inside. This was going to make things a lot easier. All they had to do was look for businesses with the Avelby Underground Tourism Group sign in their window. They wouldn't even have to feel weird about walking in and asking questions.

There was even a list of businesses on the back of the pamphlet.

"What do you think all that stuff she said meant?" asked Piper.

"It didn't mean anything."

"It has to mean *something*. She's a witch."

"She's not a witch."

"But she knew that we were special."

"She tells *everybody* they're special. She was trying to sucker us into buying stuff. Even that nonsense about rivers of spirit energy was a load of crap." She glanced back and noted that there was no Avelby Underground Tourism Group sign in the window of Everyday Magic. They probably wouldn't let a crackpot like her join.

"I don't know..." said Piper, looking back over her shoulder.

"Trust me. That woman is *definitely* a fraud."

165

Chapter 18

"You should try this one. It'd totally be adorable on you."

"I'm not wearing pink," insisted Seph.

Piper rolled her eyes. "It's not going to kill you to look girly once in a while, you know."

"How'd I let you talk me into this?" She looked around at the forest of hanging racks. It was a cute little thrift shop. If they had more time, she'd probably really enjoy herself in a place like this. But she couldn't stop thinking that the revenant must be on its way here. It stalked her all the way from Cakwetak to Sukmukwe and she didn't think for a second that it wouldn't be able to follow her here. She could feel time ticking away. They shouldn't be wasting it shopping for clothes.

"I have no idea," replied Piper. "Maybe your brain's baking in the sun because you're wearing all black on the hottest day of the year."

Seph grumbled under her breath. Maybe she was right. She *was* really uncomfortable. The skirt definitely had to go. She supposed she could settle for some khaki shorts, but she wasn't wearing any of the pastel tops that Piper kept showing her.

Why was she so determined to get her into something girly? She knew she hated that.

She found a black tank top that was more her style.

"Seriously? *More* black?"

"I *like* black."

"What's wrong with white?"

"My *bra's* black. It'll show right through it."

"Do you own *anything* that's not black?"

"I wear jeans all the time. Those're blue."

"You're impossible."

She found another tank top that was striped. "What about black *and* white? Is *that* an acceptable compromise?"

Piper considered it. It was a lighter fabric than what she was wearing now. "I...guess that'll work. I think?"

"Excellent. Can we go now?"

She gestured toward the checkout lane. "After you."

"Don't give me that look," snapped Seph.

"What look?"

"That 'you're so childish' look."

"I'm not giving you any look."

"Yes you are. Don't lie."

"I'm not lying."

"I know when you're lying, Peps. Your ears give it away. One perks up and the other lays down. It happens every time."

Piper tried to cover the ghostly ears on the top of her head, but they poked right through her hands. "Stop looking at them!"

"All set?" asked the lady at the cash register.

"I think so," replied Seph.

The woman looked to be in her early sixties, with a frilly, stuffy-looking shirt and an assortment of big, gaudy jewelry. "I don't think I've ever seen you two here before," she said.

"We're just visiting for the weekend," replied Piper.

"Yeah," said Seph. "We're doing research for a paper thingy."

"Thesis paper," said Piper.

"Yeah. That." Seph cringed a little. She was really bad at this. "Um, we're talking to people about the tunnels under the city. And how they, uh, make people superstitious?"

"How places like these tunnels gain reputations for mystery and superstition by preying on our primal instinct to fear the unknown," clarified Piper.

Seph wilted a little, embarrassed.

"It's *my* paper," explained Piper. "She's just helping me research it."

Seriously, how did she do that? It was like a superpower. She couldn't comprehend how anyone could think so fast and lie so smoothly.

The woman nodded and opened the register. "And you came to learn about the tunnels here in Avelby?"

"Exactly," said Seph. "Do you know anything about them."

"I've always heard they were part of the underground railroad."

"Really?" said Piper.

The woman smiled and nodded. "Oh yes." She laughed. "You know, I was in high school before I found out there weren't any tracks down there. I was convinced it was an actual railroad." She looked over at another woman who was hanging clothes on a rolling rack on the other side of the counter. "My dad used to say it was a good thing I was pretty because I sure wasn't smart."

The other woman laughed. "I think mine used to say the same thing about me." She wasn't dressed like the first woman. She had on a Bears tee shirt and a pair of blue jean shorts.

"So the tunnels were built for the underground railroad?" asked Piper.

"No, I don't think they were built for that reason," said the woman as she handed Seph back her change. "They were here long before that. But they made for a convenient stop along the way."

"Jacky always said the tunnels were one of the places Al Capone and other big mobsters from Chicago came to hide stolen loot and dead bodies," said the second woman. She glanced over at them and explained, "Jacky's my husband. You couldn't convince him otherwise. When he was young, he used to sneak into those tunnels looking for hidden vaults full of money."

"Boys," sighed the stuffy woman.

"You don't believe the mob ever hid anything down there?" asked Seph. Personally, she kind of liked the idea of buried mob loot. It might be nice to stumble across a few million dollars. As long as they were going down there anyway.

She shrugged. "Maybe they did. Maybe they didn't. If they did, I'm sure the government has already found it."

"You think so?" asked Piper.

"Sure. They have secret facilities down there, you know."

"Do they?"

"Oh, yes. I read all about it online." She leaned forward, as if someone might be listening in, and whispered, "It's the Democrats.

That's where they plan to freeze Clinton's and Obama's brains."

"Oh…" said Seph. She turned and looked at Piper. "Wow."

Piper just stared at the woman.

She straightened up again and gave them a big, bright smile. "Stop by again sometime, won't you?"

"Sure," said Seph. She was already nudging Piper toward the door.

"You girls have a nice day," said the other woman.

"You, too," replied Seph.

As they walked out the door, Piper whispered. "Why would they want frozen brains?"

"She was just messing with us," decided Seph.

"You think so?"

"She had to be." Clearly, the woman had a sense of humor that was grossly disproportionate to her style. Either that or she was just as nutty as the Witch of the Three Lakes.

There was a small lobby between the thrift store and the carpet and flooring business that shared the building with it. There were restrooms here, ideal for Seph to change out of these stifling clothes.

She preferred to take stuff like this home and wash it first, make it smell like the rest of her clean laundry instead of like a stuffy thrift shop. But that wasn't an option today.

Piper leaned against the door while she waited for her to change and said, "What about that stuff about the underground railroad and Al Capone? That didn't seem all that far-fetched."

"Maybe," replied Seph as she wriggled out of her sweat-soaked dress shirt. "It's possible. Chicago's not all that far from here. And all the tunnels under this town probably would've made it an ideal place to hide runaway slaves. But that still doesn't help us. What we're looking for is a lot older than any of that stuff." She sniffed the tank top and frowned at it. It smelled okay, she guessed. It didn't *stink*. But it didn't smell *new*, either. Maybe she was being snobby, but if her clothes didn't smell like new clothes, she wanted them to at least smell like *her* clothes. She pulled the tank top over her head and then paused as she unbuttoned her skirt. "Unless, of course, the mobsters sealed off the tunnel we need to find so they could stack bodies in it... *Then* I guess it would be pretty relevant."

"Please don't say stuff like that," whined Piper.

She pulled on the shorts and fastened them, then stuffed her skirt and dress shirt into the bag the crazy thrift shop lady gave her and stepped out into the small lobby. She could feel the difference immediately. This was much cooler. And her shoes didn't feel so out of place now, either, which was nice.

"See?" said Piper. "You totally look normal now."

Seph shot her a dirty look, which was completely ignored.

They walked out of the building and squinted into the brilliant sunshine. It was still hot, but these clothes didn't seem to catch and hold the heat the way her others did. She was fairly confident she could run away from huge, murderous dead guys without collapsing from heat exhaustion now. "So should we go check out that Tunnel Park place?"

"Yeah..." said Piper, distracted. She was standing next to her on the sidewalk, shading her eyes with one hand, staring out across the open park. There was a kid standing on the sidewalk outside one of the shops over there... A boy. All by himself. Was he staring back at her? He didn't look like one of the freaky black-eyed kids who scared the hell out of her outside her apartment. He looked older. His hair wasn't the same. And he was dressed like a normal kid, not in those weird, old-timey clothes that covered everything but their faces. But she couldn't help but wonder…

"You okay?" asked Seph.

"Yeah…"

A woman came out of one of the shops and the boy turned and walked with her down the sidewalk.

Probably not one of the freaky kids.

Besides, she wasn't hearing any of that weird, voice-filled static in her brain.

"I'm fine," she said. "Sorry."

"Don't go spacing out on me."

"I'm fine," she insisted. "Let's go."

They crossed the street and made their way back through the little tunnel.

Halfway beneath Main Street, Piper stopped. She turned and looked back the way they came. She tilted her head to one side, listening.

"Hear something?" asked Seph.

"I'm…not sure." She tilted her head the other way. Those ghostly ears twitched back and forth, searching. "I thought I did. For just a second there."

Seph turned and scanned the smooth, concrete walls. There didn't immediately appear to be anything about the tunnel that she found peculiar. She felt no sense of wrongness at all, no feeling that something was a little off, like she felt when she was near a secret place. There were, however, several fat, black bugs crawling around on the ceiling, which gave her a hard shiver of revulsion and made her back away several steps. "You didn't hear anything the first time we walked through here."

"No."

"What did it sound like?"

"I don't know. It was only there for a second." She looked back the way they came, expecting to see one of those creepy kids or the runner lurking under one of the trees. But there was no one there. "Maybe it was my imagination."

"Maybe..." agreed Seph. Neither of them quite knew how these extra senses of theirs worked. But what if it wasn't? What if she *did* hear something? "Come on."

A moment later, the two of them emerged from the south side of the tunnel into the larger of Raindskenner Park's two sections.

There were several children playing on the playground equipment while mothers sat on nearby benches and gossiped. A young woman was jogging on the sidewalk. A bald man was walking his dog while staring at his cell phone. An old lady was sitting by herself by the fountain.

There was not a monstrous thing to be seen.

Piper turned and looked back into the shadowy tunnel. *Was* it her imagination?

"Let's get out of here before something unpleasant *does* happen to us," suggested Seph.

"Yeah..."

She scanned the surrounding buildings as she walked. If the revenant *did* show up here, where would it come from? It didn't seem like an exceptionally large, white-haired, half-naked man covered in scars and bloody, open wounds would make it very far prowling around in broad daylight. But it managed to find her in those woods at Sukmukwe without drawing any attention. And it wasn't shy about attacking her out in the open outside her apartment building, either.

According to Piper, the black-eyed children and the runner had behaved the same way. The children might not have drawn too much attention, but a creepy, all-black shadow man running down the street should've been quite a spectacle.

The idea that these things had appeared in such blatant places worried her. It made her feel vulnerable even when she should feel safe.

What was going to happen when night fell? When everything became shadows they could hide in?

"Have you heard anything else?" she asked.

"Nothing," replied Piper. "I probably imagined it."

"Probably."

But their gazes kept drifting back toward the little tunnel, unconvinced.

Chapter 19

Tunnel Park was considerably smaller than Raindskenner, which made sense, given that it was once an ordinary residence. According to the article on Piper's phone, it was a private home until the forties, when it was bought and converted into a book-binding business, and later used as an accounting office.

The building itself was completely gone now, destroyed in a fire. The lot where it stood was now covered in neatly mown grass broken by a handful of paved walking paths. A tall elm was growing in the very center, a ring of benches built around it. The old basement walls had been replaced with gentle hills, two sets of concrete steps and a convenient, handicap-friendly ramp.

The tunnel entrances were cut horizontally into the slopes of the hills, each one topped with a safety fence to prevent all but the most determined of idiots from tumbling the eight-foot drop onto the pavement.

There was an information board mounted by the front gate of the park, telling the history of the property pretty much exactly as it appeared in the online article, but included a picture of what the attractive Victorian looked like before the fire as well as a picture of the building's burned ruins, taken from the local paper. There were also several photographs of workers uncovering the tunnels in the weeks that followed.

Seph and Piper made their way down the steps and looked around at the five openings. Each one was illuminated with strings of overhead lights and filled with the echoing laughter of playing children.

"Not exactly the gates of hell, are they?" said Seph as two boys chased each other out of one tunnel and into another.

"Nothing wrong with that," countered Piper.

That was true, but Seph had a feeling that what they were looking for wouldn't come this easily. "Do you hear anything?"

"Nothing."

She wasn't surprised. She looked at each passage, one by one, trying to do whatever it was she did back in Sukmukwe. Then, when nothing came to her, she gave up and chose one at random.

It was much cooler inside, which was nice. But she didn't care much for the smell. Earthy and damp. Distinctly subterranean. It reminded her of those other underground places where the Keeper had set his hellish traps.

About a hundred feet from where it started, the passage converged with another tunnel. A few yards to the right there was a chain with a caution sign hanging from it. Beyond that, a safe distance away, the passage ended in a pile of stone and dirt.

It had caved in years ago.

Seph walked up to the chain and peered over it.

"I still don't hear anything," reported Piper.

"I'm not seeing anything, either." But she stood there a moment, nonetheless. This seemed like a good place for something to be hidden. An apparent dead-end. A space that didn't see much traffic.

At least, these were the sorts of places they hid things in the movies.

Real life was a bit more random.

She stared at the wall of rubble in front of her, troubled. It was far too easy to imagine that what they were searching for was just beyond that point, that their only hope of saving her mother was now utterly unreachable. And if not there, then behind some other caved-in passage.

But the markers on the way to the scythe were protected. The Keeper had seen to that. There was no reason to think that these wouldn't be protected as well.

While they stood there, two young boys came running down the passage, their shoes slapping the concrete floor. They appeared to be eight or nine years old. One had blond hair, the other brown.

"This one caved in," said the blond boy. "A long time ago. Now no one knows where it used to go."

"Anything could be buried in there!" marveled the brown-haired boy.

Seph glanced over at them. "Do you think there's something in all these tunnels?"

Both of them looked up at her, their eyes wide with wonder.

"There's a gold mine down here!" exclaimed the blond boy.

"A gold mine? Really?"

"It's worth a fortune, but nobody can find it," explained the brown-haired boy. "Because the guy who found it wanted it all to himself, so he built a bunch of these old tunnels to hide the real location of it."

"Oh," said Seph. "Where did you hear about it?"

"Everybody knows about it," said the blond boy.

"My brother told me all about it," said the brown-haired boy. "He also told me that after the old miner hid the entrance, he went down into the tunnels to be with his gold and was never seen again."

"Wow," said Piper.

"They say his ghost haunts the mine to this day!" exclaimed the blond boy.

"Oh!" said Seph. "That sounds scary."

"Nah." The blond boy puffed out his chest. "We're gonna find it someday."

"But what about the ghost?" asked Piper.

"We're not afraid of ghosts," insisted the brown-haired boy. "I saw on *Ghost Hunters* that ghosts can't really hurt you."

"Oh," said Piper.

Seph smiled. "I think you're probably right about that." She'd only ever met one ghost and she'd saved both their lives. So far, ghosts had been one of the good guys. "So why do you think no one else has found this gold mine yet?"

"Because no one's found the secret entrance hidden in the tunnels," explained the brown-haired boy. "My brother says the old miner constructed such an elaborate hiding place that only the smartest and most dedicated puzzle-solvers could ever hope to find it."

"I see," said Seph, trying not to laugh. Those were big words for a couple of kids. It definitely sounded like the kind of story he'd memorized from the mouth of an older brother.

"We're gonna keep looking!" said the blond boy. "Come on!"

"Bye!" said the brown-haired boy and the two of them raced away back down the tunnel.

"Oh my gosh, they were adorable!" exclaimed Piper.

"They were," agreed Seph. "And they weren't too far off, either. I mean, I don't know about a gold mine, but we know there's *something* hidden under this city." And she was willing to bet that the part about someone building all these tunnels as an elaborate hiding place accessible only to someone with the right kind of *skills* might be dead-on as well.

Piper stared after the boys and pondered the idea. "You don't think their curiosity could get them hurt, do you?"

"I don't think so." Although she couldn't be certain. She didn't think they'd be capable of finding what was really down here, but if they were determined enough, they might find a way to break into someplace they shouldn't go. She could only hope that they weren't that reckless.

"Come on," said Piper. "Let's check the other tunnels."

They turned and walked the other way. But they soon found the path blocked again, this time by a chained, steel gate.

"That's typical," grumbled Seph. "We don't even get to explore *all* the tunnels." She walked up to the gate and pressed her face between the bars, trying to peer into the darkness beyond, where it seemed no one wanted to pay for lighting.

What they wanted could be right over there, just out of sight, and they wouldn't be able to reach it.

She had a bad feeling that this was what the Avelby Underground was going to be like. One unreachable place after another. Not just a sprawling labyrinth, but a sprawling labyrinth full of locked gates, blocked passages and no trespassing signs. Not to mention dead ends.

And if what they were looking for turned out to be on the other side of some locked gate, what were they supposed to do about it?

They went back and tried the rest of the passages, but the other tunnels proved to be the same. Only the first one had caved in. The rest were either gated off a short distance in or simply ended. One led to a mysterious, square room with no apparent purpose. Seph spent extra time in here, wandering around, staring at the walls, trying to catch a glimpse of something not quite right, hoping to find a hidden gap like the one under the Muntony library.

But there was nothing here but a few benches and a number of framed pictures and news articles on the walls.

Loud children kept running in and out, their voices reverberating off the walls like pealing church bells, quickly giving Seph a pounding headache.

Piper eyed each and every child she saw with caution. None of them looked like the little monsters that swarmed her outside the apartment. No odd clothing. No thick, bushy hair. But she couldn't be sure that *all* the creepy-eyed children would look like that.

Maybe some of them looked just like *these* kids.

The last passage they checked ended with yet another chained, steel gate.

"Nothing," said Seph as she peered into the darkness on the

other side.

"Well, we weren't very likely to get it on our first try," reasoned Piper.

"I guess not."

"Let's go check out that walking tour place. I'll bet that'll..." She trailed off.

Seph looked up at her. "You okay?"

She reached up and rubbed at the spot behind her left temple. A dull pain had begun there again. An unpleasant buzzing sensation. A sort of broken *static*. "I think I hear something..."

"What we're looking for?"

"No..." She turned and looked back the way they came, suddenly afraid. "It's the same thing I heard when I saw those kids. And when the runner chased us."

Seph scanned the tunnel behind them. "I don't see anything." Then she turned and looked through the bars of the gate again.

Something was there. A dark figure stood deep inside the shadows, its back pressed against the wall.

Was that there before?

She didn't think it was. She was pretty sure she would've seen it. It was darker than the space around it.

She put her hands on the bars and leaned as close as the iron would allow. "Pepper...?"

Piper turned and looked.

"Is that the thing that chased you and Wanda?"

The thing in the tunnel turned and took a step. As it did, it seemed to twitch and flicker. Then it was gone, vanished into thin air.

A moment later, she caught sight of it again on the other side of the tunnel, leaning against the other wall. "How did it do that?"

Piper was backing away. "We've got to get out of here."

Seph nodded. She let go of the bars and also began to back away.

The creepy thing jumped to the other side of the tunnel again.

Suddenly there were two of them.

"That's not the runner," whispered Piper.

As they continued to back away, the black figures blinked away again, then reappeared right on the other side of the gate.

There were three of them now.

"Any chance they're trapped over there?" asked Piper.

One by one, the three black forms flickered away, then reappeared, this time on this side of the gate.

"No chance at all," replied Seph.

"Can we run away now?"

"I think we should."

They turned and fled back down the tunnel.

Behind them, four black figures flickered after them.

Chapter 20

The shoes were a good idea. By the time she reached her truck, Seph was thankful that she'd let Piper talk her into buying them. Those sandals would've been torture on her poor feet before this day was out.

Piper jumped up into the passenger seat and looked back out at the little park. "Are you sure it's okay to just leave?" she asked. "What if one of those things attacks those boys?"

Seph slammed the door and started the engine. "Ian said those things weren't interested in anyone but us, remember?"

"Are you sure? I mean, I know he said that about that revenant thing, but what about all this other stuff?"

"Those things didn't appear until we got there. It was obviously us they were after."

"But what if we, like, stirred them up or something? Like a hornet's nest. What if they're all agitated now and they attack the next person who goes down there?"

Seph watched a different pair of boys than the ones they talked to chase each other out of one tunnel and into another. "I don't know," she confessed. "All I know is that Ian said no one else would be hurt if they didn't intentionally get in the way."

Piper was pinching her lower lip again, thinking. Those things *did* seem to disappear by the time they left the tunnel. Even that disturbing static sound went silent again. Maybe they slunk back into the shadows as soon as they left the area.

But what were those things? They weren't the same as those black-eyed children. And they didn't move like the runner.

As Seph shifted the truck into gear, another of those fat, black bugs dropped onto the windshield directly in front of the steering wheel. She screamed and flicked on the windshield wipers, flinging the little beast away.

"What was that?" gasped Piper, startled. She was sitting bolt upright, looking around, expecting one of those flickering figures to have appeared right outside the truck.

"Stupid bug…" grumbled Seph.

"*Seriously?* Oh my gosh, you scared the heck out of me!"

"I can't help it!" She leaned forward and looked up through the windshield, making sure there weren't more of the disgusting things falling out of the sky.

What kind of bugs were those things, anyway? They were extra gross. Some kind of beetle, she thought, with a shiny, round shell and lots of creepy little legs. They reminded her of the flesh-eating scarabs she saw in a mummy movie once. But then again, so did ladybugs…

"Let's go check out that walking tour," said Piper, relaxing back into her seat again.

Seph's heart was still pounding. She wasn't sure how many more scares she could take. "Yeah," she replied. "Sure." She laid her phone in the console next to her and let Siri do the navigating while she tried to contemplate some sort of plan. She couldn't help but think that they were wasting their time visiting tourist attractions. But she simply had no idea where else to begin.

She wondered where the Keeper was. Why couldn't he just show them where the marker was hidden? Why did it have to be such a big mystery? They were the seekers. Weren't the vaults theirs to find? The scythe and the two markers leading the way to it had sat untouched for countless ages, seemingly surviving asteroid impacts, fluctuating sea levels, ice ages and the rise of modern cities while managing to hide from countless generations of increasingly technological societies, just so two clueless Wisconsin girls could come looking for them.

This whole thing was just *stupid*.

"Do you think he's here somewhere?" asked Piper as she stared through the window at the passing businesses.

"Do I think who's here?"

"Ian."

Seph glanced out at the city streets around them. "I don't know. Probably. He's been there twice now when I've needed him." And it wasn't as if he didn't know where they were. He was the one who sent them here.

Piper nodded, distracted. "That's good."

She supposed it was. It was better knowing that *someone* out there was looking out for them. But she wondered if Piper was interested in more than just a demon bodyguard.

Siri instructed them to turn at the next intersection and then informed them that their destination was on the right.

That didn't take long.

They pulled into an open parking lot and found themselves looking out at one of Avelby's three lakes. Lots of people were out on it today. Boats were cruising back and forth, some of them pulling tubes behind them.

Seph found herself wishing she could be out on one of those boats, enjoying the water, getting a tan... Of course, pretty much *anything* was better than walking around a bunch of creepy, bug-infested tunnels and waiting for something terrifying to jump out and try to kill them.

Avelby Underground Walking Tours occupied an even smaller lot than Tunnel Park. It was one small building that served as an office, ticket counter, vending machine bank and public restroom. There were a set of concrete stairs leading down from the ticket window to a grassy lawn surrounded on two sides by concrete walls. There were two gated tunnel openings, one set into each of the walls.

On the far side of the lawn was a roped-off area by which stood a bored, chubby teenager with his nose in his cell phone. This kid, according to the overly friendly man who sold them their tickets, would be their tour guide.

Seph had her doubts that this was going to be one of those life-changing experiences she'd heard about. And yet, there were already other people here waiting for the tour. There was a plump, middle-aged woman with thick glasses, a tall, lanky man in his late sixties with a shiny bald spot on the top of his head and an uppity-looking young couple with an adorable little girl dressed like a princess.

The roped-off area turned out to be a sort of excavation site. The ground here had been dug up, revealing a sunken stretch of old rock walls. It was a section of old tunnel, the oldest Avelby tunnel ever found, according to a sign. It went nowhere. Both ends were filled in with earth and rock.

"I hope *that's* not the tunnel we're looking for," whispered Piper.

Seph hoped so, too.

The chubby teenager put away his cell phone, checked to see if anyone else was coming and then welcomed them all to Avelby Underground Walking Tours and introduced himself as Toby. Immediately, it became clear that Toby was speaking from a script that he'd had memorized for far too long. His tone was flat, as if he were running on autopilot.

"Historians generally agree that the first of Avelby's tunnels date all the way back to the first permanent structures, built by French settlers around the beginning of the nineteenth century. What historians *can't* agree on is *why* they built the tunnels. Were they to provide escape routes in case of invasions by hostile natives? Or perhaps it was the British they were afraid of. Or was it simply a way to connect the important buildings in town so no one would have to venture into the cold in the wintertime? We may never know what the intentions originally were."

Seph and Piper glanced at each other. This guy, like pretty much everyone else in the world, had no idea that those two-hundred-year-old tunnels were probably nowhere near the first.

"The original tunnels no longer exist," sighed the tour guide as he gestured at the area on the other side of the ropes. "These excavated trenches are all that remain. But modern technology is allow-ing researchers to digitally reconstruct them, allowing us an exciting glimpse into the past."

"He doesn't *sound* particularly excited, does he?" murmured Seph. While not precisely monotone, the guy clearly wasn't ecstatic about his job.

Piper nodded. "He talks just like a sociology teacher I had once," she whispered. "Hardest class to stay awake in *ever*."

Seph peered into the trench. There was something strangely tragic about the scene. The earth peeled away from it. The stone ceiling lifted away. The cobbled walls laid bare to the sun after two hundred years in the darkness. It was once something mysterious and hidden. Now it was naked and somehow sad. It made her think for some reason of a great, stone serpent laid out on the dissecting table by cold, gigantic scientists.

(*There* was an image for her sketchbook.)

"These original tunnels were estimated to span only about half a mile in total, compared to nearly fifty miles of known tunnels today. Although most of them don't lead anywhere."

"Why would you build a tunnel that doesn't go anywhere?" asked Piper.

The tour guide perked up a little at the chance to wander off his script. (But only a little.) "They all probably went somewhere at some time," he replied. "Unless they weren't finished for some rea-son. But the city's changed a lot. Buildings burned down or were torn down. Newer tunnels and underground utilities sometimes end up being built through them. Or parts of these old tunnels col-lapsed, closing them off."

"Where did these first tunnels go?" asked the mother of the princess.

"We're not entirely sure," replied Toby. "Historians think they might have linked the houses of the original settlers' families, but it's not known how the original settlement was laid out. What we do know is that a portion of these tunnels were used to connect Avelby's first courthouse to the Pulkin family home in the early eighteen-hundreds."

He turned away and started toward one of the open tunnel gates. "If you'll follow me, we'll explore some of the historic passages of Old Avelby."

Seph hesitated, her gaze still fixed on the unearthed walls of the old tunnel. The oldest of all the tunnels. Wouldn't that be what they were looking for? The beginning of this weird, little city's obsession with underground passages? If the second marker was really somewhere beneath this town, then it predated European settlement—and probably even Native American settlement—by *millennia*.

It was no different than the vault at Shawbeck Ranch. Amethyst told her that before the ranch was built, the site was a Native American village, watched over by Native American guardians who ultimately passed the burden on to the Shawbeck family. If the hidden history here was similar, then those early French settlers were passed the torch from another ancient tribe in the same way.

She doubted very much that those early French settlers simply decided on their own to dig a bunch of tunnels. It was far more likely that they got the idea from a pre-existing, subterranean vault hidden somewhere in the area. And if they knew about the vault, then they were probably the ones guarding it. Logically, that meant that the passages were designed to either provide access to whatever they were guarding, or to hide it. Perhaps both at the same time. And if that was true, then what they were looking for would be attached to *these* tunnels.

But of course the problem with that line of thinking was that *this* tunnel had been all but destroyed.

She stood there a moment longer as the tour guide's droning voice drifted away.

"Something wrong?" asked Piper.

Seph shook her head. "Just thinking."

"Come on. The tour's leaving without us."

Chapter 21

Most of what Toby the tour guide had to say in his scripted speech was of little interest to Seph. The abbreviated version seemed to be that the city of Avelby had been building tunnels for as long as it had been building houses, and that local historians had a number of apparently fascinating theories about why those original tunnels were built, but couldn't be certain of any of them. Seph, of course, already knew that these oldest tunnels under the city were most likely put there by early guardians of the chamber that was hidden somewhere beneath their feet, and would hopefully lead them to the next marker and the only object in existence that could save her mother's life. Ironically, at this point these "local historians" were doing nothing more than muddying up the truth and making her job harder. But of course, that wasn't really their fault. All the world's greatest experts, as it turned out, were tragically ill-informed about the real workings of the universe.

Just as useless was this walking tour she'd paid nearly fifty bucks for her and Piper to go on. It was interesting, as far as walking tours of boring, underground passages went, she supposed, more so than the empty, dead-end passages over at Tunnel Park, at least. The passages here ranged from smooth, concrete tubes to rustic, cobbled walls to hand-carved earth and stone, each with a different tale for Toby to tell. When the path forked and one of the tunnels was closed off, they were informed of where the other one led, which was always to either private property or to sections of the city's underground utility networks. Twice, they found themselves able to peek into old basements. One was completely sealed off, like the one they saw back in Muntony, with the stairs ripped out and the door bricked-up, its only access these dark tunnels. The second one was the sub-basement of the city newspaper building, and contained a number of interesting old printing machines and other antiques from the early nineteen-hundreds. It was interesting to see, but she wasn't looking for this kind of history. She was looking for something much older. And not once did she catch sight of anything that made her take pause and look closer for something hidden. Nor did Piper hear anything with her spirit ears.

These aren't the tunnels you're looking for, she thought.

The only part of Toby's over-practiced speech that actually interested her was his multiple mentions of the name Pulkin. It sounded as if they were the first of the city's wealthy power families. They owned all the land, the local dairy industry, the manufacturing facilities and half the businesses in town until the late eighteen-hundreds. In other words, they were prime candidates for guardians of an ancient, buried secret. Just like the Shawbecks and the Lewelsons, who guarded the vault and the second marker on the path to the scythe. If such a guardian existed in this town, they could simply find him or her. Or them. But when she asked Toby if the Pulkins family was still around, he informed her that there were no longer any living Pulkins in Avelby. The family had died out around the turn of the century.

She supposed that would've been too easy.

The entrance to the second marker could be anywhere under the city. And according to Toby's tour script, they had access to only a small fraction of the known tunnels. The vast majority of them were on private or city property. And she had a feeling that there were a lot more tunnels still hidden down here than anyone realized. If this marker was like the one in Muntony, then it would be hidden behind a secret passage that only her prophet sight could detect. But how was she supposed to find something like that in a labyrinth like this?

It seemed ludicrous when she really thought about it.

Ian was a fool if he thought they could do this on their own.

"What kind of girls do you think demons like?" whispered Piper.

Seph looked over at her, bewildered. "*What?*"

They were hanging back, letting the rest of the tour walk ahead of them, the better, hopefully, to see or hear something.

"I'm just wondering. I mean *do* they like girls?"

"You mean, like, are demons *gay*?"

"What? *No.* I mean, maybe some of them are… I guess. *I don't know.*" She shook her head, flustered. "No, I mean…do you think they like *people*? *Humans.* Do they have the same kinds of desires as us? Do they, like, have relationships with humans?"

"We're dealing with an *incubus*," whispered Seph. "That's kind of their whole thing, isn't it?"

"Oh yeah…"

Seph shook her head.

"In nineteen-nineteen," Toby droned on, "A tornado destroyed parts of the city, including the original police station and library. A lot of city records were lost that night, including many of the building plans that might've helped shed light on the mystery of the Avelby Underground. Then, during the reconstruction, a lot of the old tunnels were dug up to make way for modern updates to the sewers and storm drains. Many tunnels were sealed off or filled in, and remain buried somewhere down here to this day. This, in addition to the mysterious origins of many of these tunnels, has led to a popular surge of rumors among locals, ranging from hidden treasure to clandestine secrets lurking in the unmapped darkness of the Avelby Underground."

"So what kinds of girls do they like, then?" whispered Piper.

Seph looked at her, distracted. "Huh?"

"Like, do they like nice girls, 'cause, like, corruption of the innocent and stuff? Or do they like bad girls? You know, 'cause of demon stuff?"

Seph squinted at her. "How the hell should I know? What does it even matter?"

"I'm just curious."

"Jeez, Pi. Your brain goes to some really weird places sometimes."

Piper shot her a dirty look. "And yours doesn't? I've seen your secret sketchbook, you know. The one with those pictures of all the guys from the Avengers movies."

Seph's mouth dropped open. "*That was private!*"

"You left it laying out."

"That's not the same as saying you can paw through it!"

Piper shrugged. "Should've kept it put away, then. You know I like to look at your art."

Seph glared at her. Her face had turned a shade of red.

"Nothing has ever been found to substantiate that anything of value was ever hidden in these tunnels," said Toby. "But in the nineteen-sixties, construction workers discovered a sealed-off room under the site of the old city hall and uncovered hundreds of documents that had been lost for decades."

Piper leaned over and whispered, "You made me sit and watch all those movies with you and I don't remember any scenes like those."

Seph blushed a little brighter. "Shut up."

"Were they deleted scenes?" she asked, smirking.

"Just *stop*."

"Fine."

"This room we're coming up on now," said Toby, gesturing at an opening in the tunnel wall ahead of them, "is an old cellar, formerly connected to the basement of the old Avelby Inn by way of a secret passage. The inn was demolished in the seventies, however, and the original passage leading to the basement was filled in, leaving this doorway the only way in or out."

"How many times have you read those *Fifty Shades of Gray* books?" snapped Seph.

"Not the same thing."

"Yes, it is."

"Totally not."

"No one today knows what the original purpose of the room

was," he went on, "but it's long been rumored to be haunted by the ghost of a woman in a black dress."

"I've heard that a lot of the city's tunnels are rumored to be haunted," said the mother of the little girl. "Is that true?"

"I can't confirm or deny the existence of ghosts, but I can honestly say that every one of these tunnels has at least one rumor attached to it. People *love* telling stories about the Underground. It's something of a local pastime."

Seph stared at the empty little room. There were shelves mounted on each of the walls, but nothing on them. Nor was there any furniture in the room. It may have been an old storage room or a janitor's closet or a utility space. Or a wine cellar. Or maybe a servant's room. It was impossible to know for certain. And that only made it more mysterious.

"Hey, Persephone?"

"Yeah?"

"Who's the guy with the big horns again?"

"Loki."

"I think he's my favorite."

Seph glared at her again. Then, after a moment, she mumbled, "Mine too."

The end of the tunnel loomed ahead of them, a blinding circle of sunlight against the gloom of the dim fluorescent lighting their eyes had become accustomed to. It was literally the light at the end of the tunnel... Appropriate, Seph thought, considering that they were almost at the end of the tour and nothing useful had presented itself, meaning her mother was no closer to avoiding her own date with the light at the end of *her* tunnel. It seemed they'd wasted both their time and their money, with nothing to show for either.

Toby and the others continued on into the sunlight, but Seph lingered for a moment. She turned and looked back the way they came, willing herself to see something. *Anything.*

"What do we do now?" asked Piper.

She reached into her pocket as she walked toward the end of the tunnel and withdrew the pamphlet the witch gave her. "I guess we start looking for these signs." The Avelby Underground Tourism Group. "*Somebody* in this town must have some useful information."

But still, where did they start? Did they just get back into the truck and drive around, looking for signs at random? That didn't seem like a very good plan.

"Maybe we should ask that Toby guy where we can get more information," suggested Piper. "Tour guides are supposed to know stuff like that, right?"

"I don't know," said Seph. "I really think we might be wasting our time on this tourist stuff. We're looking for something that's been kept hidden for ages, remember? No local historian's going to—"

A loud clattering noise suddenly rang out from the silence behind them, startling them.

"What was that?" asked Piper.

"Why do you always ask me what things are?" snapped Seph. "Like I'm really going to know?"

"Did it come from that last room?"

They walked back and peered through the doorway again. No one was here. But there was a push broom lying on the floor next to the far wall that wasn't there before, as if someone had thrown it across the room.

"Was somebody in here just now?" asked Piper,

"Seriously! Why would I know these things?"

Piper stepped into the room and looked around. "Toby said something about a secret passage, didn't he?"

"But he said that passage was destroyed with the inn it was connected to. He said this was the only way in or out."

"Maybe there's *another* secret passage in here. The kind of secret that only prophet sight can see."

Seph stepped into the room. "I don't get any special vibe from it or anything." Usually, she sensed something off about the area before she actually saw anything. But this room just felt like a room.

Maybe it was a matter of looking at it from the right angle?

She turned and looked at the wall behind her, the one that separated the room from the tunnel and the one least visible from the doorway. There was something gross smeared on it. "Toby needs to tidy up a little," she grumbled, stepping closer to the wall.

"What?" asked Piper. She was prodding at the bricks where the old secret passage used to be, confirming that it wasn't still functional.

The stuff was thick and gray, but oozed down the concrete in slimy globs. Seph leaned in and carefully sniffed it, but it didn't seem to have an odor. "What *is* this stuff, anyway?"

Piper turned and looked at her. "What stuff?"

"*This* stuff," she replied, reaching out to dab at it with her finger. The significance of Piper's question struck her at the same moment her fingertip touched the goop, too late to rethink what she was doing. The instant she touched it, the world became a blinding sea of agonizing light, as if someone had just shined a powerful searchlight directly into her face.

Chapter 22

She cried out and stumbled backward, trying to shield her eyes with her clean hand, but the light seemed to be shining from *inside* her eyes, as if *she* were the burning searchlight.

The world swam away from her. She felt herself falling. Piper's voice called out to her, but it sounded so distant, as if she were shouting from somewhere far away.

Images flickered through her mind. Familiar faces. Old memories. Friends she'd known. Places she'd been. For a moment, her father's face smiled down at her, young and virile again, the way he looked when she was just a little girl. The sight sent her heart leaping into her throat. She wanted to call out to him. But he was gone as quickly as he'd appeared, sucked back into a storm of random memories.

Then she found herself back in her apartment, standing beside the door, holding her purse.

"Say hi to your mom for me," said Piper.

Seph squinted at her. Her eyes still hurt from that blistering light. "Sure," she heard herself say. Except she didn't say anything.

"Hey, my friend Evie broke up with her fiancé last week,"

blurted Meg.

What was happening? This was this morning, wasn't it?

"She's going to be looking for a new roommate."

She squeezed her eyes shut, confused.

Then she was standing in the hallway, the door swinging closed behind her.

"Bye-bye," chirped Piper.

Seph turned around, confused. What just happened.

"She's rude," said Meg, her voice drifting through the door. "I hate rude people."

"What the hell?" She reached for the doorknob again, but it was no longer there. The door was gone. The hallway was gone. Suddenly, she was sitting in her *old* apartment in Madison, her sketchbook open in her lap. She was staring down at an incomplete picture of a menacing dragon. She remembered that picture. It wasn't her best work, but she remembered clearly that she'd finished it. It was still in this sketchbook, even, somewhere in her closet, in the box with all the others.

"I don't feel like cooking tonight," sighed Amethyst. "Let's just order pizza."

Seph stared at her. She was stretched out on the couch, the television remote in her hand. She was wearing that old tee shirt that she loved, the one that was so old it was practically see-through.

"Fine by me," she heard herself say. She clasped her hand over her mouth, confused. Did she really say that? Well, she *did* say that. Back then. But she didn't think she said it again just now.

She turned and looked around. It was surreal. It'd been

months since she'd last seen this apartment. And even longer since she last saw Amethyst. She'd almost forgotten how pretty she was. And how...*busty* she was. She didn't greet the delivery boy in that flimsy shirt, did she? She obviously wasn't wearing a bra under there.

No. Amethyst was kind of flighty, but she was always appropriately bashful about her body.

She squeezed her eyes shut and tried to clear her mind. She was so confused.

"Please don't be mad at me," said Amethyst.

She was no longer in her apartment. She was standing in that bunker in Nebraska. Amethyst was standing between her and the vault, her hands clasped in front of her, pleading.

This was the moment she first discovered that Amethyst had been lying to her all that time. This was the moment she discovered that Amethyst wasn't even Amethyst.

It was the moment she lost her best friend.

She closed her eyes again and shook her head. This wasn't real. It couldn't be.

When she opened her eyes again, she was sitting at her desk at Vertical Design. It was an ordinary day at the office. The room was bustling around her. Almost everyone had their faces buried in their computers, hard at work on their projects.

Mona Yenning gave her a polite smile as she walked by on her way back to her desk.

Seph watched her until she sat down in front of her computer, then she turned in her chair and looked around the room at her other coworkers, confused. What was she doing again? Wasn't she just somewhere else?

Mr. Carrol, her boss, stepped into the doorway and looked out across the room. "Four o'clock tomorrow, Zeke."

Zeke Jenfir swiveled around in his chair and pointed back at him with one of his long, bony fingers. "Okay! Thank you!"

Mr. Carrol nodded and glanced once more over the room. When his eyes met hers, he gave her his usual, friendly nod and then turned and walked away.

She turned and stared at her monitor. Seriously, what was she doing? Something wasn't right here. Where was Piper? She was just here.

Wasn't she?

No…that was back in that old cellar at Tunnel Park.

She took off her glasses and rubbed at her eyes.

"Certain events have been unfolding recently."

She opened her eyes again to find herself staring at a chubby man in a mall security uniform. The man's name was Darren. But the thing speaking from inside him, the thing with the freaky black eyes, was not Darren. Those eyes belonged to Warner Harr. They were standing in the basement of the Cakwetak shopping mall, where she first met both Warner and Piper.

"The universe is in a state of transition," continued Warner. "Somewhere out there, a door has been opened. An ancient cycle is in motion again and in the chaos of the change, things are struggling for balance."

"What's going on?" she asked.

But Warner was no longer there. He and Darren were gone. Piper was gone. She was alone in that gloomy basement, surrounded by those dusty black windows with their security gates closed and locked, like great, black cages.

"Hello?" she called. Her voice echoed back at her.

Why was it so silent?

This wasn't how it happened that day. This was something different.

She turned to see a figure standing at the far end of the hallway, staring back at her. It wasn't a shadow, exactly, like those flickering things in Tunnel Park. It was solid. It cast shadows of its own from the overhead lights. Instead of a featureless, black shape, it was covered from head to toe in some kind of coarse cloth. The frayed fabric of its hood caught what little light there was and seemed to glow with a faint and eerie aura.

"Who's there?" she called. She tried to sound confident, even threatening, but her voice betrayed her. The fear she felt at the sight of this mysterious figure was unmistakable in the trembling creak that formed those two words.

Again, that blinding light filled her head. She cried out, both in surprise and in pain.

Things flashed through her head much more quickly this time. She saw her mother. She saw old friends. Teachers. Neighbors. She saw the house where she grew up. She saw her old art room that was in the basement. She saw her old high school. Her third-grade classroom. Her first car. Her fourteenth birthday cake. Her first day of college.

Then she saw her father again. Older now. Frailer. He was lying in the hospital bed where he'd soon take his final breath...

She forced the vision from her head. She couldn't stand it.

Even after all these years it still hurt too much.

Another vision of her father replaced it. He was in his garage, standing at his work bench, looking exactly as she remembered him looking on countless occasions. He was swinging a hammer, making it ring with each powerful strike.

She saw him glance up at her. His handsome smile. He even gave her that wink that she remembered so well, and her heart ached as if it were her first day without him all over again.

Then she was at home in her apartment. She saw Piper sitting in bed, laughing.

She saw her friends, Alton, Caitlyn and Phoenix, sitting together in the college cafeteria, drinking coffee and talking about nothing in particular.

She saw Amethyst studying on the bed in the dorm room they shared sophomore year.

Then she saw Archie Lewelson's face looming over her in the Architects' vault. The shepherd, himself, threatening to kill Piper if she didn't retrieve the Hand for him.

She saw a splash of water. A flash of metal. An imposing blade mounted on the wall of a workshop in Nebraska.

A vision of death...

Then she watched from behind the wheel of her truck as a little old woman transformed into something monstrous before her eyes.

She tried to cry out again, but she couldn't find her voice. Suddenly, she was running through a pouring rain.

Lightning flashed across a black sky.

Living fire belched from the earth and darted across a dark

field.

Snarling beasts with blood-red horns and stained, white fur bounded after her.

Darkness and chaos. Nothing and everything all at once in a violent explosion. An empty blackness blooming into existence. Earth and stone raining down from the heavens.

A flash of sparks as metal slammed against metal in the darkness. The ringing of her father's hammer again.

"Janon Tane..." said Ian's voice, drifting through the chaos. "Tane is *bad*."

Then she found herself standing on a quiet sidewalk, looking out at some small-town street. There was a curious statue on the lawn across from them. A bronze conglomeration of random shapes that swirled together like leaves caught in a whirling wind. Something about the scene was strangely unsettling, but she couldn't quite put her finger on it. Something about the people passing by...

What was going on? She was so confused. Her memories were breaking down into random little snippets that no longer even made any sense.

Then she was in a long, empty hallway with no doors.

She turned around and found herself staring across a decaying room strewn with thousands of rotting books. Her heart was suddenly pounding. A fierce panic was welling up inside her.

Something was stalking her.

She had to get out of here right now.

But then she was outside, bathed in warm, blinding sunlight. She was in some sort of scrap yard, surrounded by the corpse-like husks of hundreds of old cars.

Something was chasing her here, too, she realized. An enormous, black shape soared overhead, blocking out the sun.

She cried out, confused. She tried to run, but she only found herself stumbling through knee-deep water, surrounded by tall, shadowy trees and the foul stench of dank decay.

Again, she wasn't alone. Something splashed in the water behind her. Then to her left. She tried to turn around, but the mud had swallowed her feet, sucking her down like quicksand.

Something stirred beneath the surface, brushing past her leg as she struggled to free herself.

She reached out for something—*anything*—to use to pull herself out of the water. But there was nothing.

And she was sinking.

The mud slowly swallowed her, dragging her down into the water. She cried out for help, but there was no one to help her. She was alone with the shadowy things.

As her shoulders sank below the surface, the moon came out from behind the clouds. She had just enough time to see the old, black boathouse that loomed in front of her before the warm, stagnant water covered her face and filled her mouth.

She let out a strangled cry and sat up, gasping for air.

"Persephone!" cried Piper.

"What happened?" She looked around, but she was back in the cellar where she started her bizarre trip through memory lane hell.

"You just sort of…let out a really girlish yell and fell over."

Seph stared up at her, confused. "I did?"

207

"Yeah."

"That doesn't sound very dignified."

"It wasn't. You scared me half to death. What happened?"

"I don't know. I touched that slime and then everything went all wonky in my head."

"What slime?"

"The slime all over the wall over there, of course." She pointed at the wall.

"I don't see anything."

"Right…" said Seph. "I forget that there are things only I can see." Apparently, this slime was one of those things.

She stared at the wall. The hairs on the back of her neck were standing up.

Piper considered her for a moment, then followed her gaze. She didn't see any slime. It was an ordinary wall. A *clean* wall. Or as clean as a cellar wall could look, she supposed. "Is it still there?"

"Yeah. It's still there." But it wasn't just smeared on the wall. From where she sat now, she realized that there was a purpose to the mess. There were letters. It spelled a word. "It's a message."

"What does it say?"

Seph stared at it, her stomach twisting in her belly. A fierce, almost primal fear was suddenly growing inside her. "It says…'Gispuknya.'"

Chapter 23

What the hell was Gispuknya? And why did the very sound of the word inside her brain fill her with such unspeakable dread?

"Isn't that a kind of cold soup?" asked Piper.

Seph glanced over at her as she brushed herself off, distracted. "What? *No*. That's *gazpacho*, you dork."

"That's not what you said?"

"I said '*Gispuknya*.'"

"*Sorry*. Jeez. What's a gispuknya, then, smarty pants?"

"I have no idea."

"Then why are you acting like *I'm* an idiot?"

"I'm not acting like...ugh..." She took off her glasses and rubbed her eyes. "Can we just get out of here, please?"

Piper made an "after you" gesture at the doorway.

As she walked back out into the tunnel, Seph pondered the mysterious word. What was that slimy stuff it was written in? Why couldn't Piper see it? And why did it hurl her into that weird nightmare when she touched it? And of course there was the question of who...or *what*...put it there. Most importantly, what did it mean?

Gispuknya.

She was quite sure she'd never encountered that word before, and yet it frightened her all the way to her core.

"So what next?" asked Piper.

Seph considered the images from her dream. The shadowy figure dressed in rags. That empty hallway. The scrap yard full of junk cars. Those things were different from the others. Most of the other images were familiar in some way. They were snippets from her past, as if someone or something were rummaging around inside her brain, digging up old memories in search of something useful. But some of that stuff, like the dark figure, the swamp and that black boathouse were things she'd never seen before.

Especially that boathouse... There was something strangely significant about that particular image. It seemed different from the rest somehow.

Did those images belong to whoever attacked her? A sort of feedback? Or were they clues she was meant to follow.

"We should look for a black boathouse," she decided.

Piper stared at her, surprised. "A what?"

"It's hard to explain."

As they stepped out of the tunnel and squinted into the blazing sunlight, they found their path blocked by the chubby tour guide.

"Do you have any questions?" he asked.

"Sorry," said Piper. "We didn't mean to wander off."

"It's okay."

"We heard a noise in that room you said was haunted."

Toby looked surprised. His gaze drifted past them, toward the spooky cellar doorway. "Really?"

"I guess our imaginations were running a little wild," she laughed. "We thought there might really be a ghost in there. But I think a broom just fell over."

"Oh…" He stared into the tunnel, distracted. "I've heard stories, but I've never actually seen anything myself."

Seph was always impressed by Piper's ability to turn into a gifted actress at a moment's notice.

"We couldn't resist having a look," continued Piper. "We're both huge fans of ghost stories and creepy legends. Can you tell us more about those crazy rumors you mentioned?"

Toby looked a little uncomfortable. "I'm…uh…not really supposed to talk about that stuff. I just kind of memorize the script. If you're interested in the *real* history of Avelby, you should check out Pohl Historical Museum. If you talk to Louann, she'll be happy to tell you pretty much everything there is to know about all the area's historical mysteries."

"We might just do that," said Seph. "But we want to know about the more…*fantastic* stories about this town. Like, the really *weird* stories."

Piper stepped closer to him, her piercing, blue eyes fixed on him. "We're *really* into that kind of stuff," she purred.

Seph glanced at her, amazed. Was she actually *flirting* with this guy to get him to talk? That was crazy. She could never do something like that. She didn't have the confidence to pull it off. And who would be dumb enough to fall for something like that anyway?

"We're only supposed to talk about the facts," he replied, sounding flustered. "The owners of this place really don't like us repeating rumors. It's counter-historical and they're afraid someone will try to sneak in after hours to try to see a ghost or something and hurt themselves."

"Sure," said Piper, leaning even closer. "But you *do* know some good rumors, don't you?"

He stared at her for a moment, seemingly hypnotized by those big, pretty eyes.

"Off the record?" she begged.

This is stupid, thought Seph. There was no way he was just going to start spilling it just because some pretty blonde batted her eyes at him.

But then he said, "I suppose you could say the rumors are a part of the history. I mean, I'm not saying any of this stuff is true. So you can't quote me on it. But there're a lot of people who think most of the tunnels under the city are haunted. And a lot of *other* people think the tunnels are being used for all sorts of illegal activity even today. Some people are even convinced that there're things living down there. Really *old* things."

Piper glanced at Seph. "*That* sounds interesting."

Seph nodded. It did. "Really old things" was precisely what they were searching for.

"Tell us more about *those*," purred Piper.

Toby scratched at the back of his head and glanced around, uncomfortable. "Okay, you didn't hear this from me...but I've heard stories about a cannibalistic race of prehistoric people who live down there. Everyone tells the story a little different, though. Some say they're not people at all but some sort of lizard men. Others say they're aliens. My buddy, Mike, says they're mutants.

But nobody believes anything Mike says. He just likes telling stories." He seemed to realize that he was rambling and promptly put himself back on track and said, "I've never really believed in any of that stuff, myself, though." Although he didn't look like he didn't believe it.

"Of course," said Piper.

"If you're really interested in *those* kinds of stories, you should check out Adderbell's. All the gossipers and conspiracy nuts hang out there. They love an excuse to tell their stories. *And* they serve an amazing pub burger."

"Ooh!" Piper turned and looked at Seph. "Let's go *there!*"

"How are you hungry already?"

"Aren't *you* hungry? It's been *hours* since we had lunch."

"Not *that* many hours."

"I've never been here before. I don't want to just eat the same fast food we have at home."

"Easy for you to say. I'm the one buying."

Piper's spectral ears drooped. "Oh yeah…"

"Fine," sighed Seph. She couldn't ever seem to say no to her when she did that. "But you better not get us into another situation like you did at that diner in South Dakota."

"How was that *my* fault?"

"*I* wasn't even hungry."

Piper rolled her eyes.

"Anything else I can help you with?" asked Toby.

"Just one last thing," replied Seph. "This is probably going to sound really random, but do you know anything about a black boathouse?"

His blank expression told her everything she needed to know well before he told her he didn't.

"I didn't figure you would. Forget it. Thanks anyway."

"Sure."

Seph walked away, wondering if she'd sounded as much like a complete weirdo to him as she did to herself.

"What's this black boathouse?" asked Piper. It was the second time Seph had mentioned it.

"Just something I saw when that slime knocked me over. Might not be anything."

"You think it's related to the Gestapo?"

"Gispuknya."

"Whatever."

"I don't know. Could've just been a random dream." But she doubted it. It'd seemed pretty significant at the time. Or maybe that was just because she was drowning in swamp water at the time. "Let's go check out this Adderbell place and see where that leads us."

"I promise I'll pay you back when we get home."

"I know. Don't worry about it. I'll let you treat me to lunch a few times."

"It's a deal."

Chapter 24

Adderbell's was located just a block from Raindskenner Park on Main Street, basically returning them to where they started. It was a cozy little restaurant with a classy, modern décor. It looked like a fusion of a modest family restaurant and an up-scale bar and grill.

It smelled *wonderful*. Seph wasn't really hungry before she walked in the door, but she found that she was ready to eat the moment the tantalizing aromas of Adderbell's kitchen touched her nose.

A tall, skinny woman with long, red hair tied back into a fat, tidy braid met them and seated them at one side of the room.

Seph ordered a Coke and Piper ordered an ice water. Then, as the redheaded woman bustled off to the kitchen to let them browse the menu, Seph took a moment to look around. It wasn't very busy yet. There were only seven customers scattered around the dining room, and as she looked around at them, she couldn't help but think that they were the most mismatched group of people she'd ever seen gathered in one place. They simply didn't seem to go together.

There was an older couple sitting together at a table in the corner, chatting and waiting on their food. They appeared to be bikers. They were both dressed in leather vests, tight blue jeans and black boots. The man's head was bald, but his beard was long and shaggy. The woman had a bright red bandana holding back her frizzy, black hair.

At a nearby booth, two very serious-looking men were sitting together, both of them husky, clean-shaven and dressed in dark dress shirts and slick, black pants. To Seph, they looked like modern-day mobsters. The descendants, perhaps, of the ones the thrift store lady's husband, Jacky, liked to talk about? She couldn't decide if they looked intimidating or ridiculous.

Two old men sat at neighboring tables, chatting casually. One had a long, graying ponytail and a shaggy beard and wore a stained, oversized western shirt, long, baggy shorts and a pair of small sunglasses. In stark contrast, the other man looked like the very model of a prim, southern gentleman. He was dressed head-to-toe in a beige suit, complete with matching hat and boots. He had a perfect, snow-white goatee and a polished, walnut cane propped against one of the chairs.

A rather sad-looking, middle-aged man sat at the bar, wearing a blue work-shirt and dirty blue-jeans. He was drinking a beer and staring off into space.

And now Seph and Piper were here. Two unassuming twenty-something girls from out of town. Just to throw the room into further chaos.

Were these the gossipers and conspiracy nuts Toby was talking about?

Piper's cell phone rang. She pulled it out and frowned at the screen. "Meg," she said.

Seph rolled her eyes.

Piper accepted the call and then put the phone to her ear. "Hello?"

"Where the hell did you go?" snapped Meg.

"I was at Wanda's," she replied without a moment's hesitation. "I told you I was having lunch with her."

"No you didn't."

"Yeah. I did."

Seph chuckled. Piper never said any such thing, but Meg paid so little attention to anything anyone else said that it didn't matter *what* she did or didn't say.

"Whatever. When are you coming home? I'm hungry."

"Since when is it my responsibility to feed you?"

"Ugh. Just tell me when you're coming back."

"Not for a while. I'm not even sure I'll be back tonight."

"Seriously?"

"Sorry," said Piper, not looking particularly sorry at all.

"Any idea where Seph is, at least?"

"She's with me."

Meg groaned. "What am I supposed to do about dinner?"

"I don't know. You're a grown woman. Fend for yourself."

"Auuuuugh!"

"Sorry. Order a pizza or something."

"Whatever." Then the line went dead.

Piper lowered the phone and frowned at the screen. "She hung up on me."

Seph chuckled.

A young waitress with short, blonde hair strolled up to the table and set down their beverages. "Hello, you two. I'm Gina. I'll be taking care of you. Are we ready to order?"

"Pub burger basket, please," said Piper. "With *bacon*?"

"Sure thing. Fries?"

"Yes, please."

"Got it. What about you?"

Seph hadn't been looking at the menu. She was too busy looking at the other customers. Now she was skimming over it, trying to decide. "I guess I'll try the grilled chicken salad."

"No problem. Anything else?"

"I think that's it," replied Seph. "But, uh…" She pointed toward the front of the restaurant. "We were wondering about the sign in the window. The Avelby Underground Checkpoint?"

Gina immediately turned toward the kitchen and shouted, "Hey, Delta! You got someone asking about your tunnel!"

Everyone in the room turned to look at them and Seph felt her whole face turn red.

That…wasn't what she thought was going to happen.

"Thank you!" shouted a voice from the kitchen.

Gina smiled at them. "She'll be right with you."

"Thanks," muttered Seph as she slouched a little lower in her seat.

Piper lifted her eyebrows at her as if to say, "So *that* just happened," and sipped at her ice water.

The same tall redhead who greeted them at the door stepped out of the kitchen and yelled back, "Can you seat customers for me for a little bit, Haley?"

"Yes, ma'am, I can," replied a voice from the kitchen that probably belonged to someone named Haley.

She walked up to the table and smiled down at both of them. "You girls're here to see my tunnel?"

"*Your* tunnel?" asked Seph.

"My very own," she laughed. "I'm Delta Adderbell. My family's owned this building since prohibition drove the owners of the original pub out of business in the early nineteen-twenties. It's been fully refurbished, but the old tunnel's still there. When it was a bar, they say they used it as a storeroom for liquor and wine. But the tunnel, itself, is much older than the building and no one alive today knows for certain why it was built."

Seph and Piper exchanged an interested glance. That sounded more like what they were looking for.

Delta beamed at them, tremendously proud of her little nugget of Avelby's weird history. "You girls are welcome to see it before you leave." She turned and pointed toward the corner of the room, to a heavy-looking door with a sign for the restrooms. "Down the stairs, and past the little boys' and girls' rooms. But you really can't miss it once you've found your way to the stairs."

"We'll be sure to see it," said Seph.

"I'm Piper, by the way," said Piper. "This is Persephone."

"Seph," said Seph. "We're doing research on the area. Um…" She turned and looked at Piper. "Tell them about your…uh…science project."

"My graduate thesis," corrected Piper.

"Whatever," she grunted.

219

Piper smiled up at her. "I'm interested in the history that *isn't* in the books. The oral history. The stories, myths, urban legends, conspiracy theories. That sort of thing."

Delta's eyes had lit up. "Oh, honey, you have no idea what you've gotten yourself into."

Piper's smile melted away as most of the restaurant's hodge-podge of customers burst into laughter.

"Scooch over a little," said Delta. She pushed her way into the booth next to Piper and leaned forward. "Who've you talked to so far?"

"Um…" Seph glanced over at Piper. "We went to Tunnel Park."

"And we took the walking tour," said Piper.

Delta waved her hand at them. "Those places don't tell you nothing," she said. "Tunnel Park, especially, is all *new* tunnels. Built in the forties or fifties. *My* tunnel is much older. It dates back at least to the turn of the century. Even older, if you ask me. It's a part of the *old* network of tunnels under the city. The ones that were here before all the modern industries hacked it all apart."

That *definitely* sounded like they were moving in the right direction.

"Where does your tunnel go?" asked Piper.

"Well, nowhere, now. Someone bricked it up years ago."

"Why?"

"Well, that's the question, isn't it? It has to go *somewhere*. Why build a tunnel that doesn't go anywhere? You ask me, there's another door on the other side of that wall, probably leading into another basement somewhere. And the only reason to have a tunnel leading between two basements is if you were trying to hide something, right?"

Seph wasn't sure about that. It seemed to her that there were all sorts of good uses for a tunnel. But actually *building* one did seem like an awful lot of trouble to go to.

"There're several popular theories," she went on. "Some say the pub was a front for a band of thieves that operated in the area in the eighteen-eighties and the tunnel was their secret way in and out. Others insist that it led to a meeting place for a powerful secret society that included some of the most influential people of the time."

"Devil worshipers is what they were," shouted the scruffy-looking old man with the ponytail and dirty clothes. "You can be sure of that."

Delta rolled her eyes. "And some *impatient people who can't wait for me to finish* swear the tunnel used to lead to a satanic altar."

"There's a portal to hell down there somewhere," the old man went on. "Opened a hundred years ago with black magic and human sacrifices. Ain't that right, Ross?"

The old gentleman in the beige suit tilted his head to one side and sort of shrugged. "Anything's possible in those old holes," he said. "They say they go on forever once you go deep enough."

"All the way to hell," said the scruffy old man, nodding as if he'd just made his point.

"You shut up, Morton," said Delta. "These nice girls are here to hear about my tunnel."

Morton chuckled.

Delta never stopped smiling. She seemed to be enjoying herself, interruptions and all. "Listen up. I can't say if any of that stuff is true or not, but I *do* know that in eighteen-eighty-seven, two of the Pulkin brothers killed each other on this property."

"Pulkin…" said Seph. "I've heard that name. They were the big money in this town, right?"

"Big money and big *scandal*," she said. "Apparently, Pansy Pulkin had a habit of using the tunnels under the city to sneak around with various men behind her husband's back."

Seph saw one of Piper's ghostly ears perk up, intrigued.

"When her husband, Filbert, found out that she was sleeping with his brother, Miles, they had a terrible fight that ended with them both drawing pistols. Miles was killed here on the property. Filbert was severely injured and died a few days later."

"Wow," said Piper.

She nodded. "That same day, Pansy vanished without a trace. No one knows whether one of the brothers murdered her before the fight or if she ran away."

"Some say she intentionally played the brothers against each other," said Ross.

"A number of family heirlooms went missing around the same time," agreed Morton. "Whether she goaded them into killing each other or not, she took what she could carry and split town."

"And then there's the rumor that Pansy was seen in the company of a stranger in the days leading up to the fight," added Ross.

"What's really crazy," said Delta, "is that a locket belonging to Pansy was found in a tunnel under the old waterworks building in nineteen-eighty-seven, almost exactly one hundred years after her disappearance."

"That *is* crazy," said Piper.

Seph nodded. It was a fascinating story, but it didn't get them any closer to the second marker.

"I'd bet money that my tunnel used to be one of the ones Pansy Pulkin used to sneak around in," said Delta. "And probably not just her. I'll bet all sorts of scandalous things happened in and out of those tunnels."

"What can you tell us about the *older* tunnels?" said Seph, eager to steer the conversation toward something that might actually help them. "The *really* old ones?"

"The Pulkins began building tunnels as soon as they first moved to the area in the early nineteenth century," said Ross. "But there were already tunnels under the city when they got here. It was probably where they got the idea. Unfortunately, nobody can be sure what those original tunnels were used for or where they even used to be. After a while, there were so many tunnels being built that the old ones were completely obliterated."

"Not completely," said Morton. "Some of them are still down there somewhere."

"Maybe," agreed Ross.

"No maybe about it." Morton fixed his eyes on Seph and said, "There're still plenty of passageways under this city that people don't know about. All sorts of weird stuff goes on down there in the dark. All you have to do is ask around. People know."

"The portal to hell?" said Seph.

"And plenty more," he replied. "My dad knew a guy who worked for the city back in the day. He swore he once met a man down there with no eyes who spoke a strange language and could walk on ceilings. He was convinced there was an entire underground civilization buried down there."

Seph stared at him. She couldn't decide whether that was utterly ridiculous or exactly the sort of thing they should be looking for.

And strangely enough…a man with no eyes…who could walk on ceilings? There was something strangely familiar about that. It sounded like something from a dream she had once…

"Ain't no underground civilizations under the city," said one of the two men at the nearby booth. His voice was as gruff and husky as the rest of him. Seph and Piper both turned to look at him, and Seph decided as soon as his severe gaze fixed on her that he definitely looked more intimidating than ridiculous. "Ain't no portals to hell, either. That's all superstitious bullshit. You really want to know what's going on in those tunnels, all you have to do is take a good, long look at the Vondraseks."

"Vondraseks?" said Piper.

"Vondrasek Outdoor Apparel and Gear," explained Delta. "They're the big money in Avelby *today*. Them and the Glendengs, who own Glendeng Farms."

"The Vondrasek family practically owns the city," said the strangely intimidating man. "They've got their hands in everything. The schoolboard, the city council, the hospitals, the zoning committee. Throw enough money at it and you can own anything. And you can bet they pretty well own the utilities and highway departments around here. Ain't that right?" he asked, glancing over at his dining companion.

The other man gave an indifferent nod of his head. "I've

heard some things," he said, not really confirming or denying anything.

"The Vondraseks own this town," the first man went on. "And they do whatever they want. The law can't touch them. They use those tunnels to cover up where all that money *really* comes from."

"Murray don't like the Vondraseks much," said Morton as he leaned back in his chair, looking bored. "In case you couldn't tell."

"They do all their real business down there," Murray went on, ignoring him. "There's a secret highway that runs under all their warehouses. Trucks can drive right through, loading and unloading whatever they're carrying, completely unseen. It's a big-time smuggling operation. Drugs. Weapons. Exotic animals. Even human trafficking. They're not above any of it." He took a sip of water and then said, "There're entire warehouses buried in those tunnels filled with containers of hazardous waste materials. If anything ever goes wrong down there, this whole town's going to turn into a toxic wasteland. Ain't that right?"

The other man gave another of those indifferent nods and said, "I got a friend who says there're illegal mushroom farms down there."

"I heard that was the Glendeng family that ran those," said Ross.

"They hide the bodies of all those mutant animals they get from all their genetic experiments down there," added Morton.

"I had a friend once," said Delta, "who had an uncle who said he found an entire underground forest full of monsters down there."

Seph turned and looked at Piper. It was all she could do to maintain a straight face. What had they gotten themselves into this time? Portals to hell? Corrupt, sex-trafficking families? Illegal mushroom farmers? Monster-infested forests?

And yet…thinking about it now, hadn't they *seen* a forest full of monsters once?

What if Delta's friend's uncle had found an entrance to one of the fringe roads down there?

Was it possible?

Or perhaps it was all utter nonsense. These people couldn't be for real, could they? They were just messing with them. Just screwing with the tourists. That was how the locals had their fun, obviously.

"Lots of stuff happens here," said the weary-looking man at the bar. "It's not the tunnels. The tunnels are just another product of it. It's the *location*. We're in a triangle."

"Triangle?" said Seph.

"Like the Bermuda Triangle, but a lot smaller," said Ross.

"It's because of *them*." The man downed the last of his beer and burped. "Everything that gets caught between them gets twisted."

"Them?" asked Piper.

"Fibbel, Rennal and Deag," said Delta, nodding.

"I'm sorry…" said Seph. "Fibber…um…Fib…?"

"Fibbel, Rennal and Deag," said Morton. "The *lakes*."

"Fibbel Lake, Rennal Lake and Deag Lake," explained Ross. "The three lakes. The Old Sisters, the old timers used to call them."

"So, the *lakes* made the town weird?" asked Piper.

"There's something in those lakes," said the man at the bar. He stared into his empty mug, looking particularly sad about the fact that it was empty again. "Something unnatural. Something...*evil*."

Seph stared at him. If these guys *were* screwing with them, this guy won the prize. He was *good*. He actually gave her goosebumps.

An elderly couple walked into the restaurant, their arms linked together to support each other.

A skinny teenager with long, blue hair emerged from the kitchen and made her way toward the front of the restaurant to meet them.

"Tell them about the spaceship, Haley," said Morton.

"Spaceship?" said Piper, bewildered. The triangle thing hadn't quite sunk in yet.

"My grandpa always used to say there's an enormous, alien ship buried under all the tunnels," said Haley without looking back. "He said the government's constantly trying to seal it away, but new tunnels keep mysteriously appearing. People who go down there to snoop around sometimes end up lost in its winding, radioactive depths."

"Wow," said Seph. "That's eerily graphic."

"It's all connected," said Murray's indifferent friend. "We can't comprehend it because we can't see it all. That's the plan. That's how they keep us in the dark."

"They?" asked Piper.

With another of those indifferent-looking nods, he said, "The Illuminati."

"Oh."

"Is there anybody *not* involved?" asked Seph.

"Shame George Colnetter's not here," lamented Morton. "He'd tell you all about how the tunnels are actually an enormous time machine."

"Oh," said Seph. "That *is* a shame."

Ross turned to Morton and said, "You know, Karl Laskler always swore there was a fortune in stolen Nazi gold hidden down there."

"Remember Basil Tondry?" said Murray to his friend. "He accused old Harry Vondrasek of stealing bodies from all the funeral parlors and replacing them with dummies? He said all the real bodies are stacked in a vault down there somewhere."

"Oh wow," said Seph. "It just keeps going."

"Basil Tondry accused lots of people of lots of things," replied Murry's friend.

"Wasn't long after that he died, though, remember? Pretty suspicious."

"Wasn't nothing suspicious about it. He climbed onto his roof in January, *naked*, and got stuck there. They found him froze to death with a pair of binoculars, a laser pointer and a microwave."

Piper opened her mouth to say something, but found no words. She could only sit there, looking puzzled as she tried to wrap her mind around the microwave.

"It's never boring around here," said Delta, still smiling.

Seph had no doubt.

"You want to hear stories, you check out some of the other businesses in the Avelby Underground Tourism Group. You can start right across the street at Yoga Buns."

"Yoga Buns?" said Seph.

"It's a yoga studio and a vegan bakery."

"Oh." That made sense. She guessed.

"Be sure to check out Avelby Tea and the Hairy Knuckles Bar, too. Don't be shy. People here love to talk."

"I can tell," said Seph.

Gina appeared beside them and placed their plates in front of them. "It's all nonsense," she told them. "These people are crazy. You should probably run away."

"Oh, *hush*!" laughed Delta. She stood up and said, "I'll let you girls enjoy your food. Feel free to have a look around downstairs before you leave."

"Thank you," said Piper.

"Yeah," said Seph. "Thanks." She picked up her fork and looked over at Piper. "Get some good stuff for your paper?"

Piper blinked back at her. She was still trying to process the whole crashed alien spaceship thing.

"You know," said Ross. "My brother used to talk about strange lights over Deag Lake on dark nights in the winter."

"There's an island out there somewhere that only appears for a few hours every few years," agreed Morton.

Chapter 25

Seph finished her salad and paid the bill. Then, as Delta's menagerie of oddballs continued their endless debate on what really went on in the mysterious depths below the city, she and Piper made their way downstairs to have a look at her tunnel for themselves. Just past the restrooms was a heavy, glass door marked "Tunnel Entrance," behind which was, just as the sign promised, an open archway leading into a gloomy, underground passage.

Delta had said that it was an older tunnel than the ones over at Tunnel Park and she seemed to be right about that. Although she wasn't convinced that it was quite as old as she claimed. The floor was packed earth. The walls were rough, gray brick. The ceiling was a low archway of the same brick, with a string of wires running along the peak, connecting a series of dull, naked lightbulbs that provided just enough light to safely illuminate the tunnel without extinguishing all of its eerie, subterranean atmosphere.

Other than its apparent age, it wasn't a particularly interesting tunnel. It wasn't very long, to begin with. It only went about fifty feet, at which point it abruptly ended at a wall of considerably newer brick, just as Delta had described, with no other distinguishing features whatsoever. Whether there was another door or a secret meeting place hidden on the other side of that wall, as Delta suggested, allowing for any number of clandestine, illegal or scandalous activities to have taken place between the people of the neighboring residents who occupied these properties a hundred years ago was a question that was not likely to be answered any time soon, if ever.

It was, however, a very *clean* tunnel. There were no bugs down here. Seph didn't see a single cobweb, which she appreciated immensely.

But she didn't have a chance to savor this small stroke of luck because she immediately knew that *something* wasn't right down here. She could see the tunnel stretched out before her. She could see the bricks and mortar, the dirt floor, the lights and the wires, the wall at the far end... But she was immediately and overwhelmingly convinced that there was something else about the tunnel that she *wasn't* seeing. Not with her human eyes, anyway.

"Do you hear anything?" she asked as she stepped through the archway and looked around.

Piper cocked her head and listened. "I don't think so. What about you?"

"Something's here."

"Really?"

She started down the tunnel, trying to find whatever it was that wasn't quite as it should be. "I'm not sure where it is, though. Maybe..." She stopped and looked back, examining the archway and the bricks around it. "No..." She took off her glasses and rubbed at her eyes. "That's not right. I'm doing it wrong." She needed to relax. The harder she tried the harder it was to see through the illusions. But it was hard to relax. She just wanted to be

231

done with this nonsense and go home.

"What did you say?"

Seph returned her glasses to her face and looked at her, confused. "I'm doing it wrong?"

Piper glanced back at her. "Sorry, I thought you said something after that."

"No."

"Oh. I thought you did."

Seph turned and surveyed the tunnel again. She still didn't know what it was that felt so off about it, but whatever it was, she thought it was at the far end, closer to that wall.

She started walking toward it.

It was odd, the tunnels at Tunnel Park and Avelby Underground Walking Tours didn't feel particularly spooky, but this one was different somehow. It had a strangely eerie feeling about it. Maybe it was because those other tunnels were all open-ended. They all led straight outside into the bright sunlight while this one opened only onto Adderbell's closed-in basement.

She walked up to the wall at the far end of the tunnel and placed her hands against the cool brick. Yes, whatever was wrong with this tunnel was somewhere right around here.

She expected to find something amiss with the wall, itself, but as she ran her hands over the rough surface, nothing seemed out of place. The wall appeared to be nothing more than…well, what it appeared to be.

"What?"

Again, Seph turned and looked at her. "What?"

"I thought you said something again," said Piper.

"I didn't."

"Sorry. You keep whispering to yourself and I can't tell if you're talking to me or not."

"I didn't whisper anything."

Piper opened her mouth to say something more, but no words escaped her lips. Instead, she seemed to freeze that way. Her eyes widened a little. Those ghostly ears atop her head twitched back and forth, as if searching for something.

Seph felt a hot dread spread through her belly and an icy chill creep up the nape of her neck. She was suddenly very aware of the wall at her back and the fifty feet of closed-in tunnel in front of her. "Pi...?" she said as she watched her best friend's phantom ears swivel back, homing in on some unheard sound somewhere behind her. "What do you hear?"

Piper stared back at her, her eyes wider than ever. Her lips moved, but she couldn't seem to make the words come out.

She heard whispering. And she was *still* hearing whispering.

The same kind of whispering she heard when the revenant attacked them in Sukmukwe.

She turned and looked back the way they came. "If there's something down here, you need to find it fast," she said.

"No pressure or anything," grumbled Seph as she turned her attention back to the wall.

Where was it? What was she not seeing? And how was she supposed to find it when the whole stupid process depended on her relaxing?

Piper stood watch, her eyes fixed on the bright archway at the far end of the tunnel. Was it really the revenant? And if so, what

233

was it doing here? How did it get here? The only way down here was through the restaurant or through the emergency exit.

But Ian warned them that things like it had other, more complicated ways of getting around.

Could it appear and disappear at will, melting into the shadows like the shepherd?

That eerie whispering was getting louder. She couldn't make out most of it. What little she *did* hear was terrifying.

...kill...

...back...

...murder...

"Hurry, Persephone," she whimpered.

"I'm hurrying!" hissed Seph. But the wall refused to give up its secrets.

"Somebody's coming!"

She turned and looked. From here, they could see through the glass door at the far end of the tunnel and into the more brightly lit basement, past the restrooms all the way to the foot of the stairs. A shadow was slowly sliding down the steps.

Piper made a terrified squeaking noise in her throat.

Calm down, thought Seph. *Calm down and concentrate. Focus!*

As the shadow crept its way onto the basement floor, a shoe dropped into view. Then another as the owner of the shadow descended the steps.

The revenant didn't wear shoes.

This was only the weary workman in his dirty jeans and blue work shirt, on his way to the men's room.

"Oh my gosh..." sighed Piper as she let out the breath she'd been holding. She pressed one hand over her pounding heart and relaxed. "That was scary!"

Seph shook her head and turned back to the wall. This wasn't right. Where was it? Why couldn't she see it? Was she too close? She backed away a few steps and looked it over.

Was this better? She couldn't tell.

Then an awful thought occurred to her: what if what she was looking for was right on the other side of this wall?

Was it possible to get to the other side? Or had it long ago been sealed off like so many of the other passages beneath the city?

Piper watched the workman as he disappeared into the restroom and then turned and watched Seph as she tried to make her prophet sight work. She wished she'd hurry up and figure it out. Next time it wouldn't be a false alarm. Next time it really would be the revenant.

Then she frowned. Wait... If that was only the workman coming down the stairs...where did that eerie whispering come from?

...kill...

A deep, primal fear enveloped her like an icy blanket as she slowly turned and looked back toward Adderbell's basement again.

A great lump of flesh and bone had appeared in the archway, blocking the way out of the tunnel. It twisted and writhed, unfolding and untangling itself as it rose to its feet, slowly transforming into the shape of a man so large his white hair brushed the ceiling above him as his head snapped into place and twisted around to face her.

"*Persephone!*" she squeaked.

Seph turned around, startled, and caught sight of it.

The revenant had found her again.

Chapter 26

The stale tunnel air seemed to fill with the reeking stench of blood as the revenant stalked toward them, its gruesome, butchered body gleaming ghoulishly as it passed beneath the stark bulbs, its dead, yellow eyes flashing, its fists clenched at its sides.

The closer it came, the more visible its gruesome injuries looked. Its torn throat. The festering claw marks on its face. There was a steady stream of black ooze spilling from the gaping hole in its belly. More and more the thing looked like something out of a Romero movie.

Seph didn't know what to do. Her back was literally against the wall. There was nowhere else to go.

...*kill*... said the monster's voice inside Piper's head.

...*slash*...

...*cut*...

She pressed her hands over her ears, desperate to force out those eerie words, but it did no good. She didn't hear it with those ears. And she couldn't cover the others. It was impossible to escape the awful whispering of the approaching corpse.

...*kill now*...

...MURDER...

As the monster bore down on them, its terrible voice rising in her ears, she could find no way to escape it. She turned away, terrified, and cringed against Seph, pushing her back against the bricks.

It was at this moment, as Seph groped blindly at the wall beside her, that she saw it. From the very corner of her eye, she glimpsed an opening. A doorway in the wall of the original tunnel.

When she turned her head to look for it, there was nothing there. She was still trapped.

But that was the illusion. The other thing...the *fleeting* glimpse...*that* was the truth.

She seized Piper's arm, closed her eyes and yanked her hard toward the doorway she thought she saw.

If she was wrong, she'd slam face-first into a brick wall, likely saving the revenant a considerable amount of trouble catching and murdering her. But as luck would have it, she wasn't wrong. She didn't run into a wall. She passed through a hidden doorway and instead ran face-first into a wall of cobwebs.

In hindsight, the cobwebs were much better than the alternative. Gross spiders versus huge, murderous dead guy should've been a no-brainer. But in the heat of the moment, with her face covered in sticky gossamer and countless hairy, venomous, mostly *imaginary* spiders crawling all over her face, with every fiber of her being screaming out in sheer terror, she might've turned and fled right back into the revenant's waiting arms if she could've gathered enough of her wits to remember which way was the way back.

She screamed and thrashed, clawing at her face and arms, doing little more than wrapping herself in more and more cobwebs in her ever-growing state of panic.

Piper, on the other hand, managed to remain grounded. She pulled out her cell phone and turned on the light, scanning the space around them.

They were standing at the end of another section of old tunnel. It was much like the last one: old, gray bricks and rough, earthen floor, but it was a little smaller and a *lot* dirtier. The walls were grimy. Cobwebs hung in curtains from every surface. The floor was covered in a heavy littering of unrecognizable, dust-coated lumps that might've been anything from dust bunnies and pieces of trash to dead cockroaches and moldy rat carcasses.

The only light down here, besides the one in her hand, was what poured through the doorway they'd just passed through. Like in the basement of the library in Muntony, the illusion only worked one way. From this side, the doorway was perfectly visible. And when she looked back at that opening, she found that the revenant was right on the other side, its big hands clawing at the wall, trying to figure out where they'd gone.

And it wasn't going to take long. Even as she backed away from it, the monster's fingers crept around the bricks and into the opening.

"Come on!" she said, grabbing Seph by the elbow. "We have to get out of here!"

Seph wasn't listening. She was still screaming, still trying to brush away the cobwebs and the bugs that she was convinced were burrowing through her hair and trying to crawl into her ears.

But in her desperation to escape this horrific experience, she seemed willing enough to be led along the length of the tunnel, especially if Piper stayed ahead of her and plowed through the brunt of the webs, shielding her.

It always seemed a little surreal to her that ballsy Seph, who was always calm and cool, who didn't care what anybody thought of her, who refused to take crap from people like Meg, *who once freaking took up the Grim Reaper's scythe and cut down an ancient being of unspeakable evil,* utterly fell to pieces when confronted by some of the world's smallest and most harmless creatures.

There was another opening up ahead, a dull light illuminating it from the other side, like a beacon of hope in this otherworldly darkness.

She shined her phone's flashlight back the way they came and caught just a glimpse of something large and pale moving in the darkness.

…cut…

…rend…

…KILL…

She cried out, terrified, and pulled harder on Seph's arm.

Seph, meanwhile, couldn't hear the murderous whisperings of the dead guy chasing them and didn't seem to care. She was still too busy screaming and clawing at the cobwebs stuck to her face.

Piper pushed through the last of the dusty curtains of webbing and into the light on the other side of the opening. In an instant, they were in a much larger, concrete tube.

Seph stumbled across the tunnel, spitting and shouting as she tried to wipe away the millions of imaginary and maybe three or four real spiders that were crawling on her.

Piper wiped at the webs on her face, too, but absently. She

was far more concerned with the very *real* thing that was right behind them. But when she turned and looked back the way they came, she found that the opening they'd just run through had vanished. It was hidden, just like the one in Adderbell's tunnel.

…*kill…* whispered the revenant from somewhere on the other side of the wall.

It hadn't taken long for that thing to find its way *into* that tunnel. It certainly wouldn't take long for it to find its way out. They had to keep moving. She turned and looked one way and then the other. This tunnel was long. They seemed to be under one of the streets.

As Seph tried to shake the bugs out of her hair, she looked down to see several large cockroaches scurrying around her feet and immediately let out another scream.

Piper grabbed her arm again and pulled at her. "We have to go!"

"*Bugs!*" shrieked Seph.

"Forget the bugs! There's a really big, really mad *dead guy* trying to kill us!"

"But there're *bugs!*"

"*Priorities, Persephone!*"

She chose a direction at random and ran, practically dragging Seph behind her. There had to be a way out of here. This was clearly a modern passage. There were fat pipes and huge bundles of cables running overhead. Large electrical boxes were mounted to the walls. Bright floodlights had been installed at regular intervals, safely illuminating the entire tunnel. This was one of those places where important things happened. This was like a nerve center to a city.

Communications, utilities, gas, water, waste…any number of vital systems were run through tunnels like this. That meant that people worked down here. And that meant that people came and went. There had to be a ladder or a stairway or *something*. Given the size of the tunnel, which was more than big enough to drive a large truck into, there might even be a garage door down here somewhere.

But first they had to live long enough to find it.

…kill…

When she looked back, she found that the revenant had already emerged from the spider-infested secret passage and was even now loping after them in those strange, exaggerated lunges.

The enormity of the tunnel should've made the monster look smaller, but somehow it didn't work that way at all. It looked bigger than ever and even more terrifying.

…cut it open… whispered the terrible voice. *…spill…*

Piper screamed and pulled at Seph, urging her to go faster. She didn't have to work as hard at it now that they were away from the spiders.

…death…

Ahead of them, on the right, was an opening. A recess in the wall, about twenty feet deep. There was a door there. She ran to it and yanked on the handle, but it was locked tight. It barely even rattled.

Seph banged on it. "Help!"

Piper turned and looked back. She could see the revenant's shadow sliding along the wall as the monster approached.

…kill…

"Help us!" shouted Seph.

Piper glanced around again, desperate, and then saw it. "There!" she said, pointing at another passage. It was another tunnel, much smaller than the main shaft in which the revenant was quickly approaching, running parallel to it.

They ran for it.

...cut...

...hack...

...DEATH...

Piper wished the thing would shut up already!

The smaller tunnel followed alongside the bigger shaft for about forty feet and then abruptly turned away from it. About thirty feet farther, it intersected another passage running left and right. By now, it was no longer a tunnel at all, really. It was a hallway. The floor and ceiling were tiled. The walls were painted cinderblock. There were several closed doors with frosted glass windows. There were large, fluorescent lights mounted overhead, but none of them were on. Instead, the corridor was dimly lit by smaller versions of the powerful flood lights that lit the main shaft behind them.

"Where are we?" asked Seph.

...kill...

"Just go!" snapped Piper. She chose right and ran.

...slay...

This thing had more of a one-track mind than that last guy she dated!

"Run!"

"I *am* running!" shouted Seph.

They turned left at the end of the corridor and stepped into a huge, open room. The ceiling here was at least twenty feet high, but their path was blocked by a ten-foot-tall, chain-link fence. On the other side were towering stacks of huge, banded boxes, buckets, barrels and shrink-wrapped bags.

A warehouse of some sort?

They were standing in an empty, twelve-foot-wide aisle. Once again, they could go left or they could go right.

…kill…

Left. Piper chose left.

Seph looked back over her shoulder as she ran after her. "Did we lose it? I don't see it."

…KILL…

"Trust me, it's still there!"

Seph didn't question her about it further. She looked out through the spaces between the stacks on the other side of the chain-link fence and caught fleeting glimpses of large trucks parked in the open space beyond.

They rounded the corner and found their way blocked by a large, locked gate.

Seph grabbed it and tried to force it open. The fence shook, the metal rattling like an alarm in the eerie silence of the darkened facility.

…slash…

Piper covered her ears again. "Oh my god, shut up!"

"Sorry!" said Seph, backing away from the gate.

"Not you!"

"Oh. Wait, what?"

Piper turned and looked around. There was another corridor behind them. "This way!"

Again, they ran. There were more of those doors with the frosted glass down here. Offices? There weren't any nameplates identifying any of the doors. Except for the restrooms. Those were clearly marked. But restrooms didn't typically have more than one way in or out and if she was going to be murdered by a bloody, undead savage, she'd at least rather it not happen in a public restroom.

Why weren't there any stairs? Shouldn't there at least be marked emergency exits? What kind of workplace was this?

Piper rounded the corner and set off down the next corridor, then slowed to a stop. "Haven't we been here before?"

Seph pointed at the hallway that branched off to the right. "That was how we came in, wasn't it?"

Piper turned and looked back the way they came. They'd made a big circle and come back to where they started. But which way did the revenant go? Had it followed them into the facility? Or did it turn around and go back out the way they came?

…kill…

Wherever it was, it was still close enough to whisper those awful threats into her brain.

She crept to the adjoining hallway and peered down it.

It was empty.

"Come on," she said.

Together, they made their way back out to the locked door in the recess of the main tunnel.

"Great," grumbled Seph as she peered down one end of the tunnel and then the other. "*Now* where do we go?"

It was a good question.

They came from the left, but she could no longer see the doorway leading into the hidden chamber. In both directions, the huge tunnel seemed to go on and on, with no sign of any other doors or recesses.

At least that awful whispering had stopped.

The place they found was an active facility, most likely owned by the city. It was somewhere they clearly weren't supposed to be. If someone saw them on a security camera somewhere, they'd probably end up in big trouble. And yet they were able to get as far as that locked gate, which didn't seem right to her. The lack of any kind of door or gate on the passage leading into there probably meant that there was no need to secure those areas, which meant that *this* area probably wasn't accessible from outside.

Meaning they were most likely locked in.

They came in through one of those hidden passageways that only Seph could see, bypassing any doors or gates that might've led into this area.

"That passage you found," she realized. "Do you think that could've been what we were looking for?"

Seph was bent over, wiping at the filthy feel of cobwebs still clinging to her bare legs. She looked up at her, her nose wrinkled at the thought of going back into that filthy spider hole.

"It was hidden just like the passage in the library basement," she recalled. "Why would it be like that?"

Seph spread her hands apart and gave her head a quick shake. A "how should I know?" gesture.

Piper looked back down the main shaft, toward the hidden doorway that brought them here. "We need to take a closer look at that passage."

"You do whatever you want," said Seph. "I'm not going back in there."

...kill...

Piper snapped her head toward the passage leading into the facility, her phantom ears suddenly perked and alert. Seph stared at them, her eyes widening, and then turned and stared at the passageway, too. "Okay, fine. But you go first."

Chapter 27

They didn't have much time. The revenant's awful whispers were swelling inside her head. Like the other things she heard with her spirit ears, it had no volume, but it *felt* like it was getting louder. It was *growing* inside her head, like a balloon rapidly inflating, taking up more and more of her awareness.

The monster was getting closer.

And she couldn't remember how far it was to the hidden tunnel. The walls all looked the same. "Can you see anything?"

"Nothing."

"Do you at least *feel* something? Like in that other tunnel?"

"No. I don't…" She turned around, scanning the walls on either side. She could feel herself beginning to panic. In the tunnel under Adderbell's, she'd clearly felt that something was out of place. It was as if her subconscious mind had registered the hidden doorway that her prophet sight saw even though the rest of her brain couldn't see past the limited vision of her human eyesight. But here, she didn't feel any of that. "I've got *nothing*!"

"We *know* it's here. We came through it. We wouldn't be here if it didn't exist."

"I know! But I can't feel it."

"That doesn't make sense!"

"Of course it doesn't make sense! Why would it make sense? *Nothing* makes sense anymore!"

Piper kept looking back toward the recess with the locked door and the open passageway. The revenant's whispers inside her brain were still growing, but at least the words had melted into a sort of incomprehensible murmuring.

Seph took off her glasses and rubbed her eyes. It was hotter in this tunnel than she expected. Stuffy. It made it harder to think.

Was the opening only visible from inside the hidden passage? What good did that do? And if it was hidden, why was Piper able to see it? Why did this particular hidden passage seem to break all the rules?

"There has to be *something*," reasoned Piper. "You've got to try *harder*."

"I'm trying as hard as I can!"

Was it really a one-way door? Or was it because she was too distracted by her fear of the revenant to focus properly? Or was it simply that they weren't standing close enough to the opening?

She placed her hands on the wall and dragged her fingertips along the concrete, searching for the opening that her eyes refused to see.

"*Persephone!*" whispered Piper, her voice little more than a terrified squeak.

Seph looked up to see the revenant step out into the tunnel. It looked strangely weary. Its shoulders were slumped. Its muscular arms dangled at its sides. Its head hung.

Both of them stood frozen, watching the monster.

It stopped there, in the middle of the tunnel, as if exhausted. Then, very slowly, it turned its head and looked at them.

Piper squeaked again. It wasn't even a word. It was just a squeak. As if in her fear she'd suddenly been reduced to a mouse.

The monster twisted its head hard to one side and then the other. Even from this distance, they could hear the bones popping in the cavernous silence of the shaft. Then the thing gave its shoulders a shake. Its long, muscular arms flopped back and forth. More bones snapped and cracked. Once again, Seph was reminded of a giant puppet. Just a dark, angry soul thrashing around inside a huge, empty corpse. The thought was immensely creepy. But she didn't have time to ponder it. Its arms still flopping, the revenant turned and ran at them in that strange, loping gait.

…*kiiiiiiiiiiiiiiill*…

This time, Piper managed much more than a squeak. Her scream was loud and piercing.

Seph grabbed her hand and the two of them fled down the open tunnel. But the revenant was fast. There was no way they could outrun it for long. They were going to need to find an exit fast.

The tunnel curved to the left up ahead. But as they rounded the corner, they found the path blocked by a concrete wall with two doorways set into it. One was a normal, man-sized door, nearly identical to the locked one back in the recess. The other was an enormous garage door.

It took them only a moment to verify that the man-sized door was locked and there didn't seem to be any way to open the garage door.

To the left was some sort of office. There was a locked door and a large window looking in at several small computer stations. It wasn't exactly a high-security area. The door was locked, but the windows didn't appear to be reinforced.

Seph considered her options and then quickly stripped off her tank top.

"What are you doing?" squealed Piper.

Standing there in her bra, she wrapped the tank top around her arm, padding her elbow. "I've played enough video games to know that a room like this," she nodded toward the garage door, "is where you find the controls to a door like *that*!"

"In video games, fat plumbers break bricks with their heads!"

"It's not his head. He uses his fist. You just have to look closely." She pulled back her arm and thrust her elbow into the glass in the door.

It didn't break.

"*Ow!*"

"Why did you think that would work?"

"They do it in the movies all the time."

"You know things like that aren't based on fact, right?"

She adjusted the padding on her elbow and tried again.

"*Ouch!*"

"Stop doing that!"

"Do you have better plan?"

She didn't. She turned and looked back the way they came. Again, she could see the monster's shadow sliding across the wall. That awful whispering was swelling inside her brain.

With a loud grunt, Seph thrust her elbow into the window again. This time, it worked. The glass shattered. "Told you!"

"Just go!"

Seph reached through the broken window and unlocked the door. Then she ran inside and looked around as she shook her shirt free of any clinging glass shards.

Piper followed her in and then slammed and locked the door behind her. Then she stood there for a moment, staring through the broken window, feeling rather dumb.

Maybe the revenant was too big and stupid to figure out how to unlock it?

Seph pulled her shirt back on and cursed. There wasn't a big, highly visible button labeled "door" anywhere in the room. There weren't even any discrete, *half-hidden* buttons labeled "door" that she could see. She tried the switch by the door, but those only turned the lights on and off. If the door was controlled remotely from this room, it would've had to have been done by computer, and she didn't have the skills to hack into this place's system or even the time to let a computer boot up.

It probably didn't matter anyway. Even if they *could* open that door and escape through it before the revenant caught them, there was no guarantee that it would lead them to safety. More likely than not, they'd just find another stretch of tunnel, this one too long for them to have any hope of outrunning that monster.

Besides, Piper was right. This wasn't a video game. The doors were probably opened with normal keys found in the pockets of qualified personnel. Not by solving some ridiculous puzzle.

Piper turned and looked around the room, her heart pounding. There was another door in the corner. She opened it, expecting to find a janitor's closet. Instead, there was another corridor back here, leading into a room full of metal electrical boxes. "This way!"

As the sounds of the revenant's bare feet on concrete drew frightfully close, they closed the door behind them and slipped into the darkened electrical room.

Chapter 28

Piper was right about how useless locking the office door was. It was only a few short seconds before they heard the door crash open.

They wove through the tight maze of metal panels, making their way to the back corner of the electrical room. Seph was certain that they'd only put off being murdered by a few moments. If anything, it was now only going to take longer for someone to find their mutilated bodies. But once again, she was surprised.

There was yet another corridor back here. A narrow, concrete passageway led away from the electrical room.

Piper decided that this town's obsessions with tunnels had probably gotten way out of hand, but she was in no place to complain about it at the moment.

"Is it following us?" whispered Seph.

She looked back over her shoulder. It was dark in here, but there was enough light from the electrical room for her to see that the way back was still clear. "I don't see any—"

KILL!

She cried out and clasped her hands over her ears. The motion was pure reflex. It did nothing to stifle the booming voice that had suddenly cried out inside her head.

"Are you okay?" gasped Seph, startled.

"Keep going!"

Seph didn't need to be told twice. She turned and hurried on through the gloomy tunnel.

There was a small recess in the wall up ahead where a ladder was mounted, leading up. Farther ahead was another of those heavy, steel doors. She paused for a moment, considering her options. The door was probably locked. Every other door was. And since *up* was precisely where they wanted to be, she decided to try the ladder. But as soon as she grabbed hold of the rungs, she caught sight of a hairy, black spider crawling up one side of it. She screamed and jumped back.

"*Oh my gosh*!" cried Piper. "We can't hide if you keep screaming!"

"I'm sorry!"

"Shh!"

"*Sorry*!"

"Shut up and climb!"

Fighting back a squeal of disgust, Seph forced herself to climb past the spider.

Piper looked back. Something was moving at the far end, blocking out the dim glow from the electrical room.

The shaft was taller than she expected, climbing at least twenty feet. At the very top was a trap door of some sort.

Naturally, it was locked.

"Hurry up!" whispered Piper. She could hear the revenant's

maddening whispers swelling inside her skull again. It was in the narrow passageway, already approaching them.

"It won't open!"

"What?"

"Go back down!"

"I can't! It's coming!"

"What?"

"Shh!"

Seph bit down on her lip and fought back the urge to scream.

Piper climbed up higher and then peered down at the floor below. She could see the revenant's shadow again.

It was right there. Just out of sight. All it had to do was glance up the shaft as it approached and it would see her feet. It would have them trapped. There was no chance of escape.

Their hearts pounding, their bodies trembling, they clung to the ladder, held their breath and waited for the inevitable horror that bore down on them.

What would it do to them? How long would it take? How much pain would they feel?

Seph closed her eyes and silently prayed.

Piper tried to think of a way out of this, but there didn't seem to be any escape this time. And with her head full of the murderous whisperings of a deranged monster, her only thought was that she suddenly felt a pressing need to pee…

The revenant's muscular bulk loped into view beneath them, blocking the entire passage.

…kill…

…rend…

...MURDER...

Piper squeezed her eyes shut and felt tears spill down her cheeks.

She thought of her sister, Penny. And her parents... There was no way they'd ever know what really happened here. What would they be told? What would they think? What questions would they have to live with?

She'd never thought about that before. If everything went wrong in this crazy, screwed-up world she'd discovered, what would she leave behind?

Seph, meanwhile, could only think of one person. Her father, who fought the cancer for two long decades to make sure his only daughter could live a safe and happy life once he was gone. Everything he did, every breath he took, was to make sure no harm could ever come to his little girl.

How selfish of them...

And yet...

Piper dared to open her eyes.

The passage was empty.

The horrible whispering was slowly fading again.

The revenant had walked right past them?

Farther ahead in the tunnel, the steel door smashed open.

"Hurry!" Piper whispered.

Seph opened an eye and peeked down the shaft as Piper scurried back down the ladder. "Huh?"

"Come on! Before it comes back!"

Feeling dazed, she made her way down the ladder and back into the passage.

"Quick," whispered Piper. "Back the way we came."

With a little more luck, there would be more than a small, empty room on the other side of that busted door for the revenant to explore, allowing them the time they needed to return to the main shaft and find the exit out of this crazy place.

But she only made it a few steps before she stumbled to a stop.

There, silhouetted against the light from the electrical room, was the distinct shape of a man blocking the way back.

"What's wrong?" whispered Seph. But she didn't need an answer. She already saw the figure standing there. "Who's that?"

It was too small to be the revenant.

Was it an employee of this facility? A security guard, perhaps?

"Hello?" said Piper, raising her voice just enough to be heard by the figure, but hopefully not the revenant. "Can you help us?"

But even as she said this, she felt the pain behind her left temple again. From somewhere under the fading, murderous whispers of the revenant rose that awful static sensation she first heard when the black-eyed children arrived that morning.

Just like the black figure they encountered in the corridors of Tunnel Park, it flickered and vanished. A second later, two of them appeared, closer this time.

"Not helping…" squeaked Piper.

"Other way!" said Seph.

But when they turned away, another flickering figure was standing between them and the broken door.

They were trapped.

They looked back and forth, terrified. On one side, the one

flickering man became two. On the other side, the two became three. Five became seven. Seven became nine. Nine became twelve. And each time they multiplied, they flickered a little closer, closing in on them.

The only way out was back up the ladder.

And the ladder was a dead end.

Seph turned and climbed with Piper right behind her. Her heart racing, she hammered on the trap door, desperately hoping someone would hear and open it.

Below her, Piper crowded higher and higher, pushing her against the door.

She looked down to see a swarm of flickering black figures, all of them reaching up for them. Some had already started to climb the rungs.

Then Piper shrieked as something cold and bony grabbed her ankle.

Chapter 29

Piper screamed and kicked at the flickering men, but although she could feel them snatching at her ankles, she couldn't seem to hit them with her flailing feet. It was as if they could touch her, but she couldn't touch them.

She risked a look down and her heart leapt in her chest. They were right beneath her, hundreds of them. The floor had become a black sea of shifting, flickering forms, all of them clambering over each other, reaching for her.

And they weren't just shadows, she realized. They weren't blank and featureless forms, as they'd first appeared. They had faces. They were faint and skeletal, but they were there. Their mouths yawned open in silent screams. Their eyes were bottomless, empty sockets.

One caught her ankle and held her. Another seized the toe of her other shoe. They were pulling on her, trying to drag her down. Screaming, she held onto the ladder with one arm and Seph's leg with the other.

She didn't want to fall down there. She didn't want to sink into that flickering darkness. She didn't want to be swallowed by those awful, screaming faces. But she felt cold, bony hands on her calves, then her thighs. Something seized her shorts, pulling them down, exposing the seat of her panties.

She screamed again.

Or had she ever stopped screaming? It was hard to be sure at times like this.

Seph banged on the door hard enough to make her fist ache. She screamed until her throat hurt. And all for nothing. She, too, felt those cold, bony hands wrapping around her ankles.

This time, there was no escaping.

They were really going to die.

She was sure of it.

Then, just as the overwhelming despair of the situation began to drown her, the trap door was torn from its hinges and flung aside.

Blinding sunshine poured down onto them and the bony hands of the flickering men instantly melted back into the darkness from which they'd come.

Seph and Piper, still screaming, scrambled up the ladder and into a small room with big, open windows on three sides. A wide, open lawn was spread out around them.

"Are you all right?" asked Ian. He was standing over them, looking down at them as if they were behaving like complete lunatics.

"I think so…" gasped Seph. She was sitting on the floor, her arms propped behind her, her legs sprawled out in front of her. Her heart was racing. Her chest was heaving. Terror enveloped her like an icy blanket. Yet as she stared up into his handsome face, she seemed to get stuck there.

The fear melted away beneath his gaze. The flickering men and the gory revenant suddenly felt like distant memories and she found herself wondering why she let herself get so scared in the first place. *Of course* she was okay. Ian wouldn't let anything harm her. He'd always take care of her. He was her hero. Her protector. He was amazing…

Then she caught herself and snapped out of it. "*Where the hell have you been?*" she shouted.

"I told you I had business to take care of," he replied. "As I recall, I warned you *not* to get yourself into trouble."

"Trouble found *us*," she snapped. She sat up straight and curled her legs under her in a more dignified manner.

Piper yanked up her shorts, embarrassed, and then sat up. "I'm okay, too. By the way."

Ian smiled at her. "I'm glad to hear it."

She returned the smile, although in a far more awkward and dorky manner, she thought.

Seph shot her a baffled look, as if to say, "What was *that?*"

Piper shrugged, embarrassed, and looked away.

Seph looked back up at Ian. His tee shirt was crisp and new again. The holes he tore in it with those terrible horns and spikes were gone. There wasn't a drop of blood on them. The same was true of his jeans and boots.

Did he carry clean clothes around with him, just for such circumstances? Or could he transform his clothes in the same way he transformed his body?

Piper's gaze fell on the opening where the trap door used to be. "What *were* those things, anyway?"

Ian turned and looked down into the narrow shaft. "What things?" he asked. "I saw nothing but the two of you when I forced it open."

Seph and Piper glanced at each other, confused. Then they both crawled forward and peered down the hole.

There was nothing there. The ladder was clear. The passage below appeared to be empty again.

"Whatever it was is gone now," said Ian. He turned his attention back to Seph and held a hand out for her.

She stared up at him, freshly distracted. She was barely aware of taking his hand. He helped her to her feet, his eyes fixed on hers.

"Thanks…" she said, her voice strangely small.

"How's the search for the second marker going?"

"The what?" she asked. Then she blinked and snatched her hand back, blushing. "Pretty well just like that," she growled, pointing at the hole from which she'd just escaped. "We're either getting chased by freaks or talking to crazies!"

He gave her a patient smile and said, "What did you expect? This city conceals an ancient and extremely powerful secret. Places like that tend to attract strange things. And strange things make for strange stories. And strange stories only lead to more strange things."

Seph stared at him, confused.

"That kind of makes sense," said Piper.

"It does?" asked Seph.

"Yeah. I mean, doesn't it?"

"*No.*"

263

"It's a fascinating mechanism," said Ian. "This entire area was designed from the very beginning to befuddle anyone who came searching for the Hands. Every camp, village, town and city built on this site has contributed to the cause of hiding what's buried here. Every single member of this community, whether they're aware of it or not, is a part of a complex machine. Every crazy story, every conspiracy theory, every urban legend, is just another cog in an endlessly evolving system with the sole purpose of concealing the marker."

"That's just stupid!" said Seph. "The scythe wasn't that complicated to find."

Ian raised his eyebrows at her. "Wasn't it?"

"No, it wasn't." Then she frowned and looked at Piper. "Wasn't it? I mean, didn't we just sort of…walk in there?"

Piper shook her head. "No, Amethyst led us to it." Then she scrunched her face up. "I mean Lyla?"

"*Who cares what her name was*?" shouted Seph.

"Last time," said Ian, "the vault guardian found *you*. That was an incredible stroke of luck. This time wasn't ever going to be that easy."

"Not that easy…" sighed Seph. "You call *that* easy?" She recalled those freaky, oozing wraiths, those monstrous goat-creatures, Pappy Stan and his diner from hell… A lot of words came to mind when she recalled the nightmarish events of November, but "easy" certainly wasn't one of them.

"Miss Shawbeck can't help you this time," he said. "She has no power over the other two Hands. She has no knowledge of them. Warner Harr isn't here. Even the Keeper hasn't come to help you. I'm the only one you have this time and my powers are limited. You're on your own."

"So what are we supposed to do?" asked Seph.

"Just keep searching. What you seek may be one of the most well-hidden things in our world, but it's still yours to find. There will be clues. You just have to look for the things that no one else sees." His deep, blue eyes turned to Piper. "Or hears," he added.

Piper felt a warm blush fill her cheeks the moment their gazes locked. She suddenly felt strangely fluttery in her belly.

What was it Seph said? He had some sort of demonic *pheromone* power?

Ian held her gaze for a few seconds, then looked back at Seph. "The only way to unlock what this city's been burying all these ages is to play the game and find the truth hidden under all the lies. Look into the history of the city. Keep listening to the locals. You'll find nuggets of that truth scattered throughout every story and rumor."

"The museum Toby told us about," recalled Piper.

"The Avelby Underground Tourism Group," said Seph. "All those places Delta was talking about."

"Yoga Buns," said Piper.

"Avelby Tea and Hairy Knuckles."

Ian nodded.

"And you really think we can sort out the truth from the bullshit?" said Seph.

"I know you can," said Ian. He looked at Piper, then at Seph again. "But I'd hurry. I don't know how long those businesses are open."

Seph looked down at her watch and cursed. He was right. It was already after six. If she remembered right, the museum was only open until seven on Saturdays. Most other businesses were probably only open until nine at the latest. Only restaurants and bars would likely be open later than that. "We need to go."

"Remember," said Ian. "The Hands were meant for you to find. That means that no matter how well they're hidden, there has to be a map for you to follow. You just have to find—"

Before he could finish his sentence, the revenant leaped from the hole and onto Ian's back, sinking its bloody teeth into his neck.

Seph and Piper both screamed and backed away.

"Go!" shouted Ian. He shrugged his shoulders and flexed his muscles. From Piper's point of view, he began to shift out of focus again. Seph, however, could see the strange darkness that spread across his bulging biceps. She could see the way his muscles hardened and grew rigid. She could see his hands elongating into those strange, spiny claws. Long, curved spikes sprouted from his elbows and he drove them into the monster's sides. "I've got this!"

An instant later, Ian was human again. The monster lost its grip and dropped to the floor, where it staggered on its feet, fresh blood soaking into the waistband of its tattered jeans.

…kill…

Piper clamped her hands over her ears again. She couldn't seem to stop herself. She had to do *something* to try to stop the awful whispering in her brain.

…break…

Ian spun around and punched the revenant, knocking it backward. "Hurry up!" he urged as he stalked after the monster, punching it again and again, pushing it back toward the hole until it fell into the darkness from which it came.

It didn't fall gracefully, either. It sort of bounced against the edges of the hole, making horrid knocking noises all the way down. Piper let go of her ears and clasped her hands over her mouth to force back a cry of revulsion.

...tear apart... whispered the revenant, its ghostly voice fading as its body clattered down the hole.

She didn't have enough hands to shield herself against all the horrors that her brain was taking in right now.

"You can do it," urged Ian. He smiled back at them, seemingly unfazed by the bleeding wound on his neck. "I know you can." Then he jumped into the hole after the revenant and vanished.

Somewhere in the darkness down there, the sounds of fists striking flesh rang out from the silence.

Seph took Piper by the hand and pulled her toward the door. "Let's get out of here."

"He is *so* freaking hot," whispered Piper.

Seph shushed her.

"And he is *so* into you."

Seph's face became flushed again. "Don't be stupid!" She ran out into the sweltering sunlight and looked around. There was an empty parking lot on the far side of the open lawn. Beyond that, she could see a fence with a gate. Beyond that was a street. She recognized the buildings over there. They weren't far from Adderbell's where she'd parked the truck. "This way!"

"Is he going to be okay?" asked Piper, looking back over her shoulder.

"He's a demon. He'll be fine."

"But he was hurt."

"He's a *demon*," she said again. "He probably doesn't even *feel* pain." He didn't *look* like he felt pain. He was smiling when he followed the revenant into that tunnel. "He looked like he was enjoying himself."

Piper wasn't convinced.

Seph pulled out her cell phone and swiped at the screen, searching for the museum's website.

"I still say he's into you."

"Oh my god! Shut up!"

She found the page and scrolled down. The museum closed at seven on Saturdays, just as she thought. That wasn't going to leave much time.

"You're really not interested?"

"In what?"

"In Ian, of course."

"He's a *demon*, Pi. He's not even human." As she hurried across the parking lot, she looked around at the city. "We're not going to have time to go to the museum *and* check out all the shops around here."

"So which do we pick?"

Seph ran through the gate and then stopped and looked around. "We don't have a choice. We're going to have to split up."

Piper gawked at her. "*What?*"

"Ian said we needed to do both. It's the only way we can make it everywhere on time."

"That seems like a *really* bad idea. What am I supposed to do if that revenant thing comes back and you're not there?"

"The same thing you'd do if I *was* there: run away."

"That's not helpful."

"Sorry."

"I don't think you are."

Seph hurried across the street. She could see her truck from here. "I'll go check out the museum. You find those Avelby Underground signs. I'll call you as soon as I'm done and you can tell me where to pick you up."

"I don't like this," whined Piper.

"We don't have a choice. You start at that vegan yoga place across the street."

Piper sighed. "Fine. But *hurry*."

"I will," promised Seph.

She glanced over at her. "I wonder if Ian likes blondes."

"I don't think he does," snapped Seph. "No."

Chapter 30

Piper began at the corner across the street from Adderbell's, at Yoga Buns. It was a cute little place. But the key word was "little." The bakery was right up front, but tiny. The display counter was only about four feet long. The selection was even smaller. She saw no buns of any kind, just cupcakes. *They* were big, but so was their price. Seven dollars for a cupcake? What did they use in place of the eggs? Powdered diamonds?

There was a little seating area to the left, by the windows, completing the bakery half of this strange union. The rest of Yoga Buns was behind a wide archway, in a large, open space filled with absolutely nothing but a dozen neatly placed blue mats.

A fit, thirty-something woman walked in from a back room, dressed in skin-tight workout clothes that showed off her perfectly toned body. Somehow, she looked exactly like she belonged in a place like this. "Can I help you?" she asked.

Piper's first impression was that she didn't think she liked this woman very much. She wasn't particularly proud of it, but it was the truth. Maybe it was that, "look at me, I'm into fitness" vibe that tended to roll off people like this.

More likely, it was just the whole vegan thing. She'd learned to be on guard around people who bragged about being vegan. Too many of them always seemed to look down on her just because she ate meat.

It wasn't her fault. She didn't have any choice in the matter. But she'd learned long ago that it was better not to explain herself. Some very pompous vegetarians might look down on her, but almost *everyone* looked at her like she was a freak when she told them about her condition. She was understandably a little self-conscious about the whole meat thing. It made her a little overly sensitive.

Fortunately, she was much better at playing nice than Seph was. "Hi," she said, trying to sound cheerful. "I was just wondering about that sign in your window."

"Oh, you're here about the yoga instructor job?"

Piper blinked, confused. "Huh?"

The woman turned and stepped behind the counter. "Yeah, let me get you an application."

"What?"

"Do you have much experience instructing?"

"No. I mean…well, I mean *no*…but that's not…" She shook her head, bemused.

"How is your availability? We rotate weekends."

"I, um…"

"Oh, can you hold on a minute?" The woman handed her an application and disappeared into the back room again.

What was happening? When did she lose control of this situation? She stared at the job application, bewildered. She suddenly had a horrible image of herself in yoga pants selling overpriced cupcakes to pompous vegan soccer moms and wondering how she got there.

She hated yoga pants.

They kind of scared her.

This was new. Vegans could be mean, but they'd never bullied her into a job before… Maybe she should just run away now before this got any more out of hand.

But before she could flee, the woman walked back into the room and said, "Sorry about that. I'm Dana, by the way. What was your name?"

"Um…Piper. Actually, I'm sorry, but…" she held the application out for her to take. "I meant the *other* sign."

Dana stared at her for a moment, confused.

"I wanted to ask you about the Avelby Underground."

"Oh! Oh, I'm so sorry!" She took back the application and gave her an exaggerated grimace. "There I go again," she said, embarrassed. "Everyone says, 'Stop being so high-strung, Dana,' but I just keep doing stuff like this." She returned the application to the stack behind the counter and then smiled. "*Awkward*," she said, waving her hands in an "it's all fun" kind of gesture. Then she sort of wilted. "That's me. I'm awkward. That's my…thing…"

Piper stared at her. She didn't seem like a judgy vegan. She didn't even look like a fitness nut now. She looked like an awkward, embarrassed girl who happened to be *dressed* like a fitness nut and standing behind a tiny vegan bakery counter.

"It's okay," she said. "My fault, really. I…" she glanced back at the door. "I didn't even notice a help wanted sign when I came in. I should've been paying more attention."

Dana smiled at her. "Thanks. But really, don't worry about it. I'm totally hopeless."

Piper smiled back at her. She seemed so nice. She wasn't at all what she first expected her to be. Was she even a vegan? Just because she worked here didn't mean she was necessarily a vegan.

Oh god...was *she* the judgy one?

The thought horrified her.

"Anyway," said Dana. "Um...I just kind of work weekends. You might be better off coming in during the week and talking to Evie about the underground thing. She's the owner."

"Oh...um...I'm really only in town for the weekend."

She gave her another of those awkward grimaces. "Sorry." And she *did* look sorry, as if she'd just insulted her somehow. "I can *try* to help. What did you want to know?"

"Well...I'm working on my graduate thesis, and I want to study the stories that people share about the tunnels in this town. Not the true history of Avelby, but the history that people make up. I'm want to hear all the *weird* stuff about the tunnels."

Dana's face lit up. "Oh! You mean like how there's a tunnel to innerspace down there?"

Piper stared at her for a second, distracted. "Innerspace?"

"Yeah. You know. Hollow Earth theory? There's an entire world *inside* the earth. There're whole continents and oceans down there, and entire civilizations of people. But everything's inverted. People live on the underside of the earth's crust. And the core is actually their sun."

Piper stared at her. "Really?"

"That's what I always heard, anyway."

"Is that what you believe?"

Dana shrugged. "I don't know. I think it's kind of fun to think about. If it *is* true, I'll probably never know because I'm never going down there. I'm afraid of the tunnels."

Piper didn't blame her. She was afraid of the tunnels, too. She wished she never had to go down there again. "Does anybody know where the tunnel leading into the, uh, *innerspace* world is?"

"I guess *somebody* must know," she reasoned. "How else would anybody know it was there?"

Piper wasn't sure how to answer that. Obviously, the answer was that it *wasn't* there. It was just a story somebody told her once. But that wasn't really the point. She never expected to find innerspace. Or Nazi gold. Or an illegal storehouse of toxic waste. But she knew that *something* was down there. And according to Ian, the secret to finding it was likely hidden somewhere in all these stories about all the stuff that *wasn't* down there.

The door opened and another woman walked in. She was about the same age as Dana, but she was much smaller, barely five feet tall, with a thick mop of curly hair.

"Hi Tiff," said Dana. "Hey, this is Piper. She's doing a paper on all the weird theories people have about the tunnels."

Tiff turned and looked at her. "Oh, you mean like how the whole system is a superhighway for dead spirits?"

Piper stared back at her. "Superhighway?"

Now the crazy theories were flying at her faster than she could comprehend them.

"Yeah. Apparently, Avelby is like a layover between the worlds of the living and dead. Everyone who dies has to pass through here to reach the next life."

"Oh," said Piper.

"My grandma used to tell me all about it. That's why the deeper tunnels are so haunted. Those're the souls who wander off the tracks and the spirit guards who drag them back to where they belong."

"Wow. That's…" Piper scrunched her face up as she thought about that. Why did a spirit superhighway sound familiar? Then she remembered. Back in November, when they were rescued from the monster-infested depths of the fringe road by those curious sisters, Nadia and Max. The younger of the sisters, Nadia, told her that the fringe roads were built over the spirit highways, which were pretty much exactly what this woman had just described.

It also wasn't very different from Faith's story, she realized. The self-proclaimed Witch of the Three Lakes said nothing about departed souls on their way to the great beyond, but claimed that rivers of spiritual energy coursed through those deepest, darkest passageways, saturating the entire system. Maybe it was all connected somehow.

"You said your grandma told you about the spirit superhighway?"

"Yeah. When I was little." She frowned. "Before she died."

"I'm sorry."

"It's okay. I know it was just a story. I'm not a *total* loony like a lot of people around here. But for some reason, it makes me feel better when I think about a big highway of the dead waiting to carry me off to see her again when my time comes."

Piper smiled. "That *is* a nice thought."

"It is," agreed Dana.

Piper wondered if the spirit highway had anything to do with the second marker.

"You should talk to my friend, Josh," said Dana. "He says the tunnels are the top layer of an enormous machine that the government uses to control climate change."

"*Oh*," said Piper.

Dana nodded. "Probably powered by the sun at the core of the earth," she reasoned.

Piper couldn't tell whether she was joking or not.

Chapter 31

Piper left Yoga Buns with more questions than answers. And with Josh's email address. Because…well, it just seemed kind of rude to refuse it.

But she had no intention of using it. They were starting to drift dangerously far into foil hat territory, in her opinion.

And it didn't end there.

She walked north a few blocks, following the directions on her phone to Brendigger Hardware, where a rather gruff looking but very nice man named Edward told her that the tunnels were populated by hundreds of homeless vagrants that frequently ventured to the surface at night to scavenge for food and occasionally dragged people back to their underground home, never to be seen again.

A few more blocks north, at Rinnal Floral and Gifts, three cheerful ladies named Mina, Kimberly and Lori told her all about the ancient race of dog men who spent their lives expanding their subterranean utopia and used the Abelby tunnels to surface once every thirty years to choose a new queen, who would live out the rest of her life in lavish luxury…which was apparently okay, because the dog men, despite their names, were all gorgeous, naked, love-starved hunks who spent every spare moment showering their queens in gifts and various kinds of affection. (Just in case someone wanted to write a ridiculous fan fiction version of this already-insane story she was stuck in, she guessed.)

At the adorably named children's apparel store, Footie Pajamas, she met the bright and bubbly Kiara, who told her the lower tunnels were carved millions of years ago by ancient, burrowing monsters who were now hibernating deep in the earth, waiting for the day the stupid humans made the air toxic enough for them to surface again.

At Skilton Formalwear, Leonard and Ashton told her that the tunnels were used by witches, whose black magic had made the labyrinth unpassable to ordinary humans so that no one could see the awful things they were summoning in their unholy altars. (They didn't mention whether Faith, Witch of the Three Lakes, was involved, though.)

Caleb, at Avelby Music Company, told her that there was a secret, underground ocean down there, populated with all manner of fantastic, undocumented creatures.

Robert Lostnutter, CPA, agreed with Haley that there was an alien spaceship buried down there and added that the descendants of the ship's survivors still lived in the tunnels to this day.

At Loberly Pharmacy, a frail-looking little man named Conan claimed to know for a fact that the Waldroops, owners of Waldroop Vinyards, were hiding millions of dollars in rare and valuable wines from the government in secret wine cellars scattered all over those tunnels. And a loud, plump woman named Georgia claimed that the Masons had been using the tunnels as a secret headquarters from which they controlled all the governments of the world.

The receptionists at the office of Dr. Huber, a local dentist, couldn't agree whether the tunnels were hiding an ancient and cursed Aztec treasure, a government warehouse hoarding the cures to thousands of diseases or a secret library containing the lost works of every literary figure in history.

The amazing display of sweets at Three Lakes Confectionery made Piper wish more than ever that she hadn't left her purse at home. But by the time she'd heard from the employees and customers present about the inhumane experiments that went on in the secret labs the government kept hidden in the tunnels, the toxic sludge the Glendengs and Vondraseks were dumping into the water supply, the giant rats that were breeding out of control in the black passageways, and the flesh-eating bacteria that thrived in the stagnant waters of the lower chambers, she'd pretty well lost her appetite anyway.

Avelby Tea was one of the locations Delta specifically mentioned that she should check out, and for good reason. The store itself was on the basement level, accessed by a set of stairs from the front and a ramp from the rear, and had on prominent display, right in their store, an open section of old tunnel. It wasn't as clean as Delta's, but neither was it accessible to the public. It was separated from the store's impressive selections of teas from around the world by a heavy sheet of plexiglass, preventing her from actually exploring it. (Not that it mattered, without Seph here to scan it with her prophet sight.) But the store manager, Marcel, was perfectly happy to tell her all about how the tunnels were hiding a massive necropolis of winding, labyrinthine catacombs, housing the bones of almost every noteworthy figure in recorded history so that they could one day be resurrected and used to transform the world into a glorious utopia…which sounded to Piper exactly like one of those ideas that only ever worked on paper and turned out disastrous in actual practice…but whatever.

At Fibbel Sports and Apparel, she met Dan and Jayla. Dan was in agreement with Leonard and Ashton that the tunnels were the domain of an evil coven of witches. Jayla, on the other hand, scoffed at the idea, but was convinced that if you could find your way through the winding passageways to the chamber directly under this store, they'd find a portal that led to the restroom of a Casey's in some rural town somewhere south of St. Louis.

Beneath the Surface was a small, Graphic Design Studio run by Marshal, Dwight and Lola.

Marshal informed her that his great-great-grandfather, when he was still a young man, discovered a tiny village hidden deep in the tunnels, populated with beautiful nymphs whose naked bodies glowed radiantly in the darkness. He claimed to have returned to them many times throughout his life, spending weeks at a time with them, dining on their delicious food, learning the arcane ways of fairy magic and, of course, engaging in all manner of intimate bonding activities, often with the entire tribe at once. No one ever believed him, of course. But at the end of his life, Great-Great-Grandpa was said to have sneaked away in the still of the night to return to his beloved village deep beneath the city, never to be seen again. Marshal was a firm believer that he was still alive down there somewhere, living a life of bliss with his beloved nymphs.

Dwight was of the mind that there probably weren't any beautiful, naked spirits in those tunnels, but speculated that perhaps Marshal's great-great-grandfather might still be alive, as it was his belief that there might be a fountain of youth hidden down there. Mineral-rich waters, he explained, bubbling up from a deep, deep spring, perhaps with the help of rare, undiscovered microorganisms could be keeping him young eternally, while also filling his head with hallucinations of gorgeous, glowing women treating him like a king.

Lola told Piper that all of that was total bull and only an idiot would believe in a village of beautiful nymphs or a fountain of youth. What Marshal's great-great-grandfather found in that dark cave, obviously, was a nest of vampires.

And really, why not?

Piper's next stop was the lovably named Hairy Knuckles Bar. And after listening to all the stories about Marshal's great-great-grandfather and his harem of nymphs/vampires/hallucinations, she was wishing more than ever that she had her purse because she could *really* go for a drink right about now. Maybe even two or six.

She had to zigzag eleven blocks across town, crossing several busy streets. By the time she walked in the door, she was practically drenched in sweat and her feet were killing her.

Hairy Knuckles had a tunnel of its own, too, just like Adderbell's and Avelby Tea. But here, the tunnel was a part of the bar. There were tables there, allowing the customers to enjoy their drinks right inside a part of Avelby's historic underground.

The bartender's name was Chloe, and like Delta, she was all too eager to tell her all about the tunnel and its history. And she was even more eager to start a conversation on what she called "the dark side of Avelby," which seemed to quickly escalate into some kind of competition among everyone at the bar to see who could come up with the most absurd story.

It was Chloe's belief that the tunnels were, in fact, a cleverly concealed manufacturing facility that produced weapons for the military. Vondrasek Outdoor Apparel and Gear, Glendeng Farms and Waldroop Vinyards were all fronts for the operation and were all connected by roads built underground and all shipments for the weapons factory were hidden in the freight that naturally passed through these businesses. Copper and steel smuggled in with ferti-lizer. Assault rifles and missiles buried under boxes of hunting vests and duck calls. Napalm and rocket fuel shipped out in wine bottles. "That's where all that money really comes from," she declared, as if she'd just presented irrefutable proof. "You can't convince me oth-erwise."

An extraordinarily fat man who Chloe called Buddy—Piper wasn't entirely sure if his name was Buddy or if he was just Chloe's buddy—disagreed and firmly declared his alliance to Team Buried Alien Spacecraft.

A scary-looking man with a hideous scar covering one side of his neck told her that the secret leaders of the Republican party met once every month in a secret war room to discuss new ways to dis-credit their rivals and profit off the working class.

A skinny, older woman with bright orange hair wearing a very unflattering tube top told her the tunnels were infested with nasty little monsters that looked just like the ones from the movie *Gremlins*. "The green ones," she clarified. "Not the fluffy ones."

A goofy looking guy with tousled, gray hair said he once saw the ghost of Lyndon B. Johnson in the main storm drain that emptied into Rinnal Lake.

A pretty, drunk woman in a disheveled business dress shouted from her table that she once let Billy Logweiser see her birthmark on Rinnal Lake...which didn't seem to have anything to do with the conversation, but...whatever.

Two women sitting together at the bar claimed they'd both seen giant lizards crawling around under a storm grate once.

A man with the name Aaron printed on the breast of his work shirt insisted the tunnels were where they hid the *real* headquarters for the Obama administration and that they were at that very moment down there somewhere, plotting to destroy our freedom.

A loud, boisterous woman who, in Piper's opinion didn't have the kind of body that warranted showing off that much cleavage claimed that it didn't matter what may or may not be down there because the tunnels were rapidly filling up with toxic sludge that was oozing up from cracks in the deepest shafts, slowly eating away at the rock. And one day the whole city was going to sink into the reeking goo.

Other people—some of them in various stages of intoxication, others still seemingly stone-sober—told her about things she'd already heard before. Illegal mushroom farms. Gates to hell. Hidden vaults of gold. Stacks of bodies hidden by the mob. Hazardous waste and aliens. Witches and smugglers.

A man named Lloyd, like the weary man sitting at the bar in Adderbell's, suggested that the tunnels were a product of a single, paranormal anomaly that naturally produced wormholes, time-warps and ghost doors, leading to sightings of trans-dimensional beings, alternate time lines and elevated spirit activity. Such an anomaly could, of course, be caused by the presence of extra-terrestrial technology, such as a crashed alien ship or an ancient, hidden landing site. This made a peculiar sort of sense in spite of its ludicrousness, which left Piper scratching her head more than ever.

Chloe even went as far as to ponder the possibility that perhaps there was nothing unusual about Avelby at all. Perhaps it was the rest of the world that, for some reason, had turned blind to the true and weird nature of the world.

Piper excused herself as the conversation turned into an argument over whether the aliens came from inside or outside the solar system and then made her way back out the front door. It was much hotter out here, but also much quieter, and that was all she wanted. She was tired of this. It was getting her nowhere.

How was she supposed to find any nuggets of truth in *this much* craziness?

She took out the pamphlet and looked it over. The only other places on this list were too far away to walk to. And there didn't seem to be any point in going to any of them anyway. No one had told her anything useful all day. Even that talk about a spirit super-highway was probably only a passing coincidence.

Maybe Seph was having better luck.

She looked up and down the street. It didn't appear any different than any other city, really. You couldn't tell by looking that there were mysterious tunnels under all the streets and weird stories in everybody's heads.

Maybe Ian was wrong about this city. Maybe this wasn't even where the second marker was hidden. Maybe it was just a town full of crazy people with an absurd fascination with digging holes.

But as she reached for her phone, she glanced across the street and paused. There, in the window of a little shop called Annalisa's Treasures, was another "Official Avelby Underground Checkpoint!" sign.

She didn't notice that before...

She looked at the pamphlet again. Annalisa's Treasures wasn't on the list.

Maybe it was a new addition.

It didn't matter much. She could already guess what she'd find inside. Another loony resident of Avelby with more ludicrous stories. What would it be this time? Mutant alligators? Time traveling communists? Secret society of people who actually liked the *Star Wars* prequels? But she'd come this far, so she crossed the street and stepped inside.

Chapter 32

Annalisa's Treasures was an antique shop. It was small and cramped and filled with all sorts of things from an age Piper was still too young to remember anything about. Rocking chairs, vanities and trunks. Oil lamps and jewelry boxes. Cabinets stuffed with servingware. There were clocks, vases, wicker baskets and old suitcases. She saw fishing poles and tools, toy trucks and dollhouses, quilts and bakeware. On the floor was an assortment of jugs, crocks and cannisters. There was a very cool old bicycle standing near the door. She saw a selection of vintage cameras on a shelf on one wall, along with an old-style movie projector. She saw a homemade, wooden highchair and a hand-carved chess set. Everything in the room was distinctly *old*, but nothing looked junky. It was all clean, well-cared-for and lovingly displayed.

But no one seemed to be around.

She glanced back at the door. The sign was clearly turned to "OPEN" and the lights were all on, so she began looking around.

Some antique stores she'd been in had more of a flea market feel about them. But this place was positively *lovely*. There was something warm and inviting about the space. She walked up to the counter and looked over the items in the glass case. There were coins, pocket watches, cigarette lighters and a bunch of old pendants and broaches.

She turned around and found a shelf full of old children's books that she couldn't help glancing through. There were several old Berenstain Bears books among them. She used to love those when she was little.

She frowned at them. What was it Seph's friend, Alton, told her about those books? Something about how some people remembered the name spelled differently and that was somehow supposed to prove that they were living in an alternate dimension?

He said it was called the Mandela Effect…or something… He told her she could look it up online, but honestly, she'd never really cared that much.

She walked on, deeper into the store. There was a collection of old dolls displayed in the far corner that somehow managed to not be creepy at all.

There were also several old, black and white portraits of people who had to be long dead, which *was* kind of creepy, when you thought about it, but also kind of cool, she supposed.

Hanging on a hook on the wall was a very beautiful old wedding gown. She walked up to it, fascinated by the intricate lacework. It had such an amazingly classic look about it. It was like something from a book. She lifted the sleeves and admired it.

"You'd look absolutely gorgeous in that, dear."

She jumped and twirled around to find a sweet-looking old woman standing on the other side of a small writing desk with one of those old, manual typewriters and a basket full of colorful, glass fishing floats displayed on it. Her snow-white hair was tied into a neat tail and slung over her shoulder. It dangled almost all the way to her waist. She had beautiful, brown eyes that practically shined when she smiled. "Oh. I'm... I was just admiring it," she said, flustered. "I'm not... I don't even have a boyfriend."

The old woman gave her a sweet, understanding smile. "Oh, don't worry about that. You just be patient and you'll find someone someday."

Piper stared at her as she turned away and straightened a display of children's shoes. "I'm not in a rut," she said. Then, more to herself than to the woman, "Why does everyone keep thinking that?"

"I'm sorry, hon, what did you say?"

She shook her head and said, "I'm sorry, I just wanted to ask you about the sign in your window."

"What sign is that?" asked the old woman.

"The one for the Avelby Underground."

She looked confused. "I don't remember putting up a sign for that."

"Oh..." Piper turned and looked back toward the door.

"Or do I...?" said the old woman. Then her dark eyes lit up. "Oh, yes. I think I remember now. I put that there for a friend of mine."

"So you don't have any information about the tunnels under Avelby?"

"Nothing you'd find very interesting, I'm sure. I'm not like the people that run that group. They're nothing but a bunch of money-grubbing blowhards."

"Oh," said Piper, surprised. "Okay."

The old woman turned to a display of old tools and nudged a rusty wrench away from the edge of the table. Then she picked up an old hammer and looked at it. "These old tools are kind of neat, don't you think?"

"Huh? Um, yeah. Neat."

"Always makes me wonder... About the people who used to use them, I mean. Who were they? What were they like? Did they enjoy the work, or did they just muddle through it because you did what you had to do to survive in those days?"

Piper wasn't sure what to say to that.

She put the hammer back down on the table. Gently. As if it were a delicate relic, instead of a hunk of nearly indestructible steel that was literally made to beat things with. Then she said, "There's nothing mysterious about those tunnels. They're servants' entrances, utility tunnels and drainage channels designed to keep sewage out of the lakes. Back in the forties and fifties, especially, they were something of a fashion. You just didn't build a house without a tunnel going *somewhere*."

"So...there's no crashed alien spaceship? Or vampires? Or vagrants? Or dog people?"

The old woman laughed. "I see you've already been talking to people."

"I'm writing a paper," she said, feeling silly.

"You'll have a hard time finding reputable sources in this town, I'm afraid. Just a lot of hot air."

Piper wasn't sure what else to say. During her tour of Avelby, she'd run into a few people who rolled their eyes at the crazy stories people were telling, people like their waitress at Adderbell's, Gina, who wisely warned them to run away. But there was something surprisingly disappointing about being told, point-blank, that there was nothing weird under the streets of Avelby. Especially considering that there really *was* supposed to be something down there and she *really* needed to find it.

"But I guess there's no harm in a little fantasy," relented the woman. "Those Underground nuts are crazy, but they're pretty harmless. They're probably worth a few laughs, if nothing else."

"There *were* some pretty out-there stories," she admitted.

"No harm in it at all," she decided. "It's a pretty nice city. People love to talk. Especially when people are willing to listen. Just don't go answering any ads you see posted for that guy calling himself the Shaman of Avelby. That guy's a creep. The kind the government puts on lists. You're going to want to trust me on that."

"I'll remember that," said Piper. She made a mental list to steer way clear of any shamans while in town.

The old woman smiled at her. "What's your name?"

"Piper," she replied, snapping back to attention.

"Oh, that's a pretty name. I'm Annalisa."

"Oh, so you're…"

"*The* Annalisa of Analisa's Treasures, yes," she said, beaming. "My store. My treasures. All my special things I've collected over the years." She cocked her head to one side and looked at her, as if measuring her. "There's something a little special about you, too, isn't there?"

She stared back at her, surprised. "Um…I don't really think so. I'm just…Piper. Barely even that. Nobody ever even calls me

Piper for some reason." She realized she was babbling and forced herself to stop.

There was something a little odd about this woman, but she couldn't put her finger on it.

She seemed sort of familiar somehow…

Annalisa smiled. "No, I'm quite sure there's something special about you."

"That's what the woman at the occult bookshop told me, too, but my friend said she was just trying to sell us stuff."

She laughed. "That could be true. But Faith isn't really like the other people in Avelby. She has a pretty good head on her shoulders. She has a nose for *special things*."

Piper remembered Faith telling her that their souls shined and that they weren't like anyone else. Could there really have been whispers of truth in the witch's kooky sales pitch?

"But *I'm* not trying to sell you anything," promised Annalisa. "That's not why I'm here. My store's a little different. Sure, I sell people things when they wander in and see something they'd like to have, but this store isn't about money. Not really." She leaned a little closer, those dark eyes sparkling. "It's about uniting a person and that one, special treasure that has always belonged to them and they just don't know it yet."

Piper couldn't seem to tear her eyes from the woman's gaze. "I don't really understand."

"You will," she promised. "Because I think I have something that belongs to *you*."

"You do?"

Annalisa smiled. "Yes, I'm quite certain of it." She turned and walked back to the counter. For a moment, she fumbled with some keys and then unlocked a cabinet door behind the glass case. After rummaging around for a moment, she stood up and turned back to Piper. "Yes. This is it." She held out her hand. Dangling from her fingers was a long, gold chain with a strange-looking pendant hanging from it.

Piper stared at it. It wasn't a particularly *pretty* pendant. It was a circle of small, colored stones all connected by a rough band of shiny gold. Something about it was hard to tear her eyes from. Something about it seemed...well, it seemed *special*.

"Yes, there's no doubt about it," decided Annalisa. "This definitely belongs to you."

Piper looked up at her. "No. I've never seen that before in my life."

"That doesn't mean it's not yours," countered Annalisa. "You've never seen your heart before. It doesn't mean it doesn't belong to you."

She wasn't sure how to argue with that.

"You have lots of things that you can't see, don't you? Your thoughts? Your beliefs? All those things that make you uniquely you?"

Was it her imagination, or did the old woman's shining eyes twitch for just a second toward the top of her head?

"Trust me," she said. "This has *always* belonged to you." She placed the pendant in Piper's hand and smiled. "It's been waiting here for you."

Piper was staring at it again. Was it just that this woman was making it sound so mysterious? Or was there really something very peculiar about the pendant? It *did* feel strangely right to hold it in her hand.

"This is a very special object," said Annalisa. "As long as you're wearing it, it'll protect you from evil. Even in the darkest and deepest places."

Again, Piper looked up at her. The darkest and deepest places? "I…I didn't bring any money. I'm sorry."

Annalisa laughed. "I already told you, this store isn't about money. Besides, I can't very well sell that to you. It was already yours. You just came here to pick it up."

"I did?"

"You did," she whispered. "I was happy to hold onto it for you."

Piper shook her head. "But…"

"No buts. You take that with you. Wear it close to your heart and no matter where things lead you, you'll always be safe."

She wasn't sure what just happened, but she nodded.

"Don't let me keep you," said Annalisa, her eyes still shining. "You seemed like you were in the middle of something when you came in the door. I'm sure you have something you should be doing."

Again, she nodded. "Right…" She should probably call Persephone and see if she found anything at the museum. She was surprised she hadn't heard from her already, in fact. It was after closing time. "I should really get going."

With that same smile still on her face, she replied, "Stop by any time you're in town, dear."

"Sure," she replied, frowning as she walked away. Did she tell this woman she didn't live here?

She left Annalisa's Treasures and then stood there on the sidewalk for a moment, examining the curious pendant. Did it really have protective powers? Could it really shield her from evil?

What a curious little shop.

Bringing together people and their treasures.

She looked back one last time…

She half-expected the store to be gone, that there'd be nothing there but empty windows and a "FOR RENT" sign, but Annalisa's Treasures was right where she left it.

Because this wasn't some old cliché in one of her silly books.

The "Official Avelby Underground Checkpoint" sign, however, the one she didn't notice at first when she was standing across the street, was gone.

Had Annalisa snatched it out of the window after she left?

Was the sign only for her?

I put that there for a friend of mine.

Was she talking about *her*?

She was still trying to wrap her head around it when a petite young woman with short, black hair, ripped jeans and a gray tee shirt darted from a narrow alleyway on the other side of the street. She looked back as if something were chasing her and then quickly ran off in the other direction.

Piper watched her until she turned the corner, curious. Then she crossed the street and peered into the alleyway from which the woman had appeared.

There was nothing there. It was just a narrow, weedy gap between two brick buildings. But as she stood there, staring at it, something jangled softly deep down in her mind. It was a sound that wasn't a sound. A sensation without volume.

She recognized it at once this time.

Her spirit ears.

The "sound" didn't come again. It had gone silent. (Or whatever was the spirit ears equivalent of silence.) But she was certain she didn't imagine it. And that woman looked as if she saw something there.

She jogged to the end of the street and peered around the building.

The woman was there, heading for the next intersection. She'd stopped running, but she was still walking fast.

I'm sure you have something you should be doing, Annalisa had told her.

She felt a chill creep up her spine. But she didn't have time to ponder the mysterious old woman and her curious little treasure shop.

The suspicious young woman in the ripped jeans was getting away.

She slipped the chain over her head and hurried after her.

Chapter 33

While Piper was listening to the city's many colorful tales of what "really" went on under the streets, Seph was getting an unexpectedly grim lesson about the history of Avelby, Illinois.

Toby, the walking tour guide, had suggested she talk to someone named Louann at Pohl Historical Museum. She was expecting a stuffy, humorless old lady with a monotone voice and an endless array of boring facts about dead mayors, the construction of small-town landmarks and the importance of local industries. Instead, what she found was a spunky, quick-witted old woman with enough energy and sass to run circles around her any day of the week.

Louann seemed to be about ninety, going on *twenty-five*.

And far from boring, the stories she told were more than fascinating. Some of them were positively *chilling*.

Louann told her all about Avelby, of course. Its start as a fort near a small community of natives known as the Swambish. Its early rise as a dairy industry. She told her about the Pulkin family, which rose to wealth and success, growing the small town into a thriving city over the better part of a century, only to have their fortune squandered by the last few generations until there was nothing left of the family's once proud legacy. She mentioned the duel where the brothers, Filbert and Miles, killed each other and the disappearance of Pansy Pulkin, but she also told her about a mysterious fire that burned the Pulkin's estate to the ground not long after, and the brutal, unsolved murder of Rose Pulkin a decade later. And then there was the disappearance of four-year-old William Pulkin a few years after that.

Seph had thought that the Pulkin family sounded like the perfect candidates for the keepers of the second marker. They had all the money and the power for most of a century. But not only had they died out, they seemed to have been *cursed*. Lionel Pulkin, the last of the family line, was sent to prison for attempted murder and would've hanged, if he hadn't been found in his prison cell, beaten to death.

And the misfortune didn't end with the Pulkins, either. There was a series of grisly, unsolved murders in the early sixties, perpetrated by someone the press dubbed "the Avelby Headhunter." In the early seventies, part of a factory collapsed, killing fourteen people. Later that same year, a man was found half-eaten in Deag Lake, prompting one of the biggest monster scares in the history of the Midwest in spite of local authorities insisting the body was only ravaged by the lake's local wildlife. Two major fires ravaged the town in the eighties, killing eleven people in all. And between nineteen-ninety-two and nineteen-ninety-nine, there were three separate instances in which seemingly normal men suddenly and inexplicably woke up in the middle of the night and slaughtered their families before committing suicide in gruesome fashion. And finally, there was the disappearance of three children just a few years ago.

Louann's history of Avelby was unexpectedly gruesome. As if the revenant and those weird, flickering men weren't enough reason to fear this town.

But for all the knowledge Louann had about morbid accidents, grisly murders and unexplained disappearances, none of it told Seph anything about what might have been buried here before the city was built.

The best she could find was a map of what the original settlement looked like. According to that, the oldest areas in the city were to the south, along the northern shores of Lake Deag, which would've been consistent with what Toby told them about those old tunnels they were excavating. But the Native Americans who occupied the area before that, the Swambish, were located farther north, along the eastern shores of Fibbel Lake.

She spent a while staring at this map. In November, they found the first marker in the woods behind a local AM radio station in a little dump of a town. They found the second marker behind a secret passage in the basement of the Muntony City Library. Neither was buried very deep. Just like the marker they found in Sukmukwe, it couldn't have been more than a few feet from the tops of the chambers to the surface.

It was amazing they'd stayed hidden all this time.

What if the second marker had been destroyed? What if a construction crew demolished it at some point to make way for one of those stupid tunnels or somebody's basement?

But the Keeper, whoever or whatever he was, was supposed to be watching over the paths to the Hands. That's why he was the

Keeper. He *kept* things. Like some sort of cosmic groundskeeper. Or at least, that's what everyone made it sound like. Surely *he* wouldn't have let some stupid road crew plow a hole through the only path to one of the most important objects ever created.

And yet, it hadn't escaped her attention that the Keeper *wasn't here.*

If it was so important for them to find these things, then why didn't he just come here and tell them where to look? He had no problem disguising himself as a grubby hitchhiker and holding up a sign telling her to go to St. Paul. Or showing her the turnoff to Old Castle Road.

Maybe the reason he wasn't here was that the second Hand of the Architects was lost forever.

Louann was kind enough to sit and talk with her until well past closing time, but it was pointless. She was still no closer to the marker.

Then, just as she was leaving, she caught sight of something that stopped her in her tracks.

Hanging on one of the museum's bulletin boards were several dozen photographs that appeared to have been taken around the city. They were very artistic. There were several shots of sunrises and sunsets over the lakes. There were snow-covered park benches and trees in Spring blooms. The courthouse lit up for Christmas. The Glendeng Farm gates in fall. And among them, almost as an afterthought, was a shot from a boat, overlooking the shore of the lake in an early morning mist.

There, sticking out from the trees, was a small, wooden structure painted entirely in black. The black boathouse, exactly as it had looked in her slime-induced vision.

"That was taken by Gus Frengan a few years ago," said Louann when Seph asked her about it. "He's a pretty famous photographer these days. I heard that building started falling down right after he took that picture."

"Do you know where that is?"

"Well, that's Fibbel Lake," she said. "Not far from where the river flows out to Rinnal." She walked over to one of the maps hanging on the wall and pointed. "Right around here somewhere."

Seph stared at the spot. That wasn't far from where the Swambish lived.

A man named Jarret at Amethyst's ranch in Nebraska told them once that the vault was watched over by native tribes long before European settlers arrived, which only made sense.

"There's an orchard out on Sugly Road," recalled Louann. "If I remember right, there's an old farm located behind it. You just have to take the driveway all the way around. It's private property now. I don't know who owns it or if anybody ever still even goes there." She glanced over at Seph, curious. "Why so interested in it?"

"It just...looked familiar. I feel like I've seen it somewhere before."

"Well there's nothing out there now. I wouldn't go near the place. Probably infested with snakes these days."

Seph cringed. Why did she have to say that? She hated snakes as much as she hated bugs. "It definitely doesn't sound like somewhere I want to be," she replied. It wasn't a lie. But the fact was that, like it or not, she was pretty sure she and Piper were going to have to go find that farm.

"Well, it's time for me to wrap things up and go home," said Louann. "Is there anything else I can do for you?"

"Yeah," said Seph. She stood there a moment longer, staring at the old, black boathouse. "Just one thing. It's a little random, but..." she turned and looked at her, "...have you ever heard of something called Gispuknya?"

"Can't say I have," replied Louann.

And yet Seph couldn't help but notice a hint of hesitation in her voice. A strange tightening of her face. A flash of something in her eyes.

Did Louann just lie to her?

"Be sure to stop in again sometime," she said, a bright smile covering up whatever she might've been hiding a moment ago.

Seph nodded. "Sure."

A minute later she was back in her truck, her mind racing.

What was Gispuknya? What was with the black boathouse?

She tried calling Piper, but her phone went straight to voicemail.

Now what was going on? Given the circumstances, there was no way she'd turn her phone off. Her thoughts immediately jumped to the most awful conclusions she could think of.

She left a message telling her she was done at the museum and to call her as soon as she had a chance.

Piper was fine. She had to be. She was just somewhere with bad reception. That was all. Probably touring another tunnel like the one in the basement of Adderbell's.

...where the revenant tried to kill them...

301

She shook the thought away and glanced around at the empty parking lot. She couldn't think like that.

But she also couldn't go and pick up Piper if she had no idea where she was.

And it was getting late…

She didn't want to go check out the black boathouse on her own. But she also didn't want to go check out the black boathouse after dark.

She dropped her phone into the console and shifted the truck into gear. She'd just drive over and find the place. Have a quick look. See what it looked like over there. She didn't even have to get out of the truck. When Piper finally got back to her, she'd hurry over and pick her up.

"Easy peasy," she murmured, then immediately thought, *Famous last words…*

Chapter 34

Seph turned off Sugly Road and followed the gravel driveway around the perimeter of the orchard, like Louann described. It was a much bigger orchard than she expected it to be, reaching *way* back into the woods. But eventually she caught sight of an old, dirt road that the forest was well on its way to reclaiming. Slowly, she turned onto it and drove through the crowding branches, wincing at the sounds of wood scraping across the paint as the Ford rocked back and forth over the rough terrain.

Her poor truck. Why did these trips have to be so hard on it? It wasn't fair. She took good care of it. She kept the oil changed. She kept the road salt washed off it in the winter time. She had the tires rotated regularly. She did all the things her dad taught her to do. And then she had to go and take it somewhere like this.

She kept expecting to find a tree lying across the road, blocking her path, but she lumbered along, unimpeded, for almost half a mile before an old farmhouse finally came into view through the dense foliage.

She stopped the truck before the end of the driveway, keeping herself concealed in the trees as she surveyed the scene.

There was little about the place that was still recognizable as a farm. There was a house and a shed and even a little bit of a collapsed barn just visible through the trees that had all but swallowed it. But any semblance of a yard of any kind was utterly lost beneath waist-high grass, blackberry thickets and trees. All that was left was the occasional post sticking up from the weeds, and the rusted skeleton of an old tractor that probably hadn't moved in at least fifty years.

She picked up her phone, hoping that Piper had texted her while she was driving and she just didn't hear it, but she still had no messages. Where was she? Had something happened to her. She didn't like this. It wasn't like Piper to not return a call.

But at least she still had a signal out here.

She lowered the phone and stared out at the abandoned farm buildings. No one seemed to be here. There were no cars, anyway, nor any sign of any vehicles having left tire tracks in the grass recently.

She couldn't decide if that made it better or worse.

She *really* didn't want to go out there. Stupid Louann had her imagining snakes everywhere. There could be thousands of them in that high grass and she wouldn't know it until she stepped on one. And even if there weren't any snakes, she knew for a fact that there were going to be bugs. There were always bugs in the woods. There were probably millions of mosquitos already swarming the truck, just waiting for her to open the door. Not to mention spiders.

And yet…what else could she do? She had no idea where Piper was. And if she sat around waiting too long for her to call, it'd be dark before she got back.

And she *really* didn't want to go out there after dark.

That was the thing she kept circling back to. Nightfall. When all sorts of awful things came out. She couldn't bear the thought of poking around out here in the dark, never sure if one of those flickering shadow men might be close enough to reach out and grab her.

With a frustrated whimper, she opened the door and stepped out into the evening heat.

She could hear them. Foul, disgusting things buzzed all around her. Cicadas sang in the trees. A bumblebee was cruising over the bed of the truck.

Something buzzed in her ear and a pitiful cry escaped her as she slapped at it.

Stupid bugs. She hated them.

Her skin crawling, she forced herself to wade through the tall grass where the yard used to be, scaring up countless little grasshoppers and other icky things that lazily fled from her path. Nasty, invisible things were already buzzing in her ears.

It wasn't fair. They were just bugs. They didn't bother other people. Other people actually *liked* being out in nature. She was just being a "girl," as her dad used to say when he chided her for acting like this when she was little. She knew it was ridiculous. Especially now that she knew what sorts of *real* monsters were out there. After looking down a giant zombie worm's festering gullet, something as insignificant as a mosquito shouldn't bother her at all. But she just couldn't help it for some reason. Bugs had always frightened her.

And so did snakes.

Something moved in the grass in front of her foot and she

jumped backward, a shrill shriek escaping her before she could stifle it behind her hands.

Get ahold of yourself, she thought, frustrated. But of course, she couldn't help it.

She wished Piper were here. Piper wasn't afraid of bugs. She was afraid of lots of other silly things. Like any kind of scary movie, even the really bad ones. And dentists. Needles. Clowns. Chickens. Lawn gnomes for some strange reason. Gas station restrooms. And of course there was her intense aversion to personal conflict. She also had a sneaking suspicion that Piper was afraid of romantic commitment, because she always found a reason to turn down any guy who asked her out, and she rarely talked about any past boyfriends.

But she wasn't afraid of bugs. If she were here, she'd take the lead. She wouldn't be bothered by a grasshopper landing on her knee or a spiderweb sticking to her face.

She *really* hoped Piper was safe.

She checked her phone again, but still there were no messages. Where was she? What could she be doing?

She was starting to worry.

She made her way to the side of the farmhouse and peered in through a small, dusty window. Inside was empty and dark and filthy. It didn't look like anyone had been in there in ages.

She circled around the side of the building and looked out at the remains of the old barn. The rusty shell of the old tractor. The rotting fence posts that jutted up from the grass like the bones of a giant serpent. The little shed with its door hanging open, revealing a narrow strip of the gloom that was crowded inside it.

She didn't like this place very much. It was creepy as hell. It was too quiet. Too *still*.

Something landed on her shoulder and she slapped it away with a squeal that reminded her too much of Piper.

Stupid bugs!

She turned and looked out at the dense forest. Where was that boathouse? Which way was the lake?

If she was on the eastern side of the lake... She glanced up at the sky, took note of the sinking sun, and then scanned the tree line to the west. At first, she didn't see it. Then she did. A barely visible break in the trees. The shadow of an old path leading away from the yard in the direction of the water.

It looked so dark in there...

Her skin still crawling, she made her way through the weeds and brush and onto the overgrown path leading down the hill and to the water. Within minutes, she saw it, a dark, bulky shape behind the crowding leaves. The doors stood open and sagging, like an enormous, black eye staring back at her, watching her as she approached.

Louann was right. The boathouse had collapsed since the picture was taken. Although it looked intact as she walked up, she soon realized that the side facing the water had fallen in on one side, almost completely enclosing it.

Carefully, she stepped into the doorway and looked down at the gloomy water. An old rowboat lay rotting beneath the rippling surface, entombed here, like the tractor back behind the farmhouse.

It was curious, she realized. She could tell that it was the same black boathouse from her strange vision back in that empty cellar.

But it didn't look like this. It was still standing in the vision. And she was looking at it from the angle of the lake, almost as if the vision wasn't of the boathouse itself, but of Gus Frengan's photograph of it.

The vision was summoning her here, she realized. It was drawing her a map, showing her the way.

But why?

Why was she here? What was she supposed to do now that she'd found it? What was the significance of the black boathouse?

She looked down at her feet to find that she was standing in a puddle of that strange, gray slime.

Immediately, the hair on the back of her neck stood up. A trail of it had been dripped on the ground, leading out of the lake, through the open doors and up the path she'd just followed here. There was even a glob of it oozing down the door, as if someone had put a slime-covered hand on it as they passed…

The memory of the cellar wall flashed through her head, the mysterious word smeared in slime. (*Gispuknya.*) And a strange, strangling terror filled her.

She had to get out of here.

Chapter 35

Again, Piper's phone went straight to voicemail.

"Where are you?" demanded Seph. "Hurry up and call me back! I need you!"

She stuffed her phone back into her pocket, frustrated. She didn't like this. It was still a while until sunset, but here in these woods she was already beginning to lose light. The shadows were growing longer and deeper with each passing minute, and with the encroaching darkness she found herself growing more and more anxious.

She came out here because she decided she'd rather explore the abandoned farm alone in the daylight than after dark with Piper. She thought she was brave enough to do this on her own. But now she was starting to think this was a really stupid idea.

Every now and then she caught sight of another glob of slime on the ground or oozing down the side of a tree. If she hadn't been so distracted by all these stupid bugs, maybe she would've noticed it on her way down to the boathouse.

What was it, anyway? What manner of creature crawled out of lakes, dripped slime and left messages on walls in public places without being seen? How did it get from there to here? And how close had she come to running into it while wandering around out here all alone?

Something stirred in the branches overhead and she jumped, startled.

"Calm down," she told herself. "Just squirrels."

Somewhere far off to her right, there was a loud crack, as if a large branch had just snapped off and crashed to the ground. Again, she jumped. She looked out in that direction, her eyes wide open.

"Really *fat* squirrels," she amended. "Morbidly obese squirrels."

Something buzzed past her ear and she let out a startled squeal and swatted at it.

What was she thinking? She couldn't do something like this on her own. She acted tough, but in truth she was nothing but a big wimp.

"I'm going to die out here," she murmured, "and I have nobody to blame but myself."

Quietly, she crept out of the woods and back into the waist-deep field grass and weeds that had swallowed the old farmhouse's lawn. Where did the slime-dripping thing go? She didn't dare assume that it had gone. That wasn't the kind of luck she had. Was it out here somewhere right now, watching her? Crouched in the tall grass, perhaps? Hiding in the trees? Peering out from under the ruins of the barn? Or maybe it didn't have to hide. Maybe it didn't just drip slime. Maybe it *was* slime. Maybe it could change its shape. For all she knew, it could've soaked into the ground beneath her feet and any second now it would spring up and swallow her up like the blob in those old movies, digesting her whole.

She looked down at the ground beneath her, her heart thumping with fear.

She was seriously starting to freak herself out over this slime monster business.

Her eyes peeled for anything unnatural, she hurried off across the overgrown lawn, intending to run back to her truck. But she didn't make it far before she froze in her tracks, her wide eyes fixed on the little shed.

The first time she walked by it, the door was open just a crack. She remembered being creeped out by the sliver of darkness inside. Now, however, the door was standing half-open.

There wasn't any wind to speak of. The day was as still as it was hot. There was no reason for it to have opened by itself. Someone...or some*thing*...had been here.

Her mouth suddenly dry, her heart racing even faster, she crept toward it. She could see something inside. Not a person. Not any kind of monster. Just...a *thing*. A shape on the floor.

She glanced around again, making sure nothing was sneaking up on her while she was focused on the shed.

Was the slime thing inside when she was last here? Was it watching her through the crack? The thought gave her a fierce chill in spite of the heat.

She crept closer.

Closer...

"Dear God, please don't let me find a bunch of severed heads in here," she breathed, remembering Louann's stories about the

Avelby Headhunter and how they never found the killer or any of the victims' heads. (As if she'd needed more terrifying things to think about; she was experiencing quite enough trauma thanks to the white-haired dead guy and those freaky, flickering shadow people.)

She grasped the rusty handle, pulled the creaky door open a few more inches and peered into the shed.

The thing on the floor was a two-foot-high ring of concrete surrounding a hole in the ground. It looked like an old well of some sort, but with a rusty ladder mounted to one side. A heavy, iron disk was leaning against one wall. The cover to the well, removed fairly recently, from the looks of it.

Curious, she stepped through the doorway. She pulled out her cell phone and shined its light down into the darkness. There was a tunnel down there, much like the one connecting Adderbell's to that large service tunnel, complete with several decades of accumulated cobwebs and dust.

"Yeah…" she breathed, wrinkling her nose at a fat spider hanging out on the wall next to the ladder. "Totally not going down there by myself."

She stood up and took a step backward.

This had to be it. The tunnel they were looking for was right down there. Why else would she be lured here?

"So someone can murder you," she answered herself. "Duh."

Still, it was the closest thing she'd found to a lead. Here was a tunnel that was far enough away from the city to have not been wrecked by modern construction. It was also right around where the original village was standing. And it certainly wasn't going to be difficult to sneak in unseen.

She'd get back in her truck and go find Piper. If she hurried, they might be able to get back here before the sun went down. With a *lot* of luck, maybe they'd find the second marker, avoid whatever hellish trap the Keeper had waiting for them for a change, and then get out of this freaky town before full nightfall. That would be great. Extremely unlikely, but great.

She turned to leave, but again froze. There, standing on the farmhouse's old, crumbling porch, was a stooped figure covered head-to-toe in strange, coarse cloth.

The sight made her heart stutter in her chest. She barely managed to choke back a scream.

It was just like in her vision when she first encountered the slime. The cloaked figure standing in the basement of the Cakwetak mall. The one that didn't belong to that memory. This time, it didn't seem to be looking at her. It was staring off into the woods, toward the lake from where she'd just come.

Was it looking for her? Was it like those flickering men? Or the revenant?

Maybe it didn't know she was here.

She crouched down behind the door and peered out at it. That strange cloth it was wearing appeared to be a rough patchwork of filthy rags.

A blinding light suddenly flashed inside her head and just like in the cellar, a slideshow of images flickered across her brain. She saw her dad again, sweat on his brow, his hammer ringing rhythmically through his workshop. She saw Amethyst standing over the vault, warning them to hurry. She saw grouchy old Mr. Hallet from

Shawbeck Ranch, standing in front of a wall covered in hanging tools, chief among them a long, formidable-looking scythe. And she saw her mother lying on her couch with her blanket pulled up to her chin, a visage of death spreading across her gaunt face.

She squeezed her eyes shut and forced the images away. When she looked up again, the figure had turned its hooded face toward her.

The strangled, squeaking sound she made in her throat was one she'd heard Piper make on several occasions, but she hadn't been aware until now that she could do it, too.

You learned something new every day, it seemed.

She turned and looked around at the interior of the shed, but there was nothing here. Any tools she might have been able to use as a weapon had long been removed. She had no way to protect herself.

When she looked forward again, the figure was moving toward her.

It didn't walk, exactly. It seemed to *glide* through the grass, eerily motionless, as if its feet didn't even touch the ground.

The evening sunlight shined off a glob of slime as it oozed from the figure's ragged sleeves and into the high grass.

She wasn't going to be able to get to her truck.

She was trapped. There was only one way out. She glanced back at the hole, her stomach twisting into a knot at the thought of it.

She made that squeaking noise in her throat again.

Nope. Not going to happen. She'd rather fight the slime-dripping ghoul.

She stood up, trembling in spite of the heat. She'd never felt so afraid in her life. And that was something of an accomplishment at this point.

But she was *not* going in that filthy hole where all the bugs were.

Nothing was that scary.

The thing in the slimy rags was almost at the door. She watched its shadow as it oozed across the grass, closer and closer.

Then an awful, strangled hissing noise gurgled in the stillness just on the other side of the door, a noise so strangely inhuman it made the blood drain from her face and her knees wobble beneath her.

Who the hell was she kidding?

With an agonizing grimace and a pathetic whimper, she stepped onto the ladder and descended into the spider-infested darkness below.

Chapter 36

This was really stupid. Piper squinted into the glare of her cell phone to find without much surprise that she had no signal down here.

She was standing in another of Avelby's ridiculous tunnels, staring at what appeared to be a dead end. But she had no idea if it really *was* a dead end or not, because she came down here *alone*. Without Seph. Like an idiot.

And to make matters worse, she'd lost the suspicious woman.

Great job, Piper, she thought. *You suck as a detective.*

Seph would be so disappointed in her right now.

She'd followed the suspicious woman several blocks before watching her squeeze through a gap in a chain-link fence and disappear into a lot behind a warehouse with the Vondrasek name painted across it. The same Vondraseks, needless to say, who owned Vondrasek Outdoor Apparel and Gear and were believed by more than a few of the loony locals to be an evil crime boss family worthy of their own superhero nemesis.

She took note of the NO TRESPASSING signs and then glanced around to make sure no one was watching her before squeezing through the gap after the suspicious woman. Then she made her way across the lot, weaving between the various parked trucks and trailers, wondering the whole time whether the Vondrasek crime lords would have her arrested or simply chain a block of cement to her feet and dump her in one of the lakes with all the other nosy people who saw too much.

But the woman didn't seem to be interested in the warehouse. When Piper next caught sight of her, she was climbing over the shorter fence that ran along the back of the property. And by the time she reached the same fence, the suspicious woman had run behind a small auto body garage.

She wasn't as nimble as the mystery woman. Climbing over the same fence took her twice as long and made a *lot* more noise. So she expected when she peered around the corner that her quarry would be long gone. And to that extent, she was right. The suspicious woman was nowhere to be seen. But what she wasn't expecting was to find that there was nowhere for her to have gone. The lot was boxed in between the auto shop, the back side of a much larger, unmarked building and a high concrete wall. There were no doors or windows back here. Only a dumpster and a sizeable collection of banged-up car parts.

A quick search of the area revealed that there was no one hiding in or behind the dumpster.

With nowhere else to hide a person, the pursuit should've ended there. But as she turned to look back the way she came, wondering if she'd somehow made a mistake, she heard another one of those sounds that wasn't a sound.

This time, it was a soft sort of *tinkling*.

She spent several minutes trying to pinpoint its origin, with no luck. She wished Seph were there to tell her which way her ears were pointing. That always made things a little easier. But she could do this on her own. She knew she could. She stopped and closed her eyes. She focused on the tinkling sound and tried to ignore everything else.

Then, when she felt comfortably tuned in, she tried walking toward the sound with her eyes still closed.

Her fingers brushed against the cool surface of the larger building's metal wall and she felt her way along it, following that strange tinkling sensation as it grew inside her head. Like the other "sounds" she heard with her spirit ears, it had no volume. It didn't grow louder as she drew closer. It changed in some other way that she couldn't quite grasp. And only subtly. It was more of an instinct, she realized. She just sort of *knew* that it was getting closer.

Moving through the darkness, with no real clue what she was doing, she felt the tinkling noise pulse through her thoughts. It wasn't a rhythmic sound, like a bell. Instead, it was sort of random. Sort of *natural*. Almost like…

Sensing it was close, she reached her hand out.

Her fingers struck something cold and the *real* sound of clanging metal and glass rang out.

She opened her eyes to find several small, metal objects dangling by coarse twine in front of her, an old, glass Coke bottle hanging at the center of them.

It was some kind of junky wind chime.

That wasn't here before.

Was it?

318

She turned to find that she was standing in a little alleyway between the metal building and the tall, concrete wall, which she was positive didn't have an alley between them a minute ago.

Even if she hadn't been trying to figure out where the suspicious woman went, she would've noticed a place like this.

There were lots of wind chimes dangling from hooks and wires, cobbled together with various objects of metal and glass. Forks and spoons. Washers and springs. Shards of colored glass and old, chipped wine glasses. Large nuts and bolts. Rusty old tools. Baking pans and dinner plates. Indistinguishable strips of twisted, rust-covered steel. Coffee mugs and liquor bottles. There didn't appear to be any discernable attempt at aesthetics. There was no beauty in them, except perhaps in a strange, grungy sort of uniform ugliness. It was just junk and noise.

And the rest of the alley was no prettier.

There were strings of darkened, mismatched lights crisscrossing overhead.

Cheap, plastic patio chairs sat huddled around a small table at one end, all of them so badly sun-faded and weather-worn that she wouldn't have risked sitting in one on a double dog dare.

There was an assortment of old junk that had been transformed into flower beds. An old bathtub. A water heater someone had cut in half lengthwise. A washing machine basin. Several old tires of various sizes and an assortment of sawed-off, plastic buckets. None of them had been watered in so long that even the weeds had long died and baked to a crisp.

Several five-gallon buckets had been placed along the foundation of the metal building to catch the rainwater from its eaves, presumably for watering whatever unfortunate flowers once thrived in the recycled flower beds. Now, what little water hadn't evaporated in the heat was teeming with mosquito larva.

And at the center of all of this was a strange, rust-covered sculpture cobbled together from various chunks of scrap metal and bent iron bars to resemble a sort of sickly-looking tree from which hung even more junky chimes.

Was this someone's home?

She turned and looked toward the far end of the alley. There, in the shade of an old, tattered awning, was a wooden door with bright green paint peeling off it in fat, curled ribbons. Darkness loomed behind a single pane of cracked glass.

It was ajar.

Did she knock? Did she call out to see if anyone was there? Or did she continue trying to be sneaky and just peek inside?

This detective stuff was complicated.

She decided on the sneaky approach, simply because it seemed like the slightly less scary option at the moment, and crept toward the door, careful to dodge the various wind chimes that blocked her path. She tried hard to listen, both with her human ears and her spirit ears, but she could hear nothing with either of them except the occasional clink of metal from the chimes.

She hesitated as she reached for the handle.

This was one of those parts where something awful jumped out at her, wasn't it? Wasn't that how these sorts of situations worked? That was the payoff that came with the idiotic setup of the naïve girl nosing around in places where she wasn't supposed to be with no real idea of what she was doing?

But no slobbering, fanged thing burst from the door to devour her organs. No flickering shadows grabbed her and dragged her into their cold, dark world. No bloody, white-haired corpse leapt out to snap her neck.

The door creaked open, revealing an empty little kitchen on the other side.

Nothing stirred.

She seemed to be alone.

A quick search of the house confirmed it. There were four main rooms, laid out in a square, with a tiny bathroom crammed into the corner of one room like an afterthought.

She circled through the empty rooms, taking in the sparse, dust-covered furniture and the outdated wallpaper and carpet. A handful of photographs were hung on the wall of people who might not necessarily be dead, but almost certainly didn't look like that anymore. They looked like the sort of photographs people took in the early sixties.

More of those curious wind chimes were hanging from the low ceilings in each of the rooms, many of them in the most inconvenient places. She had to be careful not to bump into them.

What was this place? Who lived here? Why did they like wind chimes so much? And why couldn't she see it from the little lot behind the auto body shop?

And where did the suspicious woman go? There only appeared to be one way in and out of this freaky little house.

She turned and frowned at the door leading back into that colorfully decorated alley.

What kind of a house only had one way in and out? Wasn't

that a fire hazard?

Again, she turned and peered through the doorway, deeper into the old house.

There was no window in the bedroom that branched off to the side of the kitchen. But there was a window in the bedroom, looking out onto an open street, opposite the alley door.

She walked into the living room. It seemed to her that there should be a door in this room.

Maybe it was like the alley. Maybe she needed her special ears to find it.

She glanced around one last time, just to be sure she was alone, and then closed her eyes and stood there in the gloom, listening.

Seconds passed in silence.

Then minutes.

She was ready to give up when she finally heard it.

Another of those faint, ghostly chimes.

At first, she thought it was just the ones in the alley again, but something in her brain insisted that it was coming from somewhere else.

She focused all of her attention on it.

She tried to relax, to push aside all the stubborn logic that was trying to talk her out of grasping what was really there.

That way... She turned a little and took a step forward, her hands outstretched, feeling her way forward.

Her fingertips brushed against the wall paneling.

No... Over there a little...

She felt the edge of a wooden frame. Then the rough wood of

a door. Finally, a doorknob.

Without opening her eyes, afraid that she would lose it if she tried to look, she turned the knob and opened it.

A cool breeze washed over her, accompanied by a soft, harsh jangle of metal.

She opened her eyes to find herself looking down a boxed-in stairwell and a set of rough, wooden steps descending into darkness.

More of those strange, metal wind chimes dangled from the ceiling, all of them spinning and dancing and softly tinkling together in the gust she created when she pulled open the door.

And from somewhere below her... Was that voices she was hearing?

She made her way down the winding steps, careful to avoid the strange chimes. It was much farther down than a single flight. The stairs seemed to lead down at least three stories. And at the bottom awaited another door, this one clearly visible and standing wide open. There was a broken padlock lying on the concrete floor among a collection of footprints in the dust, as if someone had very recently forced it open.

Peering through it, she found a wide tunnel that was utterly filled with those metal chimes. As she shined her cell phone light into it, the various pieces of glass caught it and reflected it back at her, so that the tunnel seemed to be filled with twinkling stars.

The tunnels she was starting to get used to, but there was something about these chimes that she found unsettling. What were they doing here? Why would someone be this obsessed with them?

She cocked her head.

She was sure she was hearing voices at the far end.

Curiosity overwhelming her caution, she crept through the door and made her way slowly through the minefield of chimes, following the ghostly voices. It was far too faint to hear what was being said, or even to identify how many speakers there were, but she thought she could distinctly hear separate masculine and feminine voices. At least one man and at least one woman.

Maybe...

She couldn't really be sure.

She slipped carefully between the chimes. They were hanging everywhere, and at all heights. Some were close to the ceiling; some nearly touched the floor. Some took up almost the entire height of the tunnel.

What was this place? What was the purpose of all these chimes?

This was a tunnel. Why would you put wind chimes in a tunnel? When would there ever even be wind?

Then, as she squeezed between two chimes, sucking her belly in and mashing her breasts flat with her hands to make sure that she fit, the answer came to her with an icy chill that made her freeze in her tracks.

It was an alarm.

A crude motion detector.

But...what was it meant to detect?

She turned and looked back the way she came. Only now did it occur to her that she should've called Seph before descending those creepy stairs.

Her elbow tapped one of the chimes, making a faint "tink"

that seemed to echo through the darkness, like a dire warning.

It was too late now. It was probably farther back than forward.

But as she pushed on through the eerily twinkling darkness, she found that she was wrong about that. The tunnel went on much farther than she originally thought.

And now those voices she'd been following had gone silent.

She wondered why. Had they caught sight of her? She was hardly being inconspicuous. She needed her cell phone light to see her way through the minefield of chimes. But to someone standing at the far end of this passage, she might as well be wearing a neon sign reading "HEY! LOOK AT ME!" which would pretty well mean that she might as well forget trying to avoid the chimes and just plow right through them.

But after a few more minutes, she found that there definitely wasn't anyone watching her from the far end of the tunnel, because the tunnel abruptly ended.

And now here she was, standing in the darkness, squinting at her phone, feeling like a total idiot.

She'd let the suspicious woman get away.

Was there a hidden passageway down here somewhere? Was that where the suspicious woman had gone? And if so, why was she able to see these places?

Did *she* have spectral animal ears that no one but Seph could see?

Seph... Why didn't she wait for her?

Stupid!

It was okay.

She could do this.

It was just like in the lot behind the auto shop. It was just like in the living room of the weird wind chime house. Maybe if she just closed her eyes and listened, her spirit ears would show her the way.

She took a deep breath and focused on the sounds.

After a moment of eerie silence, she *did* hear a sound. But it wasn't with her spirit ears.

Somewhere at the far end of the tunnel, the chimes began to clang.

Chapter 37

Seph sobbed. She couldn't help it. There were cobwebs everywhere. She could feel them sticking to her face and arms and legs. They clung to her glasses. They were in her hair. They were even in her mouth!

A million, tiny, hairy legs danced across her naked skin. She couldn't see them, but she could feel every one of them. They squirmed against her forehead and skittered over her knees. Something scurried down her shirt. Something scratched at the back of her thigh. Something slithered up the back of her neck.

She stumbled and fell, and awful, squirming things wriggled out from beneath her in the gloom. Something fat and black scuttled over the back of her hand.

Tears were streaming down her cheeks and she kept making those pitiful, squeaking noises that she hated.

She was stronger than this. She knew she was. She wasn't some stupid, girly crybaby. *She'd wielded the Grim Reaper's scythe*! That was about as badass as you could get!

But there were spiders! There were centipedes! And pill bugs! And earwigs!

Oh god!

And she was all alone down here. Piper wasn't here to take her by the hand and lead her through the nightmare. Piper wasn't here to protect her from the monster that was chasing her.

She scrambled to her feet, her breath hitching in her chest, her heart racing, her skin crawling.

She hadn't even gone very far. She clawed at the cobwebs on her face and glasses and looked back at the ladder, terrified to discover that she'd barely gone a dozen paces yet.

She could see the shadow as something blocked out the light from above. She could see the slime splattering onto the dirt below.

The unholy thing that was dressed in those filthy rags was right behind her.

There was no going back. If there was going to be any chance of escaping whatever that nasty thing was, it was going to be on the other side of all these spiders.

She wasn't sure she could do it. Even now, as she watched that awful shadow swelling beneath the ladder, she didn't think she had the courage to take one more step. But then she reminded herself that if she didn't push forward, she'd *never* leave this bug-infested passage. Her body would lie in this darkness forever while the bugs and spiders and worms and maggots crawled all over it, burrowing into her flesh, devouring her eyeballs, crowding into her mouth and ears and nose, squirming around *inside* her.

She barely managed to keep from throwing up at the thought.

She turned away from the ladder and its descending horror, crossed her arms in front of her face, and with a terrified shriek, she plowed forward, carving a roughly Persephone-shaped hole through the endless cobwebs.

She was doing it! She couldn't stop screaming. She was making enough noise for every slime monster in a half-mile radius to know exactly where she was going. But she was doing it! Piper would be so proud of her!

Then she saw a hairy, brown spider scurry over her wrist and she lost it again. She threw her hands out and shook them as if they were on fire, promptly opening up her guard so that the next curtain of webs struck her right in the face, covering her mouth and nose.

She let out a piercing scream and stumbled backward, tripping over herself and falling on her butt.

Inside her head, she was screaming, *Move it*! Yet she *couldn't* move. Not yet. She had to peel away the spiderwebs. She had to get it off of her. She couldn't stand it. It was too awful.

They'll crawl into my mouth! The thought was enough to make her chest hitch in disgust.

She was sobbing again. Tears streamed down her cheeks. She could feel snot on her lip as she clawed at the webs and she knew that if she survived this she would *loathe* herself for being this way.

But she wasn't going to survive this. She was going to die down here! Because she was too much of a sniveling crybaby to do anything about it!

Stand your ass up, girl!

Seph jumped as if she'd been slapped.

In an instant, her sobbing stopped. Her body went rigid. For a moment, she forgot about the webs. She forgot about the skittering, scuttling things that danced over her skin.

That voice…

She hadn't heard that voice in five years...

You promised me. Don't you dare forget.

Another fat tear rolled down her face. "Daddy...?"

It wasn't really him. It was only a memory, coughed up by her subconscious to shock her out of her state of panic. And yet, she could almost swear she heard the voice of her late father scolding her.

She *did* promise him. She could *never* forget.

She promised him she'd always be safe. She promised him that after he was gone, she'd always take care of herself. She'd never let anyone hurt her.

And here she was, sniveling like a baby instead of getting away from the thing in the slimy rags.

She was still shaking, but she managed to stand.

She looked back to see a black shape oozing after her in the dark.

That awful, strangled, gurgling hiss filled the silent tunnel.

Clenching her teeth, she turned away and again plowed through the hellish onslaught of cobwebs.

She could do this. She wasn't her father, who was never afraid of a spider in his entire life, but she was her father's daughter. And she made him a promise!

She screamed with disgust, but she was doing it!

And was that a light up ahead? A dim glow in the hellish, spidery gloom?

Her heart swelled with hope at the thought of finding an exit from this awful tunnel and the slime thing on her heels, and she pushed herself to go even faster.

She was going to make it!

She was going to keep her promise to her father!

The iron gate came out of nowhere.

She slammed into it, barely stopping herself from banging her face against it.

"*NO!*" she screamed. "No, no, no, no, *no!*" She grabbed the bars and shoved at them. Then she yanked on them. It rocked back and forth, but refused to yield. "*No!*"

This wasn't fair! She faced her fears! She did what she had to do!

She shined her cell phone light over the gate. There was a chain holding it closed. An old, heavy padlock held the chain in place. She grabbed the padlock and tried to pry it open. Another wet sob escaped her.

She turned and shined the light back into the darkness behind her.

That eerie, black shape was there, oozing closer and closer to her.

"*Come on!*" she cried, yanking at the chain. Then she leaned forward, peering in at the larger tunnel on the other side. "*Help me! Somebody help me!*"

But no one was coming to help her.

She couldn't have gone far enough to have even left the property.

Crying, she looked back over her shoulder again.

The thing was much closer now.

How was it that fast?

She made an awful, hitching, weeping sort of noise in her

throat and yanked on the chain again.

Something shifted this time. The chain slithered out of her hands, clattering to the floor at her feet.

With a startled, "*Oh!*" she yanked the rest of it through the bars and then shoved the gate open.

The old lock must've been rusted through.

She was probably the luckiest person alive right now.

But as she stepped through the gate, she glanced once more over her shoulder. The slime monster made another of those terrible, gurgling-hissing noises from right behind her.

She screamed and stumbled, falling over the little step and landing on her hands and knees, dropping her phone. It landed at the monster's feet.

Still screaming, she crawled away from it. The phone was gone. She'd have to find another way to contact Piper. But at least she was out of the spider hole. And she didn't need the light. There was an opening at the far end of the tunnel. She was almost free!

She scrambled to her feet and ran for it.

It was only about a hundred feet away.

Eighty…

Sixty…

Forty…

She was crying again. She couldn't help it. That was easily the worst experience of her life.

Twenty feet…

The light was blinding. Again, she found herself thinking of the light at the end of that other tunnel, the one everyone supposedly traveled on their way to the next world. It was a really bad analogy, she realized. The exact opposite of what she wanted to accomplish by reaching the light in front of her.

And yet, as her eyes finally adjusted to this light, she found that it may be *exactly* the right analogy. Because this was *not* the way out. Iron bars again blocked her path.

"*NO!*"

She grabbed the bars and shook them, but this wasn't even a gate. The bars were three inches thick and imbedded in concrete at both the top and the bottom. She was looking out at a dry streambed leading into the lake.

This was a storm drain.

And like the light at the end of that other tunnel, it was *death*.

"*Help me!*" she screamed.

But no one was coming to help her.

She was too far away. No one could hear her.

No… Not no one. Someone was there, she realized. Someone was peering back at her from behind a tree, a faint shadow in the deepening shade.

"Help me please!" she screamed again.

But then the person peering back at her flickered and vanished.

A second later, there were two of them. They didn't try to hide. They stood in the open, in the middle of the dry streambed, creepy black shapes, like living shadows.

The flickering men…

She couldn't get out, but as she saw in Tunnel Park, they could easily get in.

She turned to run the other way, but the thing in the slimy

rags was suddenly standing right in front of her, blocking her path.

She pressed her back against the bars.

Another tear streaked down her face as she realized there was nowhere left to go.

She closed her eyes and screamed as cold, bony hands grabbed her wrists and arms and squeezed her ankles and thighs. Creeping fingers pulled on her hair. An arm reached around her, clawing at her belly. Another groped at her breast. Still another closed around her throat.

Then she felt another hand. It wasn't like the others. This one was wet and slimy, the hand of the thing in the filthy rags. Its palm pressed against her nose, its fingers and thumb against her cheeks and forehead, pressing her glasses against the bridge of her nose.

The slime squished between the thing's hand and her skin. It oozed into her nose and mouth. It dripped down the lenses of her glasses.

Then everything turned to darkness.

Chapter 38

Piper squeezed her eyes closed and frantically searched the walls of the tunnel.

The chaotic chiming was getting closer with each passing second, filling the passageway and her head with the awful, echoing peals of clanging iron and glass. This harsh, industrial cacophony made her think of the steampunk monstrosities she'd read about when she was younger, great, hulking machines shuffling toward her on countless robotic legs. It was a frightful image, but one that she was quite certain she'd prefer to whatever unspeakable horror might *really* be making its way toward her in this darkness.

Was it the gory revenant? The flickering men? The runner?

Or was this something new?

Whatever it was, it was related to those things because she could feel that familiar static swelling inside her head, half-buried beneath the alarming racket of the chimes.

She opened her eyes to make sure the thing wasn't already bearing down on her and saw that the twinkling, reflected lights far out in that unnerving darkness had begun to dance.

She didn't have much time.

There had to be a way out of this tunnel. The suspicious woman had to have come this way. There was nowhere else for her to go. She must've found the hidden exit. It had to be here. All she had to do was make herself listen. She had to ignore the terrifying din of the chimes and the eerie, twinkling movements and listen to the spirit noises. She just had to find the sounds that weren't sounds.

But she couldn't hear anything over the clanging chimes, her thundering heart and the desperate, hiccupping gasps of her own panicked breathing.

Why did she come down here? Why didn't she wait for Seph?

"Come on!" Where was it? There had to be something here. There *had* to be. There was nowhere else for the suspicious woman to go.

Right?

But even with her thoughts clouded by panic, she knew that there were no absolutes in this weird new world.

Maybe the suspicious woman could walk through walls. How different would that be from her own ghostly, invisible animal ears? Or from Seph's prophet sight?

Or maybe she wasn't even real. Maybe she was some kind of ghost, conjured to lure her into this terrifying trap.

Maybe the mysterious woman was just one of the flickering men in disguise.

And even if the suspicious woman *had* come this way, who was to say that the secret passage she used to escape was even at this end of the tunnel. Maybe it was back by the stairs. Or maybe there was another hidden doorway in that little house.

No. She wasn't trapped. Not really. She was sure of it.

She couldn't let herself believe that was even a possibility.

The clanging grew closer. The lights danced nearer. She could almost see it out there, a strange collection of shadows moving within the greater darkness.

She had to get out of here *now*.

She closed her eyes again, the better to block out the distraction of those dancing lights that drew nearer and nearer in the darkness, and slid her hands over the rough wall, searching for any little crack or crevice that might reveal what was hidden. She wished she could close her ears the way she could close her eyes. She wished there were a way to turn off her human sense of hearing so she could focus on the noises her other ears could detect. Maybe then she could find what she was missing.

If Seph were here, she could find it.

One of those terrified squeaks that Seph was always making fun of her for slipped out as she turned to search the other side of the tunnel.

What if Seph was the only one who could find it? What if she *needed* Seph for this? Why did she come down here without her? That was so stupid!

The clanging grew closer.

Louder.

Still, there was nothing there!

Almost without realizing it, she reached for the pendant Annalisa gave her, clutching it in one hand as she opened her eyes and peeked out into the darkness again. The tunnel was practically ablaze with dancing, twinkling lights. Any second now, the thing would come close enough to see. *"Please!"* she gasped.

The pendant was warm against her fingertips. There was something about it that she found a little bit comforting, even in this awful state of panic. But did it really have power? Could it really protect her from evil, as the old woman had claimed?

It sounded like a fairy tale.

But so did everything else she'd discovered since the day she met Seph.

"Please help me!" she whimpered.

She was about to turn and check the other wall again when her hand finally fell on something other than rough bricks.

It was a rusty, old handle.

She looked up to find that there was a door set into the wall.

She wasted no time wondering how she wasn't able to see it before. It didn't matter. All that mattered was that she'd found the exit. She yanked it open and quickly stepped into another tunnel.

This one was smaller, and almost identical to the one Seph dragged her into to escape the revenant in Adderbell's basement. There were cobwebs and dust everywhere.

Seph would've lost it again, probably, but such things didn't concern her. She'd take spiders over monsters any day.

She turned and looked back through the open door, expecting something monstrous and angry to come crashing into view.

Instead, she saw a small boy standing there. He had a mop of bushy, brown hair and was wearing the same strange, heavy clothes as those children who attacked her outside her apartment that morning. He was staring back at her with the same empty, black eyes.

As she watched, he reached up with a small, gloved hand and tapped one of the chimes, making it jangle.

Farther back in the tunnel, she could hear other children doing the same, one by one, echoing the sound.

There had to be a dozen of them at least.

Only now did she realize that the static in her head had grown loud enough for her to hear that creepy murmuring deep inside it.

The voices of the children.

The sound of madness.

A creepy little black-eyed girl stepped into the doorway and began walking toward her.

Piper covered her ears again, useless though it was, and backed away, terrified.

Chapter 39

Piper didn't wait to see what the little black-eyed freaks did next. She turned and fled through the cobwebs, desperately hoping there was another way out at the other end of this tunnel. Preferably one that wouldn't require her to have another mini-heart attack searching for another stupid invisible door.

Maybe it *was* a good thing Seph wasn't here. She simply couldn't handle spiders. And that wasn't going to change no matter how many times Piper assured her they were harmless.

When she was still young, Piper began reading everything she could get her hands on about bugs and spiders. Her sister, Penny, was as afraid of those things as Seph was. To Piper, it was the ideal way to give something back to someone she loved who always took such good care of her. So she knew as she plowed through the filthy tunnel that there were no dangerous spiders this far north. As unpleasant as the feel of cobwebs were on her skin, they were by far preferable to the nightmare children she was running away from.

Cobwebs could be wiped away, after all. Whatever those little soulless monsters intended to do to her couldn't.

She didn't look back. She didn't dare. She was afraid that if she looked back, she'd find an army of those awful children chasing right on her heels. Instead, she focused on the path before her.

It was much longer than the one she and Seph found leading from the basement of Adderbell's. There didn't seem to be an end in sight. There was nothing but the same gray bricks and grimy dirt floor. And curtain after curtain of dust-covered cobwebs.

And every now and then she caught sight of something small scurrying across the floor in her path.

Rats?

Yes, she was quite sure that Seph would not be sorry to miss out on this. Wherever she was, she was almost certainly much better off there than here.

Wherever *here* was... What was this place? What was up with those chimes? What were they guarding? Why? And who put them there?

She caught sight of a light up ahead. An exit? Or just another tunnel?

Either way, if there was light it was a better place than where she was now.

She pushed on, still not daring to look back.

It wasn't another doorway. Instead, the tunnel simply seemed to end. She shoved her way through the last of the cobwebs and then stumbled to a stop. She was standing in a large, circular room with a high, domed ceiling. The light was coming from the very top of the dome, where sunlight shined through a steel grate and onto the steel mesh of the floor.

There were two wide passageways leading out of the room,

one to the left, one to the right, both of them set at an incline. The one on the left led up. The one on the right led deeper underground.

Both passageways were unlit, but it seemed like a no-brainer. She ran toward the passage on the left.

Finally, she dared a glance behind her.

There were no black-eyed children chasing her from the dirty tunnel. In fact, there was no tunnel there, dirty or otherwise.

She stopped and turned back, trying to wrap her head around it.

There were only the two exits to this room.

The other was hidden, like at the other end. It was only visible from inside the tunnel.

How did that even work? And *why*?

It didn't matter. She had no interest in going back that way. Like, *ever*. Those creepy kids were still in there. She could hear their staticky murmuring inside her head.

They could keep it.

She turned and ran again, eager to get back to the surface and call Seph. But when she reached the passage leading up, she found her way blocked by several more black-eyed children, all of them with the same thick, overgrown hair. All of them dressed in that heavy, itchy-looking fabric.

Okay, so *not* that way.

She turned to run the other way, only to find two more, a little boy and a little girl, standing in front of the other passage, holding hands.

She stopped again and looked back. There were more of

them.

And when she turned back again, there were more over *there*.

Every time she turned, there were more of them. They were everywhere, surrounding her.

She backed into the middle of the room, where the sunlight drifted lazily down on her as the nightmare children closed in around her.

"Hi there," she tried, her voice cracking. "Aren't you guys afraid of the dark?" *Because I sure am*, she thought.

The black-eyed children said nothing. They only continued their slow, eerie approach.

She'd been in a lot of terrifying situations already today, but this was quickly becoming the worst yet. There was something utterly terrifying about these kids. And it wasn't just their creepy, black eyes. Her heart was thundering. Her stomach was kinked into a burning knot. She could barely breathe.

"Please go away. I don't want to play this game."

They didn't seem to care what she wanted. Those closest to her reached out for her, their small, gloved fingers only inches away.

She grasped the pendant Annalisa gave her again. "Please don't hurt me!" she whimpered.

As cold, little fingers brushed against her skin, somewhere in the darkness she heard a scream.

The children stopped.

All of them turned their creepy faces toward the lower ramp and stared, expressionless, into the darkness there.

Piper glanced around at them, still holding her breath, then followed their black gazes.

There was another scream, as if someone, somewhere down there, had stumbled onto the same sort of horror she was going through now.

Or perhaps it was a worse kind of horror, because the black-eyed children looked silently around at one another for a moment, then, all at once, turned and fled in the other direction, leaving her alone in her single beam of sunlight.

She stared after them as they ran away. Then she turned and stared at the other passageway.

She was pretty sure she should run now…but which way? Did she follow the fleeing monster children? Or did she run toward the screaming? Both options seemed like equally bad ideas.

She wondered how long it would take to find her way back into the dirty tunnel, but quickly decided it would be too long.

The terror she knew? Or the terror she didn't know? …which was also the terror that *scared away* the terror she knew?

Going *up* seemed like the best chance of finding her way out of these tunnels. But the way out was probably going to be locked anyway. Besides, she could still hear the faint static of those nasty little monsters inside her head.

She found herself walking toward the lower ramp.

Did she hear something down there? A soft sort of whispering? A sound that wasn't a sound, but almost?

She stepped into the passageway and peered down into the gloom.

There was another scream. Shorter than the last. Piercing. More of a yelp than a shriek.

Her cell phone flashlight wasn't going to help her see. It was just going to make her more visible to whoever or whatever might be down there, so she slipped it back into her pocket and began creeping down the ramp, staying as quiet as possible.

Someone shouted.

She paused and looked back.

The black-eyed children were still gone.

There was another of those short, piercing screams. She looked forward again in time to see a flash of white light way down in the darkness. Then another. And a third. With each pulse, it grew brighter. Whatever was making the flash was quickly getting closer.

She took a step backward.

Another flash and a huge, strange shadow streaked up the ramp.

Yet another flash and a large, lumbering form was rushing toward her.

She took another step backward, startled.

Then the shape emerged from the gloom and she realized that it was an extremely large, plump man with a *girl* slung over his shoulder. He was pumping his chubby legs as hard as he could, sweat beading on his forehead, while a pair of skinny legs bounced around, small, Sketchers-clad feet flailing in front of him.

The scene was so absurdly shocking that she couldn't even turn and run. She stood there, frozen in the middle of the passageway, staring at...the world's most ambitious kidnapper?

As he drew closer, she realized that the man was younger than he first looked, and also considerably taller, meaning the legs probably belonged to a woman, rather than a girl. But she wasn't sure that was all that much of an improvement to the situation.

She saw the big guy's eyes widen as he finally caught sight of her. He looked surprised, then frightened. He glanced back over his shoulder, swinging those skinny legs back and forth with the motion. Then he changed his course and ran straight at her.

Piper's paralysis broke, but too late to run. All she had time to do was take two steps backward before he stooped down and threw his shoulder into her, hoisting her up off her feet and over his other shoulder in a single, powerful motion.

She let out a terrified scream as she found herself bouncing along, her face just a few short feet from the concrete floor.

"Hi!" said the young woman slung over the other shoulder, as if it were the most natural thing in the world to meet while being carried off by a chubby, kidnapping giant. She had very familiar short, black hair and bright, friendly green eyes. The suspicious woman! She was holding a camera in her hands: the source of the flashing light she saw. She aimed it forward and took another picture.

The flash lit up the passage. And in the darkness, a huge pair of eyes flashed back at them from the center of an enormous shadow.

Piper screamed. "*What was that?*"

"I have no idea!" she replied without hesitation. "*But I got it on film!*" She turned and looked at Piper. "I'm Violet," she said, smiling. "The big guy's Corey."

Chapter 40

Seph didn't want to wake up. It was too cold outside. It was cozy and warm in her bed. And she'd been dreaming of her father. She wanted to stay with him. She wasn't sure why, but she felt like if she left the dream, she'd lose him somehow and she'd never see him again.

It wasn't even a particularly meaningful dream. She was just talking to him. They were standing in his workshop. He was banging away at something with his hammer again and she was telling him about something that she lost…but she couldn't remember what it was. Something important, it felt like…but she couldn't remember for sure. And he was assuring her that it would turn up.

"It's not really lost," he was saying. "You still have it. And when you need it, you'll remember where you put it."

Dad didn't fret about little things. He was always so cool and collected. Not like Mom, who freaked out over every little thing.

Mom…

Wait…

Mom needed her… She was in trouble!

The dream began to slip away and an icy panic immediately

enveloped her. She grasped for it, tried to pull it back to her, but it was *slippery*. She couldn't hold it. The harder she tried, the faster it slid into the darkness.

Dad…

Oh god…

The crushing weight of her grief came crashing down on her all over again, constricting her chest until she could barely breathe. Tears sprang to her eyes. That familiar sickness spread through her belly, sucking all the warmth out of the world.

Her heart broke all over again.

"…listen to me…"

She opened her eyes, but there was no light in this place. She wasn't in her warm bed. She was floating in an empty darkness. "Daddy?" she gasped.

"…no…"

And it wasn't her father. Her father was dead. And this was definitely not his workshop.

Slowly, it all came back to her. The deathly visage of her mother's corpse-like face. The unusually handsome stranger who called himself Ian. The bloody, white-haired corpse. The underground city. The black boathouse. The spider-infested tunnel. The iron bars.

Her heart, broken as it was, leapt in her chest as she recalled the flickering men groping her through the bars of the drainage tunnel.

"…those creatures…gone now…"

The voice, she realized, belonged to the thing in the filthy rags. She also realized that the voice was distinctly feminine. The monster was a woman? A...*slime lady*?

"Where am I?"

"...the psychic in-between..."

"The what?"

Why was it so cold? It shouldn't be this cold. It was a stifling July day.

"...a limbo...that stretches across the consciousness...of all things in this world...living and dead..." Even the slime lady's *voice* somehow oozed. The words came to her the same way the slime dripped from her filthy sleeves, in slick, sliding globs. "...it exists...only within..."

"I don't understand," she said. But she wasn't even sure if she was actually speaking. She couldn't feel her lips moving. And her voice sounded strangely far away.

Was she even breathing?

"...don't have to understand..." replied the slime lady. "...just listen..."

Did she have a choice?

"...those shadowy things that stalk you...the men who flicker...the children without souls in their eyes...all children of Gispuknya..."

Even in this cold nothingness, Seph felt a chill climb up her spine at the mention of the word.

Gispuknya.

"...the name frightens you..."

She nodded. No, she *tried* to nod. She wasn't sure she actually did anything. She seemed to be frozen and adrift in an endless void.

Or she could be flopping around like a fish. She had no clue what was really going on. This was an entirely new experience for her.

Maybe she was dead. Maybe the slime lady and the flickering men murdered her in that awful tunnel and this was some kind of bizarre purgatory.

"...Gispuknya is very old...and very evil..."

In the darkness that surrounded her, Seph heard a strange noise that made the hair on the back of her neck suddenly stand upright. It was a sort of skittering noise. A soft click-clacking of long, spindly legs. A scuttling, shuffling, *insect*-like noise.

"...it was born of ruin...risen from the rotting remains...of long dead worlds..."

In her mind, she couldn't help but picture a giant cockroach crawling out from under a pile of rubble beneath a post-apocalyptic sky.

"...it is the defiler...it desires destruction...abhors life in all its forms...and wishes to end the rebuilding of worlds...by destroying the seekers before the Architects can be awakened..."

It was getting closer. A great, shadowy thing scurrying toward her in the darkness, getting bigger and bigger. With each clack of its insectile legs, her heart beat faster and faster. She wanted to scream, but she still couldn't move.

"...you see what others can't...you know...deep inside...you've always known it was out there..."

It was right in front of her. She couldn't see it, but she could feel it. It was looming there, only inches away from her face, staring back at her with its countless, alien eyes.

"...it's why they frighten you so much..."

The feeling was far worse than the spiders and cobwebs in the old tunnel. Somewhere deep down, even *she* understood that those things wouldn't actually hurt her. But *this* thing… This thing was different. Just feeling its presence was enough to fill her with a kind of fear she'd never felt before. Her whole body trembled. Her breath caught in her throat. Did she just pee herself? It was hard to tell. She still couldn't feel her body, only the awful fear that filled it.

This thing wasn't just a bug. It wasn't even an ancient, freakishly giant bug. It was a force of nature unto itself. It was a manifestation of ultimate evil, powerful beyond imagining. It was practically a *god*.

Then it was gone.

In an instant, she was alone in the void again.

But still she trembled.

"…it was never this strong before…" said the slime lady. "…never in all the worlds that came before…something about this world…gave it new strength…made it…more dangerous…"

Seph had to make a conscious effort to breathe. Was she really up against something so monstrous? *Why?* What hope did she have of defeating something like that?

"…the black council…"

"What?"

"…it is an extension of Gispuknya…a nerve center…that holds the strings…"

The black council?

"…it is its greatest strength…but it is also a weakness…"

Gispuknya had a weakness?

"…the black council has taken something…that doesn't belong to it…take it back…cut the strings…"

Take back what the black council stole and…cut the strings? She didn't understand. None of this made sense. What did she mean by "strings"? And what was it she was supposed to take back? And how did she even find this black council?

And most of all: "What are you?"

"…something also very old…" replied the slime lady.

"But you're one of the good guys?"

"…I have no interest in good or evil…I simply am…"

Seph let that run through her head for a moment. "Is that a no, then?"

Suddenly, she wasn't alone again. Something was with her in the void. But this time, it wasn't a giant, prehistoric, godlike bug that hovered in front of her. It was…something else. Something smaller. Something softer, more feminine. But something distinctly *inhuman*.

"…I am what I've always been…and Gispuknya is my enemy…in that regard, you and I are on the same side…"

A cold, wet hand came out of the darkness and pressed against the trembling flesh of her belly. Slime squished between those slender fingers and oozed down her skin.

Seph gasped. She tried to cry out, but her body still wasn't working.

Another hand closed on her hip, dripping more slime down her thigh.

Was she even wearing clothes? Was she *naked* in this darkness?

"…listen closely to my words…" whispered the slime lady as their bodies pressed together in the darkness, cold slime squelching between them.

Was this creature *made* of slime? Or simply covered in it? Some parts of her felt solid, but other parts of her seemed to melt as the two of them came together.

"…the map points to the marsh…but what you seek lies on the *other* side…"

Maybe it was just the squishy, slime-covered body that was being slowly wrapped around her in a creepy, *Tales from the Crypt*-like lover's embrace that was making it hard to concentrate, but she was pretty sure that didn't make any sense. What map? The other side of *what*?

"…find the quiet place…" she whispered, her slimy lips brushing against her cheek. Her cold arms and legs crept around her, encircling her, submerging her in that frigid ooze. "…look for the key they left in the dark…"

It was definitely a slime *lady*. She was sure a slime *dude* wouldn't squish against her like that in those places.

"…and when the truth is finally revealed…look inside…to find what was lost…"

Seph wanted to tell her that she didn't understand. Quiet place? A key left in the dark? The key *who* left in the dark? What truth? What was lost? But the slime lady began to melt. Cold slime oozed around her, covering her body, covering her *face*, enveloping her completely in slime.

She was going to drown in it!

Panic washed over her. She tried to pull away. Then she tried to scream.

Then, suddenly, she awoke. She cried out in surprise. She

gasped for breath.

She was sitting on dirty concrete, her back against the iron bars of the drainage tunnel.

She looked around. The slime lady was gone. The tunnel before her was empty. Then she turned and looked behind her. The flickering men were also gone. She was alone again.

But the light had changed. It was getting dark out.

How long was she asleep?

Her glasses were dirty. She couldn't see clearly. She took them off and found that there was slime on her face where the slime lady placed her hand before she blacked out and went to that weird, black purgatory. It was cold and sticky and gross upon her skin. It was even on her lips. Some of it had oozed into her mouth and nose. It didn't really taste or smell like anything, but that didn't make it any better. She turned and spat onto the ground.

So gross.

At least that part about the slime lady covering her entire, naked body in slime was only a part of the dream.

But as she went to wipe her glasses clean with the tail of her shirt, she looked down and saw that she *was* still covered in cobwebs from that filthy tunnel.

A big, brown spider was crawling out of the cleavage of her tank top.

That was the final straw. After all that she'd been through, all the awful things she'd suffered, this was the catalyst that finally pushed her over the edge.

She freaked.

She screamed. She jumped to her feet, dropping her glasses.

She furiously stripped off the shirt and threw it at the tunnel wall. She shook out her hair. She slapped at her arms and legs. All reason escaped her. All that mattered was getting these awful, disgusting things off of her.

A minute later she was sitting on the cold concrete in her bra, her shorts pulled halfway down her butt, one of her shoes kicked off, her hair sticking out in every direction and panting as her heart thudded against her ribs.

Whoever decided this was a job for a girl with severe bug phobias was an idiot!

A light blossomed in the gloom and the familiar ringtone of her phone filled the silent tunnel.

It was lying on the floor, not far from where she'd dropped it.

She scrambled to her feet, not risking the time it would take to find her glasses, and ran to it, yanking at her shorts as she did. She snatched it off the ground and immediately realized that it was covered in a big glob of gray slime.

"Ew…" she whined as she picked it up and tried to fling the goop off. Some came off. She could hear it splatter against the concrete somewhere nearby. But most of it remained stubbornly on her phone.

She wiped at the screen and then held it close to her face so she could see it without her glasses. Then she swiped at it and switched it to speaker so she wouldn't have to put it against her face. "Piper?"

"Where are you?" said Piper.

I don't want to talk about it, she thought. Aloud, she said, "Long story. Where've you been?"

"Long story," replied Piper. "Can you meet me at the hotel behind the Walgreen's?"

"The hotel?"

"Room two-eleven."

Seph glanced back toward her crumpled shirt. A hotel would be a welcome change of scenery, that was for sure, but why would Piper get a room?

"I'll explain everything when you get here."

She disconnected the call and gave the phone another flick, trying to fling away more of the slime. "*So* gross…"

It was a good thing her phone case was waterproof.

Spider tunnels. Slime women. Giant, apocalyptic insects. Why did it all have to be so *icky*?

She returned to the end of the tunnel, picked up her stray shoe and located her glasses. Then she grabbed her shirt and beat it against the bars until she was convinced it was free of spiders. Then she beat it against the bars a few more times for good measure.

It was as she was getting ready to put it back on that a realization came to her: she was going to have to go back through that tunnel to get out of here.

And if she didn't hurry, she also realized, glancing through the bars at the rapidly fading light of the day, she was going to be searching for her truck in the dark.

"This totally sucks," she sighed as she trudged back toward the spider-infested tunnel.

Chapter 41

Piper opened the door and looked Seph up and down. "What happened to *you*?" she asked.

Seph stared back at her, surprised. "Why? Do I look that bad?"

"No!" she replied too quickly. "You're just...kind of disheveled is all." She made a face. "...and kind of...filthy."

She looked down at herself, embarrassed. "I am?" She thought she did a pretty good job of dusting herself off after crawling out of that disgusting well.

Piper plucked a glob of webbing and a leaf out of her tangled hair and then leaned closer, examining her. "What's all over your face?"

Seph leaned away from her and wiped at her nose and mouth again. It was still sticky from that slime. In her hurry to get here, she hadn't taken time to look herself over in the Ford's vanity mirror. "I don't want to talk about it," she grumbled.

"You look like you just got back from a really good roll in the hay!" laughed a skinny young woman with short, black hair who was suddenly peering at her from behind Piper.

"Um…thanks?" replied Seph, even *more* embarrassed.

Piper's eyes widened a little. She looked at her as if she'd just stepped out of a coat closet at a party with her shirt buttoned wrong and her skirt on backward.

Seph felt herself blush at the idea. Then she recalled the weird sensation of the slime lady *enveloping her* in that weird dream void and felt herself blush even brighter. "*Who* are you?" she asked.

"This is Violet," introduced Piper. "And that's Corey." She pointed toward a paper-littered table at the far end of the room, where an enormous young man was sitting with his nose in a cell phone *while* he was leaning over a laptop. He didn't look at her, but he lifted a huge, chubby hand in a half-assed sort of wave at the sound of his name.

Seph glanced from him to Violet and then back at Piper. "And they are…?"

"We're mapping multi-existential anomalies throughout the Midwest," said Violet.

She stared at her, confused.

"Portals to other worlds," she explained. "Wormholes. Gateways. Thin spaces between dimensions. That sort of thing."

Seph glanced at Piper, an inquisitive eyebrow raised behind one lens of her grimy glasses.

"Come on in," said Violet. "We'll show you." She turned and walked back to the table where Corey was typing on the screen of his phone with a speed that seemed supernatural given the size of his pudgy thumbs.

Seph stepped into the room and closed the door behind her. Portals to other worlds? Like the one they tumbled through in November that sent them crashing into the vault where the scythe was hidden?

That seemed a little too convenient.

"Corey's building a map," said Violet as she began shuffling through the papers on the table.

Seph leaned over the mess, surprised. Didn't the slime lady say something about a map while she was being molested in that weird, psychic purgatory?

"It looks like *lots* of maps," observed Piper.

Violet nodded. "Sorry, we're not very organized right now." She gathered all the papers and maps together and scooped them off the table, revealing the much larger map underneath. "*This* map," she clarified.

Seph and Piper both leaned over the table. It was a detailed map of the Midwest, consisting of the states from North Dakota south to Kansas and from Kansas east to Ohio. Someone had drawn circles, lines and arrows in various-colored Sharpie markers all over the map.

"This represents all the hotspots we've found since we started studying the phenomena four years ago," explained Violet.

"Color coded for intensity," said Corey without pausing from his texting.

"Yellow is pretty much just rumors," said Violet. "Urban legends. Ghost stories. That sort of thing. Green represents a suspicious number of rumors. Blue means we've found some stuff that seems legit. Purple is heavy activity and red means we've confirmed paranormal and/or multi-dimensional activity."

"Yellow to Red," simplified Corey, "Yellow means there's

probably nothing there. Red usually means we almost got eaten by something."

Violet frowned at him. "That's what I said."

"Wow," said Piper, looking at all the little circles on the map.

There were lots of yellow circles and fewer of each color along the spectrum. Only a handful of them were red, but Seph noted that Avelby was one of them. The others included Hedge Lake in Northern Michigan; Penaskee, Illinois; Letley, Iowa; Crump, Ohio and Briar Hills, Missouri.

"And you're sharing your insane-sounding hobby with us *why*, exactly?" asked Seph.

"Well, aren't you guys basically doing the same thing?" asked Violet. "I mean you're treasure hunters, right?"

"Treasure hunters?" Seph looked at Piper. "I guess we kind of are." Although she'd never thought of it exactly that way before.

Violet nodded at Piper. "We ran into this one while we were running from a nasty crosser in one of the main utility shafts."

"Crosser?" said Seph, confused.

"Oh yeah!" said Piper. "Show her the picture."

Violet pulled out her phone, swiped at it a few times, and then turned it around so she could see. It wasn't a very good picture. It was blurry, and the camera's flash had washed most of it out, but there was clearly some kind of face there, with large, ferocious teeth and shining, yellow eyes. "We call them 'crossers'," she explained.

"'Cause they cross over," said Corey. "Catchy, right?"

Piper nodded. She supposed it was. And it was easy to remember.

"These things cross into our world through various anomalies and gateways from other worlds. We've caught glimpses of them before, but *this* one was particularly strong."

"Really bad tempered," said Corey, his nose still glued to his phone.

Violet nodded. "Yeah, not even remotely friendly. But I finally got a picture of one!" She glanced back at Corey. "You backed it up, right?"

"Five times," confirmed Corey.

"Awesome. But it really was a close call. We didn't even know there was a portal down there. We were lucky to get out."

"It was lucky for me, too," said Piper. "That thing scared away those creepy kids. I thought I was done for."

Seph glanced over at her, surprised. "They came back?"

She raised her eyebrows in an exaggerated "*oh yeah*" expression and nodded. They came back all right. Just the thought of those eerie little monsters gave her a shiver.

"I don't know anything about any kids," said Violet, "but if Corey hadn't grabbed me and run like he did, we might not have gotten out of there. I've never seen a crosser that big and mean before."

Piper frowned and touched the pendant Annalisa gave her. It was supposed to protect her. And in her moment of terror, surrounded by those freaky, black-eyed children, she remembered clutching it, desperate for *any* kind of protection. Did it somehow make that portal open? Did *she* almost get Violet and Corey killed down there?

Seph glanced around at them. It was a lot to take in. Piper was attacked by the black-eyed children while they were separated?

There was a portal of some kind somewhere under the city? *And* a creepy, handsy slime lady told her that some sort of apocalyptic bug god wanted them dead?

Like the giant, white-haired dead guy wasn't enough to worry about.

She looked over the other places marked on Corey's map. There were yellow and green circles over most of the major cities, which only made sense, she supposed. Higher density populations would spawn more rumors, obviously. But several of those cities had smaller circles in and around them. Milwaukee was circled in green, for example, but she saw that Cakwetak, specifically, was circled in blue. There were also purple circles around nearby Pasoken and Creek Bend.

"It's a work in progress," said Corey.

Seph scanned the map, looking for places she knew. Messing Knob, where they tracked down the mysterious broadcast signal in November, was circled in yellow. And Fathom Lake was circled in green. But there were no circles anywhere near Muntony. Either the second marker was the only thing hidden there, or the curious pair of weirdness hunters hadn't discovered it yet. The same was true of Shawbeck Ranch. These two would probably love to find their way there, but it definitely wasn't her place to tell them about it.

"So you guys just travel around, searching for portals to other worlds?" she asked.

"Pretty much," said Corey. Finally, he laid his phone down and turned his full attention to the laptop.

"And you're just going to share all this with us?" asked Seph.

Violet shrugged. "We kind of have the same goals, right?"

Seph looked over at Piper. "I guess we do," she admitted.

Piper shrugged. "We might not be able to do all this stuff on our own. And they're definitely not going to think we're crazy."

Seph scratched at the sticky spot on her chin. That was true.

"Point is," said Violet, "we're both looking for something. I don't know what it is you're looking for, exactly, but I think we can probably help each other."

Seph considered this. It *would* be nice to have some idea where to go next. They didn't seem to be getting very far just wandering around. Ian didn't seem to be able to tell them anything more. But it wasn't like they could tell these people about the Hands.

Could they?

Piper leaned over the map. "What's this?" she asked, pointing to a red star.

"That's our hometown," replied Violet. "Tunipet, Missouri. It's where all this started for us, four years ago."

Piper looked up at her, intrigued. "What happened in Tunipet?"

Violet bit her lip. "It's...complicated."

"Long story," said Corey.

"I don't really like talking about it," said Violet, fidgeting. "Sorry."

"Oh," said Seph, unsure what else to say. So much for not keeping secrets, she supposed.

"It's just...kind of personal," she added.

"We lost a friend," explained Corey.

"Oh no!" gasped Piper.

"The short version," Violet interjected, "is that it's where we first found out that there're other worlds out there. And there're doorways to these other worlds all over the place. You just have to figure out how to see them. It's like a giant puzzle. And we've been searching for them ever since."

"And you just happened to show up in Avelby at the same time as us?" asked Seph. It was too much of a coincidence, in her opinion. It was suspicious. She couldn't help but keep her guard up.

"Actually we've been here since Monday," replied Violet. "And we didn't exactly *happen* to come here."

"Old guy," grunted Corey.

Violet nodded. "*Scary* old guy," she agreed. "We were at a place called the Plunterly Mansion. There's a huge, private collection of strange, old books in the library there. Really weird stuff."

"Rumor was that some of the books there were collected by the head psychiatrist of a mental institution, actually written by a bunch of his patients," explained Corey. "As some sort of psychological experiment."

"And you thought that if someone had ever written about finding secret doorways into other worlds," reasoned Seph, "people would probably think they were nuts, so that's where it'd end up."

"Bullseye," said Corey.

"The old man was there when we got there," explained Violet, "just sitting in a chair, reading a book, shooting us these really hateful looks every so often. Like we didn't belong there. He was really starting to give me the creeps, honestly. Later, as we were getting ready to leave, he stood up and walked out. But as he went by, he dropped *this* on the table in front of us." She shuffled the papers around and laid out a map of Avelby. Like Corey's map, someone had circled several locations and scribbled notes here and there.

Seph and Piper both leaned over it.

"He said if we really wanted to learn about the 'other side' then we should come here."

"Any idea who he was?" asked Seph.

"He didn't say," replied Violet. "He just…*left*. But…" She reached over and pointed to the bottom corner of the map, where a signature had been scrawled in neat, tiny handwriting.

"'Keeper of the Archives'," read Piper. She turned and looked at Seph, surprised. "Keeper?"

Seph recalled something the librarian in Muntony told them once. Not the *real* librarian. The real librarian was already dead. This one was the shepherd in disguise. "…he's the keeper of things," he'd said. "Lots of things."

A man named Harv had told them almost the same thing several hours earlier, so it was probably true.

She looked up at Violet, her thoughts racing. If that old man really *was* the Keeper…and if he really did send these two to Avelby…

There was also the chance that this was an elaborate trap set by Travis. But deep down, she didn't believe that. She stared at the Keeper's signature on the bottom of the map.

"Okay," she said. "Let's talk."

Chapter 42

"So…" said Seph as she seated herself on the side of the nearest of the room's two beds. "Are you guys, like, a couple? Or what?"

Violet looked up from the map. "What? Oh. No. We're just friends."

"Just friends," confirmed Corey. He still hadn't taken his eyes off his computer screen.

"Oh."

Violet wagged a finger back and forth between the two of them. "Are *you*?"

Seph stared at her, surprised. "What? *Us*? No. We're not… *No*."

"She snores," said Piper.

Seph looked over at her, surprised. "*What*? I do not."

"You totally do."

"I don't— How— *What does that even have to do with it*?"

"I couldn't share a bed with you. I'd never get any sleep."

"Seriously? That's all you…? That's the most…" She closed her eyes and shook her head. "*Anyway*…" She turned her attention back to Violet and changed the subject. "You said you've come across crossers before in your, uh, investigations?"

This time, Corey glanced up at Violet. "Few times," he confirmed.

Violet nodded. She suddenly seemed distracted.

Piper wondered if she was remembering what happened in Tunipet four years ago.

Whatever it was, it had clearly changed her life. And she could totally relate to that.

"Ever see anything else?" she pressed.

"We're pretty sure we've seen a few ghosts," said Violet. "And there was that time in Indiana, when that dog thing chased us out of that cemetery."

"I saw a UFO once," volunteered Corey.

Piper rubbed at her eyes. She was having flashbacks to her tour around town.

"What about you?" asked Violet. "You said something about a bunch of…ghost kids, was it?"

"I don't know if they were ghosts," said Piper. "But they weren't normal. They were a bunch of little kids with all-black eyes."

This actually made Corey sit up and turn around. "Black-eyed children?"

"Yeah," said Seph. "Like the ones on the internet, apparently. Although I still haven't actually seen any of them yet."

"You don't want to," Piper insisted with a shudder.

"I got another visit from those flickering men, though."

"Really?"

"Flickering men?" asked Violet.

"They look like shadows, but they kind of flicker. They appear and disappear. And *multiply*."

"Okay, *that* sounds creepy," said Violet.

"The slime lady said they were sent by Gispuknya."

"Gispuknya?" said Violet, confused.

"Slime lady?" said Piper.

Seph shook her head. "I'll tell you about it later. It's a long…*weird*…story."

"Wow," said Violet. "Who *are* you people?"

"Even longer, *weirder* story," replied Seph. "Look, I don't know how much time we have. The short of it is that my mom's life is in danger. She's…" She hesitated. She hated saying things like this aloud, even to someone who seemed to understand how weird the world was. But there didn't seem to be any holding back at this point. "She's been poisoned by a demon. We need to find something that's hidden somewhere under this city before she dies."

Violet stood up straight. "Oh! Okay. You probably should've just started with that. That's, like, *way* bigger than portals."

"Demon," contemplated Corey. "Now we're talking." He turned back to his computer and opened a new search window. "Do you know what class of demon we're dealing with?"

"It's an incubus," said Seph.

She expected some sort of reaction to this, but he only said, "Oh. That's a big one. Really strong."

"You know about demons?" said Piper, surprised.

"I know about demon *lore*," he replied. "Can't promise it'll all be accurate. Or *any* of it, really…" he amended, "…but it should give us a good start."

"Roly-Poly's plugged into all the paranormal blogs and fo-rums," said Violet as she sat down in the chair, curled her legs under her and leaned over the map. "If you've got a question about anything supernatural, he's the one you want to ask."

Roly-Poly? thought Seph. She might've laughed if she wasn't so interested in staying well away from the giant's bad side. Instead, she just said, "That must be handy."

"It is," she said.

"But how are you able to find your way into those hidden tunnels?" asked Piper.

After Corey had finally set the two of them back onto their feet, Violet led them both into a narrow corridor and around a corner, where they were abruptly returned to the dirty tunnel by which Piper entered.

"Oh," said Violet. "With this." She reached into her tee shirt and pulled out the necklace she was wearing. Dangling from the chain was what looked like an ordinary piece of clear-blue glass. "A guy on the street in St. Louis sold it to me. He said it was a piece of a mysterious looking glass and that it would show me 'anything unseen' when I looked through it." She smiled at the look Seph gave her. "I know, right? Total scam. Except when I looked through the glass, I could see an abandoned building across the street that wasn't there when I *wasn't* looking through the glass. It was the craziest thing."

Piper tipped her head to one side. "What, like Number 12 Grimmauld Place?"

"*What?*" said Seph.

She turned and looked at her. "The house from *Harry Potter*? Headquarters of the Order of the Phoenix? It was invisible to muggles?" She glanced over at Violet, who shook her head. "No? Really?" She sighed. "Never mind."

"So it lets you see hidden places," said Seph.

Violet nodded. "You'd be amazed how many of them are out there."

"That must be handy," said Seph, eying the strange, blue shard.

"It is." Violet tucked it back into her tee shirt and said, "But I can tell you guys don't need it. You can see the unseen *without* a looking glass, can't you?"

"Seph sees things," said Piper. "I can just *hear* things."

"Turns out there're a lot of people out there who can do things," said Corey.

"A lot of people," agreed Violet.

Seph stood up and walked over to the table. "So what did you find *here* with your looking glass?"

Corey reached out and placed the tips of his chubby fingers on the map. "Something about this town sort of breeds unseen things. There's the house with all the chimes." He slid his finger to another spot. "There's an entire street running between these two roads that nobody can see."

"How can people not see an entire street?" asked Piper.

"They just can't," explained Violet. "They can't even see the space these places take up. It's like they just...*ignore* their existence. It's weird."

"There's an unseen office building on this street," continued

Corey. He slid his hand over the map, from one circle to the next. "There're unseen entrances into the city's tunnels here, here, here and here, but none of them led anywhere. Here, here and here there're *alleyways* between buildings that other people can't see."

"Without the looking glass, the two buildings are built right up against each other, but *with* it, you can see there's a space between them."

Seph reached up to scratch her head and felt a lock of it sticking out, with another strand of dusty cobweb stuck in it. She flung it away and tried to smooth out her hair. "So where's the tunnel with the crosser?"

Corey planted a huge finger on the map. "Directly under here. I think." He drew a little circle around the spot. "*Somewhere* in here, for sure."

"You think that's the spot we're looking for?" asked Piper.

Seph considered it. A portal to another world was precisely where she'd expect to find the second Hand, but the Hand wasn't supposed to be in Avelby. They were looking for the second marker. And the other markers, although hidden, and guarded by scary monsters, weren't actually in another world. More importantly, weren't they supposed to be the only two people who could find the markers? Magic looking glass or not, it didn't seem like these two should be able to find it. She bent over the table again and looked over the map, trying to make sense of it all.

After a moment, she cocked her head to one side. "Hm…"

"What?" asked Violet.

"Let me see this." She turned the map and placed a finger on one of the many circles. "Here's Adderbell's. If this is the front of the building…and the basement steps were over here…then the tunnel in the basement would be about here." She traced a short line with her fingers. "So the hidden tunnel we found would go this way, intersecting with the big tunnel at about this angle… Probably directly under Greenbury Street." She drew a line where the hidden tunnel would've gone if it hadn't run into the Greenbury Street tunnel. "Running roughly north."

Piper pointed to where she found the chimes. "The one I found looked like it could be part of the same tunnel."

Seph reached out with her other hand and put her finger where the abandoned farmhouse was sitting. "And this is the other one I found behind the orchard."

She traced a line from Adderbell's secret tunnel, through Piper's house of chimes and all the way to the farmhouse. It wasn't perfectly straight, but it was close enough. "None of these tunnels are as old as what we're looking for, but they're older than most of the tunnels in this area. And I don't think it's a coincidence that they seem to be hidden from most people."

"Something at one end of this tunnel or the other," reasoned Corey.

Seph nodded. Then she leaned farther over the map, her eyes fixed on the area where Fibbel Lake spilled into the river. "Fibbel Marsh…" she said. She cocked her head. "'The map points to the marsh.'"

Piper leaned over next to her. "What?"

"'But what you seek lies on the *other* side.'"

"Huh?"

Seph wasn't sure what the slime lady meant by "*other* side."

372

She traced the line in the other direction, but that way ran straight into Deag Lake. "What is that?" she asked, pointing at a small X in the middle of Fibbel Marsh.

Corey leaned over it. "No idea. Haven't made it over there to investigate yet."

"What are you thinking?" asked Piper.

"I'm thinking the slime lady mentioned both a map and a marsh and that someone who might be the Keeper sent these two here with a map that has an X drawn on a marsh."

Violet's pale, green eyes lit up. "Let's go!"

Piper looked up at her, surprised. "Now? It's dark out."

"And scary," agreed Violet. "So you'll need us to come with you."

Seph and Piper glanced at each other. "I guess so," said Seph. She supposed they owed them for the map.

Corey closed his laptop and stood up. "This is gonna be awesome," he decided.

Seph stared up at his pudgy, beaming face. *She* wasn't going to be the one to disagree with him.

"Should we take my Jeep?" asked Violet. "There's room for all of us."

"I'd be more comfortable following in my truck," said Seph as she moved toward the door. "In case we get separated for some reason."

"Okay. Give me a phone number, then, so we can stay in touch."

As Piper pulled out her phone to exchange numbers, Seph stopped in front of the mirror. "Oh my god! I *do* look awful!"

Chapter 43

"I have a really good feeling about them," said Piper. "I think they're okay."

Seph couldn't really find a reason to disagree. Violet and Corey seemed nice. And if they were really what they said they were, they were lucky to have bumped into them. But after all she'd been through today, she couldn't help being pessimistic. She kept looking for reasons to prove they were just another of Travis' tricks.

"Besides, I didn't hear anything unusual around them, not like when all those other things showed up."

That *did* seem like a good sign. And she didn't *see* anything unusual, either. Of course, they didn't detect anything strange when they met Archie in Muntony, either...

No. The slime lady told her there'd be a map pointing to a marsh. Corey had a map—given to him by someone calling himself the "Keeper of the Archives" no less—and on that map, the old, hidden tunnels pointed straight to a marsh. That couldn't be a coincidence. It meant this was where they were supposed to be.

...right?

"So..." said Piper. "You going to tell me what happened to

you? I thought you were at the museum that whole time."

Seph gave her the abridged version of her experience at the farmhouse as she followed the taillights of Violet's Jeep Liberty north, keeping the details to a minimum. (Especially the part about the slime lady getting all touchy-feely.)

"So all the things that keep attacking us…" said Piper when she'd finished, "…the flickering men…the black-eyed children…the revenant…they're all because of this Sputnik thing?"

"Gispuknya."

"Whatever."

"Sounds like it."

Piper leaned back in her seat and pinched her lower lip between her thumb and forefinger. "So what does this spunk thing have to do with the incubus, then?"

"I don't know. I mean, if Travis wants the Hands, then he has to keep us alive. So why would he send something like that after us?"

"Same reason the shepherd sent those mall wraiths after us in November? To keep us busy so we wouldn't have time to think?"

"I don't know. This feels different."

The wraiths were the shepherd's trump card. They were the whole reason they went searching for the scythe. It was the only object in the world that could stop them. The incubus, on the other hand, had her mother. That was all the reason she needed. If anything, this Gispuknya bug and its freaky army of black-eyed children, flickering men and runners were *preventing* them from finding the second Hand.

She shook her head. "Maybe we'll learn more when we get to

the marsh." She glanced over at Piper. "What about you? How'd you meet the portal experts?"

Before she could answer, her cell phone rang again. She took it out of her pocket and made a face at the screen. "Meg."

Seph made the same face back at her.

"Hello?"

"Are we out of those little frozen quiches?"

Piper scrunched her face up, confused. "What?"

Meg sighed dramatically. "Quiches?" she said again, as if she were stupid. "You know. Little pastry things."

"I know what a quiche is."

"Are we out?" she asked again. "I can't find any in the freezer."

"Then we're probably out," Piper reasoned. Although she wasn't sure how they could be out already. She just bought them the other day. She hadn't even eaten any yet.

Meg gave another dramatic sigh. "Pick some more up before you come home."

Piper made another face. "Go buy your own if you want some so bad."

"God, Pipes, don't be a cheapskate. You sound just like Seph."

She rolled her eyes. She really wasn't in the mood for Meg tonight.

"Oh, and you're almost out of Coke again."

"How're we almost out of Coke again? Seph just bought a case *yesterday*."

Seph looked over at her, shocked. "She'd better not drink all my Coke!"

"Seph drinks *way* too much soda," grumbled Meg. "It's not healthy."

"If she drank all those, she'd better go buy some more," growled Seph.

"You ask me, she's addicted to sugar. It's totally unhealthy."

"*I* paid for those. You tell her that."

"It's no wonder she's so chunky," said Meg.

Piper's eyes grew wide. Those were war-starting shots she was firing. She glanced over at Seph. If she'd heard her say that...

"What?" said Seph, reading the horrified expression on her face. "What'd she say?"

Piper shook her head. Nothing. Nothing at all. She didn't hear anything. She was *not* getting caught in the middle of *that*.

"*What'd she say?*"

There was no way on earth she was repeating it. Seph would probably kill Meg if she heard her say something like that.

"Are you still not coming home tonight?"

"I don't know when we're coming home," she replied, happy to change the subject. She turned and looked out the window so she wouldn't have to see Seph's piercing glare. "Could be tonight, but don't expect us."

"Why is she even there when we're not home?" hissed Seph. "Tell her to go leech off her parents for a while."

"What am I supposed to do about breakfast?"

Piper threw her head back, frustrated. "Oh my god, I'm not your nanny! You can figure out how to feed yourself."

"*Auuuuugh!*"

377

Piper squeezed her eyes shut and had to force herself not to scream. She hated that noise Meg made. It was infuriating.

"You're getting to be just like *her*. You know that right? You're just *rude* anymore."

"*I'm* rude?"

"Yeah. Newsflash, I know. Sorry to be the one to break it to you."

She took the phone away from her ear and looked at it as if it had malfunctioned somehow.

"You need better influences in your life. You're turning into a total bitch."

Her mouth dropped open. "*What?*"

"I totally can't deal with you right now," said Meg. And with that, the call ended.

She stared at the phone for a moment. "She hung up on me again!"

"She's *your* friend," grumbled Seph.

Piper stuffed the phone back into her pocket and then stared out the windshield for a moment, her lips pressed tightly together.

Seph stared at her, surprised. She wasn't sure she'd ever seen her look that mad before. "Or…is she?"

"If I'm such a bitch, then I'm not covering for her anymore."

"*She called you a bitch?*"

Piper turned and looked at her. "Uh huh. And she called you fat."

"*What?*"

"Chunky. That was the word she used."

Seph called Meg something far worse than chunky. In fact,

she called her *several* things that were far worse than chunky.

Piper was pleased to discover that she didn't care as much anymore.

Chapter 44

Piper told Seph about the wind chimes house and the black-eyed children as they followed Violet past the orchard and out beyond the city limits, where the surrounding forest gave way to wet fields and marsh grass.

It was impossible to miss. A large sign pointed them to a parking lot, where a large, wooden arch framed the entrance to a walkway of wooden planks winding into the intimidating darkness of the marsh.

The entire area twinkled with fireflies, which delighted Piper, but didn't impress Seph in the least. There was nothing charming about them, in her opinion. They were bugs, just like the rest of them. Globs of glow-in-the-dark goo in their butts didn't make them any less gross.

The moment she opened the door, she knew this was going to be even more unpleasant than she expected. The sounds of crickets, frogs and night birds were almost deafening compared to the quiet cab of the truck. And her feet had barely touched the ground before the mosquitos began buzzing around her head.

She swatted at them, trying to shoo them away. But the little freaks refused to take a hint.

Plus, the whole area reeked of stagnant water and rotting veg-etation.

"I don't like it here!" she squealed.

The parking lot was lit by four tall streetlamps, each one shin-ing down from the center of a living, pulsing cloud of swarming insects.

"It sounds so pretty!" said Piper, waving absently at the air in front of her, as if the blood-sucking insects were no more bother-some than a stray strand of hair.

"Yeah, pretty like *malaria*," grumbled Seph as she slapped at something that landed on her cheek.

"They don't have malaria in Illinois."

"I'll bet they do. They just don't talk about it."

A cold, heavy spray of pungent mist struck her bare shoulders, making her scream.

"Sorry," said Corey. "Bug spray. For the mosquitos."

"No, you're fine! Keep it coming! *Please!*"

She closed her eyes and held out her arms as he walked around her, hosing down her exposed skin. Then she took off her glasses, squeezed her eyes shut and held her breath as he sprayed her face.

"All done," he said, turning to Piper. "You too?"

"Yes, thank you."

Seph stepped out of the cloud of poison, coughing, and re-turned her glasses to her face. She hated the smell of bug spray, but not nearly as much as she hated bugs. She made a mental note to buy some to keep in the Ford's glovebox, knowing she'd probably never think of it again until after she actually needed it.

Corey finished with Piper and turned to Violet, who immediately stuck out her arms and slowly twirled around for him, twisting her slender hands and arms around and tilting her neck as she did so, looking somehow as graceful as a dancer, as if the two of them had honed the simple, unromantic act of applying bug spray into a fine art during their four years of hunting for portals to other worlds.

When she was done, she walked around to the back of the Liberty while Corey held the can above his head and sprayed himself down. "I've got plenty of flashlights for everyone," she announced. "So you can save the batteries on your phones."

Seph felt like slapping herself in the forehead. "I have one too!" she remembered. "In my glovebox. For emergencies." She hadn't even thought about it. She started to go back for it.

"Leave it," said Violet. "Save it in case of an actual emergency. I have plenty." She turned and handed her two small flashlights. "Keep them. I literally buy these in bulk. I've lost track of how many I've lost."

"Thank you."

They really did seem like nice people. And they were also quite well prepared. Looking in the back of the vehicle, Seph saw ropes and climbing gear, an old tool box, a pair of dirty shovels, bolt cutters and even a scary-looking hunting rifle.

Violet slammed the lift gate closed on the Jeep—she practically had to stand on her tiptoes to reach it—and then locked it. "We ready?" she asked.

Seph wasn't, but she nodded anyway. She turned and looked

at the wooden archway and the pathway that wound out into the wet, black, twinkling, shrieking wilderness beyond it.

If this were just any ordinary bug-infested marsh at night it would be bad enough, but if her expectations were correct, this place wasn't ordinary at all. This was very possibly the location of the second marker on the path to the second Hand of the Architects. If she was right, this was a place protected by the Keeper, himself.

They would find terror here. In one form or another.

There wasn't even a moon out tonight. Only the stars and the fireflies would be shining down on them once they left the lights of the parking lot.

"So…" said Violet as they stepped onto the wooden planks and set out into the darkness. "Any chance you'll share what it is we're going to find out here?"

"Not really sure," replied Seph. "But it's probably underground somewhere."

"Probably not going to find any tunnels out here," said Corey. "Unless they're *underwater* tunnels."

"He *does* make a good point," said Piper.

Seph shrugged. "That would make sense. But nothing we find ever makes any kind of sense."

"Also a good point," agreed Piper.

"It actually *does* make *some* sense, though." realized Violet. "It's a marsh, a floodplain *and* a nature preserve. Not much chance of anyone ever building anything out here."

"If it really is what we've been looking for," added Seph, "you guys aren't going to be able to go in with us. It's boobytrapped. It sounds weird, but anyone besides us will set it off. And that would be bad."

Violet glanced over at her. "What, like poisoned arrows? Giant boulders?"

"Less *Indiana Jones*; more *Dawn of the Dead*."

"Oh… Okay…"

"First, we've got to find it," said Piper. "Did the…uh…*slime lady* tell you anything else?"

"She said the map points to the marsh, which it did. But she also said something about it being on the 'other side,' whatever that means. Other side of what?"

"Did she mean the other end of the tunnel?" asked Corey. "Maybe this is the wrong end."

"I thought of that," said Seph. "The other end leads straight toward the lake."

"Maybe it's on the shore of the lake," he suggested. "Or under it."

"I don't think so. The thing we're looking for predates white settlers in the area. According to my research, the last known Native American settlement was right near this area. Besides…" She looked out over the dark marsh. "This sort of *feels* right."

"You see something?" asked Piper.

"I don't know. I don't really know what it is I'm looking for."

They came to a fork in the wooden walkway. According to the map back by the entrance, the path consisted of several large circles. This was the first and smallest. You could take a short walk by following it in either direction and sticking to the inner path. Or you could turn at any of the other forks before returning to this point and venture farther out into the marsh.

"Hear anything?" asked Seph.

Piper shook her head. "I don't think so. Not yet. How about you? Anything at all?"

Seph shook her head, too. "I can't tell for sure. But I feel like we want to go this way." She took the path to the right.

Violet followed along behind them, peering through her looking glass pendant. "It's too dark for me to see anything unless we get closer to it."

Corey followed behind them and concentrated on keeping his eyes peeled for any kind of trouble. According to these two girls, there were bad things in this town. And having seen more than a few bad things himself these past four years, he didn't hesitate to believe them. So he kept his flashlight beam moving over the marsh around them, watching for any sign of movement that didn't belong there.

Chapter 45

For a long time, the four of them followed the rough plank pathway, swatting at the occasional mosquito that decided to ignore the bug repellent and take a bite anyway.

Bugs had begun to gather around the ends of each of their flashlights as well, and Seph kept going into spastic fits when she felt them land on her hand, making a variety of undignified whimpers and whines while her flashlight beam streaked across the boards in front of them.

"You're not really the *outdoorsy* type, are you?" deduced Violet.

"She hates bugs," said Piper. "Like, *really* hates them."

Violet nodded. "Sucks to be you right now."

"Tell me about it," groaned Seph. Then she let out a startled shriek as something much larger landed on her forearm. A moth, probably, but it might as well have been a giant hornet, as far as she was concerned.

"Wow," said Violet.

"I left the bug spray in the car," apologized Corey. "Wouldn't have helped anyway, though."

He was right. No amount of bug spray would repel this many

bugs. This whole area was infested with all manner of creepy crawly things. They were literally walking through a vast *cloud* of bugs. They shined in the beams of their flashlights wherever they aimed them and filled the air with their awful singing.

There was a constant and strangely eerie void centered over them in the endless cacophony of wildlife. Most of the creatures of the marsh fell silent as they approached and waited for them to pass before resuming their many, various songs. But the hush was only here at their feet. Out beyond the small, fifteen- or twenty-foot circle, the creatures paid them no attention at all, their voices filling the night, making it hard to concentrate on those subtle details she needed to look for.

And then there were all the little, unseen things that kept jumping into the water as they passed. Frogs, Corey had assured them, but Seph found that she didn't quite dare to believe him. Some of the splashes sounded far too big to be a frog. And others, she was convinced, sounded a lot less like a jumping frog than what she imagined it would sound like if a giant, man-eating snake or killer alligator had just slithered into the water.

It didn't matter to her how improbable such a thing was. The thing about phobias, you have to understand, is that they are, by their very definition, *irrational*.

Each time the wooden path diverged, however, Seph found herself compelled to go in one direction over the other in spite of all these icky distractions.

Something was here. She was sure of it. She just had to find it before these bugs drove her completely crazy.

But the marsh was far larger than she anticipated. It felt like hours before she finally reached a point where her strange senses told her to stop, although in reality it was probably half an hour at most.

"Can you hear anything now?" she asked as she slapped at something that was buzzing around in front of her mouth.

"I don't think so," replied Piper. "What can you see?"

"Same thing I've been seeing since we got here: a whole lot of *I don't want to be here.*"

Violet leaned over the handrail, pointed her flashlight out into the darkness and peered out through her looking glass, scanning the entire area. Then she turned and did the same thing on the other side of the path.

Nothing.

"So what now?" asked Piper.

Seph looked out over the marsh. She didn't know what she was looking for. Nothing stood out to her. And Corey was right about the tunnels. Any underground passageway built in this soup almost certainly would've flooded or filled with mud ages ago. But something told her that what she was looking for was over in that direction somewhere.

Was it really under all this mud and water? And if so, how were they supposed to reach it?

"So what do we do now?" asked Violet.

Seph wasn't sure. Her eyes kept being drawn in the same direction, out into the marsh.

"There're some little islands out there," said Corey, shining his light out over the water. "Dry ground."

"Yeah, but how do we get out there?" asked Piper.

"We just go there," he replied, as if it were the simplest answer in the world. Which, she supposed, it *was*. But it was also by far the *ickiest*.

Seph shined her light down onto the filthy, stagnant water just on the other side of the railing and felt her stomach sour at the mere thought of stepping off into that.

"Uh-uh," said Piper. "I have to go first into all the spidery places."

Violet walked on ahead and found a stretch of walkway where there wasn't a handrail. "It's not very deep," she reported.

Corey didn't hesitate. He scooped Violet into his arms as if she were nothing and then simply carried her out into the water without so much as a grimace, leaving Seph and Piper to watch after them.

The water climbed almost up to his waist before he bottomed out and began to climb back up. Then he lowered Piper into the dry weeds and started back again.

"Which way?" asked Violet as she peered through her looking glass.

Seph watched the big guy as he lumbered through the water like a great, fearless hippo. "I'm not sure. Closer to those two trees, I think."

Violet turned and scanned her surroundings. "Which trees?"

"Those over there," she said, pointing.

Violet turned and looked, confused. "You mean way over there?" she asked. "How can you even see that far?"

"Those right there," she said, pointing again. "Like, two is-lands over from you."

389

"There aren't any trees over there," said Piper.

Seph looked over at her, surprised. "What?"

Corey stopped a few paces shy of the path and looked back. "I don't see any either," he reported.

"Wait…" said Seph. "I'm the only one who can see those two trees standing *right there*?"

Violet lifted her looking glass and peered through it as she shined her light in that direction. Seph could see her flashlight beam as it washed over their mossy trunks, but she shook her head. "I still don't see anything," she said.

"Only *you* can see it," said Piper. "Does that mean it's what we came here for?"

"I guess so," replied Seph. "I wonder why that glass of hers doesn't—" But she didn't get to finish that sentence. Instead, she let out a startled, "*WAAAAH!*" as Corey swept her up into his huge arms. "*Hey!* Personal space, buddy!"

"Sorry," he said. And the deep frown that crossed over his face really did make him look sorry. But he didn't stop. He was already knee deep in the marsh. "Didn't think you'd want to get your feet wet. Want me to put you down?"

She looked down at the churning mud and water, breathed in the reeking stench of rotten vegetation, and grimaced. Without even thinking about it, she grabbed two handfuls of his tee shirt and clung to him. "I guess since you're already carrying me," she grumbled. "But *ask* first next time."

"Sorry," he said again.

A moment later, he placed her on her feet and then turned and looked back at Piper. He scratched his head, less sure about himself than he was before, and called out to her, "You wanna get carried or get wet?"

Piper didn't have to consider it. She stuck both arms out at him and opened and closed her hands several times. The universal sign of all small children all over the world for "carry me."

Violet giggled. "Corey's harmless," she assured Seph as he set off through the muck again. "He's a total teddy bear."

Seph huffed. "He seems alright," she admitted.

"He's never disrespectful. And I've known him almost my whole life and I've never seen him get mad."

He *did* seem like a really sweet guy, she supposed.

Corey came back through the water once more and put Piper on the ground next to them. Then he looked out toward the place where Seph said there were trees he couldn't see. "You want to go first? So you can show me where they are?"

Seph sighed. "Fine. But watch the hands."

It wasn't that she had any reason not to trust him. He really didn't seem like the kind of guy who might cop a feel at the first opportunity. It was more about the idea of someone just picking her up without permission. It felt like a violation. Just one step down from being groped.

And if she were to be honest, it was also the fact that she had to rely on some guy to carry her just because she was too girly and scared to wade through a little muddy water.

She didn't think her dad would be very proud of her.

"This one?" asked Corey.

"Yes."

He planted her in the dry weeds without any funny business

and then promptly turned back for Violet and Piper.

Seph straightened her clothes, swatted at the damned mosquitos and surveyed the scene before her.

According to everyone else, there were no trees here, meaning that, to them, it was just a flat little, grass- and weed-covered hill rising up above the water's surface.

But *she* could see the trees. She couldn't miss them. They were big. And now that she was up close, she didn't think they were any kind of tree she'd ever seen before. Extremely tall, with long, branchless trunks like palm trees, but with big, bristly tops. Their bases were huge, six and eight feet across, with the bottom twelve feet covered in thick moss and a sort of latticework of gnarled, thorny brambles that seemed to be a part of the tree, itself. Strange, dangling vines with large tufts of leaves that looked like shaggy fur dangled down from the tops of the tree and hung all around her.

She took a step closer, curious, and realized that there were creepy, black bugs crawling all over their bark.

They were on the ground, too, wriggling around in the grass, climbing on the weeds.

Something landed on her elbow and she yelped and slapped it away.

God, she hated it here.

Corey deposited Piper on the island next to her and then turned and went back for Violet.

"Thanks!" chirped Piper. "He's so nice," she said to Seph.

"If you like being packed around like luggage."

"Be nice. I think it's *chivalrous*."

"You would."

"So what are you seeing right now?"

Seph shined her light up into the high branches. "Two really creepy looking trees."

"Even the trees have to be creepy?"

"Looks that way. You really can't see them?"

"There's nothing here but grass," she replied, lazily waving away another mosquito. And she didn't. Seph watched her eyes wash over the surrounding area, never pausing on the huge, alien-looking trees in front of her.

They were growing close together and leaning away from each other as they stretched higher. At their gnarly bases, they were less than three feet apart, barely enough room to slip between them without snagging on those wicked-looking thorns.

And there was something behind these trees, something she couldn't quite make out from here. She pointed her flashlight between them. "What can you see over there, in the distance."

Piper squinted into the gloom. "Nothing. It's too dark."

"Better take my hand."

She didn't hesitate. She closed her hand around Seph's and then let herself be led forward. She glanced back once, to see Corey stepping out of the water with Violet in his arms, and when she looked back again, everything had changed. The marsh, with its wide-open expanse of grass had vanished, replaced by a landscape teeming with strange, tall trees and huge, shaggy clumps of thick moss.

"And now we're in a swamp," said Piper, looking around.

"We were *already* in a swamp," said Seph.

"No, we were in a marsh. *Now* we're in a swamp."

Seph yelped and slapped at something that landed on her arm. "What's the difference?" she snapped.

"Swamps have trees," said Piper.

"Well *excuse me*," she grumbled, slapping at another mosquito.

She didn't like it here. And not just because of the mosquitoes. Piper was right, after all. This was definitely more swamp-like than the marsh. And now that she was here, she remembered that she saw a swamp in that strange vision she had. She was wading through the stagnant water, running from something as things splashed around her...just before the mud began to pull her under...

"Wow," said Violet as she slipped between the two trees and looked around. "This is awesome! I wonder how far it goes." She was watching the two of them when they stepped through the portal, breaking the illusion and allowing her to follow. "Why couldn't I see it with my glass?"

"Different levels of unseen," replied Corey.

She looked up at him. "That's right! Like that theory you had when we were at Hedge Lake!"

"More than just what we can see."

"Even with the glass! That means there could be *so* much more out there! Especially with places like this! Do you think it's finite? Like that one in Crump?"

"Maybe," said Corey. Then he looked up and said, "Empty sky."

Seph and Piper looked up, too. He was right. The stars that had been shining so brightly overhead in the absence of the moon were gone. There was nothing there now but an endless, black abyss, speckled with the slow twinkling of fireflies.

"Is that something we should be concerned about?" asked Piper.

"It's pretty common, actually," said Violet as she pulled out her phone and began snapping pictures of the area. "As far as we know, most other worlds don't have stars. Or even a moon or a sun. They just sort of mimic whatever the weather is on the other side of the portal."

"Weird," said Seph.

"I know, right? And most worlds don't have their own ecosystems like this. Most of the time, they're just shadows of what's on the other side, like a darker version of our world that breaks apart more and more the farther you get from the entrance. This is incredible! You guys are amazing!"

Lucky us, thought Seph. These guys were super excited to do this stuff. Why didn't the universe make *them* the seekers?

She turned and looked around. "I guess this is what the slime lady meant by it being on the other side."

Piper nodded. "Seems like a safe bet. So where do we go next?"

Seph pointed straight ahead, to the next island. "There," she said. "Can you see it?"

"By that hill?"

"It's not…" She trailed off and aimed her flashlight out over the water.

"What is it?" asked Piper, joining her light to hers.

She shook her head. "Nothing, I guess… Just nerves."

"Are you sure?"

Of course she wasn't sure. A lot of creepy stuff was happening. It was getting harder and harder to tell which crazy things were just in her imagination and which ones were actually trying to kill her. Just now, for example, she thought she saw someone standing in the water over there, hidden in the deep shadows, watching them.

But there was nothing there now.

"Let's just go," she said, pointing at the hill rising up out of the water ahead of them. "Over there."

One by one, Corey carried the girls across the water. It was shallower this time, and the distance was shorter, but the mud was deeper here. It bogged him down, sucking at his shoes, threatening to trip him, but he made it without getting anyone but himself wet again.

Still slapping at the endless onslaught of bugs, Seph began climbing up the side of the hill.

Except it wasn't a hill at all. It only looked like a hill because no one else could see things the way she did. It was like the city she saw under Sukmukwe's lush lawns. Just beneath the surface of this mossy, stone-cluttered hill was a distinct shape. A pyramid. Not very unlike the ones found in old Mayan ruins.

But she didn't want to take the time to point that out to anybody. She wanted to get this over with and get out of this starless, God-forsaken swamp.

There was an opening at the top of the pyramid hidden within the hill, and a long, narrow staircase leading down into the darkness. She stood there, staring down into the unknown as the others climbed up behind her. Even from here, she could see those black bugs crawling around on the steps.

She gave Piper a pitiful look.

"You're not going first, are you?" Piper sighed.

"I'll go first," announced Corey, and without hesitation, he descended into that dark unknown.

Chapter 46

"Wait!"

Corey paused and looked back.

"Don't go any farther," said Seph. "Let me."

The steps led considerably deeper than any of them expected. They were at least a hundred feet down. And at the bottom was a chamber about the size of a football field. Corey's feet were on the last two steps, his meaty hand clasping the edge of the opening as he shined his flashlight into the darkness that loomed ahead of him.

Seph squeezed past him and stepped out onto the narrow walkway of packed earth that stretched the length of the room.

There was more swamp down here. Black, stagnant water covered the floor on either side of the walkway. That thick, shaggy moss covered most of the walls. A small forest of hairy-looking roots had wriggled through from above. Some of them had clung to the cracked stone and slithered across the ceiling. Others stretched all the way down into the water. And many more simply dangled overhead in bushy clumps like dead things hung out to dry. A steady drizzle of swamp water rained down through the dirt and rock, filling the silent chamber with the subtle melody of dripping water that made Seph grateful to have thought to use the bathroom in the hotel before coming here.

She walked out into the room, letting her gaze wash over every surface. This was it. It had the same feel to it as the chamber they found under Sukmukwe.

"This place looks like a boss room," said Corey.

Seph cocked her head to one side, surprised. It did, didn't it? Somehow the thought was both amusing and terrifying.

It wasn't safe for Corey and Violet to be here. If they were to get too close to the second marker, they could set off whatever horrible trap the Keeper left in this place. And if that happened, they might not even get a chance to see what was hidden here.

"You two will have to wait there," she said.

"But there's nothing here," said Violet. She'd already stepped past Corey and out onto the walkway. She was snapping pictures with her phone.

Seph turned around, horrified. "Stop! Seriously, it's not safe here!"

Violet stopped and looked around. But nothing was happening.

"Should they go back up and wait for us?" asked Piper.

"Are you sure this is the right place?" asked Violet. "There's nothing here. It's a dead end."

Seph turned and looked across the room. "No. There's something over there."

Piper cocked her head and tried to listen. "I don't hear anything," she said after a moment. Or did she? It was difficult to be certain. It was hard having two different pairs of ears for two different kinds of sounds. She glanced back at Violet. "Seriously, though, you two have to stay here. If you get too close to whatever's hidden over there, you could be in real danger."

"Plus you could mess the whole thing up and we might lose whatever we came down here for," added Seph.

"Fine," said Violet. "But you have to tell us what's in there."

Seph looked back at her.

"We helped you," she reminded her. "So you can't go leaving us out. We don't even want your treasure. We just want to know what's here. That's all. We're just looking for the truth."

Seph glanced at Piper.

Piper just shrugged.

"This isn't the…uh…treasure. It's just another part of the map. But you won't be able to read it. Only I can do that. It's like those two trees back there."

"We just want to know what's really out there," said Violet. "That's all."

Seph stared at her. "Fine. If you two don't set off any traps and get us all killed, we'll tell you everything we know. But don't blame us if you don't believe any of it."

Violet stared back at her. "Believing isn't something I have trouble with," she replied. "Trust me." Then she turned around and seated herself on the steps in front of Corey.

"Okay," said Piper. "That's settled."

Seph turned and set off across the room, careful to dodge the hairy tufts of roots that dangled from the ceiling and pooled in bushy clumps on the walkway.

"Take pictures for me!" Violet called after them.

"You know," said Piper, "it *would* be nice having friends who wouldn't think we're complete whackos if we say the universe was created by three giants and their magic tool kit."

"Let's just wait and see if they don't think we're whackos first, okay?"

"I guess you're right."

Seph glanced around at the forest of roots and the murky water. "This place gives me the creeps *really* bad," she said. "I feel like something's watching us."

As they approached the far end of the room, there was nothing to be seen but a wall. But she could feel that something was hidden there. And it only made sense that this walkway actually *led* to something. So she did her best to relax and let her prophet sight take over.

"Why is this one different, do you think?" asked Piper.

"What?"

"The other markers' entrances were all hidden behind those same illusions that only you can see, but otherwise, they were just underground. Why is this one in some creepy parallel universe?"

Seph kept her eyes on the wall in front of them, kept trying to make herself relax so she could see what was really there. "I don't know. Maybe they *were* in other worlds and we just couldn't see them."

"Hm," said Piper, clearly not convinced. "It just seems weird, is all. Like, why was this one so much harder to find?"

"Maybe because the second marker leading to the scythe had a caretaker and this one doesn't look like it does."

Piper considered this. It was true. Archie—the *real* Archie, not the impostor—and his ancestors had watched over the marker in Muntony for countless generations. This place didn't seem to have any such caretaker.

"So, *again*, why is this one different?"

"I don't know."

Piper looked back the way they came. Something felt wrong about this. She had a bad feeling. And not just because they were probably walking into another of the Keeper's nightmarish traps.

By the time Seph was close enough to reach out and touch the wall, she'd managed to make out a concealed opening in the stone. It was narrow, difficult to see, but easy enough to lead Piper through.

Behind this opening was a small room and an archway of smooth, black stone, just like the beams in the water chamber in Sukmukwe. She stepped under it and ran her fingers along the surface of it.

"Are there words?" As usual, it was just smooth, black stone to her eyes.

Seph nodded. "Yeah. There're words."

"What do they say?"

"Um…" She followed the arch all the way up, then all the way down the other side. "I think it's essentially one of those 'all ye who enter here, abandon all hope' kind of things."

"Oh. Well that's delightful."

"Isn't it? Come on. Let's hurry up and get this over with."

The two of them walked through the archway, unaware of the dripping shadow that stood watching them from the opening in the cavern wall behind them.

Chapter 47

Beyond the archway was a long, narrow passageway. There were spiderwebs here, of course, so Piper went first. But there were no more obstacles. At the far end of it they discovered a chamber almost identical to the one they found in Muntony. Large and round, with several stone columns set into dirt walls. The ceiling was a single, massive disk of smooth, gray stone.

In Muntony, there was a mural carved into the surface of the disk, depicting the three Architects (represented by giant, faceless men) standing over their freshly created world (represented by a large, table-like disk covered in images of mountains, rivers and fields). This time, however, the image looked like several coins arranged in a stack with space between them. There was a shining star at the top of the stack and a churning sea at the bottom. The coins were like the world in the other mural. They had little details on them. Mountains. Rivers. Lakes and fields. Each one was bigger than the one above it, up to the second to last one, which appeared to be covered in cracks. The last one was small and shriveled and drooping. It seemed to be melting into the waters of the sea beneath it.

Like before, Piper could see the mural. What she couldn't see, what only Seph could see with her prophet sight, was the writing spelled out in the carved lines of the mural. There were thousands of tiny, alien characters there, squeezed into every valley and crevice etched into the stone, and yet she found that she could see every last one of them.

"What does it say?" she asked.

Seph scanned the room for spiders and other creepy crawlies, and took special note of the floor beneath their feet. It was a dirt floor, like in the last chamber. Was there a giant, slumbering, zombie worm here as well? Or were there strange, alien mummies hidden behind the earthen walls like in Messing Knob? Or would another gooey blood-thing seep through the cracks and come oozing after them like in Sukmukwe?

More likely, she realized, it would probably be something new and equally terrifying.

Her heart was already pounding with the anticipation of it.

She forced herself to calm down and turned her eyes to the mural overhead. She could see the words, but for a moment, she couldn't make sense of any of them. It didn't read like any other language she'd ever seen, after all. She had to search for the hidden patterns. But eventually she began to see them.

She reached up and brushed her fingertips along the edge of one of the coins. With her other hand she traced the line of one of the waves in the water. Then her gaze drifted to the curve of a river on one of the coins above it. "Oblivion," she said. Then she traced a crack in the broken disk with one finger and one of the lines of the star with another. "Cycle. Rebirth." She traced another wave.

The curve of a mountain. "It's the rise and fall of a universe," she realized. She touched the star. "Creation." Then she moved her hand down, brushing her fingertips over each coin in turn. "Birth. Growth. An apex. Then it breaks. It crumbles. Melts." She laid her whole hand against the waves beneath the coins. "Then it sinks into the Oblivion with all the other dead things."

Piper felt a shiver. "And that's what's going to happen to *our* world?"

"It's not our world," said Seph as she dragged her fingertips through those chopping waves, her eyes distant, thoughtful. "Ours died a long, long time ago. We're just staying here until it's time to move on again."

"It's still *our* world," muttered Piper. "It's the only one any of us have ever known." It seemed wrong that it should just...*melt away* someday.

Seph studied the waves. She traced their peaks with her fingertips. She let her gaze dive deep into their depths. "Everything ends up in the Oblivion," she sighed. "It's the outermost edge of reality... It's the foundation every living thing sits on... But it's also *death*."

"You're creeping me out here, girlfriend," said Piper. "What's it say about the second Hand?"

Seph shook her head. She didn't see the Hands anywhere. "I see darkness. And I see...something about a...boat?" She shook her head. "Maybe that's not right. I don't think I know that word. But there's something about a..." She squinted up at the characters squeezed into the fine lines along the edge of one of the coins. "A weeping angel?" Again, she wasn't entirely sure if she was reading these right. This language didn't translate word for word. Going back and forth was slippery. She reached up and felt the shallow grooves of the star. "A stolen light…" she whispered. "Lost hope. Emptiness."

"This one's kind of depressing, isn't it?" said Piper. She was squinting up at it, trying to see what Seph was seeing, but no matter how hard she tried, it was just a picture.

Pictures!

"Violet wanted pictures," she remembered, pulling out her phone. "Not that she'll be able to read it, either…"

The flashes filled the room, blinding in the gloom. But Seph ignored her. She reached up and touched the coast of a tiny lake. Then the drooping edge of the melting coin. Then the smooth surface of the newborn world. "From the beginning, creation spawned destruction," she said as the meanings of the words flowed through her. "With life came poison. With light came darkness. A *flaw* in the design…" She turned and looked up at the star again. Absently, she dragged her fingers through the waves of the Oblivion. "Everything that begins ends and melts away, eventually flowing into Oblivion…" Her eyes slid back down the mural, back down into those obsidian waves. "But sometimes…sometimes things come *out* of the Oblivion. Sometimes death brings new life. *Different* life."

Piper lowered her phone and looked over at her.

"It was born from the first things that rotted," said Seph as she stared into those waves, into the endless characters carved into the tiny grooves that made up every line. "A darkness that was a contradiction to life in all its forms. The Great Enemy."

Piper stared at her. "What, like the devil?"

But Seph could only shake her head again. She didn't understand it. She just...*read* it. "And it wasn't alone," she went on. "Born from the rot and from the hatred of the Great Enemy were twelve..." She squinted up at the disk, trying to understand the word that was stuck in her head. "Twelve *somethings*," she said. "Not demons, I don't think. They're definitely different than the incubus. These were something...*more*. Twelve *terrible* somethings. Generals, maybe? No... That's not the word... But it's something like that, I think. Terrible followers of this 'Great Enemy' thing."

"So just...Satan and his twelve generals of hell? For the sake of moving on?"

Seph gave her head a little tilt. Sure. Why not. That was probably as close as she was going to get. She was pretty sure there were no words in any modern language to match the ones she was looking at.

The Great Enemy and his twelve generals. She wondered... Was this what the slime lady was talking about? Was this referring to Gispuknya and its black council? She did refer to it as her enemy, now that she thought about it. She called it the defiler.

"Don't tell me we have to take on all twelve of these guys," Piper pleaded. "It was hard enough just finding this stupid room."

Seph stared up at the disk. "It only mentions one of them." Her hands slid up from the Oblivion and back toward the star at the beginning of all things, from timeless death back to glorious birth, pausing momentarily at each of the coins along the way to let her fingertips dance through the five ages of the world in the time between. "He's the one. He's standing in front of us. Blocking our path."

"Travis?" asked Piper.

But Seph shook her head again. "*Tane.*"

The name gave Piper a shiver. "Tane? Wasn't that the name you read at the first marker? The one Ian said was *really* bad?"

"Janon Tane," recalled Seph. She stared at the name as her thoughts drifted back to what the slime lady told her about Gispuknya being the defiler. She even said that it crawled out of the ruins of dead worlds, which was essentially what the Oblivion was, according to this weird little slice of history.

Maybe *Tane* was Gispuknya.

"Okay," said Piper. She turned and looked around. The longer they were here, the more jittery she felt. They were just asking for another scare now. Any second another giant zombie worm was going to burst from the ground and start snapping its rotting jaws at them. "But seriously, *where's the vault?* It has to say *something.*"

"South," said Seph. She wasn't even sure where the word was. It just sort of jumped out at her from all the other commotion on the disk.

"Okay. That narrows it down *a little*, I guess."

"In the garden of dead children," read Seph, her eyes sliding back down the mural.

"Are you just making stuff up to scare me now?"

"Garden of dead children? Is that right? I can't…" She stood up on her tiptoes, trying to see the words better. "Is it a garden? Garden of…?"

Before she could work any more of it out, a terrible scream shattered the silence.

"That was Violet!" gasped Piper.

Chapter 48

The two of them ran as fast as they could go back down the narrow passageway, through the archway and back into the swamp chamber.

Corey and Violet hadn't moved. They were still on the steps on the far side of the room. But between here and there, dozens of oozing corpses were crawling out of the murky water and staggering toward them.

"*We didn't move!*" screamed Violet as soon as she caught sight of them. "*I swear!*"

These things weren't people. They never were. Like the ones that burst from the walls of that first chamber in Messing Knob, these weren't *human* zombies. Neither were they the same *kind* of alien zombies they encountered in Messing Knob. These were far hairier than both of them, for one thing, with mangy, matted fur covering most of their bodies. And they were far too tall—at least seven feet—and much too thin. They looked to Seph like rubber Halloween props that had been hung too close to a furnace and stretched out of shape. Except they weren't anything as unimpressive as rubber dummies. These things were well on their way to decomposing. Yellowed bones peeked out through festering gashes. Black fluids dripped from screaming jaws with too many rows of crooked teeth. Fat worms wriggled through their fur and dripped like blood from open wounds.

They were converging on the exit, rotten, skeletal hands reaching out for Corey as he backed up the steps, shielding Violet.

"*Get out of here!*" shouted Seph. "*Run! Get as far away from here as you can!*"

Immediately, the dead things turned their rotten faces toward her. She could see things squirming inside their huge, empty eye sockets and had to bite back a sudden urge to gag.

"*What about you?*" Violet shouted back at her.

"Don't worry about us! We're *supposed* to be here! They can't hurt us!"

"We can't just leave you here!"

"Corey, get her out of here! It's not safe for her!"

The look on Corey's face, even from across the room, was as clear as it was heart-wrenching. It was like watching someone cut off his own arm. He couldn't stand the thought of leaving them behind, but he also knew that he could do nothing about it. There were too many of them. What he *could* do, however, was take Violet and get her out of here. And she *did* just promise him that these monsters wouldn't harm them. He didn't want to take her word for it. He wanted to be certain. But more than that, he didn't want to risk anything happening to his best friend.

He turned around and grabbed her. He slung her over his shoulder, ignoring her protests, and then vanished up the steps with her.

Piper managed to appreciate the fact that it was both how she first laid eyes on him and how she last saw him. She prayed it wouldn't really be the *last* time. "Are they really going to be okay?"

"I think so," replied Seph. "If they keep running."

In fact, the hideous, undead things already seemed to have forgotten about them. All of them had turned around and were now slowly shuffling toward her and Piper.

"Persephone?" whispered Piper.

"Yes?"

"Are *we* really going to be okay?"

"The Keeper said his traps can't hurt us. It's what he said."

"I know that. But... *Are we really going to be okay?*"

Seph chewed her lower lip and glanced over at her, unable to hide her fear.

Piper made another of those pitiful squeaking noises in her throat as the undead monsters closed in around them.

They backed away from the approaching horde.

"The Keeper told us they're not supposed to hurt us," Seph said again. It was more to herself than to Piper. It was what she was told. The Keeper, himself, said it to her. It should be the absolute truth.

...shouldn't it?

"Do you think he told *them* that?" squeaked Piper.

Seph took another step backward. "It's okay, guys," she said, her voice trembling. "We're the seekers. The Keeper sent us?"

But they kept coming.

Maybe the Keeper forgot he was supposed to give them a hall pass?

One of them stumbled over its own dislocated foot and fell onto its face in front of Seph. Its rotten skull broke against the hard ground with a wet crack and a mass of chunky, black goo and wriggling worms and bugs spilled out and onto the toe of her shoe.

Seph screamed. It wasn't a little scream, either. It was a *big* scream. Loud. Piercing. The kind of scream that was probably going to leave her throat feeling scratchy for a while, assuming she lived long enough to suffer it.

And she kept screaming.

She turned to run back into the disk chamber, but the opening leading back to it was gone. In her panic, she seemed to have lost her ability to see it.

And there was absolutely no chance she was going to regain any kind of concentration.

She slammed her fists against the damp stone. "*No!*"

"*Persephone! They're not stopping! What do we do?*"

But Seph didn't know. They weren't supposed to hurt them. The Keeper said so. He promised!

She just kept telling herself that the Keeper told her so.

A skeletal hand reached through her hair and brushed the back of her neck.

Again, she screamed. Even louder than before.

Piper wanted to scream, too, but her voice had failed her again. All that seemed to escape the black hole of terror that had formed at the bottom of her throat were more of those pitiful squeaks.

She pressed her back against the wall as one of the gangly corpses reached out for her with its rotting hand. She turned her head and squeezed her eyes closed.

She felt the cold, wet tips of the thing's fingers slide down her cheek.

Now she found her voice.

Their screams filled the chamber.

This was when the universe was supposed to save them. This was when everything was supposed to suddenly be okay. This was when the black-eyed children ran away. This was when Ian appeared in the nick of time and threw open a door. This was when the exit finally revealed itself and let them slip away under the monsters' noses.

But that wasn't happening this time.

Bony hands closed around their necks and squeezed. The dead pulled at their hair and clothes. They clawed at the exposed flesh of their arms and legs. Rotten fingers groped at their faces in search of eyes to gouge.

This wasn't just terror. This was pain. Festering claws cut into them, tearing their flesh and drawing white-hot streaks of agony across Seph's shoulder and down Piper's arm. The back of Seph's thigh. Piper's cheek.

These weren't even the kinds of screams they used in horror movies. These were far worse. Their entire bodies shook with the force of these screams. They shrieked and howled. They thrashed against the stone wall, lost in utter, abject terror.

It seemed to go on and on.

And when death finally came for them, it came in the form of a searing-hot light that enveloped them, swallowing them whole into a silent darkness.

Chapter 49

Death wasn't as nice as Seph hoped it would be. She didn't find herself floating amongst the clouds. There was no warm sun beating down on her skin. No cool breeze. No angels to greet her. And worst of all, her dad wasn't here. He should be waiting to take her into his strong arms again and walk with her into whatever paradise came next.

Maybe she wasn't a good enough person to get into heaven. Because this certainly didn't feel like heaven. It was cold. It was dark. It was dank. And it reeked of swamp water, rotten flesh and burnt hair.

And then there was the pain.

Why didn't the pain go away?

Her shoulders and arms and the backs of her legs were burning where those things clawed her. And her throat felt as if she'd been eating sandpaper.

"Come on! Get up!"

Daddy?

"Hurry!"

No… Again, not her dad. Someone else. Someone familiar, though…

"Persephone...?"

That was Piper... Piper was the only one who called her Persephone...

Piper!

She opened her eyes to see Piper kneeling over her. There were tears streaming down her face, along with blood from three shallow, but very painful-looking claw marks on one cheek. "Pep...?"

Ian was standing over them, his crisp, white shirt smeared with mud and soot. It was *his* voice that she heard rushing them.

"*Oh my gosh!*" sobbed Piper. "*I thought you were—*" Her voice cut out before she could finish. She clutched at her raw throat and coughed.

"What happened?" mumbled Seph. She pushed herself up onto her hands and looked out at the weirdly silent chamber, only to find herself nose-to-nose with the charred face of a screaming corpse.

She screamed a scream that felt like broken glass in her throat and sat bolt upright.

"It's okay," said Ian as he helped Piper to her feet. "They're done."

And indeed they were. It looked like a bomb had gone off. There were charred bits and pieces of those weird, furry corpses littering the walkway and floating in the water. Were they really dead this time? Like, *for good* dead?

"But we can't stay here," warned Ian. "There'll be more." He held out his hand to Seph, who accepted it and let him help her to her feet. Her legs barely held her weight. Her knees wobbled beneath her. Her whole body was shaking.

She looked over at Piper again. There were more bleeding claw marks on the side of her neck and on her arms and legs. She didn't have to find a mirror to see that her own back side looked the same. The wounds were shallow, but they still burned.

"Come on," urged Ian. "Stay behind me." He turned and headed toward the steps.

Seph and Piper scooped up their dropped flashlights, then took hold of each other and followed after him. Neither of them seemed to have the strength to even ask him what had happened.

"Thank God I showed up in time," he said. "I don't understand what happened. The Keeper's traps aren't supposed to turn on the seekers. Those things should've ignored you."

"Well, they didn't," grumbled Seph, her voice hoarse from all her screaming. Just like the one at Sukmukwe that he insisted couldn't hurt them. She didn't think that thing looked harmless.

"Something must've corrupted them," he reasoned as he started up the stairs. "Scrambled their programming, so to speak. It's the only explanation. Hold up a second."

They peered past him to see a dark shape crawling down the steps toward them.

There were more of those freakish zombies up here?

Piper didn't panic at the sight. Ian was here. He had this. Instead, her first thought was that she hoped Violet and Corey didn't run into any more monsters on their way out of the marsh.

Seph watched as Ian's body rippled. That familiar darkness spread across his arms. His muscles went rigid. Then a fireball erupted from his mouth like dragon's breath, incinerating the thing on the steps.

She supposed she knew now what had torched all the ones in the chamber at the bottom of the steps. It also explained that burning flash of light she saw just before she lost consciousness. Ian's demonic powers also included some kind of hellfire breath, it seemed.

Ian continued up the steps as if nothing had happened. "We don't have a lot of time. We have to get you back to your truck. I hope you found what you needed down there."

Seph glanced at Piper. "I don't know," she said. "It's all so confusing."

"Tell me what you know. I'll try my best to help."

As they climbed the steps after him, careful not to step on the smoking remains of the crawling zombie, Seph tried to remember everything she read on the surface of the disk. "Something about Oblivion," she recalled. "And the cycle of the universe. Creation and ruin. How everything goes back to Oblivion in the end."

"I'm familiar with the concept of Oblivion," said Ian, clearly impatient. "What else did you find?"

"Stuff about darkness. Lost hope and emptiness. A stolen light."

"Uh huh." He blasted another of those strange fireballs up the steps, startling another scream out of Piper. "Sorry. Go on."

Seph shook her head, distracted. "I saw the name Tane again."

"Best not to say it aloud too much. Maybe just superstition, but let's not push our luck, okay?"

"Is he really that dangerous?" asked Piper.

"You have no idea."

Janon Tane… It wasn't just the way Ian talked about him. Something about the very *name* gave her a shiver. "Is it true that he's just one of twelve?"

Ian glanced back at her, a strange tightness in his expression, as if just speaking of them could bring doom down upon their heads at any moment. "The Twelve Teeth of the Great Enemy," he confirmed. "His twelve physical forms. His twelve bodies. They say any one of them possesses the power to tear this world in half at any given time."

"My gosh…" sighed Piper.

"Indeed."

Teeth? Physical bodies? Seph nodded. Yes. That sounded like what the disk was trying to tell her. She just didn't know how to translate the word used in that ancient language.

"What else did you see?" pressed Ian.

"Something about…a garden of dead children?"

This seemed to baffle him. "Garden of…?"

"I couldn't really read it. It might be something different."

"Hmm…"

"Oh, and something about a weeping angel."

"Weeping angel?"

"That could be wrong, too, actually. Some things don't translate well."

"Weeping angel…" breathed Ian. Then he opened his mouth and belched another blast of fire ahead of them.

A smoking lump of something came rolling down the steps, forcing them to press their backs against the wall to let it pass.

Piper watched it go for a moment, barely able to comprehend

the horror or the absurdity of it all.

"I think I understand," said Ian as he continued up toward the top of the pyramid. "When you say, 'garden of dead children'…could 'garden' maybe refer to…something like a park?"

"I don't know. Maybe. Garden was as close as I could get. I didn't know the word."

"Understandable. A lot of that stuff predates *all* known languages in this world. But I've been around a while, and there's a place I used to know of, ages ago, that was a sort of…*playground*."

Playground? Yes, that sounded similar to what the disk said.

"Ancient races used to call them 'whisper people' or 'little souls'."

"Little souls…?"

"That might be what you thought was 'dead children'."

She nodded. She couldn't quite remember what it said now, but it *did* have a similar sort of feel about it. "You might be right."

"I'm pretty sure that's where you'll find what you're looking for."

"Okay," said Seph. "So, where is this…*'playground of little souls'*, then?"

"In Tennessee. Near Horn, Tennessee, to be exact."

Seph stared at him. All the way in Tennessee?

"I'd leave right away if I were you," he said as he climbed up out of the pyramid and looked around.

Seph and Piper stepped up behind him.

The swamp was alive with undead things. They were climbing up out of the marsh and converging on the entrance to the disk chamber.

"Unless you'd like to hang around here a while longer," he added.

"No thank you," squeaked Piper.

"Didn't think so." He made his way down the side of the hill, casually ripped the furry head off the nearest zombie and then stopped and looked around. "Come on," he said. "I'll get you to your truck."

But he was going to do no such thing. As soon as the words were out of his mouth, the revenant launched itself out of the muddy water and slammed into him, knocking him over.

MURDER!

Seph and Piper both screamed.

The monster hadn't fared very well today. Seph saw it clearly in the beam of her flashlight as Ian turned and launched himself at it. Its torso was in tatters and its face had been mangled. It was missing one of its ghoulish, yellow eyes and its jaw had been horribly dislocated.

What kind of hellish determination could make *anything* keep fighting after taking such a beating.

"Get out of here!" shouted Ian. "I'll hold it off as long as I can."

Piper didn't need to be told twice. "Come on!" she shouted. She yanked on Seph's hand, pulling her down the hill and to the water's edge.

But as they approached, Seph saw something slither out of the grass and into the water ahead of them. She froze. She dug her heels into the ground, her wide, terrified eyes fixed on that awful, churning muck. "*No!*"

"Come on!" Piper shouted. "There's no time!"

She was right. There was no time. And they couldn't possibly stay here. Only death awaited them here. They were going to be surrounded soon. But she couldn't do it. There were *things* in that water. She shook her head. "I need a second!"

"We don't have a second!"

"*I can't!*"

"Persephone! There is *literally* a horde of zombies chasing you! Put on your big girl pants and *get in the fucking water!*"

Piper hardly ever swore. Seph was so startled by the outburst that she wasn't ready when she grabbed her by the arm and yanked her into the water.

It wasn't a graceful crossing. She screamed and cried and thrashed. But she screamed and cried and thrashed in the general direction they needed to go. And when she crawled out onto dry land again, she was barely on her feet before Piper was dragging her between the two trees and out of the starless swamp.

Chapter 50

Returning to the marsh, they were greeted by the welcome sight of a sky full of stars and the parking lot lights in the distance. But Seph found it difficult to appreciate such things while her skin crawled and the foul stench of swamp water still lingered in her nose.

"Come on," urged Piper, pulling her along by the hand.

Seph moaned and whined, but she went back into the water willingly enough. She was already wet, after all, which somehow made it slightly less awful. But *only* slightly. And the sooner she got this ordeal over with the sooner they could leave this bug-ridden town and never come back.

"Quit complaining," grumbled Piper. "At least it's *warm*."

"Oh yeah. Perfect temperature for *parasites*."

"Oh my gosh, *stop*." She looked back to make sure nothing was following from the swamp on the other side of the portal between the two trees, but the trees were gone. There was nothing in that direction but marsh grass and lightning bugs as far as she could see.

Maybe the Keeper's monsters were confined to that other

world. That would be a nice bit of luck.

"Are there water snakes in Illinois?" asked Seph.

"No."

"Are you sure?"

"Yes." The truth was that she had no idea whether there were or not. It wasn't something she'd ever thought to look up. But Seph didn't need to know that.

"I bet there's *something* nasty in here."

"We're halfway there. Just don't think about it."

"I can't help it. There's probably bug larva and eels and all sorts of—*oh god!*"

Piper jumped and looked around, expecting to find another of those zombie things lumbering after them. "*What?*"

Seph squealed with disgust. "*What if there're leeches?*"

Piper threw back her head. "*Auuuuugh!*" Then she slapped her hand over her mouth. "Oh god! I just made the Meg noise! You made me make the Meg noise! I *hate* the Meg noise!"

Seph rushed ahead, desperate to get out of the nasty water that she was suddenly quite certain was infested with billions of blood-sucking leeches that were probably already sinking their teeth into her flesh and feasting on her fluids. "Those dead things scratched me!" she whined. "Open wounds and swamp water! God, I'm like *walking chum!*"

"I got scratched up, too, you know! You don't see *me* acting like a baby!"

Seph climbed out of the water and onto the wooden walkway. Immediately, she began searching herself with the flashlight, wiping at every dead leaf and blade of grass that had stuck to her legs, convinced that at least one of them was going to be a squirming, pulsating leech.

"You know, we almost *died* back there," grumbled Piper as she climbed out of the water and stood over her, dripping. "You'd think that'd put this bug thing of yours a little more in perspective."

"I can't help it!"

"Were you really going to stand there like an idiot and let those things attack you again instead of just getting in the water?"

"Back off!" snapped Seph. "Go gnaw on a bone or something!"

Piper made a high-pitched gasping noise. "*Rude!*"

Seph glared at her. She hated the way her body was trembling. The way the tears kept welling up in her eyes. She hated being this *weak*. But she couldn't help it.

"I probably just saved your life back there!" Piper reminded her. "So you're *welcome*, I guess!"

"I didn't ask you to," Seph murmured. She couldn't even look her in the eye right now. She stared off into the marsh behind her. "So just drop it. Leave me…" She trailed off as she realized that something was over there. "…alone…" She lifted her flashlight and pointed it out over the water. "Who's that?"

Piper felt the hair on the back of her neck stand up. She turned around, expecting to see another of those stretched-out zombie things. Instead, there was the distinct silhouette of a woman standing in the churning water, her features buried in shadows. "Hello?"

The woman didn't move. She just sort of…*sank* straight down into the water and vanished.

"Okay that was freaky," whimpered Piper. "Even by swamp zombie standards."

Before Seph could agree with her, a long, skeletal hand shot out of the water and snatched at her foot. She screamed and jumped to her feet.

Piper grabbed her by the hand and they backed away from the water's edge.

"*Why is it still happening?*" shrieked Seph.

"Hurry!"

They ran for the parking lot. But all around them the marsh was coming alive. They could hear things splashing in the water. And as their flashlight beams bounced around in front of them in frantic jerks, they caught quick, unsettling glimpses of tall, dead things moving around in the darkness, stumbling toward the walkway, closing in around them.

The parking lot lights looked so small and far away. And the walkway wasn't even taking them toward those distant beacons of safety! They were going around them!

Rotting hands reached through the railings at them as they passed, snatching at them.

Piper was screaming again. She wasn't sure how much more of this her poor heart could stand.

The path diverged up ahead. Seph didn't try to remember which way they came. She just picked the one that promised to take them closer to those too-distant lights.

But it was also the path with a section that crossed over a dry patch of marsh and didn't have any guard rails.

Dead, hairy things were closing in from either side, forcing them to weave around them, dodging their groping arms.

The parking lot lights were getting closer, but far too slowly. And every time one of them shined her flashlight out over the marsh, there were more and more of these shaggy, alien corpses stumbling toward them.

It didn't make sense. All the Keeper's other traps didn't keep stalking them this long. Ian said they must have been corrupted. But how? Why? And by what?

Was it Gispuknya? Did the grotesque bug god do this to stop them from reuniting the Hands of the Architects? To stop the rebuilding of the universe?

If the flickering men and the black-eyed children were sent by Gispuknya, then it made sense that this shadow woman creature was its work as well. Didn't it?

Ahead of them, the pathway continued out over another stretch of water. There were railings on either side of it again there, and already Seph could see that several of the dead freaks were having trouble wrapping their rotting brains around how to get past this deceptive barrier. Several of them were reaching between the railings, groping blindly at nothing. One walked into it and then stumbled backward, lost its balance and fell into the water.

Maybe it was just wishful thinking, but it seemed like these things were getting stupider the farther they were from the second marker. The ones in the swamp chamber had moved fairly slowly, but with a definite and terrifying sort of purpose. The ones out here seemed to be drawn toward them, as if they could sense them, but their awkward movements made them look blind. Even when they came close enough to grab at them, the motion was clumsy and easy to avoid.

Or maybe she was just trying really hard to find a bright side to this apocalyptic nightmare she'd found herself in.

The walkway diverged ahead of them again, and again Seph steered Piper toward the one that seemed to go in the direction closest to the parking lot lights.

But a moment later, they found their path blocked.

The shadow woman was there. She stood before them, bathed in impossibly deep shadows that defied their lights. She was tall and slender, with long, wet hair. Black water dripped onto the boards around her feet, collecting into an inky pool. If she wore any clothes, they clung to her body like a second skin, because they made no shape around the silhouette of her lean form. She stood with her head bowed, her shoulders slumped, her dripping hands limp at her sides, as if she, too, were another of the Keepers corpses come to life.

Seph backed away, pulling Piper along with her. "Uh-uh!" she said. "I think I've seen this movie!"

They raced back to the last fork in the path and ran the other way instead.

The Keeper's AWOL zombies were here, too. Several of them were clumsily climbing through the railing, their long, bony hands reaching out for them as they ran past.

"*I don't want to do this anymore!*" shrieked Piper.

Ahead of them, one of the zombies had made it all the way through the wooden railing, only to collapse into a wet, festering pile on the planks, where it seemed to be having trouble righting itself. It could do nothing but twist its rotten neck around and slap feebly at them as they skirted past it.

A little farther, they encountered one that had found its way onto the walkway *and* onto its feet. It was staggering toward them, its arms open, as if it wanted to give them a big hug.

Not being much into sports, Seph didn't often wish she had a baseball bat, but she did now. Actually, any stick would do. Anything long enough to smack these gross things out of her way without her having to touch their matted, worm-ridden hides. But she didn't have a stick, so she simply went around the foul thing as it lumbered past her, groping blindly at the space twelve inches above her head.

But their luck wouldn't hold out forever. They might be slow and stupid, but there were more of them rising from the marsh with each passing second. Soon there were too many hands reaching through the railings to count.

"*I'm sorry I called you a big baby!*" shouted Piper. "*I know you can't help it! I didn't mean it!*"

"Can we talk about this later?"

"*I really hope so!*"

They turned at the next fork in the path and ran out over a deeper stretch of water, where the Keeper's zombies couldn't reach. The groping hands vanished.

But before they had a chance to feel any sense of relief, they found their path blocked again.

Out of the gloom ahead of them walked the shadow woman, her bare feet squelching against the wooden planks, that foul, black water dripping off her like liquid shadows.

They screamed and stumbled to a stop.

"She's not going to let us out of here!" gasped Seph.

Piper turned to run back the other way, but the Keeper's hairy zombies were gathering there, blocking them in.

They were trapped again.

Seph made one of Piper's embarrassing squeaking noises in her throat.

Where the hell was Ian? Was he still fighting with the revenant? Shouldn't he be here by now?

Piper turned and looked at the shadow woman. Now that she was thinking about it, she realized that she could hear that strange static noise coming from it. The same one she heard when the black-eyed children, the runner and the flickering men appeared. But it seemed much softer this time. More distant. The murmuring voice inside it was less a mutter than an evil hiss.

It was no wonder she didn't hear it before. It was hidden under all the noises of the marsh that accosted her human ears and cluttered her mind.

Did this freaky shadow woman do that on purpose, she wondered. Did she use Fibbel Marsh to hide from her spirit ears? It was a frightening thought. She barely understood how these things worked, herself. That an enemy understood it well enough to know how to fool them was more than a little unsettling.

She wasn't sure why, but she felt like this thing was far more dangerous than the others. It was stronger somehow.

Without thinking about it, she reached up and touched the pendant Annalisa gave her.

She'd forgotten about it for a while in all this chaos. But now that she remembered it, she found that it was strangely comforting, even in this horrible situation.

A little, anyway. She was still scared out of her mind right now. But somehow she managed to tell herself that there had to be a way out of this. She just had to look for it.

"*I'm sorry I told you to go gnaw on a bone!*" cried Seph. "*I was just really embarrassed about how stupid I was being!*"

"Let's talk about it later," said Piper as she shined her light out over the water, toward the parking lot. "Over there!" There was another walkway out there. She could just make it out in the gloom. "Come on!" Without hesitating, she climbed over the railing and jumped down into the water.

Seph stared after her for a moment, horrified at the idea of going back into that water, especially with those zombies paddling around out there. But the ones closing in from behind her, plus the horror movie chick in front of her made the decision for her. She slipped between the boards of the railing and dropped gracelessly into the water with a scream.

It was deeper than she expected it to be.

"This way!" said Piper, grabbing at her arm and pulling her along.

Already things were moving around them. Dark shapes churned beneath the surface of the water, slowly closing in from all around them.

Something grabbed Seph's ankle. She screamed and tried to kick herself free, but it wouldn't let go. "*Help me!*" she shrieked.

Piper pulled on her arm, digging her feet into the mud, trying to find leverage.

They were still moving forward, but the thing in the water was slowing them down. And other things were closing in on them.

Seph turned and kicked the arm attached to the hand. Still, it wouldn't release her. She kicked it again. And again. With the fourth kick, the stupid thing finally let go. "Move!" she screamed, rushing forward before the monster could grab her again.

The very earth seemed to fight them. The mud and weeds clawed at their feet and ankles, trying to drag them down.

…just like in that queer vision in the cellar of the Old Avelby Inn, Seph realized.

Something grabbed at Piper's arm and she screamed and jerked away.

Something tugged on Seph's hair.

Something pulled the tail of Piper's shirt.

But somehow they made it to the other side and climbed up onto the other walkway.

The parking lot was much closer now. They could make out the individual lights that shined down on it. And even better, this new walkway seemed to point straight to it, promising to take them there.

"Keep moving!" gasped Piper as she took off running again.

Seph needed no further encouragement. She raced along behind her. She was crying again, but she couldn't remember when she started. She wiped at her eyes with the back of her hand and tried to get control of herself. She could cry later. Right now she had to keep her eyes peeled for long, hairy zombies and soggy nightmare women.

They seemed to have lost the zombies for a moment. But when she shined her light out over the marsh to her right, she caught a distinct glimpse of a shadowy head and shoulders sinking into the water.

Her heart seriously wasn't going to take much more of this.

They were much closer now. They could see the truck sitting under the parking lot lights.

Violet's Jeep was there too, right where they left it.

Where were Violet and Corey? Did they make it back? Piper's heart leaped as she imagined them climbing out of the pyramid only to be beset by a horde of clawing, undead things and dragged down beneath the murky surface.

A horrible vision passed through her head: Violet's wide, dead eyes staring up through the murky, black water as she and Seph stumbled right over the top of her, utterly unaware.

The walkway split again up ahead. They could go left or they could go right. The parking lot, and sweet escape, lay straight ahead, beyond a wide stretch of grassy marsh and twinkling fireflies.

They were going to have to go around.

But even as they approached the fork in the path, they saw her. The shadow woman. She was standing in the water between them and the parking lot, staring back at them, a nightmare shadow waist-deep in the muck.

She lifted her arms out to her sides. More shadows dripped from her fingertips.

The water began to churn around them.

More of those freaky zombies rose from the murk.

Beneath their feet, something began to bang on the underside of the planks.

Both of them understood the message she was sending them.

This was her marsh now.

And they were never leaving.

Chapter 51

They were close enough to the parking lot for the lights to illuminate much of the little patch of marsh before them. The walkway made a circle around it. It didn't matter which way they went. So Seph chose left. She grabbed Piper by the hand and the two of them took off.

The shadow woman plunged back into the water and vanished.

Skeletal forms rose up on either side of the walkway and climbed through the railings, reaching out for them as they ran.

The banging under the planks grew louder.

(It was safe to say at this point that this swamp woman was probably the one who reprogrammed the Keeper's trap.)

"Hurry!" screamed Seph.

"I *am* hurrying!" She glanced to her left, keeping an eye on a zombie that had managed to wriggle through the boards and was now crawling toward her, and she caught a glimpse of the creepy woman's black form peering back at her beneath the railing.

Seph saw her a moment later, standing behind two shuffling forms on the other side of the walkway.

Gispuknya, she thought, remembering the slime lady's words. *The defiler.*

The disk mentioned a Great Enemy and its twelve teeth. Was *this* one of the twelve? Was this woman *Janon Tane*?

She'd thought Tane was a man...but Tane wasn't human. It was a creature born from the Oblivion. Perhaps it was both man *and* woman. Or neither.

Or maybe this was one of the other eleven manifestations of the Great Enemy. She supposed it didn't matter. Gispuknya's goal was to end the rebuilding of worlds. And it would do that by destroying the two of them before they could retrieve the other two Hands. They had to get out of here.

It wasn't much farther. They could see the last stretch of walkway ahead of them, waiting to take them back to the parking lot and far away from this nightmare place.

But something grabbed her ankle and tripped her. She screamed and fell. She felt Piper's hand slip out of her grip. Her body slammed against the rough planks.

"*Persephone!*"

Seph turned and kicked at the hand that held her, but the thing was strong. And it was already crawling onto her, its gaping, worm-riddled face hovering over her as its other hand closed on her thigh, its skeleton claws digging into her soft flesh.

She screamed.

Piper tried to run back, but bony hands closed around her arms, pulling her backward. She struggled to free herself, but the monster was too strong. And it wasn't alone. Another hand closed around her ankle. Another seized her hair.

Cold, slimy hands slid under her shirt, clawing at her belly.

Two more of the shaggy ghouls crawled across the planks and reached out for Seph.

Behind them, the dripping shadow woman approached from the gloom.

Piper cried out for help, hoping that perhaps Ian might still be able to hear her.

It was the only thing left that she could think to do.

Then she heard something.

Not with her spirit ears. It came through the noises of the marsh. A long, drawn-out wail that she couldn't quite identify. A scream? No...more of a yell. It grew louder and louder.

"AAAAAAAAAAAAAAAAAAAAAAAAAAAH!"

Something collided with her, knocking her onto her knees and sending the zombies tumbling away.

The shadow woman sank through the cracks between the planks, as if she were *made* of black water, and vanished again.

Then Corey was there. He was still yelling. It seemed to be some kind of battle cry, because he wasn't yelling in fear. He was *fighting*. He grabbed one of the zombies from behind and shoved it toward the railing, sending it careening over and into the water. Then he landed a kick to the face of one of the ones holding Seph down and sent the thing's head bouncing down the walkway. "Come on!" he shouted, seizing Seph beneath her arms and dragging her backward.

The remaining zombies held onto her for a moment, dragged along with her, their legs kicking uselessly at the planks until she was able to shake them off.

Corey helped her to her feet, then turned and punched another of the monsters in the face. It staggered backward and then toppled over the rail and into the water with the other one.

Piper shoved another out of her way and then grabbed Seph's hand and took off running again.

Corey sent another sprawling onto its back and then followed them. They made it almost to the parking lot before the shadow woman sprang up in front of them again.

This time, she wasn't just standing there all corpse-like. Her arms were raised. Her, slender fingers curled into dripping claws, her head lifted. Even her long, dripping hair rose up.

The marsh water churned. Great tendrils of foul, black water curled up into the air and closed in around them.

Only Piper heard the terrible hiss that rolled over them, but each of them felt the chill that rolled through the humid air.

Then there was a thunderous roar of an engine and a blinding light washed over the shadow woman.

That staticky hiss became a shriek of surprise and the monster and all her tendrils of living water came splashing down again.

Violet leaned out of the window of her Jeep and yelled for them to run.

They didn't hesitate.

Corey climbed into the Jeep. Seph and Piper jumped into the truck.

Both vehicles peeled out of the parking lot fast enough to leave tracks on the asphalt. Seph's dad wouldn't have approved of such careless driving, but she thought he might forgive her just this once, considering the circumstances.

As Violet's headlights loomed in her rearview mirror, Piper's phone rang. She pulled it out of her pocket, thankful that she'd had the good sense to buy a waterproof case for it, and put it on speaker. "Violet?"

"Are you guys okay?"

Piper glanced over at Seph. She looked appropriately freaked out after all that had just happened, but overall unharmed, she thought. "I think so."

"What the hell *was* all that? I've seen some freaky things, but you guys take the prize!"

"Thanks," said Seph, her eyes still filled with panic. "We do try to be special."

"It's a seriously long story," said Piper. "Can we tell you about it later."

"If you promise not to get yourselves killed before then."

"We'll do our best," she promised.

"Did you at least find what you were looking for down there?"

Piper looked over at Seph. "Yeah, did we?"

"I hope so," replied Seph. "I mean, we have a destination. That's pretty much what we were looking for, right?"

She nodded. "What was it called? Horn?"

"Horn," confirmed Seph. "In Tennessee."

"You're going to Tennessee?" asked Violet.

"Looks like it," said Piper.

"Should we come with you?"

Piper flashed back to that image she had of Violet's dead eyes staring up from beneath the surface of the marsh water and shivered. "No," she said. "It's too dangerous for you guys. We don't know what we might find in Tennessee, but we don't want you guys getting hurt."

"We have to do this on our own," agreed Seph.

Violet was silent for a moment as she considered this. "That *was* pretty freaky," she admitted. "I'm not going to lie."

"I got to fight zombies," said Corey from somewhere in the background. He didn't sound freaked out at all. If anything, he sounded quite pleased with himself.

"But you guys needed us back there," Violet reminded them, ignoring him.

"Yeah, but you also might've been the ones who set off the trap?" suggested Piper.

"I promise, we never moved from that spot!"

"Still…" said Piper.

"Maybe we can call you if we need you?" offered Seph.

Violet considered this for a few seconds. "Sure," she agreed. "I guess that's fair. We've still got a few things we need to do here in Avelby. But you guys be careful."

"We'll do our best," she promised.

"Okay," said Violet. "You guys stay in touch. If you ever need us for anything, just give me a call."

"Sure thing," said Piper. "And thank you! Both of you."

She disconnected the call and looked over at Seph again. "Are you okay?"

Seph shook her head. "No. You?"

"No."

"That's probably a good thing. If were okay after that I think we'd need serious psychological help."

"I think we do anyway," said Piper. "If we're actually going to go to Tennessee after that."

Seph laughed. It was short and mostly humorless. But it was a laugh. "It's not like we have a choice," she reminded her.

"Yeah."

Forget the cycle of the worlds. Forget Gispuknya. Forget the whole rest of the world. They never did any of this for any of that anyway.

This was the only way to save Seph's mom.

Violet's headlights turned off the road behind them and Piper set her phone to give her directions to Horn, Tennessee.

Chapter 52

It took about ten hours to reach Horn. Piper took the first aid kit from the glovebox and disinfected all of the scratches the Keeper's traitorous zombies had left on her. Then she did the same for Seph's shoulder and right arm while she drove out of the city and began putting miles between them and Avelby's many horrors.

They didn't talk much. Neither of them felt like chatting. They'd almost died back there, after all. The Keeper's trap that was supposed to protect the disk chamber from intruders backfired and turned on the very people it was supposed to be protecting the disk *for*.

There was something about that part of it all, in particular, that made this whole thing feel doomed. How were they supposed to succeed when the Keeper, himself, couldn't maintain control?

What horrors were they going to find when they arrived in Horn at the actual vault?

They stopped for gas a few towns south, where Seph took the time to let Piper clean the scratches on the backs of her legs and her left arm. There were also some on her lower back, where her shirt had ridden up.

They both changed their soggy shoes and socks for the sandals they were wearing when they first arrived in town and Seph made a quick change back into her dry skirt and blouse. Then she took the first shift driving while Piper slept.

But she didn't sleep well. She kept swimming in and out of dreams about dead things with too much hair and too little flesh clawing her skin and dragging her into a bubbling pit of quicksand. She awoke around daybreak, feeling only slightly less tired than she did when she went to sleep.

They made a quick stop for breakfast and gassed up the pickup again, just in case. Then they traded places and Piper took a turn at the wheel while Seph spent most of the remaining morning trying to find some fragments of sleep hidden amongst her own nightmares of giant bugs, slime women and swamp zombies.

Piper called in to work and told her store manager, Lindsey, that she'd woken up with a nasty stomach virus. Not too surprisingly, Lindsey insisted that she and her germs stay at home and told her to just let her know when she felt better.

Seph tried to call her mother, too, once it was late enough that she should be up and about, but it kept going to voice mail. If Buffy had ever found her missing cell phone, she wasn't answering it. And she couldn't help feeling anxious about it. She hoped she was okay.

Meanwhile, the roads stretched on and on before them, ever deeper into the forests of Tennessee.

There turned out to be no signs leading to Horn. Siri told them where to get off the interstate. She told them which roads to turn onto and how far to drive before the next turn, seemingly sure of herself that there *was* a Horn and that she knew how to get them there. But there was not a road sign or billboard indicating the existence of such a place until Piper finally discovered the city limit sign at a little past ten o'clock that morning on a winding, country road, nearly hidden behind a clump of low-hanging branches just around a tight curve.

"We're here," she said.

Seph sat up and looked around. "We're where?" she asked. "Where's here?" Because there was nothing here. They were nowhere. There were only woods.

"Horn. I just passed the sign."

She took off her glasses and rubbed her eyes, then squinted out at the passing foliage. "Where?" she said again.

"This is it. We just passed the city limit sign."

"How can you have a city limit without a city?"

The only sign of civilization was the road itself and a handful of gravel driveways branching off into the woods.

"I'm just telling you what I saw."

They came around another curve in the road and found a pair of big, double-wide trailers parked in the middle of a large, overgrown yard cluttered with junk cars and sun-faded toys. Just beyond that was a four-way intersection, beyond which was a chain-link fence blocking entrance to an ugly water tower.

Piper stopped at the stop sign and examined her options. She could go left, right or straight. Or she could turn around and go back the other way.

"So what're we supposed to do?" asked Seph. This place was like Messing Knob, but even smaller. There wasn't even a convenience store they could stop at to ask awkward questions.

Piper glanced up at her rearview. No one was behind her. She had a little time to think. But thinking wasn't likely to provide any answers. She had no idea what they were even looking for in this place.

"I guess we just pick a direction and drive around? Hope something jumps out at us?"

"I guess so," said Piper. She lifted her toes off the brake pedal and started to go straight across. But as she nosed into the intersection, she pressed it down and stopped again. She cocked her head to one side, listening. Her eyes drifted to the road on the right.

"What is it?"

"I'm not sure."

Seph glanced up at her ears. They twitched around in every direction, but they seemed to keep returning to a point somewhere to the right. "Go with it," she said.

Piper spun the wheel and turned right.

After a few minutes, it became obvious that Horn wasn't hiding any tourist attractions out this way. The forest and hills closed in around them and they were back out in the middle of nowhere again. But Piper's ears remained perked. And Seph kept her eyes on Piper's ears.

Something had their attention.

"What do you hear?"

Piper shook her head. "I'm not sure. I can't really explain it."

"Well it *has* to be what we're looking for. There's nothing else here. So keep following it."

Several miles dragged on, taking them farther and farther from the non-existent town they thought they were coming here to visit.

Maybe whatever she was hearing wasn't what they were looking for. Maybe it was another distraction. Another lie.

The sensation in her head wasn't anything like a sound. Her brain didn't seem to recognize it that way. Instead, it was more of a *touch*. It was sort of like the sensation of something warm caressing her skin. An almost *fuzzy* sort of feeling. Like a warm kitten snoozing in her arms. It was... *nice*.

She pressed her foot down on the brake as an overgrown turnoff emerged from the endless forest.

It was coming from down there somewhere.

Carefully, she pulled Seph's truck off the paved road and began lumbering down the rain-washed trail.

Seph watched those ghostly ears as they pointed the way forward, validating Piper's decisions.

Then Piper's phone rang. She picked it up and glanced at the screen.

Meg again.

Sighing, she accepted the call and pressed it to her ear. "What?"

"Are you going to be home soon?"

"Probably not 'til tomorrow," she grumbled.

"What are you even *doing*? You've been gone forever."

Piper rolled her eyes. What did she even care? What happened to her being a rude bitch? "I'm helping Persephone with one of her projects for work. It was short notice and they were short staffed."

Seph was never not impressed by Piper's ability to do that.

"Ugh. Tell me they're at least paying you."

"I'm volunteering."

It was amazing to her how easy it was for Meg to make the *sound* of her eyes rolling. She didn't even know that was possible before she met her. "Suit yourself, I guess."

"I'm kind of busy right now. Did you want something?"

"Do you remember when we first moved into this apartment?"

"Yeah."

"Do you remember how we got the box springs for my bed up the stairs?"

Piper was trying to focus on the narrow road in front of them. "I don't know. You had your boyfriend at the time and his two buddies hauling all that stuff up, didn't you?"

"Oh yeah."

"My gosh, I don't even remember what their names were anymore."

"Yeah, me either," grumbled Meg, distracted.

Piper blinked. "Wait…why do you want to know how to get your box springs up the stairs?"

Seph looked over at her, surprised. "What?"

"No reason. Hey, bring home some Oreos, okay?"

"Meg."

"But not those ones with too much filling that Seph likes. The *good* ones. The thin ones."

"Meg, you can't move any more of your stuff into our apartment."

"There better not be any more of her crap there when we get home," snapped Seph.

"And not those stupid vanilla ones, either. Yuck."

"Are you even listening to me?"

"Have fun with your charity work. Bye."

"Meg!" She lowered the phone and looked at the screen, but she'd ended the call again. "Oh my gosh!"

"Maybe we should've brought her with us," said Seph. "We could've fed her to those zombies and gotten away before they realized she doesn't have any brains to eat."

"Tempting," grumbled Piper.

For the next twenty minutes, they lumbered deeper and deeper into the woods.

Seph was beginning to think that this was way too much like her drive to the abandoned farmhouse. And she wasn't eager to go through that sort of thing again. She supposed she could probably tolerate another slime lady encounter, but if she had to run through another spider-infested tunnel, she was going to be pissed.

Finally, the trail opened up and they found themselves looking onto a sunny clearing with an old hunting cabin and a little pond.

Piper parked the truck and stared through the windshield at the little structure. "That's it," she said. "That's where it's coming from. I'm sure of it."

Seph didn't respond. She was staring at the cabin, too. There was something about it that didn't seem right. It was like the feeling she got in the tunnel under Adderbell's. And like what she felt as soon as she set foot in Fibbel Marsh.

Whatever magic was at work in those places…it was here, too.

She slipped her feet back into her dirty new socks and shoes (because chances were good that something here was going to want

447

to chase them) and then opened the door and stepped out of the truck. The humid Tennessee air nearly took her breath away. But she barely noticed it. She barely even noticed the buzzing of mosquitos in the air. Her eyes remained fixed on the cabin.

Piper finished lacing her own shoes and then jumped out of the truck and handed Seph her keys. "So I totally just remembered that I didn't have my license that whole time I was driving."

"Oh yeah…" She'd forgotten about that, too.

"So…yay for not being in jail right now, I guess."

"Yeah."

Piper looked out at the little cabin. "Is this where the Hand is?"

"I don't know," said Seph. "But *something* must be here. Because there's something *really* messed up about that building."

She glanced around at the woods. "Shouldn't someone be here? I thought the vaults were all protected by people like Amethyst."

"Ian told us Amethyst never knew where the other hands are," recalled Seph.

"I know *Amethyst* isn't here," said Piper, annoyed. "I said people *like* Amethyst. Another vault guard. I mean, these're the *Hands of the Architects. Somebody* should be guarding them, right?"

From somewhere in the woods behind them came a loud crack, as if a large branch had just snapped. They turned, startled. Holding their breath, they both listened, expecting at any moment that something nightmarish and blood-thirsty would emerge to devour their still-beating hearts.

When nothing did, they exchanged a worried glance and

turned their attention back to the mysterious cabin.

Seph stared at it. For just a moment as she turned to face it again, it'd looked…*different*. She wasn't sure how it was different, exactly. It was only different for a fraction of a second, while her attention was somewhere else. But it was definitely different.

This place wasn't as it seemed.

She took a deep breath, steeling herself for whatever it was that awaited her in this place. Then she began to walk toward it, with Piper right behind her.

"It's a lot quieter here than in the swamp," noticed Piper.

It was. And it *should* have been quieter. There was less activity during the day in the woods than at night in a marsh. But it was *unnaturally* quiet here. She couldn't hear a single bird singing. No squirrels played in the trees. Only the bugs seemed to be stirring, and even they seemed unnaturally hushed.

Maybe it was the heat. Maybe all the forest creatures were snoozing in the shade somewhere.

Seph found herself glancing around at everything as she approached the cabin. Something was definitely wrong here. Everything looked different from the corners of her eyes, more menacing somehow. But when she turned to look directly at them, they looked perfectly ordinary and she couldn't seem to recall *why* they looked so wrong.

She was getting a really bad feeling deep in her gut.

Something was dreadfully wrong here. Something just beneath the surface.

And yet she also remembered the slime lady telling her to "find the quiet place" in that queer, dreamlike void. Was this the quiet place? Was this what she was talking about?

"What do you hear?" she asked.

Piper glanced over at her, a sick look on her face. That strangely warm sensation that lured her here had suddenly changed. Now it sounded *cold*. It made her shiver in spite of the sweltering humidity. "Something bad," she whispered.

Seph paused at the door and looked down at the stoop. "I really hate those bugs," she said, watching several of those creepy black beetles crawling over the old mat.

Piper looked down at their feet, confused. "What bugs?" she asked.

Seph looked up at her. "What?"

"I don't see any bugs," said Piper.

She stared at her for a moment. Then she looked down again.

Wheels began turning. The first time she saw those things was in Avelby. She saw them on the sidewalks and crawling in and out of the storm drains. They were on the ceiling of the tunnel that connected the two sides of Raindskenner Park. And they were all over those two otherworldly trees at Fibbel Marsh and on the pyramid steps.

She looked down again and stared at them.

The slime lady's voice oozed through her thoughts: *...you see what others can't...you know...deep inside...you've always known it was out there...it's why they frighten you so much...*

She never said that Gispuknya was a bug. It was just the awful image that came to mind when she described it as having crawled from the rotting ruins of dead worlds, like some godlike cockroach. But it was true.

Gispuknya was a bug. He was *everything* that was creepy and crawly in the world. And he was the reason she was so terrified of those things.

Because she'd always known.

And these things were a part of it.

"Seph?"

"I'm okay." She looked up at the doorknob. She stared at it. It was just an ordinary knob on an ordinary door, but all around it, at the very edge of her vision, this cabin was anything but ordinary. "Let's get this over with."

She reached out and realized that her hand was trembling.

Piper reached out and took hold of it. She gave her a reassuring squeeze. "Together," she promised.

Seph nodded. Then, with Piper still holding her hand, she closed her fingers around the knob and turned it.

Chapter 53

Seph opened her eyes and stared up at a ceiling dripping with cobwebs.

What just happened? Why was she on the floor? She was just outside the cabin, wasn't she? Just a moment ago?

Or *was* it just a moment ago?

Everything seemed so fuzzy. She remembered turning the doorknob and then…

Nothing. Then she was just *here*.

She sat up and looked around. She was lying on a dirty, hardwood floor in a strange and empty room. There was hot sunlight shining through dingy curtains onto dusty, antique-looking chairs…and nothing more. The rest of the room was utterly empty. There was only dust, cobwebs and a strange, pervasively eerie atmosphere.

"I think I missed something," said Piper from behind her.

Seph looked back at her, relieved to find that they were still together. For a moment, she was afraid that they'd been separated again.

"What happened?"

"I don't know," said Seph as she stood up. She was still taking in the strangeness of this place. "But I think we're inside the cabin. Or…whatever kind of *Twin Peaks* hell this is."

It was too big to be a cabin. Or, at least, too big to be the *same* cabin they saw from outside.

"How did we get in here, though? Did something attack us?"

She looked down at herself. There weren't any cuts or bruises that weren't already there when they drove up. "I don't think so."

Piper stood up and dusted herself off. "This place is making some really weird sounds. It's seriously creeping me out."

Seph glanced over at her. "Weird how?"

"It's kind of…*moaning*."

Seph shuddered. "Sorry I asked…" She turned and looked around at the room. There were two doors. One, she presumed, was the front door, through which she couldn't recall entering. The other either led out the back or to another room.

There was something seriously wrong with this place. And not just the part about it being bigger inside than outside. (That sort of thing didn't exactly impress her anymore.) It was the emptiness. There were no tables. There were no shelves or cabinets. No pictures hung on the walls. No clocks. No rugs. There weren't even any lamps. There was literally nothing in this room except the dingy curtains on the windows and those chairs with their backs pushed all the way against the walls.

There was nothing to do in this room but sit.

She looked around at the chairs. Carved wood. Dark red cushions. Tall backs. No arm rests. They looked stiff and uncomfortable.

453

It was a waiting room of some sort, she realized. And for some reason, an icy chill crept down the back of her neck at the thought.

She didn't have time to contemplate it, however, because at that moment she looked down to discover a big, black roach skittering between her shoes.

She yelped and jumped back.

"I don't understand this," said Piper, ignoring the outburst. "Where are we? What does this place have to do with the Hand?"

Seph straightened her glasses, made sure the nasty bug was crawling off in the other direction and then considered it for a moment. "Ian said we were supposed to go to Horn. He said that the garden of dead children was here."

"That's still really creepy," said Piper, hugging herself against a sudden chill in spite of the heat.

"I know. But remember, even though I can read the words on the disks, I can't always translate them to English. Some of the words don't exist in our language."

"Right." She remembered now. "He said 'garden of dead children' might mean 'playground of little souls'."

"Yeah."

"That's not a lot less creepy, actually."

"Not really, no," agreed Seph.

"So you think *this* is the playground of little souls?"

"Maybe. I don't know. I'm just repeating what Ian told us."

"What does it even mean? Who are the 'little souls'?"

Seph didn't know. But Ian said they were also called "whisper people," which also wasn't much of an improvement. She glanced at Piper, curious. "You don't think it was talking about your black-eyed-children, do you?"

Piper shuddered. "I sure hope not. I *really* don't ever want to see those little creeps again."

"Yeah, that doesn't make sense. The slime lady specifically said they belonged to Gispuknya."

"Are you sure that slime lady was on our side?" asked Piper. "She sounds as icky as those creepy kids."

"I'm not sure of anything," replied Seph. "But she said Gispuknya was her enemy, so I guess that makes her our friend. For now, at least," she added, remembering that she'd also admitted that she didn't take sides.

Piper crossed her arms and looked around the room. Then she pointed to the next door. "So we're going through there, right? I mean, that's pretty much all that's left at this point. We either go forward or go back. And we both know we can't go back."

Seph turned and stared at the door. She wasn't sure what would happen with the Hands if they just walked away. She assumed that they would simply stay in their vaults forever. Or at least until this world died and sank into the Oblivion. For sure, she supposed humanity would sink with it instead of continuing on. Or maybe not. Maybe they'd just find two more seekers to do the job. Or maybe the real word was "suckers." Either way, it didn't matter to them. The world wasn't going to die in their lifetime, after all.

But there was one thing she knew was certain: if they turned back now, her mother would die.

This was her only chance.

And she might as well get it over with.

She walked over, hesitated only long enough to take a calming breath, and grasped the knob in her hand.

Like before, neither of them had any recollection of actually opening the door or walking through it. But in the next instant, they found themselves standing on the other side of it, staring back at it.

"Uh…?" said Seph.

Both of them turned and looked around.

They were standing in a room that was entirely black. All of it. Floor, walls, ceiling, even the curtains hanging over the windows on either side of the room were black. The hot sunshine that passed through them seemed to get poisoned by them. It lay on the tar-colored wood in a faint, tilted rectangle like a dying animal, too weak to fight the darkness that held it down.

The room was long and narrow, almost a hallway. And at the far end of the room, barely illuminated by the mortally wounded rays passing through the last window, were nine chairs sitting side-by side.

And sitting in these chairs, barely visible in the room's bloated gloom, were nine shadowy figures, each with its back turned to them.

Nine is thrice three, you know, thought Seph, remembering the words of Faith, the Witch of the Three Lakes. "*Very* significant," she'd said.

Piper winced as the cabin's strange moaning suddenly became a screech inside her head.

…*arrived*… said a piercing, alien voice somewhere in the pain center of her brain.

...*finally*... said another voice.

...*too long*... said another.

She clutched at her ears, trying to block out the awful voices, but it was no good. She could still only cover her *human* ears.

Seph took hold of her arm. "Are you okay?"

"What is this?" groaned Piper.

Seph turned her gaze to the nine black figures lined up at the end of the room. This time, she knew the answer. "It's the black council."

Chapter 54

...finish it...

...quickly...

...no...

...been too long...

...savor it...

...yes, savor...

...no...

...better to do quickly...

Piper cringed at each word as it entered her mind. There was something terrible about these voices. And not just because they seemed to be debating over how quickly to kill them. The very sensation of the words inside her head were like tiny explosions of pure pain. These weren't human voices. They weren't even anything remotely similar to human voices.

She wasn't even sure they were actually speaking English. The meaning of the words seemed to come independently of the agonizing sensation that was the "sound" of them.

...children did well...

...reward them...

...yes, but after...

...after, yes...

...finish first...

"What's happening?" asked Seph.

Piper clutched at her head, grimacing. "Voices..." she grunted. "Hurt..."

"What're they saying?"

She glanced up at them. "Arguing...whether to kill us fast or slow."

And they weren't even bothering to turn around and look at them. All nine of them were just sitting there, with their backs turned to them, staring at an empty, black wall.

...not too fast...

...yes, slowly...

...savor...

Piper cried out and dropped to her knees. It was too much to take. Each word drove needles of pain deeper into her brain.

"Stop it!" shouted Seph. "You're hurting her!"

...stupid creature...

...disrespectful...

...grotesque...

...kill it quickly...

...yes, quickly...

...no...

...too long...

...much too long...

...enjoy...

Seph didn't know what to do. She knelt beside Piper, terrified.

The slime lady told her she'd have to confront the black council. She told her she'd have to take back what they'd stolen. But she never told her *what* they took or how she was supposed to take it back. She had no idea what she was supposed to do now that she was here.

...pitiful...

...beneath us...

...should've let her *do it...*

...in the marsh...

...she wanted to...

...no...

...ours...

...our duty...

...our prize...

Piper shook her head. "*Shut up!*"

...do it now...

...long enough...

...yes...

...now...

Seph stood up and faced the mysterious figures. She still had no idea what she was supposed to do, but she had to do *something*. They were hurting Piper.

Terrified, her fists clenched at her sides, she walked toward them. "Knock it off!" she yelled. But even to her own ears, she didn't sound very threatening. None of those nine figures even turned their heads. They merely sat there, ignoring her. It was rude! It was insulting! After all they'd been through, after fighting so hard just to get this far, these shadowy old jerks couldn't even be bothered to turn around and look at them. It made her angry! "*Coward freaks!*" she shouted, attempting to channel that anger into her voice, making herself more threatening. But her voice cracked, betraying her.

...*amusing*...

...*it bores me*...

...*I like it*...

...*fun*...

...*disrespectful*...

...*crude*...

...*just finish it*...

...*patience*...

...*play with it a while*...

The words passed right over Seph. She didn't hear so much as a whisper. But they tore like jagged slivers of shrapnel into Piper's head, each one an agonizing migraine that dripped through her brain like drops of searing, molten slag.

"Make it stop!" she groaned.

Seph took a couple more steps toward the black council. Why were they sitting like that, anyway? Why would they have their backs to them? It didn't make sense.

She took one more step, then paused as her gaze fell on the black wall in front of them.

It wasn't a wall.

There was something there. Something moved in that darkness. Something *churned*. Shadows swam across the surface. Unsettling shapes emerged from unseen depths, blossomed into view for the briefest of moments, during which strange thoughts whispered inside her mind, like glimpses of long-forgotten horrors rising from past nightmares, before melting back into the churning blackness again.

This, she realized with mounting horror, was the living darkness from which Gispuknya was born. It was the psychic nerve that connected it to all its hideous creatures. And it all flowed through this black room, where all the decisions were made by these nine, black figures.

In a manner of speaking, she was standing inside the bug's brain.

Or *one* of its brains, at least.

The black council was watching the wall. Their attention was glued to it. This was what the slime lady was talking about. This was the strings. This was how they remained connected to Gispuknya and all its freakish minions.

Cut the strings.

But how did she do that?

Not for the first time, she wondered if the universe was putting way too much confidence in her ability to follow these stupid clues it kept passing along to her.

She stared into the black wall, watching the shadows as they swirled and bubbled. The spaces between those shadows were so deep. The wall…or whatever it really was…seemed to go on forever. It made her feel dizzy. Like staring down from a precarious ledge over a great height, it filled her with a strangely giddy sort of terror.

No, not just a wall at all.

More and more, she began to feel like there was an entire universe in there.

A universe inside of a giant bug.

Something about the idea gave her a hard shiver.

…long enough…

…do it now…

…yes, now…

…quickly…

…no…

…not too quickly…

…slowly…

…much pain…

…begin now…

…yes…

…yes…

…now…

…yes…

Piper cried out again. Covering her human ears was pointless. She knew that. But she had to do *something*. She couldn't stand it. So she pressed her hands against the sides of her head harder, mashing her ears until her fingernails dug into her scalp. "Persephone!" she screamed. "Get away! They're done arguing!"

All nine of the black figures rose to their feet.

Seph took a step backward, her heart pounding, her hands still clenched at her sides.

…the eyes first…

…yes…

…then the ears…

…make them scream…

...make them beg...

...like it when they beg...

"*Run!*" screamed Piper.

Run where? Back to her truck? Would these monsters even let them leave?

As one, the black council turned and looked at her. Their faces were terrible. She couldn't even describe what it was she was seeing. They weren't human at all. Some had two eyes, others had one or three or four, and all of them in different arrangements on their faces. The rest of their features were lost in the deep shadows of their heads, but she could see things *moving*. Things shifted and churned beneath their black faces, contorting those huge, black, bulging eyes.

She stood there, frozen in horror, unable to even scream.

The voices in Piper's mind had suddenly gone silent. The pain faded from her brain, washed away like sandy footprints in the tide.

She should've felt relieved, but she didn't. She was too distracted by the powerful presences that she suddenly realized had entered the room behind her and were now looming over her.

Chapter 55

Piper felt a hand on her shoulder. But it wasn't a cold or bony hand. It was warm. It was gentle. Kind.

She looked up, confused, and stared into the face that was bending over her.

She didn't understand.

Annalisa smiled her sweet smile and gave her shoulder a reassuring squeeze.

Three more little old ladies stepped past them and gathered around Seph.

"It's okay, dear," said one of them. "We're here now."

Seph turned and stared at her, just as confused. "Louann?" The spunky old woman from the museum? What in the world was *she* doing here?

"We'll take it from here," said the third old woman.

Seph turned and looked at her. "I know you, too," she said, confused. "From yesterday... Sukmukwe... You spoke to me on the mounds. You helped me see the footprint."

She gave her a knowing smile.

"Of course you know us," said the fourth woman. She was a

little thing, all stooped over. She looked familiar, too. "We've been keeping our eyes on you."

The black council didn't seem so menacing anymore. Those awful faces were twitching back and forth, those bulging, misplaced eyes seeming to flick from one old lady to the next.

...found us...

...betrayed...

...tricked us... said the awful, grating voices in Piper's head, making her groan.

"It's okay," promised Annalisa. "It'll all be over in a moment. You girls did magnificently."

...dishonorable...

...cheaters...

...cowards...

They began to back away from their chairs. They were actually cowering.

...from four little old ladies?

...escape...

...plead...

...bargain...

...no honor...

...cheaters...

Piper winced at each agonizing word. But it wasn't as bad as it was before. The voices had lost their imposing tone, and with it some of their power.

No. These were definitely not just four little old ladies. These women were something else.

Seph stared at the fourth woman. It was finally coming back

to her. She knew where she'd seen her before. "You were the one," she realized. "Back in November... You attacked us in that Taco Bell drive through."

She smiled that sweet smile. "Oh, I wasn't attacking *you*, dear."

Seph stared at her, confused.

"We'll talk about all that in a minute," promised Louann. "First, we're going to take back what these creeps stole from us."

And with that, all four of the women transformed into monsters before their eyes.

Just like in that Taco Bell drive-through last November, there was a grotesque series of loud snaps and the old women's faces split open at the corners of their mouths. The tops of their heads flipped back, as if on hinges, revealing impossible, gaping maws filled with giant, crooked teeth. Long, twin tongues stretched out, coiling and undulating like tentacles. Their bodies twisted and knotted and dislocated themselves, transforming them into hideous, four-legged things that were merely dressed in grandmother clothes.

They uttered a series of horrifying, ear-splitting screeches that made Seph scream and cover her ears.

But Piper barely heard the screeching. All she could hear was the horrible screaming and pleading of the black council as what she could only describe as the world's most terrifying bridge party scurried across the floor, knocking the chairs against the walls.

The monsters that had been sweet old ladies only a moment before brutally tore the black council to pieces before their eyes. Black gore splattered across the room and splashed against the walls.

Seph backed away, horrified by the scene before her, but also unable to look away. She reached out for Piper, who snatched her hand and clung to her.

And then there was silence.

The monstrous old ladies twisted themselves back into their original, unassuming shapes and then turned to see Seph and Piper gawking at them, utterly horrified. The sight must've been amusing, because it made the frightful quartet giggle.

"What just happened?" squeaked Piper.

"What just happened," replied the old woman Seph first met on Sukmukwe's East Mound, "is that you just helped us take down the black council."

"Black council?" asked Piper.

The old woman took a small mirror from her purse and glanced at herself in it. She straightened her hair and wiped a spot of black gore off one cheek as if transforming into a hideous monster and eviscerating evil shadow people were something she did every morning before lunch, and then casually put it away again. "Essentially, the creeps in charge of all the nasty stuff that's been stalking you. They've been sitting in this room this whole time, locked up where it's safe, and making the other things do all the work."

"Bureaucrats," huffed the Taco Bell lady.

The other two chuckled.

"Essentially, we just chopped off one of Gispuknya's legs," said Louann.

Seph was still confused. "Who are you people? How did you get here?"

"This is our home," replied Annalisa. "We've always lived here. Ever since this world was first created."

Seph let this sink in for a moment. "Wait... So *you're* the whisper people?"

"Some used to call us that. Others used to call us the little souls. Some just called us feints. But most of the time, they call us the Ahns."

"Ahns?" said Piper.

"Yeah. Or Anns, if you prefer," said the Sukmukwe lady. "I'm Annabelle. You've met Annalisa." She glanced at Seph. "And *you've* met Louann."

"I'm Lillyanna," said the Taco Bell lady.

Annabelle, Annalisa, Louann and Lillyanna? "The Anns," she said, getting the joke. Their names all contained "Ann."

"That's cute," said Piper.

Seph took off her glasses and rubbed at her eyes. This was all so weird. These women had been around since at least the dawn of this universe? She remembered Annabelle standing beside her on Sukmukwe's East Mound, talking about how much she wished she could've seen the long-vanished city with her own eyes. But if this were true, there was no reason she couldn't have seen it. Was she saying that she never had a chance to see the city when it was flourishing? Or was she really telling her that she wished she could see it *again*?

She could ask her. She was standing right there, looking right at her. But she was just too tired to care that much.

"Like I told you," said Lillyanna, "we've been keeping our eyes on you. And not just since yesterday. From the very beginning.

In November, at that Taco Bell, you never saw the hunter that slithered into the back of your truck. Why, if I hadn't been there…" She shook her head as if the thought were too gruesome to even consider.

"Hunter?" said Seph as she returned her glasses to her face again. "You mean one of those wraiths?" She remembered watching the monstrous old woman scurry over her windshield and drop into the bed of the truck. When she turned around, she *did* catch a glimpse of a wraith. But she thought the monster *was* the wraith. She thought it had disguised itself as an old woman.

She supposed that explained why none of the other wraiths ever did anything like that.

"So do you guys work for the Keeper, then?" asked Piper.

The Ahns all giggled again.

"Hardly, dear," said Lillyanna.

"We don't work for anybody," said Louann.

"But we're all on the same side here," added Annabelle. "We all work for the cycle."

"The cycle of creation," said Seph.

"Of course," said Annalisa. "Without the cycle, everything would end. Even the Great Enemy works for the cycle."

"Wait…" said Seph. "I thought Gispuknya *wanted* everything to end."

"Gispuknya *does*," said Louann. "We're talking about the Great Enemy, born from the toxic depths of the Oblivion after the decay of the first universes. The Dark Creator. The Great Deceiver."

"The Great Enemy doesn't want the cycle to end, because

then it, too, will end," explained Annabelle.

"No one to deceive if no one's around anymore," said Lilly-anna.

"Makes sense," said Seph. "I guess…"

"The Great Enemy wants to *control* the Hands," said Annabelle. "It wants to use them, not destroy them."

"So they're different?" said Piper, still confused.

"Oh yes," said Louann. "Gispuknya wasn't born from the Oblivion. He was born from the ashes of a dead and corrupted world and the sins of its people. He's a sort of disease. A 'bug', if you'll pardon the pun. He's been around for many cycles now, but he's never been much of a threat before. He was just another pest."

"Something about this world made it stronger," said Seph, remembering what the slime lady told her.

Louann nodded. "Yes." She looked down at her, her expression softening. "I'm sorry I had to lie to you when you asked me about him before. I couldn't risk blowing my cover."

"Sure…" replied Seph. "I…think I understand." It made her feel a little dazed to think that the spitfire museum lady was an otherworldly creature watching over them like a hellish guardian angel. "What I *don't* understand is what we're doing *here*."

"Isn't it obvious?" said Annabelle. "This is the location of the vault for the second Hand of the Architects."

Piper's expression lit up. "It's here?"

Annabelle frowned. "Well, no, actually."

Her face fell again. "What?"

"That's the problem," said Annalisa. "A long time ago, Gispuknya came to destroy the second Hand. And he almost succeeded. He slaughtered the vault guards and even managed to break the seal before we could drive him back. So the Keeper asked us to move it somewhere safer."

"Wait…" said Seph. "So you moved the Hand?"

"We did," said Louann. "We hid it somewhere Gispuknya's minions couldn't find it."

"So after all this, we have to keep looking?"

"Well, you shouldn't have to look too hard," said Lillyanna. "It's not like it's lost. We can tell you exactly where it is."

"Okay," said Piper. That was good news at least.

"So where is it?" asked Seph.

"It's in its new vault," replied Louann, "hidden at the Baptist church on Leviner Street. In Avelby."

Seph gaped at her. "*All the way back in Avelby*? You couldn't've told me that while I was talking to you at the museum?"

"No," she replied. "I couldn't. First of all, we needed you."

"The black council wouldn't let us in so we could face them," said Lillyanna. "Bunch of cowards. We needed you to come here and let them lure you in."

"So we were bait?" asked Seph.

"Yes," said Annalisa. "But you were never in any harm. We were here the whole time, hiding, waiting for them to stand up and disconnect themselves from the black room. As soon as they did that, we were able to enter and take back our playground."

"Besides," said Annalisa. She raised her arm and gestured at the far end of the room. Although they'd barely noticed, the black room had been fading to lighter and lighter shades of gray. Now it was moving toward white. The "wall" where all the things were churning and swimming had vanished, revealing the space behind it. There was a large block of stone sitting on a raised platform. "You can't open the vault without the key."

Seph stared at the stone. She'd seen one like it before. In Amethyst's queer bunker inside the crazy warehouse on the flip side of her multi-dimensional ranch. It was a vault keeper's tomb. The entrance to the vault where the second Hand was supposed to be resting.

There were two differences, however. First, this one had an enormous crack in it. Something, at some point in time, had broken it nearly in half. Second, there was a carving mounted to the front of it. A large, white bird with its wings spread apart, as if ready to take flight. There was a strange symbol carved into its chest.

Look for the key they left in the dark, she thought. The slime lady's words sent a shiver through her body.

It was all part of the game.

Every single thing.

It wasn't so unlike November after all. They were still the pawns, being danced across the board without a clue. Only the players had changed.

"The Incubus already knows it's there," said Annabelle. "He'll be there waiting for you. You're going to have to face him."

"How can we face an incubus?" asked Piper.

"You have everything you need," promised Annalisa. "You still have what I gave you, don't you?"

Piper pulled the pendant from her shirt.

"Keep that on you. It'll protect you." She turned her eyes on Seph. "And you'll know what to do when the time comes. I know you will."

"That makes one of us," she murmured.

"The vault we created is strong, but not as strong as the Architects' vaults," warned Louann. "The incubus will try to force you to open it because that'll be the easiest way in. But he won't need you. Given enough time, he knows he'll find a way to break through it. That gives him an advantage. Beware of that."

Seph nodded, but she still wasn't convinced they could do it.

Lillyanna glanced around at the mysterious cabin. "We've crippled Gispuknya for the time being. He won't be a problem. As for the incubus, the universe will always give you a way. Trust in that and make sure the Hand finds its owner."

"But we still don't even know what the Hand is," said Piper.

Annabelle looked at her, surprised. "Really? You haven't figured that out yet?"

"How were we supposed to figure that out?" asked Seph. "We haven't been given any clues."

"Of course you have. You already know what the Hands are. You're the seekers. They *talk* to you."

"They're not saying much, then," she countered.

"Are you sure?" asked Annalisa, stepping closer to her. "You don't have any recurring themes in your dreams? No thoughts that you find your mind going back to? A happy memory? A favorite place? Someone beloved who you've lost?"

Seph stared at her. Her father was often in her dreams. It wasn't anything strange. She just missed him. That was all.

"There's nothing...*odd*...about these dreams?" she pressed.

"He's just there," she replied. "Like he always was. Standing at his workbench."

"*Just* like he always was?"

She frowned. She could see him as clearly as if he were here right now. Banging away at some project. Beads of sweat on his face. The way he used to glance over at her and give her that smile.

"An object that can change the form of anything it touches," she whispered.

Bang.

Bang.

Bang.

Her eyes grew wide.

"There it is," giggled Lillyanna. "I knew she'd get it."

She could remember him standing there with a screwdriver or a ratchet. But why in the world would he just be standing there swinging a hammer? He was a mechanic, not a carpenter or a black-smith. Sure, he used a hammer, but not every time she saw him.

"A hammer that can bend anything in existence into any form you wish," said Annalisa. "You could craft anything with such a tool. A house. A city. A country. A *society*. You could even build a vessel capable of carrying all life in an entire, dying world through the very cosmos and sail them to a new home."

Seph and Piper both stared at her.

"Noah's hammer," said Louann.

"And you'd better get to it before that filthy incubus does," added Lillyanna.

"Good luck," said Annalisa.

And then, without warning, Seph and Piper were standing outside, next to the Ford. The cabin and the pond were nowhere to be seen. Instead, they were standing in an empty meadow.

This was the same place as before. Seph could tell. But it was much different now. That darkness had left. It was a peaceful place now. A *happy* place.

Even the light had changed, but that didn't have anything to do with the black council being gone. Seph looked at her watch and was shocked to see that it was already after five o'clock!

"How long were we in there?" she stammered. How long had they lain asleep on that waiting room floor?

"It couldn't have really been that long," reasoned Piper. "I would've, like, *died* if I'd missed lunch *and* dinner."

That was true. And her own belly wasn't rumbling as if she'd skipped two meals, either. She was only just starting to feel ready for lunch. But the sun didn't lie. The day was mostly gone already. Did time move differently inside the black council's cabin?

Piper's phone alerted her to four missed calls and six text messages from Meg. She frowned at the screen, baffled, and then just returned it to her pocket and shook her head. "I can't even right now," she sighed. "So... Back to Avelby?"

Seph looked over at her, feeling exhausted. "Yeah. Back to Avelby."

Chapter 56

They stopped to eat twice. Once just to make sure Piper's furiously carnivorous belly wasn't going to spontaneously realize that it was way past due for its required sacrifice of flesh and begin brutally punishing her for it, and then again around midnight, when it began to complain for its dinner in loud, embarrassing gurgles, letting them know that the clock in her gut was still set to the time it was *before* they entered the black council's hunting cabin.

That seemed to be proof that they'd actually lost those hours somehow, rather than simply sleeping through them. But it was odd that their watches had kept time. Shouldn't *they* have lost those hours too?

Whatever. She was too tired to think about it too much.

They also lost an hour to a traffic jam in Southern Illinois, so by the time they arrived back in Avelby and located the Baptist church on Leviner Street, it was already a little past five o'clock in the morning and the first light of the day had begun to push back the gloom ahead of the rising sun.

Seph parked in the empty lot and stepped out of the truck. She could already tell it was going to be another hot day, but for the moment it was actually comfortable out. For once, there weren't even any bugs buzzing around her.

But it was hard to enjoy these little comforts as she stared up at the church's towering steeples with her stomach twisted into a burning knot.

"So it's in there?" asked Piper. "Noah's hammer?" It sounded so weird to say it aloud. Was it the real Noah's hammer? The hammer that he used to build the real ark? Or was that only a metaphor? When Annalisa spoke of a vessel capable of carrying all life in an entire, dying world through the very cosmos, sailing them to a new home…was that the story that inspired the biblical tale of Noah's ark? Or was she using Noah and his ark as a metaphor to describe what the Hand was capable of? She supposed it didn't matter. In the end, it was probably just like the scythe. It was a tool of such awesome power that it found itself attached to anyone, real or imaginary, who was ever known to wield a hammer. It could just as easily have been Thor's hammer. Or Hephaestus' hammer, with which he forged all the weapons of the gods. Or even John Henry's hammer. And since the scythe was less a literal scythe than a physical manifestation of one of the slumbering Architects themselves, then it could just as easily have been almost any other mythical tool capable of changing the world around it in even subtlest ways. Anything from the Pied Piper's pipe to Johnny Appleseed's sack.

It was all a little overwhelming when she really thought about it.

Seph nodded. "It's in there all right. And so is Travis."

"The incubus."

She nodded again.

The windows were all lit up. Every light was on inside, seemingly inviting them in.

"How do we beat an incubus?"

Seph had no idea. "I guess we just have to believe what the Ahns told us. The universe will give us what we need."

"That seems like a dangerously optimistic plan."

"It does. But aren't you the one who's always telling me to be more optimistic?"

"This wasn't what I had in mind."

"Well, it's the only plan we've got. So let's get it over with."

Piper reached up and clutched the pendant Annalisa gave her. Then the two of them crossed the parking lot toward the heavy, wooden doors of the church.

There was a large, white stone in front of the building, standing at the center of a large flowerbed and surrounded by a decorative brick border. Seph paused as they walked past it and read the illuminated plaque set into the ground at its base. The stone was a city landmark. "The Weeping Angel," she read.

Piper stared at it. "Weeping Angel... Wasn't that one of the things you read in the disk chamber?"

Seph nodded. Her mouth tightened. Suddenly, things were starting to click into place. It all made a little more sense now. "Come on."

She didn't bother sneaking around. It wouldn't do any good anyway. You couldn't sneak up on a demon. She opened the door and walked into the church without hesitating. Then she stood there, Piper at her side, looking over the scene before her.

The place was a wreck. The pews had been piled in a corner.

There were huge, gaping holes in the walls. The floor had been ripped up in several places. Almost a dozen men wielding crowbars, sledgehammers and power saws were hard at work destroying the place. One by one they stopped what they were doing and turned to stare at them.

There were others elsewhere in the church. They could hear them working, unaware of the interruption here. But this wasn't some ordinary renovation crew. They weren't wearing safety glasses or hard hats or even gloves. They were just men with tools tearing holes in a church.

They *were*, however, all armed. Several of them drew pistols from holsters on their hips. Two had shoulder holsters, like police detectives wore on television. Several others threw down their tools and snatched up rifles that were leaning against the walls near where they stood.

Piper squealed and crowded behind Seph, but Seph didn't cower. She wasn't afraid. "Relax," she said. "They aren't going to shoot us. Their boss might still have use for us." She raised her voice and called out, "Isn't that right, Travis?"

From somewhere in the back, someone knocked something over. Footsteps echoed through the suddenly silent church as the incubus approached.

Seph glared at the shadow that slid across the wall. "Or would you rather me call you *Ian*?"

He walked out into view. His shirt was new and crisp again, his jeans and boots perfectly clean, in spite of the fact that the last time they saw him he was wrestling with a bloody corpse in the stagnant mud of the Keeper's swamp. His handsome face showed no sign of surprise. "Take a break, guys. I've been expecting them."

His deconstruction crew lowered their weapons, but didn't put them away.

Elsewhere in the building, a saw screamed to life. At least two more people were swinging hammers. They could hear debris crashing to the floor.

"I see you finally caught on," said Ian. "Took you long enough."

Seph glared at him. It was a lie from the very beginning. Amethyst never sent him to meet her at Buffy's apartment. He'd been there all night, waiting for her. She was willing to bet that he even stole her phone so she couldn't cancel their breakfast date, ruining his plans to confront her. He wasn't there to help her save her mother. He was only there to trick her into searching for the hammer. He only wanted to keep them alive long enough to find the location of the Ahns' vault.

"The Weeping Angel," she said.

Ian/Travis nodded. "That rock was sacred to the people of this land a few hundred years ago. Now it's landscaping. That's humanity for you. You ask me, that's the *real* flaw in the cycle. People. Selfish, greedy and cruel. But *I'm* the demon. Go figure, right?"

Seph didn't give him the satisfaction of a response. She hated this. They handed it to him. They gave him exactly what he wanted. It was while they were climbing out of the pyramid in the Keeper's swamp. When he offered to help her make sense of the riddles she'd found on the disk. As soon as she mentioned the Weeping Angel, he knew exactly where to find it. "I take it you were hoping the black council would kill us in Tennessee."

He shrugged. "That would've been fine with me, yeah. But I knew those old hags wouldn't let that happen. No, I sent you there because I knew you'd squash the bug for me."

This caught her off guard. The bug? Gispuknya?

"Now that it's gone," explained Ian, an infuriatingly smug look on his face, "it's safe for me to take the hammer."

"And now you're wrecking a church?" said Piper. "I thought demons weren't allowed in churches."

"That's stupid," said Ian. "Superstition. It's a *building*. Wood and brick. I'm not going to burst into flames because I'm not human."

"Oh," said Piper. That was disappointing. She rather liked the idea of nasty demons not being able to walk into a church.

"Besides," he added, "it's not a church. It's a vault *disguised* as a church. The hammer belongs to me. As far as I'm concerned, that makes this my property. I can do with it as I please."

"Doesn't look to me like you have any idea what you're doing," said Seph, eyeing the mess.

Ian's lip curled into a slight smile. "Yes. I'll give you that. It could take weeks to find where the vault entrance is. But I'll take this place apart, brick by brick, until I do." Then that smile spread a little wider. "Unless, of course, you'd like to help me find it."

"Why would we do that?" asked Piper.

He turned his gaze to her. That creepy smile turned into an evil grin. "That's a very good question. Remember when I said I had some business to take care of in Sukmuke?" He turned and gestured at a long, wooden crate lying on the floor in front of the pulpit. "I brought you a little something. Go on over. Take a look.

Don't be shy."

They both stared at the crate, but neither of them moved.

"Go on," urged Ian. "You're going to love it."

Seph didn't trust this demon as far as she could admire those bulging biceps, but she also didn't exactly have a plan. Lillyanna told her the universe would give them a way to defeat the incubus. She told her to trust in that. And it appeared that trust in the universe was all they had.

Hand-in-hand, they started across the room toward the mysterious crate.

"Spread out, guys," said Ian. "Let the ladies through."

Seph had no idea where he found these guys, but they were obedient enough. They stepped back, giving them room.

But they never took their eyes off them. Not for a single second.

The crate was about eight feet long by three feet wide and about two feet deep, made of rough pine. The lid was on a hinge and lifted up.

Seph and Piper stood over it for a moment, uncertain. Then Seph bent, braced herself for something horrible, and opened the lid.

Inside was Wanda Janger.

"Oh my god!" cried Seph

"*Wanda!*"

She was dirty and bruised, her immaculate makeup badly smeared. Her wrists and ankles were bound with duct tape. Another piece of duct tape covered her mouth. A fat chain was looped around her with several of the links bolted directly through the crate and into the floor, making it impossible to move her.

She was alive. Her long eyelashes fluttered as she squinted up into the bright lights of the church.

She was wearing the same clothes as when they left her at Sukmukwe. How long had she been in this box?

Seph turned to face Ian, furious. "You son of a bitch!"

"It's easy," said Ian. "Tell me where the Ahns hid the entrance to the vault…and I won't incinerate that box."

Chapter 57

Piper yanked at the chains, but they wouldn't budge. Even if she had the right tool, she doubted she'd be strong enough to loosen the bolts holding them down. Wanda was trapped in there. If Ian did to this box what he did to those zombies in the disk chamber, she'd be cremated alive. They'd have only two options: jump out of the way and watch their friend die or stand their ground and die with her. And that was a decision she desperately didn't want to have to make.

She reached in and pulled the tape off her mouth, wincing at the painful way it pulled on her parched lips.

"Wanda!"

"Babs..."

"Take it easy. We're here."

"He grabbed me before I could leave the park. I'm sorry. I messed everything up for you."

"No. You didn't do anything wrong. I'm sorry. We never should've left you."

"We trusted him," said Seph. "He said she'd be safer if we left her. He told us nothing would hurt her." She stared at Ian with hatred in her eyes. First her mom and now Wanda?

And if he grabbed her in Sukmukwe, she realized, then that must've been *him* who sent that text to Piper, telling them she'd made it home safely.

This guy was really pissing her off.

So much for "demons aren't necessarily evil," she supposed.

"It's your choice, really," said Ian. "It doesn't matter much to me. I've waited ages to get my hands on the hammer. I can wait a little while longer. Either way, I'm going to find it. But I'd rather do it fast and be on my way, so I'm willing to make a deal. Show me the entrance. Let me take the hammer. And all three of you can go home."

Seph continued to glare at him. She said nothing. She had no idea what she *could* say. The bastard had backed her into a corner.

Did she do something wrong? Was it a mistake to just walk through the doors and confront him like that? Sneaking in couldn't have accomplished anything. Surely they wouldn't have been able to sneak past all those armed goons. This wasn't a video game. There wasn't anywhere to hide. It wasn't a sprawling cathedral with high, shadowy walkways and secret passages. It was just a simple little, small-town church.

And it wasn't like they were going to be able to spirit Wanda out of here. They never would've even known she was here. Even if they'd found a way to sneak in, find the hammer and vanish, Ian would likely have murdered her as revenge.

Maybe the Ahns were wrong. Maybe the universe didn't have a plan this time. Maybe it had picked the wrong seekers after all.

Ian spread his arms out. He raised his eyebrows. "Take it or leave it."

Seph wanted to tell him to go to hell, but she found her throat locked.

"No? Nothing? I really thought your friend meant more to you than this."

"Babs…" whimpered Wanda.

"Shhh. It's okay. I promise."

Ian dropped his arms. "*Tell me*!" he shouted. And Seph saw curls of smoke billow from his mouth.

"We don't know where it is!" screamed Piper.

But Ian turned his blue eyes toward Seph. "Oh, *she* does. Don't you?"

Seph stared back at him, her teeth clenched, her fists trembling at her sides.

Piper looked up at her. Tears welled up in her eyes.

Seph looked down at her. She didn't know what to do.

"Last chance," said Ian. "Or this place reeks of burning meat."

They stared at each other.

"Three," said Ian. Smoke rolled from his mouth.

Seph turned her gaze to Wanda. She was staring up at her, her eyes wide with terror.

"Two." His body began to change. That strange darkness spread across his arms and his body became rigid. Clusters of reddish horns began growing from his shoulders. A hot flame belched from his pursed lips.

Her heart was racing.

"One."

She didn't know what else to do. If the universe was going to give them a way to win this, it had better come up with something fast.

She turned and looked up at the stained-glass window behind the pulpit. It was facing east, and the morning sun was beginning to rise. It glowed with the morning light. And at the very center of it was a white bird. A dove. Just like on the tomb in the cabin.

She saw it when she first entered the room.

Ian followed her gaze. "Of course," he said, that evil grin spreading across his face again. In an instant, he was back to his human form. Or as human as a murderous monster could be. "I would've gotten there eventually," he decided. "But I appreciate the help."

"Now let her go!" shouted Piper.

He looked down at her, still grinning. "Actually, I think it'd be safer to just kill you all now. Nothing personal."

Before they could react, the incubus transformed himself again and stretched his mouth into an impossible, gaping, tooth-filled cavern of a maw. A ball of blistering fire erupted from the demon's throat.

Piper leaned over Wanda.

Seph threw her arms around Piper.

All three of them screamed.

But although a sweltering heat passed over them, the flames never reached them.

A heavy object slammed against the floor in front of them, its bulk shaking the entire building.

Both of them looked up to find the revenant crouched in front of them, inexplicably shielding them from the demon's flames.

...*FINALLY*... the monster screamed into Piper's head.

Seph and Piper watched, horrified, as the flames died away and the burning revenant collapsed onto its knees and then onto its face.

Ian stood there, human once again, staring at the smoldering form in front of him. He wasn't grinning any more. "Aw crap," he said.

A black shadow streaked across the room and up the wall, knocking a cross onto the floor. It vanished. Then it reappeared on the other side of the room, zigzagging back and forth.

Across the room, Ian's small army of thugs were turning in circles, their guns raised. They had no idea what was going on.

Then one of them turned and fired at the others, killing two of them before the rest opened fire and cut him down. But before the first gunman hit the floor, another turned and blasted the one beside him. Chaos broke out. Bullets flew.

Three more men ran in from nearby rooms to see what was happening, only to either be shot dead immediately or to suddenly turn his weapon on the others before being gunned down.

Seph and Piper clung tighter to each other and huddled over Wanda, trying to make themselves as small as possible and praying that no stray bullets flew their way.

In a matter of seconds, the church fell silent again.

One gunman remained. A barrel-chested man in a dirty tank top and tattered jeans, with his back to them.

His rifle dropped from his hand and clattered onto the floor.

Ian stared at him for a moment, uncertain. "Glen?" he said.

"Buddy? You okay?"

Slowly, Glen turned to face him. There were bloodstained bullet holes in his tank top.

And his eyes were as black as coal.

"Aaaaand...Glen's gone," said Ian, sounding deflated. "Hello, Warner."

Seph and Piper both stared at the bloody gunman. Warner? Warner Harr?

"No hard feelings?" tried Ian.

Warner twisted Glen's neck, making it crack in the silence of the church. His hands curled into fists at his sides. "You stuffed me in that festering carcass and left me there for *three weeks*," he snarled.

"So...*lots* of hard feelings," said Ian, nodding. "I understand."

Three more gunmen ran into the room from upstairs, weapons raised, their wide eyes immediately drawn to the dead bodies.

"What happened?" demanded a skinny one with no shirt and tattoos all over his arms and torso.

"Don't—" said Ian, but it was too late.

Glen collapsed onto the floor and the gunman standing behind the other two opened his black eyes and shot the other two dead.

"...come in here," Ian finished with a sigh. "Fine. Let's get this over with."

He transformed again and launched himself at Warner, knocking him back and then slashing at him with those spiny claws.

Piper grabbed Seph by her shoulders and leaned close to her. Her eyes had suddenly gone black. "Only you can stop him now," warned Warner.

Seph stared at him. Her? No, *him*. No... She was so confused. She couldn't think straight. Her heart was still racing. She was scared out of her mind. "What can *I* do?"

But then she was only staring into Piper's wide, blue eyes. She was staring back at her, equally confused.

Ian stood up straight, his body still rigid, his claws dripping with the blood of the gunman. "Where'd you go now?" he growled.

One of the downed gunmen stood up and emptied one of the pistols into Ian's back.

Ian twisted around and launched himself at his attacker.

Inside the box, Wanda lifted her head and stared up at Seph. Now *she* was Warner. "The scythe!"

Seph stared down at her. "I don't have the scythe anymore!"

"Impossible!"

"The Keeper said it went back to one of the Architects!"

"The scythe *is* one of the Architects!" countered Wanda—no, *Warner.*

"It's gone!" shouted Seph.

Wanda stared up at her, her eyes red and swollen instead of black. "What?"

Ian slammed the gunman against the wall with a snarl, only to be shot in the back by the next one. He turned around, opened his mouth wide and set him ablaze.

"Use it!" shouted Piper, her eyes black again.

"The Keeper said it went to serve its master!" replied Seph. She remembered him telling her that. Those were his exact words.

"The Hands only choose *one* master!"

Seph stared at her.

Piper stared back at her, those blue eyes wider than ever. "*What's happening?*"

She barely heard her. Somewhere in her head, she heard her dad's voice. "It's not really lost," he said from somewhere in a dream. "You still have it. And when you need it, you'll remember where you put it."

Ian cut down another of his stubborn gunmen and let out a roar. Then he bounded across the room, past Seph and Piper, and scurried right up the wall.

He was going for the window.

He was going for the hammer.

Seph watched him as he clawed his way up to the glass, distracted. The sun was higher now. The window was ablaze. The white bird shined like an angel.

What was it the slime lady told her? When the truth was finally revealed, she should look inside to find what was lost?

But if there was anything lost to be found, there wasn't going to be time to look for it.

Ian pulled himself up onto the narrow ledge and, with a satisfied roar of victory, he plunged his claw into the blazing glass to claim his prize.

Chapter 58

A kaleidoscope of glittering colors rained down from the shattered window and onto the floor.

And then there was only silence.

Seph and Piper crouched over their bound friend, motionless, staring up at the frozen form of the demon still perched on the ledge.

He was staring out at Avelby as it lay bathed in the warm glow of the morning sun, confused.

Nothing happened.

"Huh," said Wanda as she stared up at the broken window with Warner's black eyes. (Or was it Warner who was staring up at the broken window with Wanda's face?) "You lied."

"I thought it would buy us some time," said Seph.

Ian turned his head and looked down at them. He wasn't handsome anymore. His face was positively monstrous. A twisted, broken shape with blazing, broken eyes. "*You...*" he snarled.

"In my defense," said Seph. "I never actually *said* that was the entrance. I just kind of looked up at it. You make a lot of assumptions."

With a roar, the incubus turned and hurled itself off the ledge, its massive bulk shaking the building as it struck the floor. It was bigger than it was before. Much bigger.

It charged at them, spreading its arms—more arms than it had before—and more gleaming claws than either of them could count. A long, snake-like tail whipped back and forth in the air above it.

Piper screamed.

But Seph merely stared at the approaching beast. Suddenly, she wasn't afraid anymore.

Time seemed to slow to a crawl.

"Find what you were looking for yet?" asked her father.

It was as if he were standing right behind her. But she didn't bother looking for him. She wouldn't see him. That wasn't how things worked. Instead, she looked down at her hands.

She was soaking wet.

Her entire body glistened, her skin and clothes completely covered in a fine layer of crystal-clear water.

"Yeah," she said. "I found it."

He was right. It was never lost. She'd just put it away somewhere until she needed it again.

The light flashed off the edge of the blade as the Grim Reaper's scythe cut through the air.

Then Ian was standing over her, his blue eyes wide with shock.

"That was for my mom," she told him.

Then he melted before her eyes. Like a Styrofoam cup tossed onto a bonfire, his entire body shriveled away, starting at his side, where the blade cut through his demonic form, and racing outward.

In the space of a few frantic heartbeats, he'd disintegrated into dust and was gone forever.

"What just happened?" asked Wanda.

Piper looked down at her. "Oh. Uh. That was the Grim Reaper's scythe I was telling you about."

"Oh. Okay. Cool. Can someone get me out of here now?"

Seph looked down at her hands. A thought occurred to her. When she was running from the slime lady in that nasty tunnel and ran into that gate, the lock gave out in her hands. She'd assumed at the time that it'd been rusted through. She remembered thinking she must be the luckiest person alive. But maybe it wasn't luck at all.

She bent over the box and took hold of the chains.

She thought it might take a while. She had no idea how this worked. But it was like a reflex. Almost without thinking, she clenched her hands and the chains came apart, clattering to the bottom of the box around Wanda's body.

"That's pretty cool," said Seph.

Together, she and Piper removed the tape binding her wrists and ankles and helped her out of the crate. She was a little wobbly. Her body was stiff. But she didn't seem to be in pain.

She sat down on the step and her eyes suddenly flashed black.

"Warner!" gasped Seph.

He lifted Wanda's arms, turning them this way and that. He flexed her fingers. He stretched out her legs. "This body is a little dehydrated," he informed them, "but unharmed. Your friend will be all right."

"That's good," sighed Piper.

Warner looked up at Seph. "I owe you an apology."

"You do?"

He nodded toward the charred corpse of the revenant. "My behavior while I was trapped in that monstrosity was...erratic at best. It was hard to think straight. The incubus told you the monster was indestructible, but in reality, it was only impossible for me to kill myself. I targeted you because I thought you would use the scythe on me. I had no idea you didn't know how to use it yet."

Seph shrugged. "Nobody ever gave me an instruction manual, I guess."

"So all those times you showed up," realized Piper, "and I kept hearing you say things like 'kill' and 'hack' and 'murder'...all that time you were trying to tell me how to set you free?"

Warner nodded Wanda's head. "As I said, it was hard to think straight."

Seph found herself remembering how weary the revenant had looked after they fled from the facility. It walked out into that shaft with its head hung low and all slumped over, as if defeated. Suddenly, it was all too easy to imagine Warner trapped inside that thing, frustrated that the people he was struggling to protect couldn't understand him. "It's okay," she assured him. "It all worked out. Right?"

"You still have to claim the hammer," he reminded her.

"Oh yeah," said Piper. She looked up at Seph. "Where is it?"

"It's right outside," she replied.

A moment later, the three of them were standing in the flowerbed next to the weeping angel stone.

"In all honesty," said Seph. "I didn't realize it at first." She ran her hand over the surface of the rock. Unseen to Piper, there was a symbol carved into one side of it. It was exactly like the symbol on the white bird in the cabin.

The rock itself was probably called the Weeping Angel because if you squinted at it and used a lot of imagination, it kind of looked like an angel stooped over as if sobbing. But she realized that if you turned and looked at it upside-down, from the other side, it looked a lot like the bird in that carving the Ahns showed them.

"I was so mad to realize what it meant that I didn't see what was hidden. When I walked into the church, I thought it *was* the bird in the glass. But it was missing the symbol. *That's* when I realized I'd walked right past it."

"Clever girl," said Warner.

"You're not hurting her in there, are you?" asked Seph.

"It's as if she's asleep," he assured her. "I'll return her to you as soon as I know you're safe."

"Okay then," said Piper. She glanced at Seph. "So what do we do?"

Seph stared at the Weeping Angel. "It's just like the tomb in Amethyst's warehouse. It's the gateway. We're the key."

"But what about the gate?" asked Piper. "Amethyst isn't here to open it."

That was true. This time there was no vault guard.

"You don't need a gate to open it," Warner informed them. "You have the scythe."

Seph looked back at him. (Her? Them?) Then she looked down at her hands. "Will that work?"

497

"No reason it shouldn't," said Warner. "The Hands are pretty much all-powerful."

Seph turned back to the stone. "Okay then," she said. She took Piper's hand, squeezed it, and then placed her other hand on the stone.

Together, they leaned forward.

And then they fell.

Chapter 59

A moment later, they were both lying on the cold earth, still holding hands.

"You okay?" asked Piper.

"Uh huh. You?"

"Uh huh."

They rose to their feet and looked around. They were standing in another tunnel. (Of course.) But this wasn't like those other tunnels. It was clean. And it didn't reek of dirt and mud. And it wasn't entirely dark, either. A brilliant light shined down on them from somewhere high overhead.

The morning sunlight in Avelby?

And at the far end of the tunnel was another light.

A red light.

Since it was the only thing down here, they began walking toward it.

It took a while. Something about the tunnel seemed to struggle with the simple concept of distance. They kept looking back over their shoulders, puzzled. It was as if for every ten or fifteen steps they took, they only progressed one or two.

"It's like a glitch in a video game," observed Seph.

"It's kind of disorienting," said Piper. "I don't like it. Something seems wrong about this place."

"Maybe it's because it was built by the Ahns instead of the Architects."

"Maybe."

It was slow moving, but gradually they approached the red light.

It was fire. Something up ahead was burning.

Minutes passed. Slowly, they drew closer.

In spite of the light from the flames, the tunnel only grew darker and darker, until they could see nothing but the red glow in front of them and the blinding glare behind them.

Then, when the darkness finally began to ebb again and the red glow of the fire was close enough to illuminate their surroundings, they found themselves in a shadowy place filled with…antiques?

"I know this place," said Piper, looking around at the little shop. It was dark now. And extremely spooky. But everything was exactly the same as it was in that warmly lit shop across from the Hairy Knuckles Bar. This was Annalisa's Treasures!

Or rather, some flip-side version of it.

The fire was burning on a table just ahead of them.

Piper knew what they were going to find as soon as she recognized the shop. She felt dumb for missing it all this time.

Annalisa had even picked it up and showed it to her. "Always makes me wonder…" she'd said. "About the people who used to use them, I mean. Who were they? What were they like?"

The hammer lay on the table with the rest of the tools, engulfed in eerie, red flames.

She supposed Annalisa couldn't have just handed it to her while she had it in her hand, showing it to her. That would've been too easy. Or maybe that was only a shadow of the hammer and you could only claim it by approaching it on this side.

Because of reasons, she thought. Just reasons.

They stood there a moment, staring at it.

Noah's hammer. The second Hand of the Architects. The tool that shaped everything that ever was and ever would be into existence.

The only thing that could save Buffy's life.

"So do we just, like, reach out and take it?" asked Piper.

Seph frowned at it. "I don't want to just reach out and take it. It's on fire."

"I know."

They stood there a moment longer, unsure how to proceed.

"What about the scythe?" asked Piper. "Isn't it basically made of water?"

Seph glanced over at her, eyebrows raised. "I don't know."

"Give it a try."

Seph looked down at her hand. For a moment, she didn't move.

"What's wrong."

"I don't really know how it works."

"Oh. Um… Concentrate?"

"I *am* concentrating."

"Then I've got nothing."

Seph stared at her hand. Maybe it only worked when she was in extreme danger? Maybe she couldn't control it consciously. Maybe it only worked when it wanted to work.

This sucked. But at least they didn't have to worry about a deranged monster holding one of them hostage while they tried to figure it out. This time, she'd dispatched the monster *before* entering the vault.

"Why's it so different from last time?" wondered Piper.

Seph closed her eyes and tried to relax. No. The scythe was a part of her now. She could feel it now that she knew it was there. She and it were a part of a symbiosis. They worked *together*.

When she opened her eyes, she found that her hand was wet. She held it up, turning it around in front of her face, watching the water dance over her skin, defying gravity.

"That's pretty awesome," said Piper.

It certainly was.

"So...can you touch it?"

Seph looked down at the hammer. Touching one of the most powerful objects in the world to another of the most powerful objects in the world? What could go wrong?

Gingerly, she reached out her hand.

Two things happened. First, the flames withdrew from her hand and the water climbed up her wrist, leaving her fingers dry. It was like bringing two opposing magnets together. They pushed each other away. Secondly, the hammer on the table faded away, as if it were only an illusion.

"Okay, that doesn't work," said Piper.

Seph pulled her hand back and watched the water vanish. It

was as if her hand absorbed it. And perhaps that was exactly what happened.

She took a deep breath and tried it again, this time with a dry hand.

The same thing happened. The fire all shifted to the far side of the table, away from her hand, and the hammer vanished from sight.

Seph took a step backward. "I don't think it likes me. You try it."

Piper looked uncertain, but she stepped forward. "This is kind of freaky."

"It makes sense. I mean, *I* already have one of the Hands. Maybe you're not allowed to have more than one."

She glanced back at her. "Then who gets the third one?"

She shrugged. They'd deal with that when the time came, she supposed.

Piper turned her attention back to the flames and took a deep breath. "Okay," she sighed. "Here goes nothing."

She reached out slowly. She could feel the warmth of it on her fingertips.

"I think it's working."

Then the flames flared up, startling her. She jumped back.

"Did I make it mad?"

The hammer vanished. All the tools on the table vanished. All of Annalisa's treasures vanished, leaving only the fire, which was suddenly a twisting, writhing ball of flames floating in front of them.

Then, in a flash, the flames darted between them, trailing fire behind it like a shooting star.

They turned around, surprised.

There was a dark figure standing at the far end of the tunnel, a black silhouette against the brilliant sunlight shining down from above.

The ball of fire shot straight to the figure's hand, where it took the distinct form of a blazing hammer.

The two of them stood there, shocked, as that mysterious figure stared back at them.

Then the figure, and Noah's hammer with it, vanished.

An icy panic washed over both of them and they ran.

But the strange physics of the tunnel that impeded their progress on their way in worked in reverse on the way out. In an instant, the blinding sunlight washed over them and they were ejected face-first into the flowerbed on the church lawn.

They both looked up to see Wanda standing over them, Warner's black eyes still staring out from her face. "What happened?" she asked. (*He* asked? *They* asked?)

"There was someone else down there," said Seph. "A man, I think. He took the hammer."

Warner stared at her, a grim look on Wanda's face. "Tane."

"Tane?" said Piper. "Janon Tane?"

"You saw him?" asked Seph.

"No. Tane's like the wind. He comes and goes unseen. But I felt him."

"We have to get it back!"

But Warner shook Wanda's head. "If Tane has the hammer, then it's gone."

Seph stared at him. "No. It can't be gone." She scrambled to her feet, panic overwhelming her. "We *need* it."

Piper stood up, too, her eyes wide.

That hammer was the only thing that could save Seph's mom.

Seph stared off into the distance. Tears had sprung to her eyes. They failed? They actually lost Noah's hammer? No. It couldn't be. That wasn't how it was supposed to go. They were supposed to save her mom.

Oh god…

What had they done?

"I'm sorry," said Warner. "Go home. I have to go report this."

"You can't go!" cried Piper. "What about Tane? What about Buffy?"

"Tane has what he wants. He's long gone. There's nothing more you can do. Go home."

And with that, Wanda blinked and her eyes were her own again. She stared at the both of them for a moment. Then she turned and looked around, trying to figure out why she was suddenly outside. "*What keeps happening to me?*"

Chapter 60

Seph was mostly silent as she drove back to Cakwetak. She kept replaying the events of the past two days over and over in her mind, trying to understand where she went wrong.

It wasn't fair. They beat the incubus. They beat Gispuknya. How could they lose the Hand?

And now there was nothing in the world that could save poor Buffy. She was going to wither away and die, poisoned by that sick demon. And why? Just so he could try and fail to get his hands on the hammer?

And what was going to happen now that Noah's hammer was in Janon Tane's possession? What would an evil creature like him do with the power to remake anything in the world to suit his own twisted desires?

What had they done?

Beside her, Piper was keeping the promise she made to Wanda in Sukmukwe. She told her the whole story. Every detail, no matter how unbelievable.

Wanda, who'd been kidnapped, roughed up and locked in a closet somewhere for most of this crazy weekend before being locked in a wooden crate for the last six hours, wasn't having any trouble believing in tools of ultimate power, godlike architects or incubi.

At least her attackers hadn't abused her too badly. Most of the scuffs and bruises she'd received in the ordeal came from the fight she put up when that creep first grabbed her, which she thought was pretty impressive, given that she was fighting an actual demon. Ian's goons must've been terrified of him, because none of them ever seemed to even *consider* laying a hand on her. They even gave her water and regular bathroom breaks, right up until they bolted her into that god-forsaken box.

That was terrifying. She thought for sure that they were going to bury her alive or something. If she wasn't claustrophobic after today, there was probably something wrong with her.

And she'd very nearly wet herself when she heard the demonic creep threaten to set the box on fire. She was probably going to have nightmares about that the rest of her life.

They dropped her off at Sukmukwe, where her bright yellow bug with its pretty pink bow was still waiting for her.

Seph promised her that if she ever felt freaked out by any of this, she was more than welcome to come over any time and talk about it. She could even stay over any time if she ever felt scared of being home alone. Their door would always be open to her.

For her part, though, Wanda seemed to be okay. She was more concerned with how she was going to explain to her boss why she didn't show up for work the past two nights.

After leaving Sukmukwe, Piper got in touch with Violet and Corey. They were safe. They'd received a tip from one of Corey's online buddies and were now on their way to Minnesota.

They promised to call the next time they passed through the Milwaukee area. They could do lunch and exchange crazy stories.

It was good to have friends who knew how weird they really were.

And then there was Meg. She called as they were entering Cakwetak, asking if they were ever going to come home and make some breakfast.

Piper told her that McDonald's served it until half-past ten and then gleefully hung up on her.

They didn't go home. Seph decided she needed to go to Buffy's place, instead. She wanted to stay by her. She wanted to make her as comfortable as possible for as long as she had left. And Piper refused to go home without her. She was going to stay by Seph's side. No matter how long it took.

And when Seph found herself stepping out of the truck and looking down the sidewalk that led up to her mother's door, she'd never been more grateful to have a hand to hold in her entire life.

She wondered how long it would take? Would it really take a week, as Ian had warned? Or would it happen in just a few days? Or would it drag on for a month or more?

As she walked up to the door and rang the bell, clutching Piper's hand for dear life, the worst idea yet occurred to her. What if Buffy was already gone? She never did answer her phone. What if she didn't answer the door, either? What if she had to use the key she gave her, only to walk in and find her lifeless, withered body?

Oh god…

She'd faced a lot of terrifying things this weekend, but she wasn't strong enough to go through this again.

The door opened.

"We were wondering when you'd show up," said Lillyanna.

Behind her, Buffy's apartment was bustling with little old ladies.

"What's going on?" asked Seph, bewildered.

"Come in, come in," she insisted. "It's nice and cool in here."

Seph stepped into the apartment. For some reason, it didn't stink of cigarette smoke anymore. It smelled *clean*. Like Pine Sol and Pledge. And there was a hint of something savory on the air. Homemade stew?

She walked into the living room to find Buffy sitting up straight, a hot cup of tea in her hands, smiling. Annabelle was sitting beside her, going on about how much prettier her *real* name was. Marianne was such a *perfect* name. *So* much better than *Buffy*.

"You made it back!" exclaimed Louann.

Buffy looked over at them. Her expression lit up. "Seph!"

"Hey…" said Seph, still trying to take it all in. "How're you feeling?"

"So much better! These ladies are the absolute *best*! I had no idea you knew such nice people!"

Me neither, thought Seph. She glanced at Piper, who only shrugged.

"Oh, Seph's been a *huge* help in our charity organization," bragged Louann. She glanced at Seph and winked. "We have no idea what we'd do without her. When she told us you weren't feeling well, we just knew we had to help out."

Annalisa stepped out of the kitchen, wiping her hands on a

dish towel. "How did it go in Avelby?" she asked.

Seph glanced around. "Um…"

"Let's talk over here." She turned, smiling and walked back into the kitchen. Along the way, she gestured at several women she hadn't met yet. "That's Loriann, Annalee, Annabeth and Carolann." Then she pointed across the room. "Over there's Roxanne and Polyanna." Two more ladies were standing in the kitchen. A huge pot was sitting on the stovetop, steaming. The smell was heavenly. And there were three pans of homemade rolls rising on the countertop. "And this is Arianna and Annice."

Seph looked around at them, surprised. She'd seen many of these women before somewhere, she realized.

"I was in Raindskenner Park on Saturday," said Arianna, reading her expression. She was peeling potatoes for the pot.

Seph nodded. "Sitting on the bench. Right about when Piper heard something in that tunnel that ran under Main Street."

"Gispuknya's little creeps don't like it when we're around," she whispered, smiling. "If they notice us, they run away."

Piper stared at Annice. She was cutting up carrots and celery. "And you were there when that runner was chasing us," she realized. "You looked right at me and smiled."

"Why do you think the runner stopped chasing you?" she asked, winking at her.

Piper blinked. *She* was the reason the runner just disappeared?

"That's one monster that won't be chasing anyone ever again. I promise you that."

They didn't have to ask her what she meant by that. They both saw what happened to the black council. The runner had almost certainly been dismembered and devoured by this sweet, unassuming old woman.

"It's like we told you," said Annalisa. "We've *always* kept our eyes on you. And we always will."

"But not in a creepy way or anything," said Arianna. This made all three of them laugh.

Seph and Piper glanced at each other. This was so weird.

"So how did it go?" asked Annalisa.

Seph felt sick. "It didn't," she replied. "We screwed up."

Her kind old face fell. "What do you mean?"

"Janon Tane has Noah's hammer."

She stared at her, confused. "And?"

Seph blinked. "And what? Tane has the second Hand of the Architects. He took it right out from under us."

"Of course he did."

"Huh?"

Piper scrunched her nose up, confused.

"That *is* bad, right?" said Seph. "I mean, *Tane has the hammer.*"

Annalisa smiled. "Tane *always* gets the hammer."

Both of them stared at her.

"The Hands choose who wields them," explained Annice. "The scythe always chooses a seeker and the hammer always chooses Tane."

"It's kind of like a balance thing," said Arianna as she rinsed the freshly peeled potatoes. "Good and evil and all that."

"But won't he use it to wreck the world or something?" asked Piper.

"I'm sure he'll use it to his own ends," said Annalisa. "He always does. But only the Architects, themselves, can utilize their full power. All three of them have to come together and awaken."

Seph took her glasses off and rubbed her eyes, exhausted. "Do you think, maybe, someone could've told us these things?"

"If you knew the Hand was just going to go to Tane," said Louann as she walked into the room with Buffy's empty tea cup, "then you wouldn't have fought so hard to reach it. And then that demon might've found it. Or worse still, Gispuknya."

Seph considered this. She supposed it was true. But it still seemed pretty unfair.

"You stopped the incubus from taking it *and* landed a crippling blow to Gispuknya," said Annice. "That's what you call a job well done."

"So…" said Piper. "Everything actually worked out?"

Seph turned and looked out at Buffy. "My mom…"

"Oh, she'll be fine," Annalisa assured her. "I mean, you *did*…" she drew her finger across her throat, "…the incubus, didn't you?"

"Yeah. He's…definitely gone."

She spread her hands out. "There you go."

"But I thought she'd still die anyway."

Annalisa tilted her head to one side, confused. "Who told you that?"

Seph stared at her, awareness blossoming across her face. "Ian did…" Her cheeks flushed with color as she realized that the whole thing was a lie. Even her mother's imminent demise. "That lying… *Ugh*! Stupid!"

Annalisa giggled. "It's okay. We all get a little fooled once in a while by a pretty face, right?"

Seph rolled her eyes. "He wasn't even all that pretty."

"Sure he wasn't," said Louann.

Annice and Arianna giggled.

"Oh," said Annalisa, "and you don't have to worry about the whole Travis thing. We took care of that."

Seph stared at her, confused.

"Your mom's forgotten all about him. She won't even remember he existed."

"Oh…" She turned and looked out at her again. "That's good." And it was. But also…she couldn't help feeling a little sad for her. Travis was really a murderous demon…but for a while there, she really believed she'd found someone special in her life.

It wasn't fair…

"So what happens now?" asked Piper.

The Ahns' expressions all turned serious. All at once, the atmosphere changed.

"Now the real struggle begins," said Annice.

"The first two Hands have been claimed," said Louann as she stirred a fresh cup of tea for Buffy. "The third is the one that breaks the tie. If Tane claims it, he'll have the power to create the next world in his own image."

Seph stared at them, horrified. "Has that ever happened before?"

"Only once," said Arianna, her expression grim.

"And what happened?" asked Piper.

"The Architects created the Black World," said Annice. "Where all the dark things came from."

Seph felt a shiver run down her spine. "All the dark things?"

"All the shadowy things in the world," explained Annalisa. "Everything that's true form is black and monstrous."

Seph remembered the oozing black forms of the wraiths. Warner Harr's oily, black shape. The black council and that black wall of churning, writhing things.

"It was where Gispuknya began," recalled Annice. "Where greed and malice built the first of those awful machines."

Seph felt a chill creep down her back. Awful machines? What *was* Gispuknya, anyway? What was the horrible story behind it?

"And where our first ancestors were born," added Louann. "We mustn't forget that."

"I suppose not," sighed Arianna.

That was right. Piper had almost forgotten that these women weren't human.

"Humanity almost went extinct in the Black World," said Annalisa.

"So we have to find the third Hand before they do," said Seph.

"Not just find it," said Annalisa. "*Claim* it. You'll have to convince it to choose you. It's the only way."

"And don't forget," said Louann as she walked away. "Gispuknya isn't dead. It'll be back. And it'll be *angry*."

Annalisa nodded, a grim expression on her face. "It's a three-way war now. The fate of the universe, and of the great cycle, has never been in this much peril before."

Piper hugged herself against a sudden chill. "What do we do now?"

"Just be ready," said Annice. "The next move will be Tane's."

Seph and Piper exchanged an uneasy look. A three-way war for control of the creation of the next universe?

"Don't worry yourselves too much about it," said Annalisa. "When the time comes, we'll all be here for you. No matter what."

"Did you girls have breakfast?" asked Arianna? "We stocked the fridge with all sorts of good stuff. How about some bacon and eggs?"

"*Ooh!*" said Piper.

Seph smiled. That did sound good.

She turned and looked out at her mother again. She wasn't going to die. The incubus was gone. Even Gispuknya had crawled off into some god-forsaken hole to lick his wounds for a while.

And they had a lot of new friends. The Ahns. Violet and Corey. They could talk to Wanda now, too. They didn't have to keep these awful secrets from everybody.

They didn't even really lose Noah's hammer. It was always going to end up in Tane's hand. So…everything was just the way it was supposed to be.

Everything was really okay.

For now, anyway.

Piper turned and smiled at her.

Today, all that mattered was today. And today was looking like a beautiful day.

ABOUT THE AUTHOR

Brian Harmon grew up in rural Missouri and now lives in Southern Wisconsin with his wife, Guinevere, and their three children.

For more about Brian Harmon and his work, visit

www.BrianHarmonBooks.com

www.ingramcontent.com/pod-product-compliance
Lightning Source LLC
Chambersburg PA
CBHW051933020726
47501CB00001B/109